SECRET HEIR FOR CHRISTMAS

LAQUETTE

AN OFF-LIMITS MERGER

NAIMA SIMONE

MILLS & BOON

First Published in Great Britain 2023
by Mills & Boon, an imprint of HarperCollins*Publishers* Ltd
1 London Bridge Street, London, SE1 9GF

www.harpercollins.co.uk

HarperCollins*Publishers*
Macken House, 39/40 Mayor Street Upper,
Dublin 1, D01 C9W8, Ireland

Secret Heir for Christmas © 2023 Laquette R. Holmes
An Off-Limits Merger © 2023 Naima Simone

ISBN: 978-0-263-31770-1

1023

SECRET HEIR FOR CHRISTMAS

LaQUETTE

To my late grandfather, James Davidson. I still feel your guiding hand on my shoulder and your dedication and love surrounding me. You were my Ace Devereaux in the flesh, and I will never forget just how much you meant and still mean to me.

One

"There you are?"

Stephan looked up to find his uncle, David Devereaux, taking the last step on the staircase on the opposite side of the foyer door. Although younger than Ace by just shy of a decade, he and Ace were almost identical. So much so, there used to be a time where Stephan had difficulty telling the two men apart when he was a child.

But now, without the shroud of sickness and pallor around him, the distinction between the two men was sharply emphasized.

"Hi, Uncle David" Stephan stepped in, closing the foyer door and trying to leave the November chill outside. He quickly hung up his coat in a nearby closet and then stepped into the waiting hug David had for him.

He was grown. Thirty-eight years grown to be exact, and he had not a shred of shame in the absolute comfort he felt in being embraced so lovingly by his uncle. With the exception of his mother—whose normal disposition was icy, if he were being nice, and downright mean if he was telling the truth—most everyone in his family was down for a good hug whenever, wherever they could share one.

And right now, in the midst of all they were dealing with, it was almost impossible not to pass each other without doling a handful out.

"How you doing, Unc?"

David's eyes brightened and he cupped each side of Stephan's face with a warm hand.

"My baby nephew is standing before me instead of being more than three thousand miles away on another continent, and my only brother is still here for me to hold and tell him I love him. Add to the fact that Amara and Lennox are about to give me my first great-grand, and there's not much to complain about. Even if I wanted to."

Stephan marveled at how a man who'd lived to see his late sixties could carry the "I won't complain" motto around with such grace and humility. But even while losing his only brother, he still found a reason to hold on to joy.

Stephan closed his eyes, trying to soak up the love and warmth radiating from his uncle's hands, permeating his skin, and filling him with the strength he needed, that they all needed at this moment in life.

"Uncle David, you trying to make me feel guilty about being in Paris. You know I was over there working, right?"

"I know, nephew." David's smile grew. "But I still missed seeing your face every day while you were there. If nothing else comes of Ace's decline in health, at least it brought you home to us. I hope you're considering staying for good now that you're back."

Stephan's gut twisted into knots and the skin on his arms prickled with anxiety. Return for good? He hadn't even intended to be here for this long. He didn't regret coming home for Ace. There was no way he could've given up this time to spend Ace's last days with him. But being home wasn't a good thing for Stephan. Not when his mother's bitterness dogged him, and not when his presence threatened the well-being of his sister-in-love, Lyric.

David stood there, hope lightening his deep brown eyes, and Stephan had no idea what to say. It wasn't that he had a problem with being honest with his family members or telling them no. But David wasn't a stupid man. He was thorough, methodical, and analytical. It's why, until recently, he'd held the position of lead counsel for Devereaux Incorporated since the company's inception. Whatever Stephan said, he had no doubts his uncle would turn his answer over in his head, that eventually, he'd figure out why Stephan had left in the first place.

Because my lies broke the family.

"Is that my brother-in-love?" The boulder of guilt lodged in Stephan's gut shifted slightly.

Lyric Devereaux-Smith was his late brother Randall's widow. While Randall had been twenty years Lyric's senior, she was only a few years older than Stephan. This meant she'd fallen easily into their cousin group more than two decades ago.

"Come here, girl, and let me love on you."

Lyric squealed the same way she did every time she saw him after any time apart. Whether it was two days or two years, she always delighted in his presence. It was just one of the multitude of reasons staying away from his family hurt so much. Yet, he knew the alternative would bear even greater pain. Not just for him, but especially for the gentle soul who had her arms wrapped around him as she peppered his face with kisses the way only a sister could.

"You staying long? Josiah and I were gonna leave to go get something to eat. But if you're gonna be here for a bit, we can order in and hang with you"

He looked over Lyric's shoulder to find her man sitting in the living room off to the side of the foyer. Josiah gave him a quick nod to acknowledge Stephan's presence, followed by a light thumping of his fist over his heart.

Admittedly, he and Josiah didn't know each other that well. But as long as his beloved Lyric kept that ridiculous smile on her face, Stephan had no objections to Josiah whatsoever.

Stephan loved Lyric.

She'd been more than Randall's wife for two decades. She'd been his sister from the moment Randall had brought her home. He'd adored his big brother, but the love he had for Lyric and the way she'd made him feel wanted, cherished, and not a nuisance, as his mother and brother had, it meant there wasn't much in this world Stephan wouldn't do to keep her happy and safe. Something his brother and mother hadn't been so concerned with.

"Nah," Stephan replied. "I'm running behind for something I have to do anyway."

He lied. There wasn't a damn thing he had to do later. He just couldn't stay in her presence. Not knowing what he'd done. Not knowing the harm he could still do if the truth ever crossed his lips.

"I just came to sit with Uncle Ace for a bit before I head out."

He hugged her again, and by the time he released her,

Josiah was behind her, extending one hand to Stephan as he wrapped the other around Lyric's shoulder.

"Good to see you again, Stephan."

"You make sure to take good care of my sister."

"I always do, my man. I always do."

Satisfied, he left his three family members standing in the foyer and made his way upstairs to Ace's room. The door was large, sitting at the top of the stairs, looming, making it impossible for him to forget what lay on the other side of it.

He took a breath, as he always did since he'd returned home to find his uncle slowly succumbing to cancer's hold. It was time to put on the mask. Time to find the joy and love he needed to impart to Ace.

The love part was easy. Ace had showered him with so much love growing up, he'd been a decidedly neutralizing effect on Martha's acrid and detached demeanor.

But finding the joy right now, when he knew how Ace was suffering, when he knew how much it hurt to think of not having his uncle in his life anymore, that was the hard part.

One last breath in, then Stephan squared his shoulders and knocked lightly on the door before twisting the knob and slowly opening it.

There, in the center of the room was his uncle, Jordan Dylan Devereaux, I, aka Ace. His thin frame was covered with his signature silk pajamas. Today's were a royal purple, a stark contrast to Ace's pale brown skin. Regardless of how sickness dogged him, he sat in the middle of his bed, the perfect statesman, waiting for his next visitor to enter.

"There's my favorite nephew."

Stephan shook his head. "I win that prize because I'm your only one?"

Ace shook his head. "Not the only, just the only one..." Ace stopped as if he couldn't bring himself to say the words. Stephan didn't blame him. Thinking of Randall in the past tense was still difficult for him too.

Ace looked to the large clock sitting on a far-off wall and brought a reprimanding gaze back to Stephan.

"It is well after dinnertime on a Friday night. Why are you not out and about doing what young people do?"

"Thirty-eight ain't all that young, Uncle Ace. After work there are only two places I want to be—here with you, or in my bed asleep."

The amount of pity in the old man's eyes told Stephan exactly what he was thinking.

"You have life. Take it from an old fool who wasted too much of his, go out and live. Go meet new people. Go find love. And if you can't find love, have a whole lot of fun practicing. Don't waste any time on me."

Stephan stepped closer to Ace's bed, sitting slowly next to the spot the man had patted with his hand.

"There's no place in this world I would rather be than here with you, old man. Why are you trying to run me off when I just got here?"

"Because I've lived my life, baby boy. I want you to do the same. I won't be here for much longer."

Stephan bristled at the truth in Ace's words. "Uncle Ace, the last time I checked, God wasn't one of your names. You've beat this thing longer than the six months the doctors originally gave you. Who's to say you won't continue to put cancer on its ass?"

Ace pointed a finger at himself as a weary smile hung on his mouth.

"I wouldn't exactly call this beating cancer's ass. I'm still here and I'm grateful for that. But I'm tired, Stephan, and the only reason I'm still here is because I haven't yet fulfilled my promise to my dearest Alva. When I know in my heart that all our babies are all right, then, and only then will I take my leave. As it stands, you're the only one left I need to look out for."

Stephan snickered. Not that he found anything remotely funny about this situation. But he knew if he didn't laugh, the ball of grief growing at the base of his throat would be too large to breathe around soon if he didn't disrupt it.

"I don't want to talk about this, Uncle Ace. It's morbid. And if death wants you, he's gotta go through me. And for the record, I'on think death's really ready to catch these hands."

Ace's eyes lit up with amusement until laughter shook his frail frame. Stephan was sure it was the absurdity of the image of him literally coming to fisticuffs with the Grim Reaper that had Ace's infirm voice sounding the slightest bit fuller and lighter, and he didn't care. The joy illuminating Ace's face was enough to fill Stephan's heart with a lifetime of contentment.

Ace wiped the sides of his damp eyes while finally exacting some control over his amusement.

"While I would definitely pay money to see that brawl, I don't think it's one you will win."

Ace reached for Stephan's hand, giving it a squeeze.

"A foolish man wastes his time trying to run from death. A wise man embraces it and spends his time enjoying and appreciating every moment he's granted."

Stephan could definitely see the truth in Ace's words. It didn't mean it made his heart hurt any less, though.

"Stephan, I know that if I tell you not to worry yourself trying to take care of the rest of the Devereaux cousins, you'll just ignore me. You're very much like me in that respect. Taking care of those we love is instinctual. It's encoded in our DNA."

There was no need for Stephan to deny the veracity of Ace's claim. The fact was, he'd hightailed it on the first thing smoking back to the States as soon as he'd heard Ace's condition wasn't as stable as the old man had led him to believe. If that wasn't proof that he had helicopter parent written in his future, Stephan didn't know what was.

"You can't stop loving your people, Stephan. But if you're going to pour so much into them, suffer so much for them, you must have someone to pour into you so that beautiful light of yours doesn't go dim."

Ace's words were precise, cleaving his heart in two like a heated scalpel cutting clean through his flesh.

"All of the Devereaux cousins will have a role to play in this family once I'm gone. You're all gonna try to give your all to cover up your broken hearts. Which means all of you will need a rudder to help you navigate. Your cousins have that, Stephan. If you don't find something or someone to hold you together soon, I'm afraid you will destroy that big beautiful heart of yours. And we both know that if you fall, you have secrets that could tear this family apart."

Stephan stood up, walking to the window. It was almost winter, so the sun had disappeared into the horizon long ago leaving behind a midnight blue sky, whose inky hue felt like a replica of the darkness floating around in his soul.

"Are you asking me to keep those secrets to the detriment of myself?"

"No." Ace's response was clear, even in his frail state. "I would never ask that of you. I've begged you to let me set you free of these secrets for a long time. I never agreed with you having to swallow all of this down. You were so busy protecting everyone else, you wouldn't even take time to mourn the brother you'd lost."

Stephan shoved his hands into his slacks, his heart beating in his chest and his emotions welling up so fast that he was afraid he'd shatter into pieces right there.

He'd mourned his brother.

Every day of the last two years. Even more so when he was away from his family in Paris, paying penance for the secrets he held to protect those he loved the most. He hadn't stopped grieving as far as he was concerned.

"I don't know what you want from me, Uncle Ace."

"I want you to give yourself permission to be free so you can open your heart up again and let love in."

"There's no room for anything but this weight that my brother forced me to carry. You know that, Uncle Ace."

"Come here, baby boy."

There was nothing like the elders in your life reminding you that no matter how grown you got, you'd never be more of an adult than them.

He'd like to say he hated it. Well, he certainly hated it whenever his mother tried to pull rank like that. But when Ace did it, it always seemed so loving that Stephan could never find even a sliver of anger to toss at Ace.

He returned to Ace's bedside, lowering himself on the mattress and waiting for his uncle to speak again.

"Let me take this burden to the grave with me, Stephan. I should never have allowed you to take it up in the first place. You were hurting so much, and you insisted this was the only way. But if I'd known it would take you from me, I never would've gone along with it. Please, let me take this from you."

Stephan could feel the fire of pain filling him. His entire body tensed, trying to cage it all in.

"I can't do that, uncle."

Ace's smile was sad, his mouth slightly drooping as he took in the picture of Stephan.

"I somehow knew that would be your answer. So, here's my counter."

Ace held up two fingers as he looked Stephan directly in the eye. "I have two conditions." Even in his current state with his body appearing so thin and feeble, a light breeze could probably topple him over, Ace was still the ultimate businessman. He'd wheeled and dealed, until he'd made his company a household brand and his name a bright star in the sky. Stephan should've known that dying of cancer wouldn't be the thing to deter the man's command and spirit.

"I cannot have you sitting here waiting for me to die. If you won't let me lift this from your shoulders, then I want to see you spend a little time every day finding joy outside of this family, outside of our business, and outside of me."

Stephan tilted his head, watching Ace, trying to suss out exactly what Ace was playing at.

"So, you're saying I can't come visit you?"

"No." Ace chuckled and shook his head as if to say, *this simple boy.* "I'm saying that when you do, I want you to share verifiable proof that you are out there living and experiencing life."

"What the hell does that mean, Uncle Ace. How am I supposed to prove that I'm living life?"

Much like when Stephan was a child and Ace had given him a directive, the man simply sat back, raised a brow, and dared Stephan to say another word. In Ace's generation, grown folks didn't explain themselves to the younger generations. Apparently that dynamic hadn't changed even now when Stephan was nearing forty.

He took a deep breath, realizing being ticked off with a dying man probably wasn't going to gain him any brownie points in the karma department.

"What's the next condition?"

Satisfied with Stephan's acceptance of the situation, Ace continued.

"I want to experience joy myself. And as time slips away from me, my mind keeps drifting back to those wonderful Christmas parties we used to have. You remember them, don't you?"

He certainly did. Every year, Ace would go all out hiring the party planner de jour to turn Borough Hall into a Christmas delight. Devereauxs from all over the globe would gather and literally eat, drink, and be merry throughout the night until the wee hours of the morning.

Those parties, more like galas, were the high point of the year, and Stephan had always looked forward to them. Until two years ago. Randall's passing, and Stephan's departure immediately after the funeral, had seemed to erase Ace's drive to put it all together.

"Your Aunt Alva began the tradition when we married. I kept it going after she died to keep her close to my heart. I want to experience one last Devereaux Christmas and I want you to plan it for me. This way, you'll know how to carry on the torch when I'm gone."

"Uncle Ace. I don't think anyone in the family is up for a party right now, least of all you."

"I am still the patriarch of our family, and my word is still law as far as our bloodline is concerned. You will do these things I have asked, or I will set you free of your burden whether you want to be free or not. What say you, young man?"

Ace squared his shoulders as best he could, daring Stephan to challenge him again. The old man's ability to control the room, even from his deathbed, was unmatched and Stephan knew he was outranked immediately.

He scratched his hand lightly against his beard pretending consideration of his imaginary options. They both knew he was caught and there wasn't a thing he could do about it. Not if he wanted to protect his sister-in-love, and even though she deserved it least of all, his mother.

"I guess it's a good thing mistletoe is in season. Seems I'm going to need a lot of it."

Two

Stephan walked Gates Avenue, to get to his Grand Avenue home. Walking through Brooklyn had always been a way to clear his head when he needed it, and right now, after dealing with his difficult uncle, the crisp air and the concrete sidewalks were exactly what he needed.

He'd just crossed Washington Avenue when his gaze landed on Brown Memorial Baptist Church. The bright red brick building had been standing since 1958. The purplish-blue sky of the evening already settled over the large structure, but even in the coming night, it stood as a beacon to the community.

It reminded him of Ace, strong, vivid, and able to weather the test of time. But now where slightly visible wear on the building stood as a proud reminder of what it had endured, Ace's frail shell showed anyone at a glance that he'd soon leave this world. And as much as the old man aggravated him tonight with talks of Stephan settling down and planning a blasted Christmas party, knowing he was leaving soon plagued Stephan like an ulcer eating away at his insides.

"Well—" he leaned his head upward as he looked at the church "—if the sight of you can't bring me comfort, then I know what will."

He opened the Lyft app on his phone and typed in his destination. Walking to Fulton Street and Franklin Avenue wasn't that long of a trek, but he just couldn't spare the energy to take the first step on his journey.

Brooklyn neighborhoods were densely populated with attached homes and buildings lining each street. Like many places in New York City, real estate was built up not out. That meant fitting more people into homes while minimizing how much land was needed. That translated into a large amount of people in the area, but also meant there was less space for things like parking and driveways.

His cars were stored in a private parking facility nearby. He didn't really need them. He never traveled more than walking distances in any direction from his house. If he needed to, there were always rideshares or buses and subways to get where he needed to go.

When his ride was confirmed to be a few moments away, Stephan shoved the phone in to his pocket, knowing his refusal to chart another path was just the reason Ace was strong-arming him into this proof-of-joy nonsense. He understood that completely. He also understood that Ace was trying to help, not harm him, as a means for Stephan to open up and not keep everything so bottled up inside.

But sharing who he was had only ever brought pain, and so there wasn't a chance in hell he was going to willingly cut himself open for all to see his flaws and failings, not even for Ace.

The world thought it was so easy being a Devereaux.

That was a whole lie.

Nothing had ever come easy to Stephan, not the things that mattered anyway.

People only wanted to be around him for what he could do for them, in both the professional and the personal. And after the last time he'd dared let someone inside, they'd repaid him by blackmailing him in his darkest hour.

That had been the case with Dexter. The last man Stephan had ever let get close to him. Dexter and Stephan had met in Jamaica six months after Randall's death. Stephan had gone there on official Devereaux Inc. business, but the real reason he'd volunteered for the trip was one, he needed to make sure the secrets the beautiful island held for his brother would never come to light. But most of all, he'd gone there hoping to find some kind of closure.

He'd met Dexter in a club for the elite and they'd instantly been on fire. Finding that sort of happiness when you'd suffered a tragic loss turned out to be dangerous. A month later, Dexter was living with him in Paris. And when he caught Dexter with another man in Stephan's bed four months after that, the nightmare he'd have to endure to rid himself of Dexter, began.

Dexter had apparently figured he'd need an insurance policy just in case shit went sideways between them and he lost his meal ticket. To find what he needed, Dexter had bypassed Stephan's security on his personal laptop and discovered enough information about Randall's death to blackmail Stephan.

Evicting that man out of his life had cost Stephan his already compromised ability to trust, the trouble of having his legal team put together an ironclad NDA, and a five-million-dollar payoff.

After that debacle, people in hell had a greater chance of getting ice water than Ace had of getting Stephan to let anyone else inside.

Just as he'd come to that conclusion, his ride arrived, and within minutes he was standing in front of Crown Fried Chicken on Fulton Street and Franklin Avenue. He was certain his salvation couldn't be found in this place. But his momentary comfort, yeah, it had that in spades.

Stephan stepped inside of the storefront that barely held enough room to house more than a few customers at a time. The entire food counter was shielded behind a wall of plexiglass, so he had to bend down from his six-two height to speak into the order window.

No, it wasn't the most ideal dining experience, but the salty, fried goodness of the dirty wings would more than make up for that.

Stephan ordered from memory, even two years of fine dining in Paris couldn't dim his recollection of everything he liked at chain stores like this. Dirty wings were fried crispy, seasoned well enough to give a mythical giant high blood pressure, and best of all, cheap. He was a billionaire, that didn't mean he didn't enjoy a good bargain too.

As he pulled out his debit card to pay for his food, he wished decisions regarding his real life—especially where matters of family, trust, and love were concerned—were as sure and uncomplicated.

He stepped outside, watching the hustle of Fulton Street rush hour traffic, filled with cars and B25 MTA buses and bicyclists and pedestrians weaving their way through the smallest of openings to get to their destination.

The chaos of it all calmed him, made his brain stop thinking and the unsettled anxious feeling that had shrouded him since he left Ace's house, quiet. But soon enough his order was up and he was walking the remaining five blocks to his home. All he wanted to do was get inside his house, strip out of his suit, and plop down on his living room floor as he ate his dirty wings and watched trash TV.

After the shitty day he'd had, that shouldn't be too much to ask, right?

"Hey, mister!"

Stephan couldn't focus on the small distant voice. He ignored it, allowing it to fade into the background noise of a Brooklyn street.

He stood at his door, balancing his key in one hand and a large red slushy and a bag with a twelve-piece of fried wings, fries, and a sweet potato pie.

After spending two years in Paris with all its fine dining, being a car ride away from one of his old Brooklyn haunts was a familiar joy that he'd desperately needed at this moment.

He'd been home for four months now, but spending nearly every day at Devereaux Inc.'s Brooklyn headquarters and every night at his Uncle Ace's bedside, there had been few opportunities to venture off to hit up the hole-in-the wall spots like Crown Fried Chicken that only born and bred Brooklynites could appreciate.

Sure, he could've used a food delivery app to get it. However, he figured if he wasn't going to employ any restraint when it came to indulging this way, if he wanted it bad enough, he should at least go get it himself.

Between the sodium, fat, sugar, and carbs in the bag, he

was certain he could put himself into a food coma so he wouldn't have to deal with the pain of impending grief trying to swallow him whole from the inside out or the frustration that Ace had forced on him.

He'd just gotten the door open when he heard the small voice again, closer this time, three seconds too late.

Just as he looked around, he saw a little girl with wild brown curls in every direction that fell all around her shoulders. She was waving her hand, trying to get Stephan's attention, and by the time she did, he felt something small and furry bump across his ankle.

He jerked back, losing his balance as a blur of black fur ran in circles around his ankles before darting inside of Stephan's half-opened door.

Stephan felt himself falling backward as wet cold spread across his pecs when his cup tipped over and the red slushy bled all over his Armani shirt and suit jacket, and his wool peacoat.

Stephan expected to hit the hard concrete steps in front of his door, but instead, he hit a wall of hard flesh instead.

The only voice he'd heard he assumed belonged to the brown-skin sprite that had been calling him before. She couldn't have been any more than five, maybe six. There was no way she had the strength or the muscles to hold up his six-foot-two-inch frame.

"I gotcha."

The voice was deep and smooth, like a fine bourbon that you sipped to savor its rich flavor.

When Stephan could feel the ground beneath his feet again, he turned to finally lay eyes on the owner of the voice, the person who'd saved him.

Deep brown eyes, tan skin, and high cheekbones filled

his gaze. Of their own volition, his eyes continued to take in his apparent savior. Jet-black hair combed back off his face. It was tapered on the sides, and Stephan could see just the tiniest hint of gray teasing at his hero's temples, and a few more sprinkled into his neat, close-cropped beard.

Damn, he's pretty.

Pretty was an understatement. Now that Stephan was standing mostly on his own, he could see the man was an inch shorter than him, but matched him in the same lean but muscular build.

"Mister—" Stephan could hear that little insistent voice again "—can I go get Ebony?"

Tugging on the hemline of his coat broke through the mesmerizing hold the stranger's gaze had on Stephan, finally making him look down to see a smaller version of the same gaze staring up at him.

"E-ebony?" Stephan stammered. "Who's Ebony?"

"My puppy," the little girl said.

Stephan blinked, trying to figure out what the child was talking about. If he wasn't so busy staring at the beautiful man standing in front of him, he might be able to make some sense of what was going on.

"Nevaeh." That molten voice spoke and Stephan was forced to look into those hypnotic eyes again. "I think we've disturbed this man enough. Go and ask your grannie to fix you a snack. I'll get Ebony."

The little girl nodded, nearly skipping down the stairs and walking to an older woman waving from the stoop three to four doors down the block.

"I'm sorry. This is a hell of a way to introduce myself to my new neighbor."

A crooked smile tilted his tempting mouth, dragging Stephan's eyes directly to it.

"I'm Carter Jiménez." Carter held out his hand. "That little busybody tugging on your jacket was my daughter Nevaeh, and the little menace that escaped into your house is our new black lab, Ebony."

Stephan instinctively went to shake Carter's hand until he saw the red sticky remnants of his slushy all over his palm.

"Are you new on the block?" Carter's voice pulled Stephan's attention away from his very messy state. "I don't recall seeing you around much."

Stephan's personal alarm went off. As a Devereaux, he was always suspicious when random folks asked questions about him. Not that he believed himself to be so interesting, but when folks knew you came from a wealthy and powerful family, sometimes, they did strange things like sell information. The next thing he knew, he could end up on the Shade Room, being dragged for some filth he hadn't even had the pleasure of curating himself.

"I travel overseas a lot for work, so that's probably why we haven't run into each other before." He pulled a small pack of wet wipes out of his coat and cleaned his hands, then shrugged. "Or, just because it's Brooklyn and nowadays folks quietly mind each other's business without actually physically getting in each other's mix."

That comment garnered Stephan a wide grin from his neighbor that put him somewhat at ease.

"This is true." Carter's huff of laughter felt like sunlight poured directly into his soul. Stephan had the unrecognizable urge to cut loose and join in. "I remember growing up on the block in Bed-Stuy. You couldn't get away with anything, because at least one nosy adult was gonna rat you out to your moms, and all hell would break loose when you walked in at the end of the day."

At that, Stephan did laugh. He'd had quite a few of those experiences when he was a kid too. But as he aged, those informants went from being the caring residents on his block to newshounds and business competitors trying to use Stephan for one thing or another.

Suddenly aware that they'd been standing outside for more than a handful of minutes, Stephan placed his hands back in his pockets. He didn't hang, he didn't dawdle, and as alluring as his neighbor's smile was, standing outside long enough for prying eyes to catch a glimpse just wasn't his thing.

Carter must've managed to understand Stephan's unspoken desire to wrap this up, because he stepped up another step, bringing him closer to Stephan, making him more aware of just how good-looking Carter was. Hell, the man's edge-up game was so nice, Stephan was damn near mesmerized by how crisp those lines were around his forehead and his beard, and how badly they made him want to trace his fingers across them.

"I'm sorry about this little accident. Those wings look like they were good as hell."

The mention of his wings cleared his head. Looking down, Stephan saw his delicious wings spread out on his stoop, taunting him.

"Dammit," the expletive slipped from his lips. "I really wanted those, too."

"Again, I'm sorry…"

"Stephan." He took another longing glance at his wings before lifting his gaze to find remorse written all over Carter's face. "I guess my Friday night buffet isn't going to happen after all."

"Hey." Carter gave him a wary smile. If his remorse wasn't so cute, Stephan might be mad as hell. He really did want those wings in the worst way. "Your evening doesn't have to be tanked. I own The Vault."

"The VIP lounge?"

"Yeah," Carter replied. "Why don't you stop by tonight? I'll comp you all the wings you can eat. We don't sell red slushies, but I have a delicious, imported beer on tap that all my regulars seem to love. What do you say?"

Stephan had come home to wallow in his grief and fear, and somehow, he found himself covered in red slushy, his comfort food all over the ground, and a fine as sin man standing on his steps trying to give him all-he-could-eat wings and beer. Grief was the furthest thing from his mind right now, and at the moment, Stephan wasn't exactly put out by that.

"That…um…that sounds like a plan."

Stephan gave Carter one last smile, determined to get away from this man's unprecedented magnetism and out of his very sticky and essentially ruined clothes.

"See you later, Carter."

Stephan turned around to walk away.

"Stephan?"

He turned back around to find Carter pointing toward Stephan's door. "My dog?"

What the absolute hell is wrong with me?

"Sure." Stephan opened the door. "Let me get her. It's been a while since I've been home. I'm not sure what condition I left the place in."

Stephan left Carter standing on the stoop and went inside. He found his uninvited guest chewing on the edge of his very expensive silk rug like it was her favorite chew toy.

He should be mad. This little ball of fur had ruined his dinner and his rug. But when Stephan bent down and picked the little menace up, she instantly snuggled into his arms, licking the side of his face.

"All right, Ms. Ebony, you should know Black folks don't believe in kissing their dogs in the mouth." The dog ignored him and went right back to licking his jaw.

He chuckled. "Just like so many of the women in my family, you're just gonna do what you wanna do anyway, huh?"

The dog proceeded as if she hadn't heard anything. Stephan scratched behind her little floppy ears, smiling as the little thing showered him with affection.

"You're lucky you're cute and your daddy's even cuter, otherwise I'd have an attitude."

Stephan stepped outside and was greeted by Carter's megawatt smile, and once again he was transfixed and his reaction to this man was beginning to piss him off. He was Stephan Devereaux-Smith, a member of the most powerful Brooklyn family there was. People were caught up with him, not the other way around.

But when Carter took the small creature out of his hand and their fingers touched for the briefest moments, Stephan was open all over again.

"Thanks, Stephan. I'll be looking out for you tonight at the lounge. I'll see you soon."

Stephan watched as Carter's long legs carried him down one set of stairs and up another. It was only when his neighbor disappeared down the block that Stephan smiled, shoving his still slightly sticky hands in his slacks. Life was hell right now and Carter had presented Stephan with a distraction. Things would still be terrible in the morning. Ace would still be dying all the same. But maybe, just maybe, the pretty man with the cute kid and dog could make Stephan forget for just a little while.

"You certainly will."

Three

Stephan stood in front of his floor-to-ceiling mirror in his closet, trying to settle on the final touches of his outfit.

On his worst day, Stephan could always throw a look together without much effort. But tonight, even though he'd been dressed in Armani when Carter's dog assaulted him, he wanted to make sure his outfit said "in control, yet chill." He wanted Carter to see him as an everyday brotha just dropping in to enjoy some wings.

He shook his head, unable to believe the story he was trying to sell himself. He knew this was about something more than his "fit" being together. This was about making a good impression on Carter. He didn't know why he cared what Carter thought of him. He hadn't known the man for more than five minutes. But in that short amount of time, Carter had definitely made an impression on him.

He was friendly, outgoing, and Stephan could tell he had a great sense of humor. When you grew up with everything you did being scrutinized because of your family's social position, sometimes humor was all you had to help you keep your sanity.

He moved to his jewelry display case, going back and forth between the Rolex and the Cartier, before the sleek yet bold platinum link bracelet from Tiffany and Co. caught his eye. Satisfied with his choice, he quickly put it on and then grabbed the matching chain and secured it around his neck.

Deciding he'd fiddled enough with his clothes and accessories, it was time go. Better that than sitting around trying to analyze which demon he would attempt to ignore at present.

Besides, it's not like he was going to allow his interest in Carter to go beyond the superficial. He'd learned long ago that allowing anything deeper, meant inviting hurt into life. And right now, dealing with Ace's illness and Stephan's long-suffering entanglement with guilt was all the hurt he had tolerance for.

He grabbed his jacket, took a deep breath, and then headed out the door. Happy that he didn't have to care why he wanted to impress Carter. No, he didn't have to care, not one bit at all.

"Carter, you expecting somebody?"

Carter barely glanced at his best friend Lennox Carlisle as he vigorously wiped the bar top while looking at the main entrance.

"Why do you ask?" Carter managed to answer Lennox's question with a question, which he knew would annoy his friend.

Serves him right. Lennox was actively distracting Carter's ability to watch the door like a hawk in anticipation of seeing a certain tall, dark, and sexy man walk into his lounge.

"Because you've been shining the same spot on the bar like you're trying to take the paint off it. S'up?"

What was up, indeed. Damn if Carter knew. He'd been walking with his daughter and their puppy when his little princess had ignored his warning about holding on to the puppy's leash. The next thing he knew, he was taking two steps at a time to keep an innocent bystander on the porch a few houses down from Carter's from hitting the concrete.

"Nevaeh lost control of Ebony's leash and the little miscreant nearly tripped one of my neighbors, causing him to lose the bag full of dirty wings and his red slushy all over his shirt front and porch."

"You worried he's gonna cause a fuss?"

Carter shook his head. "Nah. Most of all, he just really looked sad. At first, I thought it was over his lost food. But when I looked at him, it seemed to run deeper than that. Like he was going through something. So, I told him to come down here and I would comp him all the wings he could eat."

Lennox leaned against the bar, his pointed eyebrow acting as a bullshit detector.

"And so, you thought the wings you serve here would somehow magically make this stranger happy?"

Lennox tilted his head, looking Carter up and down with suspicion until he had a wide grin settled on his face, and he asked. "What's he look like?"

Carter immediately went back to wiping down his bar. It wasn't just an action to keep up with the city health code, it also calmed his mood when his best friend was getting on his last nerve.

"Carter," Lennox sang, placing a hand on top of Carter's, stilling his repetitive motion.

Carter huffed. "He was a walking wet dream, okay. An inch or so taller than me, lanky build with broad shoulders, and rich, dark skin. But no matter how attractive he was, that wasn't the reason I invited him."

He waited for Lennox to crack a joke, but true to form, his friend could tell there was something more happening here. And just like always, Lennox was there for him with no judgment at all.

"I looked in his eyes and I saw something familiar reflected in them, something I've seen in my own whenever I looked in a mirror."

"What's that?" Lennox asked, waiting patiently for an answer.

"Grief." Carter met his friend's eyes and watched them soften at the utterance of the word.

After tragically losing his wife, Michelle, in an accident five years ago, grief had become an unwanted guest that had barged into his life uninvited.

"And so, you just want to give him a little bit of grief therapy?"

Carter shrugged, not really knowing how to answer Lennox.

"I just know that some days, the grief was so powerful I could hardly breathe. But whenever I wanted to crumble under it, you or my mom or Gracie came through to throw me a lifeline."

Carter threw the cloth over his shoulder as he looked his friend in the eye.

"I just know what it is to need a little kindness when life has its foot on your neck. I'm just trying to pay it forward, man, you know?"

"Yeah," Lennox agreed before taking the last swig of his

beer. "But don't be so disappointed if he doesn't take you up on your offer. If you remember, you weren't the easiest person to help either, and we had a lifetime of friendship under our belt when you went through that hell. Maybe he's just not there yet, and that's okay."

Lennox stood up, taking a few bills from his pocket and laying them on the bar.

"You leaving already?"

"Yeah," Lennox replied with a little more excitement than was necessary. "Amara's at that point in her pregnancy where she can't get enough of me, and as much as I love you, ain't no way I'm missing what she's offering to sit at your bar."

"God, you're a pig," Carter replied.

"A well-satisfied pig. Can you say the same?"

Carter certainly could not and they both knew it. He'd dated here and there over the last two years, but when you were a single dad and a business owner, dating, even hookups that required no dating at all were a luxury Carter didn't always have the time or the energy for.

Lennox winked at him, chuckling as he headed out the door. Carter spread his hands flat on the bar, enjoying the slow pace of his lounge. The Friday night rush hadn't come in yet, and there were just a few members scattered throughout the front room.

The Vault was a members-only VIP lounge. There were three floors open to the patrons. On the main floor, a bar, a dining area, and a private dining room for private parties. Carter's office was also on the main floor down a private corridor off to the side of bar. The upper level was for gaming tables and TVs, which were flanked by another bar and lounge area. The third floor held a dance floor, a DJ booth,

and yes, another bar. They served brunch, lunch, and dinner, or for those patrons that just wanted a drink and some
apps, they were more than welcome to eat at any of the bars.

Although the food and drinks were top-tier, that's not
why his clientele came. At The Vault, the Brooklyn elite
came to get away from the public world. Here, other than the
house security cameras, which no one had access to other
than Carter and his head of security, no cameras, electronic
devices, or audio equipment were allowed. Each member
had to deposit those things into an assigned locker in the
coatroom that was always staffed with two attendants.

There was a zero-tolerance policy for breaking the rules.
Carter was that protective of his members' privacy. You
couldn't even enter through the street level. While there
were emergency exits that let out to the street, allowing for
safe evacuation if necessary, you had to actually drive or
walk down a ramp and be cleared to enter the building by
a host and a security team.

Membership was a rigorous and expensive vetting process that included background checks, personal recommen-
dations from other established members, and an okay from
Carter's gut as the last checkpoint. So if you could get past
all those hurdles, The Vault was a place for you to let go and
be a normal person for the time you were here.

It was born out of Carter's inability to get away from the
eyes of the world when he was at his lowest and the world
just wouldn't let him be human for one damn minute.

Five years ago, thirty-two-year-old Carter had been living a completely different life. He was married to his beautiful wife, Michelle, and they were new parents. He was on
top of his career as one of the most sought-after actors in

mainstream Hollywood. A feat doubly impressive for a bi-sexual Puerto Rican boy from Brooklyn.

But as quickly as his star rose, it came crashing back down, shattering into a billion tiny pieces when his wife was ripped from his life.

Refusing to revisit the pain that came with allowing his mind to venture back to that very dark time, he went about setting up for the crowd he knew would be coming soon.

Glancing up from the glass he was drying, Carter's gaze came to an abrupt halt when Stephan seemed to just appear. His presence quickly filled the room like thick smoke.

There, his neighbor with the sad eyes and beautiful lips stood still, his gaze combing the room until he found Carter.

Carter knew the exact moment Stephan spotted him. It wasn't just because of the flicker of fire in Stephan's dark eyes. No, it was because he felt it, like a jolt of electricity sizzling through him, burning each layer of his skin as it dissipated throughout his system.

Slowly, he moved across the room and Carter took a mo-ment to really soak up this vision of a man.

Stephan had traded his Armani, slushy stained suit for a red Billionaire Boys Club helmet varsity jacket paired with a black Henley and black straight-cut jeans.

Carter let his eyes drift to the floor to get a glimpse of the wheat nubuck Jimmy Choo X Timberland boots that brought the entire outfit together, and he smiled.

Outside of his brownstone, Stephan had seemed a lit-tle stiff if Carter was to be honest. But if this was relaxed Stephan, Carter wasn't mad at all. Brothas in a pair of Timbs had been his weakness when he was in his teens and early twenties.

He'd thought he'd outgrown that particular quirk, possibly because, once he'd met Michelle, he'd fallen so hard for her, no one caught his notice but her. But there was something about the confident way that jacket hung on Stephan's broad shoulders, and the rhythmic swag in his walk that woke up something Carter hadn't felt in a long time...lust.

He was still processing that when Stephan sat down on the stool directly in front of him.

"Well," Stephan began slowly as he took a moment to look around. "I'm here. Where are these amazing wings and beer you promised me?"

"I'll put in an order for you now. It's should take a few minutes. But while you wait, here's the beer."

Carter filled a glass from the tap and handed it to Stephan, an innocent action he'd performed countless times in the five years he'd owned this lounge. But tonight, Stephan's fingers grazed Carter's and fire burned where their flesh met.

The heat made him want to draw his hand back, but somewhere between Stephan's touch and Carter's brain, the message was lost.

"Thank you, man."

The deep timbre of Stephan's voice rattled through Carter, drawing him in, making him lean onto the bar to get closer.

It was only so he could hear Stephan better. It had nothing to do with the fact that the sight of this man made his pulse jump or that being this close, the spicy sweetness of his cologne was more intoxicating than any of the alcoholic beverages lining the mirrored wall behind the bar. No, it had nothing to do with any of that.

"What are you thanking me for? You haven't even tasted the wings yet."

Carter tried to make his tone light and fun, but his words

seemed breathier, and he wondered where the hell had his hardcore Brooklynness gone? He was a real one. No matter that his face used to be plastered on big screens all over the world, he'd never lost his down-to-earth "carismático" persona.

"You did me a solid I didn't even know I needed."

Carter watched Stephan's eyes fill with an ache that rang so familiar in his chest. Carter wanted to press to ask what he had lost, but remembered Lennox's warning.

He didn't know this man and he had no right to push into his life, even if his intentions were good and he just wanted to help.

He filled a glass for himself, stepping back, trying to put space between them and give Stephan room to breathe.

"I know I'm probably gonna sound so pathetic. Like a stereotypical bar patron crying over their beer."

"This is a no judgment zone. I've needed to cry over my beer a time or two in my life, and my friends always let me do it, so I'm paying it forward."

"So…" Stephan raised a brow as he peeled away the label on his now-empty beer bottle. "We're friends now?"

"We're neighbors," Carter said between sips, trying his hardest to keep things cool and unbothered. "I don't see why we can't be friends too. I'm new on our street, after all. I could use someone to give me the rundown on the haps on the block."

"I don't know how much good I would be on that score. I've been in Paris working for the last two years. I bought my brownstone a year before I left, so I haven't exactly bonded with any of the neighbors either."

Carter tipped his beer toward Stephan and offered him

a playful wink, again trying to keep things light, even if everything about his reaction to this man was over-the-top.

"Even better reason we should link up. We're the two newbies on the block."

Stephan locked gazes with him, his stare unwavering, as if he were attempting to see if there was more to Carter's nice guy act than just him trying to be, well…nice.

Stephan looked up at him again and the grief was still there, but there was something else, something more intense and it made Carter squeeze his beer tumbler so hard, he worried he might break the thing in his hand.

"I don't know how much of a friend I could be right now. But I sure as hell wouldn't mind a distraction."

Stephan licked his lips and every muscle tightened in Carter's body, wondering what those thick pillows would feel like pressed against his skin. Was he this hard up that he was actually standing here low-key, letting a man who was obviously going through something hit on him?

"You wouldn't happen to know of any distractions I could get into around here, would you?"

If Carter were a better man, he'd turn down the innuendo etched in the sharp lines of Stephan's face, that burned so deeply in his soulful eyes. But he wasn't a better man, apparently, because when he opened his mouth, instead of saying no. He said, "Yes, I certainly do."

Four

"This is certainly not the distraction I was expecting."

Stephan watched the corners of Carter's mouth curl into a devious grin. It was at that moment Stephan understood that Carter was extremely aware of what Stephan had been expecting and was enjoying Stephan's enlightenment. Obviously, Stephan was the only person in the room who'd assumed they'd be partially disrobed by now.

"Oh, I know exactly what you were expecting." Carter leaned down, aligning his shot on the ebony pool table with the bloodred velvet top. "And don't get me wrong, I wouldn't mind it. In fact, I very much want it."

"Then why not take what I'm offering?"

Carter stood up, holding his cue stick at his side. Stephan could tell the man was choosing his words carefully, thinking before he spoke. It showed a thoughtfulness and awareness the businessman in him appreciated. But the flawed man in him and his half-hard cock weren't as appreciative of this quality.

"Are you married?"

While Stephan's question may have appeared cynical, it wasn't. He didn't believe every devastatingly hot man he encountered was a devoted husband by day and trolling for hookups by night. Unfortunately, that didn't mean he didn't have to always be cautious. There were too many wealthy, powerful men who presented one face to the world so they could enjoy the privilege their apparent heterosexuality brought them.

But when they thought no one could see them, they would forget about the wives they had at home and slake their desires with men behind closed doors.

Stephan wasn't about that life. Being on the DL, more formally known as the "Down Low", didn't appeal to him one bit.

Yes, he was a wealthy man. But what little he did expose to the public about himself, hiding who he was wasn't part of that. He also wasn't for knowingly or unknowingly hurting someone else's spouse. He had enough dirty little secrets to carry. Knowing about someone else's deception regarding their sexuality wasn't a confidence he had any desire to hold. His life was complicated enough being part of the Devereaux family. Upholding the public image of perfection—an image needed to keep the family name and the business profitable—while knowing how flawed they all were was sometimes more weight than he could bear. He didn't need to add being someone's side piece to the mix as well.

"No, I'm not married." Carter paused for a second before he continued. "I've been a widower for the last five years."

Stephan's back straightened at the word *widower* and his stomach tightened with remorse. When death was stalking someone you loved, the knowledge that very soon you would walk the same painful path others had rang loud, like the knell of a bell filling a cathedral.

"I'm sorry."

Carter took a deep breath, allowing what looked akin to peace to soothe his features.

"Thank you," Carter replied. "But please don't feel sorry for me. I had the love of my life for ten years and she gave me a beautiful daughter. That's more than most people get."

Stephan saw a twinkle of heartwarming nostalgia mixed with the ache of loss, and the fact that Carter could still smile and grasp even a sliver of happiness from his memories made envy hang in Stephan's belly.

You have to first accept Ace's fate before you can move on to that sort of peace.

The thought caught Stephan off guard. Sure, in his head he knew that Ace was dying. That very soon he'd lose someone so precious to him, he wondered if he'd survive. But knowing, and experiencing the finality of it in real time were two different things.

"My late wife has nothing to do with the reason I put the brakes on the very clear subliminals you were throwing."

Carter's voice broke through Stephan's grim musings, pulling a chuckle from him. "Was I that obvious?"

"I'm a fan of obvious honesty." Carter turned away from the pool table in his office, walking to a mini fridge in the corner and returning with two beers in his hand. "We live on the same street. I just don't want to make things awkward. It can get a little weird running into a one-night stand when you're pulling up on the block. I've only lived there for a year. My daughter and I are just feeling settled. I don't want to rock the boat for her."

Stephan took a sip of his beer, nodding briefly. He could

respect Carter's perspective. But he'd certainly be an outright liar if he said the thought of peeling every stitch of the fine silk shirt and fitted black slacks Carter wore away from his skin didn't have the lick of desire still burning through his veins.

"Well, since you're not interested in sleeping with me, why did you invite me back to your office?" Stephan stepped in a circle around the large room with its slate gray walls and black furniture that made the room both stylish and inviting. "I mean, the office is great and the pool table is top-tier, but if you didn't plan on letting me have my way with you on top of it, why bother?

Carter hung his head as his muscled form shook in laughter.

"There's that honesty again."

When Carter brought his head up again, Stephan's gaze caught the gleam of Carter's wide grin and his chest tightened.

Since when had he ever been into a man's smile? Never, in the history of ever, as far as he could remember. Not even as a besotted teenager who'd fallen hard for the upperclassmen in high school who hadn't known his young freshman self was alive had his stomach fluttered over a man. And when Carter's deep brown eyes sparkled with the right mix of mischief and "I'm sexy and I know it" mojo, Stephan's stomach definitely felt like it was on the high spin cycle of a washing machine.

"For the record, I never said anything about being uninterested."

Carter's heated gaze slid down the length of Stephan and back up again, taking him in as if Stephan were a tasty treat locked behind a display glass.

"I brought you here because you looked like you were going through something and I know what that feels like. And I can tell you, when life was kicking my ass, sex wouldn't have fixed anything, even if I could've ignored the pain long enough to get lost in someone else."

Carter put down his beer on a nearby table and walked across the room until he was standing so close to Stephan, he could smell the subtle spice in Carter's cologne.

Stephan's skin felt tight with need and his muscles ached with desperation as he tried to keep himself still so he didn't do something stupid like pull this man into a kiss and do his damnedest to discover what that beautiful bow in Carter's upper lip tasted like.

"If sex didn't work," Stephan ground out, his voice like sand over rough gravel, causing his throat to burn as he spoke. "What did?"

"Having friends who checked in on me even when I didn't want them to. But most of all, having someone to talk to without judgment. And for some reason, I get the sense you don't have that readily available to you."

Stephan pulled in a ragged breath, placing his hands on his lean hips to pull his rib cage up so he could force more air into his lungs.

"I live in a world where opening yourself up can mean your literal destruction. Sharing anything other than what people need to know isn't something I can readily do."

"I can't believe there's no one, Stephan."

Carter's words forced Stephan to go through his mental Rolodex. Friends and acquaintances were out. He couldn't chance what he'd done being leaked to the authorities or the press. It would ruin the family, and Devereaux Inc. would take a hit he wasn't sure it could recover from.

Yes, his cousins loved him and would do anything for him. But if they found out he'd lied and run like a coward for the last two years to cover it up, they might not want anything to do with him again.

Especially Lyric.

Lyric could never know the truth he was hiding.

He could never trade freedom from his own guilt if inflicting pain on her would be the result.

Uncle David would bear the secret if he knew. As the family lawyer, that would be his job. But he wouldn't use legalities to bind that man to a secret that would break his heart.

And his mother, she was so filled with anger and the desire for vengeance since his brother's death, there was no way he could tell her the truth. He couldn't trust that she wouldn't use the information to harm Ace. Hell, she'd already tried to enact a hostile takeover of Devereaux Inc., If Stephan opened his mouth, looking for someone to lighten his load, he just couldn't be sure Martha wouldn't use it to her own ends, even if that meant cutting her one remaining son down at the knees.

No, there was only Ace. Ace, who had been by his side. Ace, who had helped him protect the secret all these years. Ace, who was dying, and Stephan didn't have the heart to ask the man to bear another thing for him.

"You don't know anything about me, Carter. Why do you care whether I have someone to talk to or not?"

"Because I was you, and now I'm not. I'm proof that you can survive loss, however significant that loss is. I'm proof you can live again."

Carter's words hit Stephan in the middle of his chest, and if he hadn't had his hands on his hips, the sheer impact of them would've folded him over like a soggy French fry.

Living? What the hell was that? He hadn't lived since he received the news that his brother had died. All he did was exist. He existed to bear the secret that could destroy his family and their business. He existed to protect his sister-in-love's heart and peace of mind. He existed to do whatever was needed to calm Ace's fears as he transitioned from this life unto the next. Living? No, that wasn't part of the equation at all.

Carter kept staring at him, his warm brown eyes offering Stephan a soft, warm place to let down his armor and rest.

He was tired. So tired of bearing this weight. Every moment he held on to all this sadness, pain, and secrecy, Stephan felt like the walls were closing in on him.

Maybe it can't hurt to share just a little of your woes? His mind whispered that to him like a pusher seeking to hook a new user. Stephan was strong and smart, though. Surely he could share a tiny bit—just enough to release just a little of the pressure—without baring his complete soul, right?

You don't need what this man is offering, Stephan. The timing was all wrong. Somehow that did nothing to slake Stephan's desire for him. But more importantly, it did not extinguish this unnatural urge in him to share his burden with Carter. Someone who knew exactly how corrosive loss was.

"My uncle is dying."

Stephan fought every lesson he'd ever been taught about keeping the family's business private.

Keep our business out of the street. Never break the cipher.

He closed his eyes to quiet the clanging alarms sounding off in his head. It wasn't his sheer will that made them stop, however. It was the sliver of relief that was beginning to weave its way through every sinew of his body.

"I'm so sorry, Stephan."

Carter's reply was just the push he needed to make him continue, even though it went against all Stephan's instincts.

"My uncle raised me, loved me through some pretty rough times. And he's never asked a single thing from me in return, until today."

Carter folded his arms, waiting for Stephan to continue. His attentive but soft gaze letting Stephan know if he wanted to end the conversation, he was okay with that too.

"He asked me to throw him a Christmas party, a nod to happier days in my family."

"That doesn't seem like such a strange request."

"It's not." Stephan rubbed a hand down his face, pursing his lips as he figured out how to say what he needed without exposing Ace to this perfect, albeit hot, stranger. "It's just, there's a very real possibility he won't make it till Christmas and celebrating right now feels wrong."

A flash of a Christmas past at Borough Hall with he and his cousin Amara fiddling underneath the tree with the other Devereaux kids while the adults drank eggnog cocktails and laughed about old times that Stephan and Amara hadn't been old enough to understand. And now that he was in fact old enough to understand, that wonderful warmth that surrounded him was disappearing forever.

"To you," Carter replied. "But have you considered that this may be the last time for him to see all of his loved ones before he goes?"

"My uncle practically said as much when he asked me to throw him the party. I just can't see myself celebrating the fact that he's leaving us."

Carter shook his head and shared a comforting smile as he laid a gentle hand on Stephan's shoulder.

"Not happy that he's leaving, happy that he's still here for another holiday with you and the rest of your family."

Stephan's mind took in Carter's words, planting them somewhere in his consciousness, where things began to take root.

Carter was right. Ace did want a final memory of all his family together. He knew this would make the old man happy. But an event for the family included his mother too. He knew Ace had probably already considered this, but in his nostalgic and sickly haze, Stephan wasn't sure the man really accounted for how bad things were between Ace and Martha. Knowing how much tension there was between the two, could Stephan really give Ace the loving Devereaux Christmas he longed for?

"My family's complicated, Carter." Stephan shrugged, trying to shake the tension building across his shoulders.

"All families are complicated, Stephan. That shouldn't stop you from doing this for your uncle, if this is what he wants."

"Trust me," Stephan huffed. "My family's built different. The standard rules don't always apply."

Carter's unrelenting optimism was painted across his mouth in a comforting smile, letting Stephan know whatever excuse he came up with, Carter had an answer for it. That, however, didn't mean Stephan wasn't going to try to find a suitable justification anyway.

"This sounds good in theory, but the truth is, I don't know if my uncle will make it until Christmas. With Thanksgiving being three weeks away, I don't really see getting this thing done as quickly as it would need to happen."

Stephan took another swig of his beer, hoping this would quiet the mild throbbing in his head and loosen the ache in his back.

"Listen. It doesn't matter if it were August at the height of a sweltering New York summer. If your uncle wants this and you're able to do it for him, I don't see the harm in giving him what he wants. And if you need any help, you can always call me. Party planning is part of the job of owning this place."

Stephan released a long huff, relieved that some of the tension in his neck was starting to fade away.

"I think I'd like that." Stephan tried to find the strength to offer a warm smile. "Thanks for the offer." It was probably just out of pity. Who would want to get involved with planning something like this, especially when there wasn't any history between the two of them? Knowing that didn't stop Stephan from appreciating Carter's gesture nonetheless.

"Are you free tomorrow night?" Stephan's eyes widened at Carter's question. This man couldn't be serious, could he?

Stephan nodded and waited for Carter to continue.

"You have any food allergies? I make a mean paella, along with a few other dishes I could bring for you to sample for the menu that will make you forget about everything that ails you."

Stephan seriously doubted Carter's claim. But the warmth radiating in the middle of his chest told him to give it a try anyway.

"No allergies. Paella and whatever else you want to bring sounds great."

"Good. I'll bring the food, and while we eat we can brainstorm about this party."

More warmth spread through Stephan as he listened to Carter. No romantic interest had ever touched Stephan like this. And since he hadn't actually had the opportunity to act on his attraction to Carter, he couldn't truly call him a romantic interest—which only baffled him further.

"You're bringing me food and helping me get this last-minute Christmas party for the ages together. The least I can do is have some wine for you to drink and a dessert for you to enjoy. I make a delightful lemon sorbet, and unless the cleaning service I've used to keep the place together while I was away has hit my wine cellar, I think I should have the perfect wine to go with it. Is eight too late. I've got work and then a family thing immediately following."

"Eight is perfect," Carter replied. "See you then."

This man had set aside Stephan's advances, and instead of telling Stephan to kick rocks with open-toed shoes on, as he deserved for acting like a creep, Carter was offering to help him heal his family.

This was all very strange to Stephan. Strange, but enjoyable.

Carter's mouth curved into a bright and wide grin that nearly stopped Stephan's ability to breathe.

What the hell?

This wasn't a date. This was a nice guy doing him a favor. So the excitement fluttering in his stomach shouldn't have been there.

But it was.

Stephan took a swig of his beer, wondering when he'd reverted into a teenager with no impulse control instead of the grown, disciplined man he was.

He put his half-finished beer on a nearby tabletop, gave Carter a brief nod because he couldn't trust himself not to stay, and not to touch Carter. When he was arm's length away from escape, Carter stopped him.

"Oh, and Stephan," The way that Carter's rich baritone

enveloped his name made him bite down on his bottom lip to keep a satisfied moan from escaping his mouth. "If anyone was going to be having their way tonight, it would've been me having my way with you."

Every muscle in Stephan's body tightened as the rumble of Carter's voice trembled through him. That wasn't an empty threat or just one Brooklynite joking with another. Game recognized game. Stephan had thrown that tone around a time or two. It was a voice so deep it was as if it were bathed in whiskey. Stephan had used it only when he'd needed to take control of a rudderless ship and give clear guidance on what the next step on the journey was. This, however, was the first time he'd been on the receiving end of it.

Control and organization kept things running smoothly and kept the people he loved from getting hurt. Ace had taught him that and Stephan had held tightly to that lesson. But standing at the edge of this room, held in place by the sheer will delivered in Carter's voice, for once, everything in him ached to let someone else control him and his situation.

Five

November in Brooklyn meant the night encroached upon the day before five. Streetlights and stars lit Clinton Hill in a soft amber light that always comforted Stephan. Yes, he'd traveled all over the world and seen iconic places that were praised in lofty circles. But to him, the rhythmic hum of a concrete Brooklyn street would always, always be a thing of beauty.

He took one last gaze outside of his office window at Devereaux Inc., comforted by the familiarity of the Dekalb and Clinton Avenues intersection. This was home. And even though his family situation weighed on him, he would always be happy to let his gaze linger over these streets.

"And what about the preliminary numbers for the upcoming quarter?" Stephan rejoined his conversation with the second-in-command of the Paris office.

"Are already in your inbox."

Stephan smiled as he looked down at the computer screen, finding the lifted brow his assistant Henrí offered.

Henrí was just as much of a perfectionist as Stephan. He triple-and quadruple-checked everything before he let it grace Stephan's inbox or desk.

Leaving Paris as abruptly as he had upon getting the news of Ace's decline, Stephan had only had enough time to pack a bag and get on the first flight he could book back to the States. Once notified of the situation, as Stephan's second-in-command, Henrí seamlessly took over the operations of the Paris office of Devereaux Inc.

Both knew Henrí could do both their jobs in his sleep, so the fact that Stephan was nitpicking over quarterly reports was a glaring sign that he was still feeling unmoored after last night's encounter with Carter.

"Thanks, Henrí," Stephan managed. "I'm slightly concerned that I'm obsolete with how well you've been running things these last five months. When I left, I never imagined working remotely for so long."

"I know you didn't. But honestly, knowing how much you love Mr. Devereaux, there was no way I could imagine you not going home to spend his remaining time with him. You made the right choice, Stephan. And the blessing of technology is that you can still do your job while being so far away."

Devereaux Inc. allowed for flexible schedules and remote options for its employees. Unless your work required you to be in-house, it wasn't mandated that you be bound to a Devereaux Inc. desk. Stephan had never imagined when that policy had been enacted, he himself would need to take advantage of it. But here he was.

Stephan shook his head. "No, the blessing is having you as my second. I couldn't leave the office in anyone else's hands."

Henrí gave Stephan a brief nod before the tentative fur-
row of his brow signaled there was something more he
wanted to say.

"How is Ace?"

Stephan leaned back in his chair, one elbow bracing his
tired torso up against one of the arms. He hated this question. Especially when he was at work.

Devereaux Inc. was the one place he could pretend his
world wasn't ending. But as loyal as Henrí had been to both
Stephan and Ace, he knew the man's concerns deserved to
be addressed.

"His prognosis is the same. He's dying. When he ended
up in the hospital this summer, we thought he was leaving
us then. But he just seems to be holding on for something.
I think he's fighting to see Amara and Lennox's baby be
born. That's the only loose end I can think of."

A sad, but loving smile curved Henrí's lips. "I'm sure Ace
would love to meet a new Devereaux. But the only thing
I've ever heard him talk about fighting for was his 'babies,'
and if I remember, that's pretty much all of the cousins in
your generation."

Stephan narrowed his gaze. He and Henrí weren't the
closest of friends, so if he knew that, it was because he'd
heard it come from Ace's mouth. That man was worse than
any grandparent with pictures of their new grand. Ace had
doted on Amara, Lyric, Jeremiah, and himself forever and
always. Now that Ace's estranged granddaughter, Trey, had
returned, falling in love with Jeremiah and marrying him,
she too was included in that overarching "babies" that Ace
always lovingly spoke of.

"You're right, he does love us. But everyone is boo'd up

and Amara is even cooking a human. As far as all his old-fashioned markers go, Ace's 'babies' are doing just fine."

"Maybe in your eyes, Stephan. But maybe Ace sees something that you're blind to. Something only the love of an elder can recognize."

The crack in Stephan's heart spread just a millimeter more every time he thought about Ace leaving him. He'd like to say it was just his specific connection to Ace he was grieving, but Stephan knew that wasn't the case.

For all the Devereaux cousins, he'd been a rock, a pillar, a cheerleader, and if you went left when you should've gone right, he'd been the correction they'd needed too. Having someone who just knew—without you having to say a word—that something was going wrong, it was a gift Stephan was ashamed to say he hadn't truly appreciated until it was slowly being taken from him.

Stephan placed a finger at his temple as he leaned into the cushions of his chair, trying hard not to crumble under the wall of sadness that seemed to get higher—brick by brick—with every day.

"God—" Stephan cleared his throat "—you're over three thousand miles away and you're sounding like him, Henrí."

"For the most part, I've never known the old man to be wrong, so I'll take that as a compliment. Anyway, you have all the documents you need. If there's nothing else, I have a bottle of wine chilling and a beautiful young woman on her way to help me drink it. I'll see you next week, Stephan. Give my best wishes to Ace and the rest of the Devereauxs. Call if you need me for anything."

Stephan gave him a mock salute before the screen went black.

He was just about to exhale all the tension Henrí's gentle

demeanor had helped soothe when he could hear a slight disturbance on the other side of his door.

"He's on a conference call right now and not taking visitors. If you would kindly make an appointment, I'll see that you get on his calendar immediately."

Stephan sat up quickly and he could feel the tension his body had tried to release, bunching the muscles of his neck into a hard knot.

His executive assistant, Andre, had on his professional but defensive voice. He only used it when people were crossing the boundaries he'd asked Andre to enforce.

And since no one in the office had an issue with those boundaries, Stephan knew he could only be talking to one person.

"Five, four, three, two, one." He counted slowly, and exactly on cue, the cold but familiar voice spoke.

"I am not some business associate to be handled, my dear. I am his mother, and I will see him right now."

Within seconds, his door flew open and the very last person he needed in his presence right now entered with a frantic Andre running behind her.

He silently waved Andre off, letting him know he'd deal with his mother from here.

Martha Devereaux-Smith stood in the middle of his office, wearing a wide-leg black pantsuit covered by a fashionable white wool coat. Her use of color against her rich, tawny brown skin, coupled with her gray hair pulled into her signature bun gave her an elegant, aristocratic appearance that made most people fearful to cross her.

But he'd been raised by this woman and was immune to her toxicity. And more than anything, that was the reason he was never her favored son. That honor went to one man only, his late brother, Randall.

"Your brother would never have had me wait in the waiting room like some commoner."

He snorted. Martha never missed a beat to bring the drama.

"Mother, contrary to your delusions, you are not royal or noble, so I think that means you are in fact in a commoner."

"You were always too rude and ungrateful for your own good, boy. A lingering effect of my poor choice in allowing you to spend so much time with that wretched Ace."

"Don't"

His voice was intentionally sharp, slicing through the air and hitting his target dead center. To most, his mother still seemed cold, unfazed by his command. But he knew Martha Devereaux-Smith better than anyone else. He'd grown up in her house and seen how she maneuvered and manipulated people to get exactly what she wanted. Though he wasn't skilled enough to master her as a child and use her powers against her, he had learned to stay out of her way, keep her eyes off him so he could hold on to some semblance of peace. And the best way to do that was by disappearing to his uncle Ace's house, where he was cared for instead of weaponized or trained to dominate the world like the heir apparent, Randall, had been.

The narrowing of her gaze, the sharp jut of her jaw, those were her tells. The instinctive tells she couldn't keep in check that revealed when her control was disturbed by something she either hadn't seen coming or didn't know how to restrain.

"If you want to spew your ugliness about Ace, do it somewhere else. But what you're not going to do is disrespect him in his own company, Mother. Not while I sit here."

That man she'd referred to as *wretched* was one of the only adults in his life who didn't see him as a nuisance. He was an "oops" baby. Conceived just as his mother was embarking on menopause when she'd thought she'd be free to focus solely on making Randall Ace's heir. The universe had another plan, and here he was, born more than twenty years after her first child with none of the insatiable need for power Randall seemed to inherit in doubles from her.

She'd had no use for him because she'd had her precious. When his father died just a few years before Stephan's first double digit, Martha had had no idea how to deal with a sensitive boy who didn't want to bend the world to his will. But Ace had.

Ace… Ace had taken every moment he could to let the lonely little boy in the family know that he was loved, wanted, and appreciated.

It was punishment enough that there were only a finite number of moments he had with Ace left. He wouldn't let Martha sully even one of them with her long-held hatred of her brother. Especially…when he knew the reasons for her hate were his fault, and not Ace's.

Stephan took a breath, trying to find some compassion for his mother, but it was so hard when she worked so diligently at erasing even the smallest crumb of empathy in his heart.

"You defend him so profoundly." Her words were strong, but appropriately reserved. She was a diva of the highest order, and never would she allow anyone to see her act out of character in public. "What a joy it would be if you could find that kind of love and vigor for me, the woman who gave *you* life."

"Mother, I'm sure you didn't come all the way down here for this. Did you want something?"

"I want my son to act like he can stand to be in a room with me for more than five minutes. You've been home over four months, and yet, I've only seen you a few times. When am I going to rank on your list of priorities, Stephan?"

"Mother, Ace is dying. Can't you find the slightest bit of grace. He's your brother, for God's sake. The patriarch of this family, and this entire family is hurting from the fear of his loss. Do you understand that, Mother? He's dying. Can't you find it in your heart to put your differences aside to work things out before it's too late? Can't you have the slightest bit of concern for those of us who love him?"

She straightened her shoulders, pulling them back as she arranged her coat around them.

"That man cut my heart out when he killed my son. And even though you didn't hold your brother in high enough regard to stop following behind Ace like a little puppy, I will either find a way to avenge my son or I will dance on Ace's grave. At this point, I'm just as partial to one as the other."

Stephan had to squeeze his hands into tight firsts to keep himself from speaking the words that had lingered in his heart and mind for the last two years. But as Martha turned on her designer heels and exited the door, Stephan knew he'd have to watch her. Whatever scheme she was up to, he knew it would not be good for Ace, Devereaux Inc. or anyone else in the Devereaux clan.

Six

Carter stood in his large master bedroom, standing in front of the mirror that stood in the corner.

The room was decorated in warm browns, burgundies, and creams. Being raised by a mother who was born in the Caribbean, Carter had always been surrounded by bright, exciting colors. But when he'd lost Michelle, he could never seem to bear that brightness again. When they moved into this place, Carter had instructed the interior decorator to create a space that was warm and nurturing but had just a splash of the masculine. As the only man living in this house, sometimes he needed something that was distinctive and something all his own that didn't appear in any of the other rooms of the house.

"So, this boy you're going on a date with?" His mother continued through his speakerphone with a tone that told him whatever it was she was about to ask, she had a stockpile of information on the topic already. "Is he nice?"

"Mommy, I told you, this isn't a date. I'm helping someone plan a Christmas party for a sick relative. There's no dating involved."

"Carter, mijo?"

He shook his head. Anytime she started with his name, followed by the loving endearment for *my son* in Spanish, he was looking at a serious guilt trip session.

"Mommy, I'm serious. I know you want to see me happy and married off again. But the truth is, Michelle was it for me. And I'm raising your granddaughter. I don't have time to devote my attention to a relationship."

"Carter," she huffed, and if she were here with him, he knew she'd be looking up at the ceiling as she mouthed *Dios mio* to the heavens. That was always how she dealt with him when his exasperating obtuseness was on display.

"You know I'm not telling you to marry if that's not what you want. But you gotta stop hiding. You have to engage with the outside world."

"I do," he added.

"No, you don't. You work and you take care of Nevaeh, and now you have this dog… What on earth possessed you to get that dog anyway. Don't you have enough on your plate?"

He most certainly did, and adding a puppy to it really made him question his own sanity most days.

"Nevaeh asked me for a sibling. I knew I couldn't give her that, so a puppy was the next best thing."

"Carter—"

"Mommy, I'm not there. Losing Michelle, the way I did, I just don't know if I can open up myself enough to let someone in."

He could hear compassion softening the breath she released through the phone.

"I know, mijo. I loved her too. We all did. But Michelle

would want you to live fully. To love again. You know that, don't you?"

"I know, Mommy. I just…being in the world without her, sometimes it hurts so bad. And I don't know if I have enough strength left to give my little girl all she needs and love someone else too. So, until that passes, I'll just keep doing what I'm doing. Because the last time I let the world in, it took my wife. I couldn't survive another loss like that."

"Daddy, are you upstairs?"

Joy blossomed in his chest at the sound of his daughter's voice. She was his reason for living, and knowing she was happy and thriving would always bring him joy.

"Ven, mija." He called over his shoulder then walked over to where his phone rested on a nearby dresser.

"Mommy, I gotta go. Nevaeh and Gracie just came back from walking the dog, and I don't want them to walk in on this conversation."

"Okay," she agreed. "Just kiss my little nieta and tell Gracie to take care of my babies while I'm gone."

He lovingly agreed and ended the call just before little footsteps thumped into his room.

"Oh, Daddy, I like that color on you."

Carter turned around to find the light and center of his life, Nevaeh. Her deep brown skin and her wild curls proudly displayed both her African American and Puerto Rican heritages. His pretty, brown-eyed girl, who was so full of life and joy it made his heart burst with love for her, leaned into the doorjamb, giving him a grin so big he was sure it brightened the room.

"You like the blue on me, mija?"

She squinted her eyes as if she were really taking him in, and knowing just how perceptive the mind was behind those deep brown orbs, he knew she really was taking in every inch of the electric blue Brett Johnson cashmere turtleneck, his black slacks, and black ankle boots. She allowed her gaze to scan him from top to bottom and back again before she nodded her approval.

"It looks good on your skin. I bet your date's gonna like it too."

Carter turned and lifted his gaze to meet his daughter's, trying to see if she was joking or not.

"Little girl—" he tilted his head and lifted his brow to let her know she'd gotten his attention "—just because I put on a nice outfit doesn't mean I'm going out on a date. I wear dressier things than these when I go to work."

"Yeah," she agreed. "But you never fuss so much with your clothes when you're just going to work. So this has to be a date, right?"

Out of the mouths of babes.

Every time his little one opened her mouth nowadays, Carter found himself wondering if this kind of awareness was usual, or was he just lucky, and by lucky, he meant not so much in this instance, to have a kid who managed his personal business better than he did.

"I'm not going on a date, date, mija. I'm going to see if I can offer our new neighbor some help."

"What kinda help?"

Carter walked over to the foot bench at the bottom of his bed and motioned for his daughter to meet him there. When they were both seated, he covered her fingers with his, giving them a playful squeeze to get her to look up at him.

"Mr. Smith needs help planning an event for one of his family members who is very sick. Since party planning is a big part of my work, I offered to help him."

She tilted her head back and forth as if she were tossing his words around in her head until the motion made meaning.

"So it's not a date?"

"Not in the traditional sense, no."

She looked up at him, the way only a six-year-old could, calling his bullshit with pursed lips in one moment and then tiring of the adult game of vocabulary keep-away he seemed to be playing in the next.

"Well, I hope his family member feels better. And even if it's not a *date* date, use your manners and smile a lot. That always makes you happy when I do those things. Maybe it will make Mr. Smith feel better if you do 'em too."

God, her innocence twisted something deep in his soul. This, this was the reason he'd walked away from everything in Hollywood after his wife's death. Michelle, more lovingly referred to as Mish by all her friends…losing her had nearly broken him. But being responsible for this little cherub of his made Carter hypervigilant when it came to her protection.

There was no way he could've kept a mind as curious as hers innocent out in LA. Even worse, there was no way he could protect her privacy there either. Out there, she was always going to be the daughter of superstar Carter Simon, the man who'd tragically lost his wife to the perils of fame.

By its nature, New York was a town where folks were nosy but tried hard not to get involved in other folks' business. That, and New Yorkers, especially Brooklynites, never thought anyone was special enough to hold up traffic or get special favors. Dammit, they had places to be and not a whole lot of time to get there. Because of that, here, his little girl was just Nevaeh Jiménez, a beautiful brown girl with big curls and an even bigger smile. And that was exactly the way he wanted her to remain. After losing her mother before she had a chance to even know Mish, Nevaeh deserved at least that much.

Carter turned back to his mirror, trying hard to keep it together. Thinking about his late wife, especially when it came to their daughter, always made him feel like his skin was tight and itchy and uncomfortable. Not because he didn't want to think about Mish; he'd loved her with every beat of his heart. But loving someone so wonderful and having her snatched away in one unforgettable moment, it sometimes made it hard for him to walk that fine line of happy father and grieving widower.

There was no end to grief. It came in waves. For years you could be fine, and then a memory crosses your mind and you're right back in the thick of it, feeling like you're being pulled beneath the undertow of dark, icy waters.

He was fortunate that he hadn't experienced one of those lows in over two years, and he didn't want to find himself adrift now. Tonight, he wanted to focus on the twinge of excitement that meeting his new neighbor had sparked in him. Yes, this wasn't a *date* date, but he didn't want to show up to Stephan's place with red swollen eyes. Considering everything Stephan was going through, Carter was sure Stephan wouldn't allow Carter to be of any help to him if he worried about Carter's emotional well-being.

"I promise to use good manners and smile, baby girl." He pointed toward his door and motioned for her to walk through it. "Now, go get ready for bed, and don't give Grannie Gracie any problems tonight."

"Daddy," she admonished him with just the flourish of her voice and the slightly disrespectful roll of her eyes. "I never give Grannie Gracie problems. We're besties."

He chuckled. His daughter was right—she and his former mother-in-law were besties, and Nevaeh never gave her problems because Grace affectionately called Gracie, always spoiled the little girl rotten. Carter knew it came from that soft place where loss and love dwelled, commingling to make you cherish every moment with your loved ones. Hell, before his own mother had taken her annual sabbatical to ride out most of the New York cold weather in Puerto Rico a few weeks ago, she'd worked just as hard as Gracie to prove Nevaeh was the most loved little girl in the world.

"I know. But I'm your dad. I still gotta state the rules so you can remember them.

He could see the laughter light up her eyes as if she were calculating all the mischief she and her grandmother were going to get up to tonight. Figuring it was easier to pretend either of them was going to listen to his so-called rules, he fiddled with his clothes again.

You just told your daughter this isn't a date, date. Why are you still primping?

Why indeed?

This wasn't the first time he'd met someone that sparked his interest. He'd been on quite a few dates in the last two years. But those were just one-offs. A means to a satisfying end. None of those dates, however, had him hyper focused on making sure his mousse worked to secure his naturally curly hair into coiffed perfection.

"Daddy?"

Nevaeh's voice pulled him from his thoughts of hair products and casual but cute attire.

"Yes, mija?"

"Try to have some fun too. I like it when you smile."

He scrunched his brow, walking toward her and then squatting down so he was closer to her eye level.

"You talk like I don't smile. I smile all the time."

"Yeah, but sometimes I can tell you're smiling 'cause you don't want me to know you're sad..." Her words drifted off, leaving the *about mom* part floating on the wind.

His throat tightened. He dropped his gaze for just a moment, trying to pull himself together. He was supposed to be the one looking out for her happiness. Not the other way around.

"Hey, it's okay to be sad sometimes, especially when we're missing the people we love. But that doesn't mean I'm sad *all* the time. Because I'm not. You wanna know why?"

She nodded, her curls bopping eagerly as she awaited his answer.

"Because I have you. Getting to be your dad makes me the happiest man in the world, even if I get sad sometimes because I miss mom."

"You sure?"

"Never more sure of anything in the world."

She launched herself at him, giving him just enough time to brace for the impact of an excited six-year-old, wrapping her arms around his neck while he was still squatting.

After she'd squeezed her little arms as tightly as she could around him, she gave him a quick kiss on the cheek and a, "Love you, daddy," as he put her down and she bounced out of his room.

He turned to the mirror, taking one last look at himself. Satisfied with his reflection and deciding that sans a full glam squad, his appearance wouldn't get much better by his own hands, he headed out of the bedroom, down the stairs, and through the front door.

"Ready or not, Stephan, here I come."

Seven

"Hey, you made it."

A snap of excitement crackled inside Carter's chest as a flash of delight sparked in Stephan's eyes and wide grin.

"Yeah, the commute was a beast, but I'm here."

Stephan's cheeks turned a deep mauve under his espresso brown skin, and Carter had to fight the urge to swipe his thumb against one cheek to see if the skin there was as warm and supple as his mind imagined.

The only thing stopping him was the nagging voice in the back of his head telling him how repugnant he'd be if he went through with that desire.

Oh, he knew this wasn't supposed to be about his attraction to Stephan, but his helping the man do something nice for his dying uncle and providing a bit of friendship for someone who was going through something difficult. But that didn't seem to stop the want curling in his stomach.

It was all so unsettling for him. Not twenty minutes ago he'd told his mother he wasn't ready for any romantic entanglements. But then he was here, in front of Stephan, and now he had to remind himself that Stephan was off-limits.

Carter had been around plenty of attractive people. Between being an actor and being the owner of a very successful VIP lounge for the elite, it meant good-looking people weren't an oddity to him. But his reaction to Stephan was something altogether different.

Because it wasn't about finding him attractive. And boy, did Carter find everything about Stephan's tight broad body appealing. But it was his haunted eyes that called to Carter, that made him want to dig deeper and provide support wherever he could.

He felt compassion for the guy. That's all it was. That's all it could be. Because, like he'd told his mother, he wasn't ready. He might not ever be ready to invest his heart in someone else again.

Carter focused on Stephan once more, loving the flush under the man's skin despite the fact that he'd just chastised himself for his poorly timed, foul thoughts.

"Oh, let me get that." Carter could tell the moment Stephan realized he was grinning like a child in a toy aisle because the man cleared his throat, downplaying his zeal by swiftly taking the insulated food bag out of Carter's hand.

"Thanks for agreeing to do this, Carter." He stepped aside and politely ushered Carter in. "I know we don't know each other well, and I can't figure out for the life of me why you'd want to spend your time doing this, but I appreciate it."

Carter stepped into the foyer and followed Stephan into the back of the house and into his modern kitchen. Everything from the cabinets to the appliances and countertops were white, giving a crisp, showroom look to the space that Carter envied. There was no way he could indulge in an all-white anything with the hurricane that was his daughter constantly exploding all over everything.

He motioned for Carter to take a seat in the breakfast nook in the corner by the large window that looked into the well-kept backyard.

"The mudroom's behind that door if you wanna wash the commute off you before I serve the meal."

Carter smiled, liking the fact that Stephan could take and make a joke, then made quick work of getting up to wash his hands.

When he returned to the kitchen proper, Stephan was bringing two heaping plates to the table.

"Carter, this smells amazing by the way."

"My mother's recipe." He used his fork to shift around the food on his plate before answering. "According to her, good food lifts the spirits. And since eating her food always makes me feel good, I'm inclined to agree with her."

"Well, if the menu you have in mind smells anything like this, I might actually believe we can pull this off. My uncle isn't much for fancy food. He likes food that speaks to a people's culture. Soul food, Asian, Mediterranean, hell, even American classics like a good cheeseburger—he loves it. But if he can't pronounce it, chances are he won't eat it, so keep it elegant but simple."

Stephan sat down, looking over his plate before lifting his eyes up to Carter.

"Do you get to do that often—eating your mother's food, I mean?"

Carter relaxed at the mention of his mother. Although she knew how to ride his nerves like any good mother did, she was his greatest supporter. No matter the challenge, she always had him, and he adored her for it. "Yes. She lives further up on Bedford. But right now, she's snowbirding in Puerto Rico for the next few months. When she's home, Nevaeh, Gracie, and I spend as much time with her as all our schedules allow. The four of us are pretty close"

Still feeling too raw after the conversation he just had with his mother, Carter pointed his fork at Stephan's plate.

"Eat up before it gets cold. You look like you need a good, hot meal."

"Is your superpower as a VIP lounge owner that you can always anticipate the needs of your patrons?"

Stephan took a bite and waited for Carter to respond.

"It's more likely something I pulled in from my old life."

"Old life?" Stephan snorted. "You make it sound like you were part of the mafia."

"In a way," Carter replied, "I guess you can say that's true. I used to work in Hollywood. To succeed there, you have to sell your devotion and obedience to the machine. Any act of defiance or disloyalty can ruin, if not take, your life."

Stephan's fork stopped midway between his plate and his mouth, as he stared at Carter.

He recognized the look blooming across Stephan's face. He'd seen it plenty of times when people realized who he was and what he had been.

His stomach tightened, tension stiffening his limbs as he waited for the expectant excitement and over-the-top fanfare that usually made him feel like he was being put on display.

It always made him uncomfortable. And when Stephan hadn't seemed to make a big deal about him, he'd figured either Stephan didn't care, or he simply didn't know who Carter was. Either way, it suited him just the same.

But this rapport the two men seemed to be building from

their very first interaction was now threatened. Because the last thing Carter needed in his life was a fanboy looking for access into Hollywood.

But just as quickly as recognition flared in Stephan's eyes, it passed, and he focused on his forkful of food.

He took the bite, wiping his mouth with a napkin before reaching for a nearby glass of water.

"You don't have to hold back on my account. I'd rather get this out in the open if it's gonna make things weird."

"If you're asking if I've always known you were actor Carter Simon, Hollywood heartthrob, the answer is no. I didn't until you just mentioned your work in Hollywood. The beard makes you look totally different."

Carter blinked, wondering if this was a facade, or if Stephan was really this at ease with Carter's past.

"That was the whole point. I wanted a normal life again. I didn't want Carter Simon to intrude on the life I was trying to build for us here. The beard, the new profession, it all was the exact opposite of who I was when I was him."

"Except, your lounge is literally an exclusive hot spot for the who's who in New York. Celebrities, politicians, business powerbrokers, they all come to The Vault for a good time away from the cameras."

Carter leaned forward, raising a brow.

"So you did look me up?"

Stephan shook his head. "No, I looked up the lounge when you invited me for wings. I live by 'the who all gon' be there' query. So I checked it out before I showed up. The search fails to mention anything about you being a renowned actor, though."

Carter nodded at Stephan. "Carter Simon and Carter Jiménez are two different people. Simon has nothing to do with Jiménez. With the exception of my late wife, my daughter, and my best friend who works in politics, I hate everything about Hollywood and the celebrity lifestyle. Notoriety is a cancer that destroys, and I have no intention of ever inviting it back into our lives."

Now that Stephan knew who he was, he assumed the man knew how he'd lost his wife. Carter Simon's life put her in the path of the paparazzi who chased her to her death. There was no way he could remain associated with that world and protect his daughter and his sanity.

"It's why I came back here. I needed to be around real people and protect my daughter from the vile truths of living in that world. It's also why I'll never go back."

"So owning a club that the rich and elite patronize is…"

It was a fair question. But the truth was, it had nothing to do with keeping a foothold in that life.

"Membership to the club isn't offered to the who's who because of who they are. It's offered to them because I understand what it is to live in a fishbowl. My place offers them a safe space to be normal without fear of having their normalcy exploited or broadcast around the world."

"So, this really isn't an act, I take it?"

Carter grimaced as he tried to figure out what Stephan was talking about.

"This pay it forward thing you have going on?" He took another bite of food and continued. "I thought it was a ploy to get into my pants at first. But now, knowing who you were, I can honestly understand why you do what you do."

Stephan's statement struck Carter in the middle of his chest with as much force as a sledgehammer on a tiny nail tack. Somehow, he got who and why Carter was, and as unnerving as that should've been, it drew Carter in.

When your career was becoming everyone's fantasy, the reality of who you are didn't often matter. As an actor, he was always on. As a Puerto Rican actor who also happened to be bisexual, that meant he was never allowed to do something as simple as look like he'd rolled straight out of bed and out on the street. He had to be perfectly coiffed at all times for fear the tabloids would paint him as having some kind of breakdown that would put his employability in harm's way.

He knew it sounded far-fetched, but the reality was, just because he could pass for white in the right lighting didn't mean that Hollywood execs ever forgot for one moment that he wasn't. And from the moment he'd landed his first big role, he knew the deck was stacked against him, and he had to play by a different set of rules to win. It was fucked up. That was for certain. But it was fact, nonetheless.

Sitting here with this man, who didn't seem to care about his past fame, it felt good. It felt good enough that he kept himself from asking a bunch of questions to dig into Stephan's past. He would learn him—so he could help him, of course. But he would learn what would made the handsome man with the soulful eyes tick.

"Now I'm curious." Carter put his fork down, giving Stephan his complete attention and making it decidedly harder to keep his hand-mouth-eye coordination in check while he was eating. "When most folks find out who I used to be, they're never this chill about it. Not even New Yorkers."

Stephan understood why. There was a time you couldn't go to the movies and not see a promo poster with Carter's clean-shaven face staring back at you.

Stephan opened his mouth to speak but hesitated. He too had his own issues with fame and notoriety. And right now, he wasn't really sure if Carter was someone he should share that with.

First, he seemed cool enough, but Stephan had to protect Ace and his family at all costs. Trust was a precious commodity in his world. Sharing it with the wrong person could destroy you.

However, it was the next reason that weighed on him more heavily. Would Carter be able to disassociate Stephan from the world he lived in?

If Stephan remembered the headlines correctly, tabloid reporters had surrounded his wife while she was on the street and chased her when she found a break in their human wall. She ran blindly into the street, putting her into the path of oncoming traffic. Fame literally cost her her life.

After experiencing something like that, and given Carter's disclosed hatred of Hollywood, Stephan worried that Carter wouldn't be able to discern the difference between who Stephan was and the world he was forced to live in by virtue of his last name.

"My work often puts me in contact with people from all walks of life."

"What exactly do you do?"

Stephan could feel a slight twitch in his sharp jawline. He struggled to control it, hoping it would look like more of an involuntary muscle movement than a reaction to Carter's question.

"I run the Paris branch of an American-based venture capitalist company."

That's it. Make it sound as boring as you can so Carter drops the subject.

"So you're on leave now to be with your uncle?"

"I'm back in the States to be with uncle. Fortunately, my job allows for remote working when necessary. If I need to go back, I will. But with the advent of video chats, I don't have to go back at all, if I don't want to."

Stephan's conscience howled at the colorful version of the truth he was presenting. Yes, he was telling the truth. But the fact that he was keeping Carter in the dark about who he really was nicked at him for reasons he didn't understand.

It wasn't like Stephan wasn't justified in this behavior. Time had taught him over and over again that people would screw him over in a second if it benefited them. Or that he was only valuable as long as he was doing something for them.

Dexter had never made that point clearer. Six months after his brother died in Jamaica, Stephan had gone back there partly for Devereaux Inc. business and partly looking for some sort of peace. It wasn't that he hadn't accepted Randall's untimely death; he had. It was that Stephan's soul was so full of hurt, anguish, and guilt about shoving family secrets so far down his throat, he felt like he was choking.

He'd run into Dexter over the course of his business, and they'd hit it off. Laughing, playing, and relaxing, the time he spent with Dexter had healed something in him. Until he'd discovered it was all a ploy to cash in on the bank of Stephan Devereaux-Smith.

Dexter was just one in a long line of people who had proven to Stephan he couldn't let his guard down or let people in.

As a result, Stephan stuck to his "no new friends" policy, and after assholes like Dexter, he never felt the slightest bit bad about being vague about his life, work, and background. That's why the sliver of guilt tugging at the back of his brain didn't make any sense. This was standard operating procedure. Don't let anyone in, and you don't have to worry about them using you.

What the hell was wrong with him? What the hell was Carter doing to him?

"Well…" Carter beamed as he picked up his glass of water and held it up for a toast. The momentary darkness talking about his past cast over him disappearing quickly. "I know being home must be hard for you right now. But I'm glad the universe saw fit for our paths to cross. I can never have too many real folks around me."

Stephan picked up his glass, clinking it to Carter's. Real? Stephan couldn't remember the last time he'd been allowed to be his real self. But sitting here with Carter, Stephan desperately wanted to be the real him again.

"Now," Carter said with a bit of exuberance in his voice. Let's finish this good food, and get to planning the best Christmas party that ever was. I know someone that can make the walls look like snowcapped mountains if you're into that kind of thing."

The idea of gaudy fake mountains in Borough Hall should've made Stephan choke on his food. But seeing the outright joy beaming on Carter's face as he said it, Stephan was pretty certain he'd suffer that level of tackiness any day of the week if it meant he got to watch Carter smile like that.

Because more than anything, Stephan was realizing that every time Carter smiled, he did feel more and more like the real Stephan Devereaux-Smith. It was just too bad being the real him would mean he'd have to push Carter away. And that, even though it galled him to admit it, wasn't what he wanted.

Eight

<u>"A</u>re you gonna share why you have us in this early as hell meeting, or are we supposed to guess?'

Stephan looked to his side to find his cousin Amara squirming around in her chair trying to find the perfect spot to support her back. From what he'd heard, with only two more months to go in her pregnancy, there wasn't really a comfortable spot to be had.

Make no mistake, Amara wasn't a bowl of sunshine before her pregnancy. But this baby was raising her hackles in such a way, everyone who crossed her path was on notice.

He laughed off her grumpy response. Hell, if he had to do the work of cooking a human, he'd be pissy all the time too.

"Because, cousin…" he replied with as much compassion as he could muster, which was saying something, because Stephan didn't coddle most people he encountered. "We're the cousin crew and I wanted to let y'all in on a few things."

"Everything okay, *cousin*?" Stephan watched as Trey, the newest edition to both the Devereaux family and Devereaux

Incorporated, walked into the room and sat at the head of the conference table. Her taking that seat was a reminder to everyone in that room she might be new to the crew, but she was definitely in charge.

She was Ace's estranged granddaughter, someone who managed the impossible by bringing Ace and her father, Deuce, back into each other's lives again.

A miracle worker like that, Stephan understood without question why Ace had chosen her as his direct successor as owner and CEO of the family's billion-dollar company.

She'd married, Jeremiah, Ace's ward from the time he was sixteen years old, and an honorary Devereaux cousin, around the time Stephan had returned home for Ace. She was smart, headstrong, ambitious, and her Brooklyn glam girl fashion sense was on fire. But the thing that made him embrace her openly was the fact that she was just as loyal to Ace as he was. Up until Ace's mandate that he go out and find a life, Stephan had seen Trey and Jeremiah at Ace's bedside or downstairs in the family room of Devereaux manor almost every night.

And when they were all huddled in that big bedroom of Ace's, she loved on that old man the way only a devoted granddaughter who thought her granddaddy hung the moon could.

I'll admit," Trey continued, "I get a little worried when my branch directors call for an unexpected meeting like this."

"Everything's fine, Trey." Stephan tried to assure her, although he wasn't exactly sure any of them would find what he had to say agreeable. "I was just waiting for you and Jeremiah to get here so I could begin."

"Where's Lyric?" Amara interjected. "If I gotta be here, so does she."

"Lyric is filming this morning. She couldn't make it, but I plan to call her later to fill her in."

"Then let's get to it so we can start the rest of our workday. Is something going on with the Paris branch you need us to know about?" Jeremiah gave him a nod. He was co-CEO with his wife, so he would have just as much of an interest in this meeting as Trey did.

"Everything's more than fine with the Paris branch. This isn't about the business. This is about the family, specifically Ace."

He could see worry literally etch into their faces. Every one of them was aware of Ace's poor prognosis. Mentioning Ace nowadays created an immediate call to attention. He meant that much to every one of them.

"Ace wants me to throw him a Devereaux family Christmas party."

"I'm sorry," Trey replied. "A Devereaux what now?"

"A Devereaux family Christmas party," Jeremiah, Amara, and Stephan said in unison.

"It was a tradition long before any of us was born," Amara continued.

"It was still a thing even when I came to the family at sixteen," Jeremiah added by way of answering his wife. "It was this grand Christmas party where all the branches of the Devereaux family came together to celebrate Christmas under one roof. It was the biggest event in the family until two years ago."

Amara looked up at the ceiling as if she were looking back into Devereaux Christmases past and Jeremiah was beaming too. There was a distant smile on both their faces that Stephan couldn't help but match.

Just the mention of those Christmases past made him

think about some of the loud boisterous times they'd had with their family, where the kids played with their toys while the adults talked. Where Ace would lead the family in a solemn prayer they said before they sat down to a feast. And the best part, the best part was when they'd get to the call and answer portion of the evening where Ace would use his rich baritone to lead them all in spiritual or devotional songs that had been sung through the generations of the Brooklyn Devereauxs since time began.

It was love, plain and simple. And it had all stopped because of him, because of what he'd done, the secret he still carried to this day.

"Sounds like a wonderful time. What happened two years ago to make it stop?"

Stephan watched his two cousins as their smiles faded and their gazes fell on him. They were looking to him. His stomach roiled and his neck tightened. Two years and speaking these words still hollowed out his soul.

"My brother died two months before Christmas, and I left home and refused to return. To Ace, having Christmas without his only living nephew wasn't going to happen. So, he refused to have another one until I was ready to come home."

Silence in the room was overpowering. Not because he thought his family was judging him. No, because he was judging himself. If he'd only known Ace's time was nearly up, he probably would've made another decision. But being so overrun by the guilt of secrets and lies, Stephan ran, leaving Ace to deal with the family so Stephan could keep the ticking time bomb of truth locked down far away where it couldn't do any damage.

"It's my fault this family has been fractured for the last two years. I owe Ace this." After everything Ace had done for him, after taking all the blame Stephan should've shouldered himself, he owed this debt.

His words hung in the air as they all stared at each other, trying to figure who would say what next.

"Stephan." Trey stood as she called his name, making her way to his side of the conference table and placing a comforting hand on his shoulder. "I think my dad broke the family when he married my mom thirty-some-odd years ago. You don't have to take that burden on all by yourself. Not the blame for the family nor the load of planning this party on your own."

The tension that made his neck ache was joined by pain that lanced through the center of his chest like a sharp knife. If she knew, if they all knew, none of them would be so eager to help him appease his conscience.

"I appreciate it, cousin. I do. But if you don't mind, if none of you mind, I'd like to do this myself. He asked me to do it, and it's the least I can do after all he's done for me."

"I'm surprised you agreed to anything that would take you away from Ace's bed." Amara's voice broke through the heavy emotions weighing down his rib cage, making it hard to breathe. "Let me guess, you're planning the whole thing from the chair at his bedside?"

"No, smart-ass," he countered. "I've actually connected with a friend who has experience in party planning. He's agreed to help me get this thing together." He stopped to look at his watch as a reminder of how little time he had left between now and when the party would take place.

"We sketched out some plans the last time we met up and he's agreed to help me get this thing together quickly."

Jeremiah sighed heavily, drawing the attention in the room to himself. "He might not have that long, cousin."

The words were heavy, somber, and quiet, yet they all heard them as if they were spoken through a megaphone.

"I know," Stephan answered quietly. "That's why I'm gonna make this happen quickly. The date's set for two weeks from this Saturday."

"Two days after Thanksgiving?" Trey asked the question, but Jeremiah and Amara were nodding in unison while she did.

"Yeah. It's the earliest I can make it happen. It seems even Devereaux money can't move mountains for the holidays."

"Well," Trey continued. "We're here for you, cousin. Whether it's to plan this party, or talk whenever something's wearing you down, we're here for you."

Jeremiah joined her, stopping to give Stephan a warm hug before he and his wife left the room. Realizing Amara was still there, he reached out to help her out of her chair.

"You are such a good man, Stephan. Regardless of whether Ace makes it to see this party or not, you are the best there is."

She kissed him on his cheek and left him in the large conference room by himself. As always, the familiar darkness that dogged him for the last two years closed its cold fingers around his throat and squeezed tightly and he struggled to breathe.

But somewhere through the anxiety building in his head, he could hear the chiming of his cellphone in his pocket. With shaking hands he turned it over, and when he saw Carter's name flashing, his airway opened up again, and sweet air traveled freely into his lungs.

"Hello." Stephan's voice was raw, and he knew Carter would probably sense something was wrong.

"You were on my mind, so I decided to call and see if you

were up for lunch today. It's pretty quiet this time of day at The Vault, so I could hang out a bit. You free?"

Stephan's shoulders relaxed and he managed a weary, grateful smile. He had a ton of work to do and his emotions were all over the place. But for some reason, the idea of spending more time with Carter made every anxious thought in his head go silent.

Carter was fine and then some with his dark hair and eyes, and a body that wouldn't quit. Stephan could definitely see why he'd been such a sought-after actor in the past. Yes, his looks had attracted Stephan in the beginning, but between spending time with him at his club and having dinner at Stephan's place, Stephan had been way more interested in just talking to Carter.

He was funny, a typical doting dad who adored his daughter, and even though Stephan had only met the girl once in passing, he never tired of the flash of joy that streaked across Carter's eyes when he spoke about her. However, above all else, the thing that Stephan cherished most about Carter was his compassion. His need to check in and make sure someone was all right.

Stephan assumed this was something Carter did for all the people around him. He hadn't really known him long enough to determine otherwise. But if he were honest, he liked knowing Carter cared enough about him to make sure Stephan was okay.

He hadn't felt cared for like that in a long time.

That had to be the reason, right?

"What other reason could there be? Stephan wasn't built for anything else.

Sure, it wasn't like he made their visits and calls all about him. In fact, he was way more interested in listening to

Carter go on and on about garland versus tinsel. Stephan didn't remember which he'd chosen, because he'd been so busy watching the animated delight on the man's face as he talked. It was all perfectly natural and harmless.

At least, he could pretend it was all harmless until Carter was near him, like bending over a catalog to show Stephan a new option for the winter wonderland Carter was helping him build—that's when things went straight to hell in a handbasket. That's when he had to fight his base need to touch Carter, to smell and taste him, and have him do the same to Stephan.

The need to smell him was almost an uncontrollable urge at this point. Stephan's dick had never been hard over the way a man smelled. But every time Carter wore whatever the hell that sweet and woodsy scent was, Stephan had to damn near sit on his hands like some uncontrollable child who couldn't be trusted not to touch the new shiny thing in front of him.

His conscience chose that moment to wag its metaphorical finger in Stephan's face. He was wrong for this. He was essentially using Carter as if he were human Valium at best and spank bank material at worst. Carter deserved better than that. But no matter how terrible Stephan knew he was, he couldn't resist the euphoric high he knew he'd experience being in the man's presence. If that made him an asshole, he'd accept it. He'd certainly called himself worse.

He took a breath, trying to temper his excitement. "For you," he said calmly. "And your club's wings, I'm always free."

Nine

"Hey, boss. Where'd you want these?"

Carter smoothed out the linen on the table he'd had set up in the corner.

"Just bring the rolling cart over here. I'll set the food out when I'm ready."

Ian, his bartender/server/jack-of-all trades when Carter was in a staffing crunch, pushed a small cart filled with a few platters.

"You entertaining a potential big client? Because this is an extensive menu list."

From the variety of foods Carter had brought to Stephan's house, Carter figured the best way to tackle the menu for this event was the same way he handled the menu here at The Vault.

Brooklyn was made up of many little neighborhoods with strong ties to ethnic communities. He had everything from soul food, Asian, Latin American, and Caribbean cuisine, to Italian at The Vault. So, coming up with a diverse menu wouldn't be the problem. The problem was they didn't have a great deal of time, so everything they added would have to be locally sourced and available in abundant quantities.

Carter decided to put a heavy emphasis on soul food because of the time-constraint issue, but also because Stephan said it was his uncle's favorite. He'd use Latin and Caribbean cuisine to round out everything nicely.

Ian made a show of shaking the order list out before reading it aloud. "First up is your bread service. Honey corn bread and buttermilk biscuits. You've got your starters— lime-pepper wings, crab cakes, mini Jamaican beef patties, plantains, and pasteles. You've got your entrées—blackened catfish, braised oxtails, pernil, smothered pork chops, and short ribs. Next are your sides—Jamaican rice & peas, collard greens garnished with smoked turkey, baked macaroni and cheese, candied yams, potato salad, and Spanish rice. The dessert should arrive before you get to the entrées. The sweet potato pie and peach cobbler were just coming out of the oven when I was leaving the kitchen."

Carter began checking the lids to make sure everything was to his specifications when he felt Ian's heavy gaze on him. As Carter met it, he could see Ian's eyes processing every detail of Carter's behavior. Five minutes in his presence, and he could read anyone. That particular superpower along with his unmatched skill at mixology made him one of the most popular and well-tipped bartenders in his employ.

"I don't have a big client. Just a friend I'm helping plan an unexpected party. We're on a time crunch, so I needed to come up with a sample menu he could taste in one setting so we can get the ball rolling on things."

That's all Carter could say by way of explanation. It's all he would say to Ian, and more importantly to himself.

Carter would not admit that he never took this much care with setting a table for a client. Hell, he wouldn't even do this for his best friend Lennox.

Then why are you doing this?

Nope, not going there. Not even for a little bit.

He lifted his gaze from the table to Ian and caught his employee offering him his signature slick smile that he usually reserved for patrons who made a habit of lying to themselves as they made themselves the victors or the victims of their tales. That grin screamed, *You see this fool right here? He actually believes the crap he's spewing.*

It was always hilarious before, an inside joke that he'd found entertaining so many times in the past. But now that Carter suspected he was playing the role of the fool in today's scenario, he wasn't amused at all.

Ian didn't wait for further explanation. He just gave Carter a knowing wink, then left as quietly as he'd entered.

Carter didn't want to think about what was going on here. For one, Stephan had a lot of emotional upheaval going on right now and people made really bad decisions when they were hurting.

Not that Carter was looking for forever, but he'd meant what he'd said the last time he and Stephan were in this room. They were neighbors, and getting close could become problematic if things went left. He didn't want his daughter impacted by that. She was safe here. The world of the rich and famous wasn't coming to Brooklyn to find her, not like they had her mother in L.A. And above all else, Carter had to protect the sanctity of the fortress he'd built for them here.

He rubbed the back of his neck, trying to self-soothe the nervous energy that was coursing through him.

There was no harm in being attracted to Stephan. He

was the walking depiction of tall, dark, and handsome. Add to that his deep soulful eyes and his big heart, and Carter would be a fool not to be attracted to him.

He wasn't afraid of being attracted to Stephan physically. He'd be grateful if that's all it was.

But that wasn't all there was to it and therein lay the problem.

He wanted to connect with Stephan. He'd felt this intense need to check on him, make sure he was all right from that first moment on Stephan's stoop. He wanted to make it better, whatever *it* was.

Carter had blamed it on the brokenhearted recognizing a heart currently breaking, but now that he was helping Stephan, now that he'd had a little tiny glimpse into who the man might be, Carter wanted to keep digging until he'd uncovered it all.

He realized how trifling it was to want to be firmly planted into someone else's business when he'd literally moved across the country to keep people out of his. But the more time he spent with Stephan, the more he hoped he'd open up to Carter, give him a little more insight than he had. Because from the tiny bit he could see, Stephan, by all accounts, was a good man. And good men going through hard times deserved a break.

That was it. That's all it could be. He wanted to connect because he wanted to give this gorgeous man, who loved his uncle enough to come home and spend the man's last days with him, a break. Anyone that selfless deserved all the fucking breaks in the world as far as Carter was concerned.

Nice guy or no, Carter still had to pay close attention to himself and his motives. Codependence was a real thing, and just because Carter was on an even keel now with his grief, didn't mean he couldn't subconsciously be looking for a literal partner in grief.

He couldn't do that to Stephan when his heartache and loss was so present. And he couldn't upend his own healing process either. Not just for him, but the beautiful little girl who depended on him. He needed to be whole.

Then why was he standing here setting the perfect mood for an afternoon delight?

The answer was simple. He wanted Stephan Smith. He wanted to know him. Listening to him talk the other night about his work and then brainstorming the initial planning stages of the Christmas party had made Carter feel at ease with the man. So at ease in fact that he'd revealed his past to Stephan.

He never let people in that far. But part of him had wanted to know if Stephan could be trusted or not, and so he'd shared his truth. The man had come through with flying colors, understanding Carter's reticence around fame and his absolute hatred of the business that had stolen his wife from him.

The relief he'd felt at Stephan's reaction had broken something free in him. The hesitance and trepidation he always felt around new people drifted away.

And now, much to his dismay, all that remained was this want, this desire to just be in the man's presence. Hence this impromptu lunch—he still couldn't bring himself to call it a *date* date, though.

That would mean he was looking for something more, and he wasn't actually sure if either of them was ready for more than food and a little emotional support at present.

"I hope whatever's under those covered silver platters tastes as good as its packaging looks."

The trepidation of his reasonable mind vanished and Carter's entire being buzzed with excitement at the sound of Stephan's voice.

"Please prepare to be impressed, sir." Carter lifted the cover for the small center dish. "These are our famous wings for starters." He placed the covering on the rolling cart and then pointed to the larger covered dishes still remaining on the cart. "And these," Carter uncovered the remaining dishes, pausing to give Stephan a chance to take the presented bounty all in. "are everything else."

"Damn, Carter." Stephan beamed as he stepped into the room, closing the door behind and making his way to the table in the corner where Carter stood. "All this is for me? To what do I owe the pleasure?"

What indeed?

It was a fair question. And he didn't really have an answer except for the fact that he just really wanted to pamper Stephan, take care of him.

"Well, for one, I appreciated how you treated me after finding out about my past. Usually when someone discovers who I was, things immediately get weird. You treated me like a normal person, and I appreciate that."

Stephan gave a slow nod, raising a brow to bid Carter permission to continue.

"And second?"

His voice was somewhere in his lower register, as if his words were meant for Carter alone. Of course, that intent should be obvious because they were the only two people in the room. But the way the richness of his deeper notes teased Carter's ears and ghosted over his skin, leaving goose bumps behind, he knew Stephan was speaking this way solely for his benefit.

A small smile curved his lips in appreciation for this constant volley that seemed to pass between them.

One moment, Carter was the one being forward with all the double entendres, and the next, Stephan was turning the tables on him. They didn't just shift dominance, this space they were creating between them allowed for either of them to be vulnerable when they wanted or needed to be.

Carter liked it. He liked it too much. So much so he kept his hands clasped behind his back for fear that he would cross a line that neither of them could afford to ignore right now.

"I pulled some strings and I was able to get a venue for this Christmas gala."

"Oh yeah? Where?"

"I know you didn't think we'd be able to get it at such late notice, but if you want it, Borough Hall is available," Carter answered. "That is, if you're not too worried about budget. And even if you are, I'm sure my people can get us a steep discount."

Stephan stepped closer until he was on the same side of the food cart as Carter. He was so close, the mix of spice and soap, with a slight twinge of sweetness filled Carter's senses, making it hard to focus on anything but those full lips that were so close to him, all he'd have to do is lean forward just so, and he'd know what they tasted like.

"I'm not worried about the budget. There are enough of us Smiths that if we need to chip in to cover the costs, I'm sure it won't be a problem."

"Good." Carter swallowed. "I gave the contact your number, so you should be getting a call either later today or tomorrow."

Stephan gave Carter a slow nod, his gaze drifting to Carter's mouth as he stepped so close that Carter had no choice but to step back until he felt his desk pressing into the backs of his thighs.

Stephan picked up his hand, cupping Carter's cheek, caressing the line of his jaw with his thumb. Every inch of his skin the man's thumb slid across burned, aching for Stephan's soothing touch.

"You are a godsend, Carter, and I find myself wanting to show my appreciation to you right now."

"You don't owe me anything, Stephan." Carter tried to keep his eyes open, but being this close to Stephan with his hands touching Carter's bare skin was making him dizzy with need.

"Oh, you misunderstand me. I want to show you my appreciation because I want you. Not because I feel obligated to you. Will you let me?"

Carter knew the correct answer to Stephan's question should've been no. He knew allowing this was going to cause trouble down the line that he would more than likely regret. But with this fine-ass-man all in his face, taking up all his good air and replacing it with the most enticing aroma Carter had ever encountered, he knew damn well he wasn't going to turn this man's request down.

"Yes."

A small, simple world. But damn, did it hold so much power. Just that small utterance was enough to unleash all the repressed desire they'd both haphazardly juggled since they'd met.

Stephan's first press of his lips was soft and tentative. Seeking, as he tried to learn what Carter liked. But the fire that burned between them elicited such a deep moan that within seconds, Stephan had skipped passed tentative and his lips pressed firmly against Carter's, teasing, tasting, tempting him until the only thing his body could do was burn and quiver.

Stephan's hand slipped from Carter's jaw, to the back of his head, raking the scalp beneath his buzzed fade, and the heat that had been coursing through him turned into a full-on blaze, making his cock twitch as it ached for some personal attention of its own.

His hands were on Stephan because he wanted to touch him, but also because he needed something to brace against, since this kiss had snatched his innate ability to remain balanced on his own two feet.

Carter wasn't sure who ended the kiss, although the desperation raging inside of him made him believe it had to be Stephan who'd had strength enough to step away. Because everything in Carter, and he did in fact mean everything, wanted that kiss to continue and move on to the point where they were stripping each other's clothes off and humping on Carter's desk.

It's not like it would be the first time. Lennox and Amara had conceived their soon-to-be-born baby on this very desk. A little more action wouldn't hurt the obviously sturdy piece of furniture.

"Now…" Stephan stepped away, a sexy twinkle in his eye beckoning Carter to follow him as he sat down at the perfectly set table. "Who exactly's going to have their way with whom?"

The smirk on his lips should've pissed Carter off. The sheer arrogance of the statement, and he knew he had a lot of audacity to see it as such, considering he'd said much the same to Stephan a week ago. But mad was the furthest thing from Carter's mind at this moment.

No, he wasn't mad, he was turned on beyond all recognition and had not the slightest bit of shame in admitting he wholeheartedly wanted Stephan to have his way with him as often and in whichever way he deemed fit.

Because that kiss had him reciting the rosary in his head to get his cock to relent and his blood to stop boiling him from the inside out.

Oh, Mr. Smith, it is most definitely on.

Ten

Stephan stood in front of the white double brownstone mansion that seemed to have stood on Clinton Ave from the beginning of time.

Devereaux Manor, the place where Ace had created a legacy and a home for his family. Even though Stephan had never technically lived here, he'd spent so much of his life within its walls that it was hard to find very many memories of his childhood that hadn't started there.

He hesitated slightly as he took the first step across the threshold and into its hallowed halls filled with family portraits of those who came before and those still here. And every time he stood before them, gratitude and pride filled him that he was granted access to such a legacy.

Even in the depths of his guilt for the lies he'd told and the secrets he'd kept, he knew he'd done it to protect his family. The people he loved more than himself. The people who deserved happiness, even if it was at Stephan's expense.

He didn't see anyone lingering around when he came in,

so he quickly headed directly for Ace's room, taking the steps two at a time. When he reached the landing, he gave himself a shake, trying to douse the good mood flowing through him. He'd kissed Carter last night, and even the weight of his sins couldn't stop Stephan from feeling like he was on top of the world.

Before he could let go of the memory of how good Carter tasted, he took a settling breath and stepped toward the door. Laughter greeted him, so Stephan tapped quickly on the door and walked inside.

Remember, be chill and don't act different.

"Heyyyy, family! What we got going on here?"

Both Ace and Trey stopped laughing to look at Stephan and then each other. Their searching gazes told him his greeting was just a tad bit over the top.

"Hey, nephew," Ace greeted him, waving him into the room that held a light energy Stephan knew came from the laughter he'd heard through the door. "Trey was just telling me about how upset she made some of the more seasoned board members at the last quarterly meeting."

"My day isn't made if I'm not making one of them mad." Trey stood next to the small wet bar in the corner, pouring herself a healthy glass of water from the Svalbarði bottle Stephan recognized. When she was done, she came over and wrapped an arm around him. They were still getting to know each other, but the bond, that thing that forced the Devereaux family to stand against the world together, that was strong and present. "How you doin', cuz? You looking good. Got a little sparkle in your eye and pep in your step. Anything new you wanna share with the class?"

He stilled his features, trying hard to lock everything

down. He was a grown man—a kiss shouldn't be enough to make him lose all his chill like this.

Don't be that goofy dude, Stephan.

He cleared his throat and tried again to make his face impassive so he wouldn't give anything away. There was no way Trey could've known anything about the kiss Stephan and Carter shared. But he'd seen this cunning woman in the boardroom. If she sensed the slightest bit of blood in the water, she would pounce like the apex predator she was.

"Nothing's happening, cousin. It's just a beautiful day outside and I'm happy to spend a little time with my family."

Trey stepped around him as she watched him with a lifted brow, then stopped to take a sip of water from her glass. When she was done, she sat back down in her chair with a suspicious gleam in her eye and broad grin on her face.

"If you say so." She crossed one thick leg over another as she settled back into her seat.

"So, anything to report, nephew."

"Can I take my coat off first, Uncle Ace?"

The old man waved a pointed finger in the air. "No you may not. As per our last conversation, you're only supposed to come here if you've got proof of joy."

Stephan faked a shiver, rubbing his hands up and down his arms to drive his point home. "Damn, you're talking to me in professional clap-back now? Uncle Ace, that ain't right."

"If I were you, cousin," Trey interjected. "I'd give the old man what he wants. He's got a nasty way of gathering us when we don't cooperate."

She wasn't wrong, but Stephan couldn't let that comment fly without a response. With a fake scowl on his face, he removed his jacket and sat down in a nearby chair before he spoke again.

"You know minding your business and drinking your water is free, right?"

Trey took a long sip and then lifted her glass in Stephan's direction.

"You's a damn lie," Trey replied. "A month's supply of this Svalbarði Limited Edition water cost more than some people's rent.

Stephan held his laughter for as long as he could, but the moment he snickered, Trey and Ace followed suit.

Once they recovered, Trey excused herself, leaving Ace and Stephan to face each other with no barriers.

"My granddaughter is right," Ace began slowly as his gaze took Stephan in much the same way Trey had. "You do seem to have little spark about you."

Kissing a sexy man who had great conversation, a compassionate heart, and a sweetheart of an ass would do that for you. But seeing as he couldn't share that or rather he wouldn't. What would be the point? He already knew that nothing serious could come of a liaison between him and Carter. Getting Ace all excited about something that would amount to nothing in the end seemed cruel to Ace, to Carter, and Stephan.

His decision further cemented, Stephan found something else to talk about.

"A friend of mine has agreed to help me plan this party of yours, and he's been sharing some great ideas I think you're gonna like."

"Such as?'

The old man's smile looked as innocent as the sky was blue, but knowing what a mental ninja Ace was, Stephan didn't fall for the sweet old man act Ace was playing right now. If Carter could see Ace, he'd probably nominate this performance to the Academy. Yeah, *could* being the operative word here.

Enjoying his good mood too much to let the realities of his situation bring him down, he decided the best thing he could do in this situation was play along.

"I told him you're pretty much royalty in our circles, so he found some tablecloths that were owned by an Ethiopian empress he's going to see if we can rent. It's going to cost a mint if he can come through, but from what I could tell from the photos, they'll be more than worth it."

"And that's all you're excited about?" Ace asked again. "These royal linens?"

"Of course," Stephan answered quickly. "What other reason could there be?"

Ace narrowed his gaze, his cheeks rising with a slightly sinister gleam in his eyes.

"Okay, nephew," Ace said. "Tell me about these party plans you and your *friend*—" Ace put emphasis on the word, letting Stephan know he wasn't fooled by his bullshit "—have come up with for this event."

Stephan stepped out into the cold air, bundled into his North Face and a beanie as he left Devereaux Manor and walked the seven blocks up Gates Avenue to his home. He was just about to turn right onto Grand Avenue when a jolt of restlessness hit him. It was still Saturday morning and since he didn't have any plans, he figured he might as well stop into his favorite local café and get some pastry and a coffee. CUP aka Coffee Uplifts People, was located just five blocks away from his brownstone at the intersection of Gates and Bedford Avenues. It was a Black-owned coffee shop with a mission to source from Black and Brown growers around the world.

Even though he was part of the notorious 2 percent of the superwealthy in America, he wholeheartedly believed in supporting the businesses and people the world often forgot about. And being one of the few Black-owned billion-dollar businesses, not only in the United States but the world, Stephan, his family, and Devereaux Inc. felt an unshakable commitment to giving back in meaningful ways to their community. The only time that promise had ever been in jeopardy was when his cousin Amara had made a fast deal for the wrong reasons. But his uncle David had gathered her quickly, and she'd gotten herself, and the company's focus back on track. As a bonus, she ended up with a husband, a baby on the way, and was about to become the First Lady of New York City in the new year.

Feeling it might be a tad early for him to get so hopped up on his urban renewal stance, Stephan hurried into the coffee shop, sighing his relief when the warmth enveloped him. He waved at the owner, delighted that his usual table in the corner was available.

"Stephan? Is that you?"

He followed the voice until he found Carter sitting at a table with a tiny person who was currently wearing an oversized white sweater that in conjunction with the fuzzy cap on her head, looked like a human plushie.

Stephan waved, not sure if he should walk over to their table.

To be clear, he wanted to walk over to their table and kiss Carter hello. But the man was sitting with his young daughter; now might not be the best time to act on his desire to tongue the man down.

Not to mention, there were Carter's hang-ups about drawing attention to himself in public, all of it making his usual confidence when it came to matters of attraction seem ill-fitting at present.

"We're having cocoa, Mr. Smith."

Once those big eyes found his and that wide grin spread across the little girl's face, there wasn't a chance Stephan was walking away.

"Thank you for the invitation, Nevaeh." Stephan sat down, reciprocating her grin, then lifting his gaze up to find the same wide eyes looking at him, just in a bigger, sexier form. But the effect was still the same. Both father and daughter had Stephan Devereaux-Smith, the smoothest talking brotha in the world, wrapped up in endless lashes that shielded dark brown eyes deep enough to drown in.

If he didn't get control of this situation, he'd have to return his player's card.

"What are the two of you doing here today?"

"Having breakfast after washday."

"Is that so?" Stephan replied, trying his best to give his finest attentive face to the little girl.

"Yeah. My mother-in-law and I take turns doing washday. Today was my turn and I was too tired to think about cooking after that."

Stephan didn't blame him. He'd kept his hair long until his teens and braiding that much fabulously coily hair was a whole job, even when a salon professional was doing it.

"I can imagine. My cousin and I used to take turns doing each other's hair when we didn't want to sit in a salon all day. It was a lot of work, but our hair was always styled to perfection, especially when we wore matching cornrows and beads."

Carter's jaw dropped, making something in Stephan's chest swell with delight.

"You wore cornrows and beads?"

"I did. My joints were always on point too." Stephan was speaking absolute fact. He and Amara really did slay back in the day. A sad ache tried to horn its way in on Stephan's mind when he had to resist the urge to grab his phone and show Carter.

That was the problem with secrets. They wound their sneaky tentacles into even the most innocuous and innocent aspects of a person's life.

"Mr. Smith." Stephan's ears perked up at the small voice using such formal language, and he smiled.

"If it's okay with your dad, you can call me Stephan too, Nevaeh."

When she turned to him, Carter met her with a nod, and she hurriedly brought her gaze back to Stephan's.

"Stephan," she continued. "Do you still know how to do cornrows. I asked Daddy, but all he knows how to do are boring ponytails."

Stephan hissed at that body shot Nevaeh had thrown at Carter.

He waved off Stephan's sympathy. "Kids don't care nothing about your feelings. I'm used to it by now."

Without pausing, Nevaeh jumped right back into her line of questioning. "Do you think you could do some for me today?"

Stephan blinked, unsure of how to respond. Yes, he knew how to cornrow hair, but this was Carter's daughter, and doing hair was such a personal and intimate thing in the

Black community, Stephan didn't think he had the right to cross such a line. Not when he knew he couldn't allow either of them the same kind of access to his own life.

Stephan's eyes caught Carter's and he could see a slight tenseness growing there. Had he wanted Stephan to say yes?

"Nevaeh, I'm sure Stephan has a bunch of things to do today. Cornrows can take a long time. If Grannie Gracie is too tired to do them after spending the weekend with her cousin, maybe we can find an African Hair Braider to do them for us."

"It's fine." Stephan watched as Carter's brows rose. Yeah, he'd surprised himself with that one too. He should not be doing anything that was going to further entangle their lives. But when Carter's surprise turned into the corner of his mouth lifting, Stephan couldn't remember all the reasons he was supposed to be staying away. "I can do it."

"I warn you," Carter fake-whispered. "She's tender-headed."

Stephan gave Nevaeh a conspiratorial wink. "No one is tender-headed if the folks doing the combing would learn how to properly detangle the hair attached to sensitive scalps."

"Yeah, Daddy," Nevaeh chimed in. "You gotta be gentle."

Carter was chuckling and Stephan's heart felt like it stopped as he watched this dedicated father with his child. And that's when he realized he was definitely in danger of allowing Carter to get too close. But for some unexplained reason, he couldn't seem to find the panic that should've come along with that realization.

"Now that we've settled that," Stephan continued, "let's go around the corner to the beauty supply store and you can pick out some pretty beads, then we'll catch a Lyft and go down to Targét so we can pick up a bunch of Pattern Beauty products to keep the ouchies away."

"Targét?" The confusion on Carter's face was so adorable Stephan had to fight to keep from laughing.

"Target is for basic—" Stephan caught sight of Nevaeh's gaze locked on him and bit his lip to keep the explicative from leaving his mouth "—folks," Stephan continued. "We're too fabulous for all that, so when we walk in it's Targét."

Nevaeh was excitedly bouncing on her feet as she stood and started putting her coat on. Carter took that moment to lay his hand across Stephan's on the table, forcing him to laser in on the warm pressure his hand provided.

"I'm sorry you got roped into this. You really don't have to do it."

Carter attempted to pull away and Stephan caught his hand, lacing their hands together. "I want to do this," he murmured."

It was the truest statement he'd ever made.

There was something so special about this man and his daughter, Stephan just wanted to experience their magic for a little while. That wasn't so wrong, was it?

He knew it was, but if they were willing to share their joy with Stephan for just a little while, he'd soak it up the way dry hair sopped up cheap hair products."

"Look at how pretty I am, Daddy!"

Carter couldn't help how a wide smile bloomed on his face when his baby girl stood up from the bar chair Stephan had her seated on, with an intricate pattern of braids that were adorned with red and clear beads at each end.

"You are the prettiest girl in the world. Did you thank Stephan for taking such good care of your hair?"

She nodded.

"Good, then go upstairs and get your tablet and FaceTime abuela so she can see how pretty you look."

His daughter left the two men alone, and Carter still couldn't tamp down the excitement and joy he'd been experiencing since he'd spotted Stephan at CUP.

"You have to let me repay you for this, Stephan."

Standing tall and lanky in Carter's living room, he folded his arms and shook his head.

"Nope. Beauty days are always a gift whether I'm on the receiving end of them or not. Not to mention, doing Nevaeh's hair gave me a reason to flex my skills, so I'm calling it a win."

It had taken them more than an hour to get all the supplies Stephan insisted they needed, and then it had taken more than two hours with built-in snack and bathroom breaks, for Stephan to finish.

And that little traitor of his, who started bawling the moment Carter came near her head with a brush or a comb, had sat so sweetly for Stephan, Carter could hardly recognize her.

"That was labor. Also, you've gotta show me how you keep her from crying. That girl can burst an eardrum with her crying when it's time to get her hair done."

"No secret, just have to know what products to use to really detangle without traumatizing the girl. Those products I brought in will work wonders. Just follow the directions on them and take your time."

The moment stretched out between them. It was so full with unspoken words. No man gave up his entire Saturday to braid a child's hair when that child wasn't his. And yet here Stephan was.

Stephan was being a perplexing enigma to Carter, and more and more his curiosity wanted to explore, seek as much information as he could to have the man make sense to him, or more importantly, help Carter understand why he wanted to know so much about him.

"I really enjoyed myself today, Carter."

"Did you?" When Stephan nodded Carter asked, "But why?"

"Because spending time with you and your daughter made me forget about everything else in the world at the moment. It helped me remember just how fun it was to be with family and friends before life added so much pressure, I couldn't breathe."

He stepped closer to Carter, leaning in slowly until all Carter could do was shiver in anticipation of a repeat of their kiss.

"But most all, because you have a great kid and she has a great father, and I'd be out of my mind not to want to spend as much time as I possibly could in your collective presence."

Before Carter could respond, Stephan pressed his lips to Carter's in such a sweet and gentle kiss, Carter had to actually wonder if it had happened at all.

By the time he found his bearings again, Stephan had stepped away from him, grabbing his coat and yelling his goodbyes up to Nevaeh. And just like before he let himself out of Carter's door he said, "Can't wait to do it again."

Eleven

"Hey there."

Carter bit his lip to fight the moan that was circling the bottom of his throat. Dammit, in the week since he'd seen Stephan last, since he knew what that man's lips felt like against his, just the thought of Stephan Smith turned Carter into a puddle. Hearing the rumble of Stephan's voice tickle his ear was somehow signaling to his dick that this was the appropriate time to stand at attention.

God, how hard up must you be, Jiménez?

Very, apparently.

"Hi, Stephan," Carter replied softly. It was Saturday morning and his nosy daughter always seemed to find her way to him when he was on the phone. Usually, he didn't mind so much. Considering his current state of partial arousal, he figured it was probably best he stayed off her radar.

"Did I wake you?"

"No," Carter replied. "I've been up for a bit. Did you

need something? Aren't you supposed to go meet with my connect at Borough Hall today? Is that still happening?"

Stephan's gentle laughter put Carter at ease, forcing him to take a breath and pull himself together.

"Everything's fine, Carter."

He was still chuckling as he replied and although Carter knew that laughter was at his own expense, hearing it somehow eased something in him, as if knowing Stephan was all right soothed him somehow.

"I'm actually on my way inside Borough Hall now to secure the venue. But, after I take care of that and a few other errands I need to run today, I was hoping you'd be available to have dinner with me tonight."

"Dinner? Have we forgotten anything off the party list? We finalized vendors last week for everything."

The sultry chuckle slipped through the phone lines again, forcing Carter's micromanaging tendencies to relax.

"No, everything for the party is set. Once I pay for the venue, the stationery company has the go-ahead to hand deliver all of the invitations to my uncle's family, friends, etc. I wasn't asking for more of your help with planning the party. I was asking you out on a date."

"A date?"

"Yeah," Stephan replied. "You know, when people who are interested in getting to know each other romantically, so they go out to eat and maybe entertain themselves to sort of help that process along?"

Carter sat up, unable to stop the smile from bending the corners of his mouth.

"And you want to get to know me, romantically?"

"Well, I certainly don't go around sharing fantastic kisses like ours with just any random on the street."

"So, I'm special?"

Stephan let a moan of his own escape, and Carter had to admit he liked knowing Stephan was just as affected by him.

"Baby, you're so much more than special. And the truth is, I have no idea why. Everything about you has called to me from the moment I met you. And I thought it was just because I wanted a distraction from my family issues. But that's not it. There's something about you, Carter, something I'd probably leave alone if I knew what was good for me. But after knowing how that mouth of yours tastes, I just can't get you out of my head. So, since you don't necessarily seem like the type of guy who's into hookups—"

"Hey," Carter interrupted. "You don't know me like that. I could very well be into all of the hookups. Would that turn you off if I were?"

"Your unruly dog ruined my damn dirty chicken wings and I still wanted to be around you, touch you. Your hookup history wouldn't even faze me. Besides, I've never been a saint, so I definitely can't point fingers when it comes to someone having a healthy sexual appetite."

Carter's insides churned into a hot sour mix of jealousy. He didn't have to even think about it. From its first lick inside his belly, he wanted to lay waste to anyone who'd ever had the audacity to touch Stephan.

Was that response rational? Not the tiniest bit. They weren't even an item. They hadn't even gone on their first official date, date. Did that make the fire and tension growing inside Carter any less real? Not in the least.

Carter had held back from pursuing anything physical with Stephan because he firmly believed sex would've only complicated whatever his issues were. And even though Carter had no doubt those issues were nowhere near resolved, after the kiss they'd shared in Carter's office, there was no way in hell Carter could deny how much he wanted Stephan.

God, he was such a hot mess of contradiction.

"If it's a nonissue, why did you say I don't seem like I'm into hookups?"

Stephan chuckled, and Carter could tell by the rich tones of his voice he wasn't just BS-ing. He was absolutely enjoying himself.

"Because, that first time I came down to The Vault, the only thing I had in mind when I walked into that place was finding a sturdy enough surface with enough privacy that I could tease and taste as much of you as I wanted for as long as I wanted. But you put the kibosh on that ASAP. Those are not the moves of a player who's just looking for the next available body."

Why was this man so good at reading him so well. If he was this good at it out of bed, Carter hoped like hell it was an indicator he'd be just as good when there was nothing between their bodies but air.

Heat burned across Carter's skin. Just the thought of being naked with Stephan was searing him, burning through each layer of skin, leaving Carter exposed in a way that should make him so uncomfortable.

But he wasn't.

To the contrary, he was excited by the idea. So excited in fact, he knew there was no chance in hell he wouldn't let Stephan strip him naked if he had the opportunity.

He pinched the bridge of his nose. As he gave in to the realization that this was probably going to happen, and soon, Carter thought they had better set some ground rules first.

He'd fought like hell and given up his career to protect

his daughter from all the messiness Hollywood peddled in. He'd be damned if he upset the happy, healthy peace she had here in Brooklyn just for a chance to satisfy this damn itch he had where Stephan Smith was concerned.

"Okay, you've convinced me."

"Great," his reply was smooth and even. "I'll make reservations for us at Negril BK, it you're okay with it."

"Well, I love Negril BK, but after working most nights in the service industry myself, I'd really prefer just sort of Netflix-and-chilling when I'm off."

"You don't want to be seen in public with me?" Stephan's voice was strong, but quiet, as if he were trying hard to put his strength on display, bracing himself for unwanted revelations Carter's reticence had obviously prompted. It clawed at that part of Carter that had wanted to be a lifeline for Stephan from the first day they met.

Knowing that his hang-ups with public life would hurt or disappoint Stephan even a tiny bit made him wish that he was much further along on his healing journey. Because if he could ever get past what the celebrity press had cost him, he knew he'd parade Stephan around for the world to see. Carter shook his head, trying to figure out how to say everything rolling around in his head without sounding weird or offensive.

"It's not that, Stephan—I just, I need to keep my life private. I know that may not make sense to you, but for me, whatever happens between us, I need to be able to trust that this stays our business and no one else's."

"Carter, you don't have to say it. I get it. You don't want to draw attention to yourself. Brooklyn is your safe space and being out and about drawing attention to yourself isn't in your best interest. No worries. I think I can do this first-date thing justice and keep prying eyes away. Trust me to take care of you."

For some strange reason, Carter instinctively knew he could trust Stephan.

Maybe it was the way he worried over the uncle who'd raised him. Maybe it was because he just seemed to read Carter and anticipate his needs.

Whatever it was. He wholeheartedly believed Stephan would protect him. And no matter how foolish it was to espouse that belief, Carter was all in.

"Whatever happens between us, I need to be able to trust that this stays our business and no one else's."

Stephan bristled as a cold gust of air passed through him. He attributed it to the usual Brooklyn chill that came with living where there was so much stone, concrete, metal, and glass. Deep down, however, he knew the weather had nothing to do with why he felt so off.

Stephan should be happy Carter didn't want to make a big spectacle of whatever this thing was that kept pulling them together.

Should be was the operative phrase.

When this ended—and it would certainly end—there would be no messy split if Stephan agreed to what Carter wanted, a clandestine affair that only they were aware of. They'd simply say their goodbyes and go their separate ways.

But somewhere deep inside Stephan could sense disappointment spreading through him, tainting the delight he always experienced when he was in Carter's orbit or simply thinking about him.

This isn't about you. It's about Carter and what he needs.

So just swallow whatever this is that has you feeling on edge. It's not like it's the first time you've had to ignore discomfort for the greater good.

"You really can't walk two blocks in Brooklyn without running into a Devereaux."

Stephan turned around to the familiar voice to find Lennox standing in the corner of the Starbucks, presumably waiting for his order to be called up. Stephan shrugged and tilted his head toward the man.

"That should be an obvious truth for someone who's married to one of us."

Lennox shared a good-natured laugh as he grabbed Stephan into a big hug.

"S'up, man. I meant to call and congratulate you on your win. My cousin-in-love, the next mayor of the Big Apple. I'm surprised you're even allowed to walk around by yourself anymore. Shouldn't you have secret service surrounding you at all times."

"Bruh, you've only been in Paris two years." He held his hands out in a WTF manner. "That shouldn't be long enough for you to forget how our government works, and what agencies work together within that government. Secret Service is the president, dude. NYPD protects the NYC mayor."

"If it ain't about money, or making money, it doesn't really cross my mind."

Lennox pursed his lips. "You're a Devereaux, so that tracks."

Both their names were called at the same time. They each grabbed their coffees and moved in a corner to get out of the way of the door.

"Listen, man." Lennox took a sip of his coffee before he continued. "I've got a million and one meetings today.

I only came down to make sure a favor I needed done for my best friend was taken care of."

"You're not even mayor yet and you're out here doing political favors for friends?"

Lennox lifted his brow, managing to scold Stephan better than his mother used to as a kid.

"Don't even play like that, man. My best friend has a client who was looking to rent out Borough Hall for a private event. I just put him in touch with the person he needed to deal with."

Stephan's mind stumbled over Lennox's words as he repeated them in his head and then spoke them again.

"Your best friend?"

Lennox nodded. "That's right, you've never met Carter. I know you've been holding it down where Ace is concerned, so you haven't had a lot of time to hang out with us."

"You two are newlyweds, Lennox. You don't need me underfoot."

"You're family, Stephan, and you're always welcome. But seriously, our little one is gonna be here before you know it. You gotta come check us out before then. Let me know when you're ready and I'll make sure Carter is there."

Stephan stiffened. What would be the odds that his cousin's, husband's best friend is the same man he'd been fantasizing about doing dirty things to?

Could fate really take that kind of sick pleasure in dicking him around like this?

"We could have dinner at our place, or if you're up for going out, we could probably eat at The Vault. Carter owns it."

The few sips of coffee Stephan had ingested left a sour taste in his mouth that made him feel like retching in the middle of Starbucks on Court Street.

"I think you'd like him." Lennox continued as if he needed to drive the imaginary dagger deeper into his chest.

Like him? I want to strip him naked and run my tongue against every inch of skin he has. I'd say that goes well beyond liking him.

He was sure Lennox would agree if he was aware of all the moving pieces to this particular puzzle.

"I'm sure I would." Stephan barely maintained his composure, even if alarms were sounding off every two seconds in his head.

"Look, man—" Lennox hooked a thumb over his shoulder in the direction of the door "—I've got another appointment to get to. But don't be scarce. Your cousin's thrilled to have you back home. Drop in soon."

Lennox went out of the building, and a half dozen people who seemed to come out of nowhere encircled him before they stepped out of the door.

Stephan looked at his watch and saw he had another twenty minutes before he had to make it across the street and secure the venue for Ace's Christmas gala.

That was more than enough time for him to have a controlled freak-out about this mess.

He was attracted to Carter, a man who hated the elite and worked his best to stay out of the limelight. He was certain that's why he hadn't seen Carter anywhere near Lennox's campaign trail.

Realizing he and Carter had barely a degree of separation between them, let alone six, the game was changing.

Next to Lyric, Amara was the closest thing he had to a sister and Lennox was her husband. If he handled this poorly, this thing had the potential to blow up in all their faces.

Yes, Stephan had exiled himself away from his people for

two years. But he'd always known they would be waiting for him with open arms when he was ready to return home. But Carter's connection to his cousin, it was too close for Stephan's comfort. It threatened the delicate peace his loved ones enjoyed as long as Stephan guarded the ugly truth like a hardened warden.

They'd never see that he was protecting them. They'd only know Stephan had lied. And no matter how much he loved them and they him, he wasn't sure they'd ever be able to forgive him. How could he be certain when the truth was he couldn't forgive himself.

He tightened his fists, wondering who in heaven decided Stephan was the person who should bear all the volatile shit that had—and could again—blow up the family. Because right now, Stephan sure as hell felt like asking for a meeting with the manager, because this for damn sure didn't make the slightest bit of sense.

He took a breath, calming himself. He couldn't make rash decisions under this type of duress. When he felt he was calm enough to think about this chaos with a clear mind, there was only one conclusion he could draw.

He had to tell Carter who he really was. Which meant, he'd also have to face the very unpleasant reality that Carter wouldn't want to have anything else to do with him.

And didn't that just suck large donkey balls.

Twelve

"You rented a yacht?"

Stephan couldn't help the slip of laughter that escaped his lips. Although Carter moved and once resided in a world of luxury, having access to a yacht in Brooklyn wasn't exactly commonplace.

Just one of the perks of being a Devereaux. *Common* wasn't part of their vocabulary, so things like asking your cousin if you could borrow his yacht so you could spend some quality time with your date was just as normal as asking to hang out in their furnished basement.

He was about to share that thought with Carter when he realized the man wouldn't find it the least bit funny. It was the reason he'd walked around with a boulder sitting in the pit of his stomach since he'd run into Lennox that morning. Carter hated where Stephan came from and who he was.

Notoriety was a birthright of every Devereaux. The only reason Stephan didn't receive as much fanfare as the rest was that he'd spent most of his life working behind the scenes. But if he'd stood at Ace's side the way the rest of his cousins had, the world would know his face as well as the others.

"It's a work perk. I thought our first official *date* date was a perfect reason to splurge a little. Don't you?"

Carter's grin radiated, its gleam reaching the depths of his dark eyes.

"Now, let's get below deck," Stephan said, eager to have Carter all to himself. "Being on a yacht might be cool, but since it's November and this water is brick-as-a-mug, I'on wanna spend too much time admiring the vessel up here.

"Man, you have no idea how much it warms my heart to hear terms of measurements like 'Than/as-a-mug'.

"I think I do," Stephan replied. "I've lived in Paris for two years, remember?"

Stephan led him below deck, taking his wool coat and scarf.

Carter continued their conversation. "My best friend, who's a Black man born and raised in Brooklyn, came to visit me on set out in LA once and he used it while we were talking to this Beverly Hills type. Blond slick hair, crystal blue eyes, polished from head to toe, and the luxury watch and sports car as the perfect accessories.

"He looked at my boy like he had two heads, then turned to me, because I'm the white-passing Puerto Rican, to ask what the hell he meant, like I was his walking 'hood-to-standardized-English translator."

"Did you explain it?"

Carter shook his head. "No, I was inclined to tell him to google it. But my best friend took pity on him and told him 'a mug' represented the most extreme condition/state of something. When using it as a comparative, you're saying that whatever your subject is, it's in a more extreme state than 'a mug', i.e. , it's extremely cold outside, so it's colder than, or cold as-a-mug.'"

"Let me guess," Stephan replied. "Even once he got the explanation, he still tried to act like he was confused. Like AAVE isn't a whole language?"

"You know it. But being back home in Brooklyn, where phrases like that are common, it just feels so good. I don't care where I go in the world, there's just no place like Brooklyn"

Stephan could definitely relate. He was well-traveled the world over. But his heart was right here in Brooklyn, and as he looked at the happy spark in Carter's eyes, he realized that phrase might literally be the case if he didn't curb things with this man soon.

"Did you get a whole lot of that in Paris?"

"A lot of what?" Stephan thought on Carter's question, realizing what the man was talking about.

"People dismissing the significance of Black American culture?" When Carter nodded, Stephan continued. "Everyone loves to consume Black American culture, but when Black Americans put their own culture into practice, it's often not received well.

"My job gives me access to money and power the way very few Black Americans are expected to possess. It means wherever I go in this world, I have to navigate people's expectations in the boardroom, in the bedroom, and everywhere in between."

Paris had allowed him to build an emotional fortress around himself so he could heal. But as a Black gay man who could access money and power, it meant men who were drawn to both wanted him not only for his money and power, but because he was the object of their "Black guys have big dicks" fantasies, and they wanted to see if the rumors were true.

So, after Dexter, Stephan had stayed protected in his fortress, because trying to deal with his brother's death and Dexter's deception, Stephan understood that the only person he could trust was himself.

Feeling the twinge of discomfort from old wounds being abraded, he shoved them back down and turned to his guest.

"Listen Car—"

Carter inhaled once they reached the cabin. "Is that oxtail I smell?"

"Yes, oxtail pizza to be exact from Cuts and Slices."

Carter moaned and the rich sound did more for Stephan's libido than his appetite.

"The spot on Howard and Halsey Avenues?" Stephan nodded, pointing toward the two large pie boxes settled on the bolted coffee table. "That smells divine. I've always wanted to try their offerings, but they usually have a line around the corner."

"Well," Stephan continued as he sat down and motioned for Carter to sit down next to him. "I had time to kill, so I figured why not."

"You are really trying to impress your way into my pants, aren't you?"

"Is it working?"

Stephan was master of the quiet flex. Oh, he could definitely do flash with the best of them. But when it came to the people he cared about, subtle was always the best way to show he cared.

"Yes, but the truth is, good food is a bonus. I came here with every intention of giving you what we both want."

"Straight and to the point, huh?"

Carter grabbed his hand. "I'm a single father and a business owner with very little time to myself. I don't plan to spend one moment tonight playing coy. I don't need the buildup, I just need you. Can you give me that, at least for tonight?"

"Carter, I do want to give you that, give us both that."

He really did want to satisfy them both. But if he crossed that threshold with Carter, he wasn't so sure he'd be able to easily walk away. Every moment with Carter made Stephan feel like a new person, like he didn't have to hide in his lonely old fortress. Being with him gave Stephan the tiniest hope that maybe, just maybe, he could let someone else in. Which was exactly why he needed to slow things down and tell Carter the truth about his identity and his life as a member of the Devereaux family.

As surely as he recognized his own name, Stephan knew that the moment Carter's body touched his, he'd be too far gone to walk away, to do the right thing, to accept that Carter wouldn't want anything else to do with him.

"Then what's the holdup? Are you having second thoughts? I'm not looking for forever. I just want to enjoy the here and now."

"I get that," Stephan replied. His voice was rough, scraping against the inside of his throat. Stephan knew he couldn't say with such clarity that he just wanted to have fun with Carter. Because fun had gone out the window for him once he pressed his lips to Carter's and tasted him for the first time. "But I feel like there are important things we need to discuss."

Like the fact that I am part of the very world you despise, the world that took everything from you.

Life was so damn cruel. Here was this beautiful man with eyes only for him. Carter's skin was flushed with desire, body trembling in anticipation of his touch. It should've been so simple. Have fun, enjoy what he hoped was going to be phenomenal sex, and go back home in the morning.

Carter was helping him plan a Christmas gala. In addition, him having no expectations beyond this night, and Stephan could see the proverbial cherry on top of this scenario.

Stephan rarely saw that kind of selflessness. Its display was complicating things, making him ache for more when he should detach himself and move on. His feelings for Carter were deepening. The truth was he didn't want to ruin their chance at something real by deceiving Carter one moment longer.

"Carter, I—"

He never got the chance to finish his sentence. Carter pressed his lips against Stephan's. The urgency and strength demanded Stephan's submission, his compliance, and his reciprocation.

Carter teased until Stephan's lips were open and he dipped his tongue inside of Stephan's mouth, eagerly tasting every inch his tongue met.

Stephan had never been at a true loss for words, but having Carter's mouth, and now his hands which were currently reaching under the hem of Stephan's turtleneck and touching the sensitive skin there, had him dizzy, unable to determine which way was up.

Soon, Carter was pressing Stephan's back into the sofa, straddling his thighs and lowering himself over Stephan's clothed cock. He shifted his hips, driving a needy moan from Stephan that tested the limits of his restraint. And when Carter moved his hips again and Stephan's cock went from half-hard to fully erect in two and a half seconds, those restraints that he'd been struggling so hard to maintain, snapped.

Stephan placed a firm grip on Carter's neck, pulling him flush against him and loving the sweet moan he gifted Stephan with. He locked his remaining arm around Carter's waist, making certain he stayed right where he wanted him, pressed firmly against his cock, making Stephan ache, and hopefully feeling just as achy himself.

Stephan growled as he turned them sideways, flipping Carter beneath him and thrusting his hips forward so Carter was aware of what he was doing to him. He needn't have bothered, though. Because the sweet smirk placed firmly on Carter's lips told Stephan the eager man beneath him knew exactly what he was doing.

"Ah," Carter mewled. "There he is. There's the man I've been waiting to show up and show out."

"That mouth of yours is going to get you in so much trouble." Stephan knew Carter was egging him on, but the bait was too inviting not to take.

"Promise?"

The man was playing with fire. Lying beneath him with his brow arched and his bottom lip tugged between his teeth, Stephan knew he didn't have a shred of control left in him.

"Fuck it."

He leaned up long enough to remove his shirt, and when Carter lay back on the couch still clothed, Stephan gritted through his clenched teeth, "Are you waiting for an invitation."

"No." Carter beamed. Just enjoying watching you lose the blessed control you fight so hard to keep."

Carter was right. He did have a need to control all the emotion, fire, the secrets that dwelled within him. If he lost control for even a second, the fallout would be chaos.

But tonight, he didn't have to hold on so tightly. Tonight, he would give Carter what he was asking for, what they both so desperately wanted, and enjoy the pure bliss of letting go in this silent space where only the two of them existed.

He leaned back on his haunches, unbuttoning his pants, then stood so he could finally free himself of the rest of his clothes. When Carter wasn't moving fast enough for his liking, he growled, "Strip."

A spark of something hungry flashed in Carter's eyes and a lightbulb went off in Stephan's head. Carter said he was waiting for this take-charge man to show up. He said he wanted Stephan to lose control, but from the way he scurried off the sofa and began removing his clothing, Stephan wondered if what Carter was looking for was someone who knew how to manage *him* in the bedroom.

The outside world often thought that when someone asked to be dominated when it came to sex, it meant they were weak, that somehow they weren't real men. But it was the furthest thing from the truth. To submit meant you allowed someone to have control over you in the ways in which you deemed appropriate.

Carter managed every part of his life: his family, his business. It would make sense to Stephan that Carter possibly needed to let his guard down. Could he need something, or perhaps, someone, to take control so he could enjoy being cared for?

Was Carter here because he trusted Stephan enough to take care of him, to give him what he needed and keep him safe?"

Stephan didn't get off on needing to control others. Yet, the idea of Carter submitting to him had him hard enough to cut glass. As someone who didn't find it easy to trust, he knew what kind of sacrifice it was to allow yourself to be this vulnerable when you had so much to lose.

It had ruffled his sense of well-being when Carter had said he only wanted tonight. But realizing how much trust Carter was putting in him, Stephan knew one night would never be enough.

He was an asshole for allowing that realization to stroke his ego. Especially when he was aware that they might be walking their separate ways by the end of the night. But everything in him wanted to please Carter right now and if this man needed to stop taking care of everyone in his life for this brief moment they shared, Stephan would make this so sweet for him, Carter would never be able to forget it or re-create it with someone else.

Carter went to lower himself to the sofa, and Stephan pulled him into his arms, placing his hand at the front of Carter's neck, allowing his thumb to barely touch his Adam's apple and basking in the beautiful tremor Carter gave him in response.

"You don't want this to be gentle, do you?"

"What gave it away?"

"That smart-ass mouth of yours, for one. I think if you have this much air and brain power to talk slick, you might need something to fill it."

Carter closed his eyes and shivered and Stephan wanted nothing more than to bury himself as deeply as he could in Carter's body. But he was a man living on borrowed time as far as Carter was concerned, so he would savor this for as long as humanly possible.

"So, all that strong talk about having your way with me, that was just for show?"

Carter swallowed, licking his lips as if they were dry from the heavy breathing he was doing.

"Maybe." Carter's voice was gravel over concrete, rough, scraping over every nerve Stephan possessed. "Or maybe—" he breathed deeply, opening his eyes and looking into Stephan's "—maybe this is exactly the way I wanted to have you all along, and I needed to know if you could handle it. If you could handle me."

That was the proverbial straw that broke the camel's back. Stephan pulled Carter's body into his, loving the sensation of hard flesh against hard flesh. With one hand, Stephan held Carter's head where he wanted it as he devoured the tender flesh of his partner's mouth.

He used his other hand to stroke Carter's cock from root to tip, letting his thumb glide over the domed cap. The pearl of pre-cum there set him aflame, making him ache to taste it. But tonight was about giving Carter what he needed.

Carter thrust into Stephan's hand, the smooth silk of his flesh in Stephan's palm made him want to spill his pleasure right where they stood. He was already addicted to the way Carter's skin felt pressed against his. He'd have this every night and twice on Sundays for the rest of his life if he could. But he knew the likelihood of that was nil, and if by chance tonight was all they had, Stephan was going to give Carter everything he'd asked for.

He pulled his mouth from Carter's, leaving the man chasing his mouth as if it were a lifeline.

"I need to get you to one of the staterooms before I lose it right here on this damn sofa."

"I've…" Carter stopped to catch his breath, "I've got whatever you need in my inside coat pocket."

"Keep us busy then, while I grab it."

Stephan sat down on the sofa, taking Carter by the hand so he would follow, straddling Stephan's legs. He took Carter's hand and wrapped it around both their cocks, showing him the slow rhythm Stephan wanted him to keep while he grabbed the hem of Carter's coat to bring it closer.

Stephan's head lolled against the back of the couch at the delicious and distracting friction Carter was creating. Fortunately, he was able to find the exact pocket Carter had mentioned easily, otherwise, his next move was to rip the thing to shreds and shake it until its contents fell on the sofa cushion next to them. Because there was no damn way in hell Stephan was moving away from Carter.

His fingertips could make out the square foil and a small plastic tube he knew had to be lube. He lifted the foil, opening his eyes to glance at it and then placed it into Carter's hand.

"Get me ready."

Carter made such quick work of getting the condom on Stephan, he'd almost had to laugh. But since he was just as needy as Carter, he knew he couldn't.

He opened the lubricant, applying it to his fingers and gently rubbing at the puckered skin of Carter's entrance, trying to hold on to what little restraint he had, because as eager as he was to bury himself inside of Carter, he didn't want to make this uncomfortable for him.

"Are you sure you're up for this tonight?"

"I told you I don't want gentle."

"Carter, look at me." The deep rumble of his voice cleared

up any misunderstanding Carter might have about how serious Stephan was right now.

"Not being gentle isn't the same thing as hurting you. So, I'm asking are you sure you're up for this. Because it isn't a requirement for either of us to be satisfied tonight."

Carter's eyes morphed from a deep brown to a bottomless inky black. Stephan might've been alarmed until he saw the corner of Carter's mouth lift into a sly grin.

"I prepped myself before I got here."

Stephan's lungs seized as his brain processed what Carter was saying. "How?" he wheezed out. "With your fingers?"

Carter leaned in, licking and then nipping Stephan's earlobe before he whispered, "I had to take the edge off for fear I'd explode when you touched me. So just before I jumped into the shower, I reached into my toy drawer and pulled out old faithful." Carter gave Stephan's cock a squeeze before continuing. "He's a lifelike dildo with all the ridges, girth, and length I need to get myself ready for fun with a partner."

"God, Carter," he hissed through clenched teeth. "You're trying to kill me with that image."

Carter's smile broadened, and since Stephan was the master of one-upmanship, he sank two fingers into Carter's entrance, and reveled in the pleasure-filled moan that Carter let loose into the air.

Satisfied that he wouldn't hurt Carter, he removed his fingers and lined his cock up pressing slowly into Carter's body.

Blinding heat enveloped him as Carter lowered himself gradually.

Carter's body tightened just before they were completely joined.

"That's it, baby," Stephan crooned in his ear, wrapping

his arms around Carter, giving him something to brace against as Stephan pressed further into his body. "Take all of me. Take me like you took your toy."

Carter swirled his hips, giving Stephan the go-ahead to move. The next time Carter moved his hips again, Stephan thrust up to meet him, and Carter moaned so pretty, Stephan slid his hands down to Carter's hips and dragged him forward again.

"Ride me like you rode that fake cock."

Carter picked up the tempo, meeting Stephan's powerful thrusts with just as much vigor. They were already slick with sweat and tense with pleasure, and if Stephan could stay like this for the rest of his life, he'd die a happy man.

Carter's cock was hard and dripping against Stephan's stomach, trapped between both of them. He was so blissed out, so overwhelmed with the dual sensation, his eyes were closed and his mouth hung open as if he couldn't figure out how to breathe through it.

Stephan wasn't far behind. He would be falling soon too, but not until he wrung ever drop of pleasure from Carter that he could.

"Did you come with that toy deep inside you?"

Carter's body shook.

"Did you clamp down on it like a damn vice?"

"Stephan…please… I"

"I know what you need, baby."

Stephan tightened his grip on Carter's hips, pistoning into his body until Carter keened in ecstasy, his body milking Stephan for his essence, his strength, his ability to focus on anything other than the point where their bodies were joined and how damn good Carter felt clasping him. And when he couldn't hold his release back any longer, he buried himself so deeply inside Carter, hoping to erase the memory of every toy, be they plastic or of the human variety, he'd ever let enter his body. Because the only cock, the only name he wanted this man to ever remember was his.

Once they cleaned up, Stephan pulled Carter into his arms, needing to hold on to this moment longer. Because now that he knew what they were like together, Stephan didn't think there was any way he could willingly walk away from this man now.

Thirteen

"Not only does he avoid me when he's away from me, but he ignores me when I'm in his presence too. A girl could catch a complex dealing with you."

Stephan blinked the thick fog in his head clear just in time to bring Lyric, who was now sitting in front of his desk, into focus. He'd spent most of his morning replaying the time he and Carter had spent since their first night together a week ago.

Every touch, every smile, every whispered plea or outburst of laughter had taken up every working brain cell in his head. That's exactly how he'd forgotten to call Lyric and update her on this gala. Being with Carter made Stephan forget everything, especially the really bad things that made his heart ache.

"Sis, you know it's not even like that."

"Do I?"

Stephan knew Lyric's tone was supposed to be light and amusing, fun between two siblings-in-love getting at each other. But Stephan knew Lyric, and she didn't play like that. So although that "Do I?" was posed as if it were a joke, for damn sure, Stephan knew she was dead serious.

"You call a cousins' meeting and tell everyone you're going to update me, but then you don't actually update me. You've been home for months, and we've barely spent any time together. My husband dies, and the little brother I think I'm going to grieve with just ups and leaves no sooner than his brother's in the ground and doesn't come home for two years. Exactly what am I supposed to think other than you don't want to be around me."

Stephan stood up, walking around the desk and kneeling down in front of her.

"I know I've been a shitty little brother, Lyric, and I'm so sorry about that."

"Why, Stephan?" she whispered. "Is it because I moved on, because I'm with Josiah?"

He shook his head. "Sis, this has nothing to do with you, and everything to do with me. I'd like to say this has all been part of my grieving process, but I won't even insult you by telling you that lie."

"Then what?" She leaned forward, taking his hand between hers, doing the Lyric thing and finding a way to comfort him even when he'd been the one to cause her pain. "Is everything okay?"

"Am I safe? Yeah. But, I've just been going through a lot of emotional ups and downs and returning home just brought it all to bear. Add to that everything that's going on with Ace, and sometimes my feelings are just too big to force anyone else to be around me and them."

"Is that what's going on right now," she asked. "When I came in, you seemed like you were in another world."

His sister-in-love was always so good at reading him. It was one of the things he adored about her, but also the main reason why he couldn't stay after Randall died. If he'd stayed around her, there was no way he could've protected her from the truth.

"I've… I've been seeing someone and it's sort of messing with my head. I'm just trying to figure out how best to handle it."

Her smile was soft and supportive. "I don't think I've ever heard you say out loud that you're seeing someone before. This must be serious."

"The only thing serious about it is the sex."

"I'm sure it is, Steph, but the fact that you're actually sitting in your office brooding over a man tells me it's much more than sex."

Again, she knew him too well, and if he wasn't careful, she'd have all his secrets out on Front Street if he didn't bring this impromptu "let's talk about our feelings" session she was trying to have to a close.

"When Ace leaves, so will I, Lyric. So, there's no way for this to be more than it is. His entire life is here in Brooklyn and he has no intention of ever leaving. It can't work."

She leaned forward, squeezing his hands lightly.

"What was that old saying Ace used to always say to us?" She fake-scratched her head as if she was looking for the answer in the air. "Oh, I remember. 'Old man Can't been dead a long time.' So, by my calculation, that means you literally can."

"Please don't quote that old man to me. You know he refuses to see me unless I have some proof of joy to share with him."

Stephan waited to see her astonishment at such an unreasonable request, but all she did was smile.

"Can you blame him? With the exception of Trey and Jeremiah's wedding, all you've done since you returned home was work and sit by his side."

"Lyric, not you too."

He threw up his hands in exasperation, sitting on his desk as his shoulders slumped in familiar despair.

"Stephan, he's leaving us. As scary as that is for us, think about what that might feel like for him."

Fear? Ace? Those two words never took up the same space in his head.

"Ace is afraid, Stephan. Ace loves two things in life, Devereaux Inc. and the Devereaux family. He has put so much into the business, but it's cost him his sister, his nephew, and for a long while, his son and his granddaughter. He's using what time he has left to try to make sure the current generation will always look to love and not a bottom line for the answers."

Stephan's brow furrowed as he tried to make sense of Lyric's words. She was the empath in the family, the one who always sensed what was happening with everyone else. Was she once again seeing through another Devereaux man in this family who looked like polished gold on the outside, but was drowning silently in all his unspoken pain?

This conversation was beginning to hit too close to home for his taste.

"Sis, I think you're making more of this than necessary."

"No, I don't think you're paying close enough attention."

She shifted in her seat, leaning forward a bit, as if she were making sure he heard what she was saying.

"He wants us to be better than those that came before us. And you're the last holdout."

"Are you really standing here telling me you ended up with Josiah because Ace told you to?"

She smiled at the mention of her lover's name and part of him braced, not because he was against love and all its supposed splendor, but because part of him knew that he'd never be worthy of a man smiling at the mention of his name the way Lyric did at the mere whisper of Josiah's.

How could he be when there was just so much to atone for?

Outside of Lyric, Carter was the closest thing to a saint Stephan had ever seen. He was loyal, friendly, so compassionate that he reached out to Stephan simply because he looked like life was kicking his ass. Who does that? No one. That alone made Carter special. When you added in his dedication to his daughter and his mother and mother-in-law, his near sainthood was pretty much solidified.

Carter deserved someone better than Stephan, a man who'd lied to his family to protect them. A man who'd sold his own soul just to keep a very ugly truth from destroying the people he loved. Did he do it because he was selfless? Not likely. And now, knowing that he'd eventually have to give Carter up at some point, he didn't want to tell them because he didn't want to lose them. He didn't want them to hate him and abandon him.

That wasn't selfless. That was as selfish as it came and Carter deserved better.

"I didn't fall in love with Josiah because Ace wanted me to. But I was open to him being part of my life because Ace made me realize I had so much love left to give, that I didn't die with my husband."

She stood, then placed a gentle kiss on his cheek. "I don't know what burdens you bear that keeps you so closed off from love, Stephan. But whatever it is, Ace is trying to tell you that you don't have to carry it alone, that you're worthy of love despite whatever thing in your heart and head is telling you otherwise. Just do like the rest of the cousins did, and listen to him. Maybe if you do, things between you and this secret lover of yours won't seem so bad."

There was so much hope in her smile that Stephan wanted desperately to hold on to. If Lyric said it, then maybe it really could be true. Then…then there might be a way to keep this thing that warmed him from the inside out whenever he was near Carter.

"When you've got a better handle on what you're feeling for this mysterious man, come tell me about him."

She was halfway out the door when he called to her. "Wait, I really do have to update you on the cousins' meeting."

"You know doggone well the cousins crew can't hold water. Two minutes after y'all completed that meeting I had two different sets of voice mails relaying what happened. I've already marked the day on our calendar. Josiah and I will be there to support you in whatever way you need."

She dashed out of the room, leaving him with a big grin on his face and his heart feeling a tad bit lighter. How his brother had treated her so poorly, Stephan would never know. But he'd always known what a gem his sister-in-love was, and that's why he'd go to his grave to protect her. No matter the cost.

Now he just needed to figure out how to keep Carter from falling victim to a Devereaux-Smith man too. The only problem was Carter made the perpetual ache he'd carried around for two years go away. And Stephan knew no matter how much he didn't want to hurt Carter, he was also selfish enough to keep him in his life to stop the slow hemorrhaging of the blood his family unknowingly demanded.

Well, that should be no big deal, right? All I have to do is figure it all out and everything will be just perfect.

He laughed at his nonsensical response to this impossible situation he'd placed himself in. And as the panic and ache began to spread, pushing against his chest, making it difficult to breathe, he knew exactly what, or more aptly who, he needed to make everything all right.

"Dammit!"

Carter grabbed a nearby bar cloth and wiped furiously to stop the coffee he'd just prepared from spilling all over the bar rim and possibly scalding the patron seated on the opposite side.

"I'm sorry," Carter apologized. "I'll get you another coffee as soon as I get this cleaned up."

The patron nodded and Carter continued to rub the cloth back and forth until all the liquid was absorbed.

He turned around to find Ian with a hip leaned casually against the shelves, watching Carter as if he was trying to figure out some kind of puzzle.

"You okay, boss?"

Carter had to think a minute on how to answer that. He wasn't slow to respond because he was searching for the answer. No, he paused because he had to decide which of the varied answers to that question he was going to share.

"It's been a rough week and I haven't been getting as much sleep as I obviously need."

"If you need to head out early, I can hold it down for you."

Ian's offer was so tempting. To put it mildly, Stephan had spent the last week wearing him out. Between finalizing the details of the party including finding a Christmas tree large enough to rival the one at Rockefeller, and having some of the best sex he'd had in the last few years, Carter was exhausted. Not just physically, but the emotional high he'd been on had him wired, and Carter was afraid of the crash that would inevitably happen when he came down.

This was supposed to be fun. But fun was quickly turning into an addiction, and Carter couldn't afford to let anyone, especially someone as closed off as Stephan get underneath his skin like this.

Oh, he was fun, and selfless in his acts. But there were moments Carter could tell he was manic with desire because he didn't want to face whatever it was that was happening in his family life.

Carter understood needing that distraction. He'd been there himself when Michelle died. But this connection Carter had with him, how vulnerable he felt when Stephan held him in his arms. This was dangerous territory.

If he were smart, he'd work his shift and then take his ass home and get some sleep. That's exactly what he needed to do.

But, God, the sex was everything Carter needed it to be.

Energetic, passionate, fun, and so damn hot, Carter didn't understand how they hadn't burned through every surface they'd slammed each other against in an effort to get naked and connect to some part of each of their bodies.

"Thanks, man. But I've got a bunch of invoices to go through this afternoon. I need to dig into them."

"Okay," Ian replied. "But the lunch crowd won't be in

for about an hour. At least try to catch a few winks in your office before then."

"Will do."

Carter finished making the fresh coffee and handed it off to the eager patron. He was about to make his way to the back when the bell over the door chimed, and Stephan, walking in big and bold, sucking all the oxygen up in the room with his unbelievable sex appeal, entered Carter's establishment.

Every muscle in Carter's body tensed in delicious anticipation, as if he was supposed to be ready to give or receive pleasure on sight of the beautiful man walking toward him.

Carter wanted to wring his own neck for lacking self-control where Stephan Smith was concerned.

How did this man's mere appearance still render this visceral reaction from Carter, where his body, that was two seconds ago asking for a catnap, was now craving Stephan's touch like he'd never seen the man nor spent nearly every night this week making love to him.

Like clockwork, he'd leave Stephan's bed in time to wake Nevaeh up for school, feed her breakfast and get her out the door for school. Then, he'd catch a few hours of sleep and then run errands for The Vault or for Stephan's Christmas gala. Next, he'd pick Nevaeh up from school, help her with her homework, and spend quality time with her. And once he'd tucked her into bed, he'd go to work, then tell her grandmother he was staying late because they'd been swamped.

As soon as he closed, he'd make a beeline for Stephan's house, where the man would systematically dismantle every part of Carter simply to put him back together and send him on his way in the morning.

It was so exhausting and exhilarating, and even though

he walked away satisfied every time, Carter still craved something more.

More time, more tenderness, more intimacy where they opened up and let each other in. But he'd been the one to tell Stephan he only wanted it to be about the sex, so he couldn't very well be the one to change his mind now. Could he?

Did he?

Did he want to change his mind and reach for something deeper, stronger with Stephan?"

He was a father and he always had to consider his daughter first. He was sure she'd be thrilled if Carter pursued something more significant with Stephan. After the way he braided her hair in cornrows, she was happy to be his best friend. But after he came back the next weekend with some beads and other hair accessories to add to the latest style he'd given her, he was sure Nevaeh loved Stephan more than him.

Too bad relationships couldn't be based on something as simple as one's ability to cornrow and style a little girl's hair. No, they were based on things like being open with each other. And he still didn't know enough about Stephan to leap headfirst into a relationship with him.

He was a good man, Carter was sure of that. The way he talked about his uncle, the fact that he was giving his time, and several pretty pennies to boot, to make his dying uncle happy, that definitely said something about the man's character. But outside of knowing that his brother passed away a couple of years ago and that he grew up with a cousin whose hair he used to braid, he had no idea about Stephan's past.

Why have you let it get this far without asking him about his family and his background?

Because having his privacy violated on almost a daily

basis when he was an actor had taught Carter to be protective of not just his, but everyone else's too. When Michelle had died, the press had been relentless. They'd even paid one of the funeral home employees to sneak a picture of him kneeling at Michelle's opened casket when he'd gone in to approve her final appearance. Before he could put her in the ground, that picture was all over the news cycle.

It wasn't enough that they'd chased her into traffic and taken her life, they needed to exploit her death too.

He knew how deep betrayal like that went, and as a result, he'd never barge his way into someone else's life, even if that man seemed to be taking up so much space in Carter's.

And no matter how much Carter's curiosity wanted to know everything about Stephan Smith, there was one last reason he would never push for more: he wanted Stephan to offer that information freely. Because if he did, Carter wouldn't have to stand behind his bar wondering if he should try to deepen his relationship with Stephan. Carter would know beyond a shadow of doubt that Stephan Smith was the man for him.

"Hey," Stephan said, pulling Carter out of his rambling thoughts. His voice was pleasant, respectable, and no one in the room, including Carter, would assume he'd had Carter bent over the back of his sofa, calling for every deity his addled brain could remember in both English and Spanish.

"Hey, yourself," Carter replied. "Did you need something?"

"Actually, I did. I have a question about some of the details for the gala." Stephan pointed his chin toward Carter's office in the back. "You got a minute?"

Carter signaled to Ian he was going to the back and he led Stephan into his office. The second he closed the door, he found his back pushed against the nearby wall with Stephan's body flush against his and Stephan's mouth devouring his.

Carter should put his foot down—this was his place of business and he didn't make a habit of taking sex breaks in his office. But when Stephan's tongue licked into his mouth, Carter thought sex in his office in the middle of the day with the hot guy who sexes you stupid might be the best work perk he'd ever heard of.

"Mmmm," Stephan moaned as he gentled the kiss.

"You said…" Carter cleared his throat, "You said you had a question about the gala."

With his head tilted and his gaze locked on Carter's, he tucked his bottom lip between his teeth and nodded. "Yes," he began. "I needed to know, how can I be expected to focus on finalizing the details we've set up for this gala when I miss you so damn much?"

Before Carter could utter a word, Stephan buried his face in his neck, nibbling the sensitive spot just beneath Carter's ear as he palmed Carter's instantly hard cock through his pants.

"Fuck, Stephan. You better plan on doing something about that."

"So damn bossy." Stephan squeezed again and Carter flattened his hands against the wall trying to find purchase.

"Stephan, please."

"Ssshhhh," he whispered, tickling the same spot underneath his earlobe. "I promise to take care of you. You just have to do one thing for me first."

This son of a bitch literally had Carter by the balls and had the audacity to try to strike up negotiations right now.

If that wasn't the coldest, yet sexiest thing he'd ever heard, Carter didn't know what was.

"Anything, please."

"You know I love it when you beg so pretty, baby."

"Stephan, I swear I'm gonna resort to violence if you don't stop playing games and get me off."

He could feel Stephan's smile against his cheek. This damn man was enjoying ruining him and Carter was helpless to stop him.

"Promise me that after you put Nevaeh to bed that you'll come spend the night with me again."

Carter hissed. "I need to go home and sleep, Stephan."

"You can sleep at my place."

Stephan pushed Carter's hands above his head, gripping his wrists in one hand and using his free hand to undo Carter's belt and zipper and pull his cock free, stroking him from root to tip.

"Stephan, please."

"All you have to do is give me what I want, and I'll make it so good for you. Don't you want that?"

Damn if he didn't. Not just because Stephan's hand felt like silk against his skin. It certainly did. But really, it was because at that moment, Stephan found his gaze and Carter saw need and hunger that exceeded his own. It flashed like lightning in those deep brown eyes, and Carter, for the briefest moment, could swear that Stephan's hunger wasn't all about the sex.

"Yes," Carter moaned, and Stephan set his hands free, taking a step away from him.

Before Carter could speak, Stephan was on his knees, pulling Carter's pants down, shoving his nose where thigh met pelvis. He took a satisfying breath, stroking Carter's cock with one hand and letting his fingertips graze Carter's balls.

"What the hell are you doing to me, Stephan. What would you do to me if I let you?"

Stephan gazed up at him, then took one ridiculously long lick of his cock and smiled.

"Anything and everything, you want me to."

And with that, he took Carter so deep into his mouth Carter was convinced in that moment, he'd lost his soul to this man.

Fourteen

"Oh, look who the wind done blew in?"

Stephen narrowed his eyes to throw just enough shade at the supposedly frail old man sitting in the middle of the huge bed.

"Uncle Ace, weren't you the one who told me not to come around?"

"See?" he grumbled. "That's the problem with you young'uns right there. You think you know so much and don't know a thing. I told you not to come back unless you had something to share. Have you at least tried to find some joy since you were last here?"

"Uncle Ace, I check in with you every day on the phone. You know exactly what's going on with me."

"Don't sass me, boy."

If Ace wanted to know where Stephan had found his smart mouth, all he'd have to do was look in the mirror. He got that sass from Ace, and watching the man serve him up a heaping helping of it was just the kind of thing he needed to keep his earlier good mood in place.

"Is that a smile I see on your face, nephew?"

"If it is, it's because I'm happy to hang out with my uncle again. I've missed our daily meetings."

Ace pursed his lips, silently conveying an entire conversation, the way only an elderly Black man could, with such a small gesture.

"You must think I got Boo-boo the Fool written across my forehead. You ain't ever been that happy to see me. Is this about my gala? Did you get those linens you told me about the last time you were here. The ones you said were used by an Ethiopian Empress?"

Stephan inwardly laughed. He didn't know who Boo-boo the Fool was, but he'd heard about him repeatedly from almost every Black parent he'd encountered throughout his lifetime.

Trying to get his thoughts back on track, his shook his head to clear his mind. Carter had managed to get those royal linens for him, and the memory of how they'd celebrated that victory burned through him like molten lava slipping into the sea.

Stephan opened his mouth to reply as Lyric's words about Ace wanting to make sure he was bound in love and not the business crossed his mind. As Ace sat there staring at him, his eyes bright and eager with anticipation of even the smallest sliver of personal happiness for Stephan, he realized she was right.

And that's when it hit him.

The only sliver of happiness Stephan had in his life *was* Carter.

"I met someone, Uncle Ace."

He moved closer to Ace's bedside, sitting just on the edge.

"Do you remember when I told you a friend of mine was helping me put your Christmas gala together? Well, we sort of hit it off and started seeing each other." His uncle didn't say anything. He simply nodded and Stephan continued. "He's a really a good man, Unc."

"He'd better be if he's managed to catch your eye."

Ace's protective streak warmed him. "I like him a lot, Uncle Ace."

Ace's eyes softened and the tense lines of illness receded ever so briefly.

"Just how much is a lot, nephew?"

Stephan paused to consider Ace's question. There was just so much about Carter that pleased Stephan, they'd be here all day if he tried to explain in detail what "a lot" meant.

The way Carter always looked after him when they were together, whether it was bringing him something to eat or drink, or checking in with Stephan to make sure his day was going well, for example. He could even talk about the way Carter was with his daughter and why seeing him with the little girl made Stephan happy, especially when he tried to be strict even though it was obvious that little one knew just how to play her daddy. Or his favorite thing about Carter, the way he sought Stephan out in his sleep, curling his body into Stephan's and humming a sleepy sigh of relief when he unconsciously found him.

And then there were the things he liked that he wouldn't share with Ace. Not that he couldn't find a way to be both truthful and respectful about the sex while speaking to his uncle, but being with Carter in that way was so special, he just didn't want to share it with another soul. Not even Ace.

Fam, that don't sound like, like. That sounds like love.

His head snapped up, looking at Ace to see if those words had come from his uncle, but the way Ace stared at him, Stephan could tell he was still waiting for him to answer Ace's previous question.

Those were *his* thoughts not Ace's words.

Too afraid to face his realization he tried to remember what Ace had asked him.

"How much do I like him?" He ran his hand down his face, pursing his lips as he tried to find the words. "I like him enough that sometimes, I want to be able to tell him the things I can't say to the rest of the world."

Ace tilted his head and Stephan could see understanding settling on the older man's face.

"So why don't you tell him…everything."

"If I do, he'll hate me."

The bright glimmer of hope was dashed as a cloud of sadness seemed to fill the edges of Ace's eyes.

"That's not possible. How could he hate my nephew when my nephew is one of the best men I've ever known?"

"You're supposed to say that. You're my uncle."

Ace waved a dismissive hand around between them. "I'm old and I'm dying. I say what I want. Not what I have to. Now what's this nonsense about him hating you?"

Ace leaned back into his pillows as Stephan told him the entire story of how he and Carter had met and what fame had cost him and his young daughter.

"Well, I don't blame him for wanting to stay out of the limelight. And I see how that might make being with someone in this family a bit trying."

Ace lifted a shaky hand and placed it on Stephan's cheek and smiled. "But I think you have to give him the choice of whether what he feels for you is stronger than his fear. You can't make that decision for him, Stephan."

"Uncle Ace—"

His uncle placed a finger across his lips to silence Stephan. It was something Ace had done many times over when Stephan would get too excited or afraid to hear beyond his own thoughts.

"You didn't think Lyric could deal with the truth, and because of that decision, you took on a burden that wasn't yours to bear. Why is it you believe everyone's feelings are more important than your own? You deserve to be happy too. And this young man deserves to know all of you. Not just the tiny pieces you think he can handle."

Stephan kicked off his shoes and crawled into the bed, laying his head in his uncle's lap and wanting so desperately to go back to a time when things were so simple that comfort from Ace made all his worries slip away.

"Eventually I have to go back to Paris. What sense does blowing up his world with the truth make when I won't be here to help him deal with it?"

"Running won't make it hurt any less, Stephan. It will only make it bigger."

"Uncle Ace."

"You made a choice because you were afraid that Lyric wouldn't choose you. That your word wouldn't have been enough and that she would've hated the messenger. You're doing the same thing now. You're keeping this young man in the dark for all these selfless reasons you've concocted in your head. But the truth is, you're just afraid you're not enough for him to choose you."

Ace rubbed his head, soothing away so much of the pain he'd lugged around like permanent luggage.

"You're worth choosing, Stephan. And from all that you've told me about your Carter, I think he'll come to that conclusion too if you let him."

God did he want Ace to be right.

"If you want this Carter of yours to accept this very complicated truth, then you've got to accept it yourself and begin your own journey of healing. But until you're ready to face some of the events and people linked to that truth, it will always haunt you, and you will never be free to love your family, Carter, or yourself.

Stephan lay still until Ace eventually fell asleep, then he slipped from the bed and exited the room.

Ace had given him so much to think about, his head was spinning. But as always, the old man's words felt like a weighted, heated blanket swaddled around Stephan, comforting him, while keeping him safe.

He walked a few doors down until he found the guest room he used whenever visits to Ace turned into sleepovers. When the door was closed, he pulled out his phone, scrolled through his contacts, and pressed the one he was looking for.

Ace was right; he needed to be free. He wouldn't offer himself up to Carter any other way. If that meant facing his past, then he would start right here.

"Well, to what do I owe the pleasure of a call from my only living son?"

God, his mother was dramatic for no damn reason. He looked up to the ceiling, suppressing a chuckle. As much as her melodrama plucked his nerves, Stephan had to admit it kept things interesting, to say the least.

"Mother, I don't want to fight. I just want to talk. I want to be able to reach out to my mother and ask her to do something for me without us having to go through military-grade strategies before we do so. I want things to be different between us, Mother. I need them to be different. I need to be free, and that can't happen until we can talk without our usual defenses being engaged."

He let it all out, not stopping to give her a chance to interrupt him. It was the only way he could get all those words to cross the threshold of his lips and travel across the air and through the phone lines. And when he was done, his breathing ragged as if he'd just climbed a mountain, he called to her again.

"Mother, are you still there?"

She cleared her throat and Stephan thought she was gearing up to deliver her usual cold and still cadence. But then she said, "Son," so quietly he almost didn't hear her. Her voice was devoid of any of her usual venom. Instead, for the first time in as long as he could remember, her voice was thick and inviting. "Tell me what you need, and I promise I will make it happen."

He'd made the first step, and some of the weight he'd carried all these years slid off the planes of his shoulders like a rockslide. It was scary, and exciting, but most of all, it gave him hope that he could actually share his thoughts, his wants and desires, with Carter too.

Stephan turned onto his block and nearly crashed into a small body wrapped in every insulated layer of winter wear there was. It wasn't until he looked up and realized who was under all those layers.

"Hi, Stephan."

Nevaeh waved an uncovered hand and Stephan wondered how she managed to maintain that level of freedom. Back in his day, the old folks would've never let him leave the front door without gloves to go with the hat, scarf, face mask, and feather-lined coat.

"Hi, Nevaeh."

"Goodness, mija, where are your gloves?"

Stephan couldn't help the bark of laughter that escaped his throat.

"I was just wondering how she managed to sneak out without full winter armor."

"I left them on the couch."

"Your fingers are gonna freeze off by the time we finish walking the dog."

Stephan looked around to see the dog at the other end of the leash in the child's hand.

Carter shared a pleading look with him.

"Would you mind waiting with her while I run inside and get her gloves?"

Stephan nodded and they all stepped inside Carter's front yard. Stephan and Nevaeh took a seat on the bottom step of the front stoop while Carter took the stairs two at a time and headed inside.

"My daddy smiles a lot when your name comes up. Do you smile when you hear his?"

Straight to the point, huh, kid?

"I do."

"My *abuelita* and Grannie Gracie say that's because my daddy probably likes you…a lot." She didn't even blink before the next questions spilled out of her mouth. "Do you like my daddy…a lot?"

Stephan lifted both brows as he tried to figure out what to say next. He didn't think he'd get far BSing this kid, so he decided to be as age-appropriately truthful as possible.

"Yes, I do like your daddy…a lot. Is that okay with you?"

She leaned her head up to look at him, tucking her tiny fingers into her pockets. At that moment, Carter stepped out of the front door and onto the stoop, smiling down at the two of them as if he were taking in something precious.

Nevaeh returned her gaze back to Stephan and gave him a sure nod.

"Yeah, it's okay with me."

Carter handed the little girl her gloves and motioned for Stephan to follow him to the other end of the yard away from little ears.

"Everything okay?" Carter asked as Stephan turned around and glanced at the carefree little brown girl and her dog having fun on a cold night.

"Yeah," Stephan replied, feeling like he'd answered that question truthfully for the first time in years. "Everything seems to be just how it's supposed to be. And as long as you keep up your end of the bargain tonight. I think that'll remain the case. Can you still get away?"

"Ian is closing up tonight, so as soon as we get rid of the last customer, I'm on my way to you."

"You want me to pick you up?"

"We go through this every night. The place is like three blocks away. I will call when I'm leaving, and you can watch me walk up the block from your living room window like you always do."

Carter looked over his shoulder to see if Nevaeh was paying attention to them. Satisfied she only had eyes for the dog, without warning, he leaned in to sneak a quick peck from Stephan, then strode to where his daughter was standing

"Ven, mija. Let's hurry. Daddy's got to put in a lot of work tonight."

Stephan's gazed was fixed on the trio's retreating frames. As they turned the corner, Stephan couldn't help inserting himself into the wholesome vision father, daughter, and their dog made. What he wouldn't give for his fantasy to become truth.

"What's all this?"

Carter stood in the middle of Stephan's en suite bathroom, taking in all of the hard work Stephan had managed in the few hours since he'd shoved Carter against a wall in his office and sucked his cock until Carter melted into a satisfied puddle and Stephan's jaw had a pleasant ache.

It had definitely been the mood lifter he'd needed after talking to both Lyric and Ace about his emotions. But now, as he welcomed the man into the room, handing him a champagne flute to help get the night started, all Stephan could think about was taking care of Carter.

"You don't like it?"

"Like it?" Carter's eyes widened as he focused on Stephan's. I love it. But I'm a New Yorker, and we're naturally suspicious of people doing nice things for us for no apparent reason."

Stephan reached down and pulled his own flute to his lips, taking a sip before he replied.

"Maybe I just want to do something nice for you?"

"Getting me pizza from Cuts and Slices was nice—which I thoroughly enjoyed by the way."

Stephan could tell by the sexy, sated smirk on Carter's face that he was fondly remembering all that happened before and after the pizza too.

"But a rose petal trail from your front door to your bathtub, dimmed lights, flickering candles, a Jacuzzi filled with what smells like a sort of lavender bath scent, and damn good champagne?" Carter took an exaggerated gulp, emptying his glass. "I mean, it's not my birthday, is it?"

"Unless you lied to me during that whole 'what's your name, what's your sign' part of our hookup, I'd say we're a few months too early for that, Carter."

"Okay, then what's this all about? I came here for the express purpose of letting you inside my pants. This level of romance isn't necessary to get what you want."

Stephan's body tensed. Everything in him rejected the idea that Carter shouldn't have this kind of treatment just because it was a day ending in *y*. Yes, Stephan had tried to keep things light because he knew he couldn't do a long-term relationship with Carter. As he stood here, he realized it wasn't solely because he didn't want that kind of attachment to the man.

Carter was attentive, fun, caring, and sexy as all hell. Not to mention, the few times he'd seen the man with his daughter, Stephan's heart melted in his chest at how sweet and patient he was with her.

Who wouldn't want all of that in a partner?

Yet, knowing all those incredible things about the man, the one thing that kept Stephan from reaching for more is that he knew beyond a shadow of a doubt that Carter would not live in his world.

Once they left the protectorate of Brooklyn and stepped out on the global stage together, between Carter's former celebrity and Stephan's current position as a member of the global elite, there was no way their relationship would stay secret for long.

After everything Carter had lost, he could never ask Carter to risk it, even though everything in him wanted to.

"You presume the only thing I wanted tonight was to sex you." Before Carter could answer, he placed a finger over his lips to stop him from speaking. "It's a given that whenever you're near me, I want you, Carter. But I'm also concerned about you burning the candle at both ends. So, I wanted to just take care of you tonight."

He put his glass down, then took Carter's. He stepped into Carter's space, placing a gentle, yet teasing kiss that held so much promise. He'd meant it as a gentle introduction, but he could tell by the way desire burned in Carter's eyes and the way his chest heaved, he was ready to forgo this pampering session Stephan had in mind and get straight to the point where they were naked, panting, and sweaty with need, and later, satisfaction.

Carter tried to deepen the kiss, get them to that frenzied place faster, but Stephan refused.

"Carter, just let me take my time, please. I promise I'll make it good for you."

He always did. Stephan would never leave Carter unsatisfied. But the end of their time together was drawing nigh. Learning who Lennox was to Carter, there was no way he could continue their relation and risk hurting so many people he cared for, including Carter.

He wanted to savor Carter, let him know how treasured he was, even if only for one more night.

Stephan stepped into the Jacuzzi and held Carter's hand as he followed, sitting down and pulling Carter's back into his chest before completely surrounding Carter, trying desperately to show he was safe here. That his needs would always be met if Stephan had a say.

"You are a wonderful man, Carter Jiménez."

He kissed Carter's jaw as he stroked slow circles with his

hands on Carter's chest. He tweaked one nipple and then the other, loving how Carter pressed his back and ass against him in response.

"And if you'd let me, I'd show you off to the world."

"Hmm," Carter sighed. "Would you?"

Stephan slid one hand beneath the water, motioning for Carter to widen his thighs. When he did, Stephan's hand cupped Carter's heavy sac, gently kneading his balls with deft fingertips that had committed Carter's reactions to memory.

The soft sigh Carter shared in response meant he was aroused, ready for whatever pleasure Stephan decided to gift him with.

When Stephan slid his hand up and closed his palm around Carter's thick cock, the indecent moan Carter released was a garbled, "fuck yeah" meant to encourage Stephan in his current course of action.

And when Stephan's hand picked up a sensual tempo, lovingly caressing Carter's beautiful cock from root to tip while his tongue plundered Carter's mouth, and the man's body shuddered, that meant he was ready to splinter, and Stephan wanted so desperately to watch him fall apart.

"If you'd let me, I'd show you off to the world. I would take you downtown to Brooklyn Bridge at night and show the world that you were the real jewel of Brooklyn."

Carter moaned, his face tightened in impending pleasure.

"I'd take you back to Paris with me, take you to the height of the Eiffel Tower so everyone could see how it pales in comparison to your beauty."

Carter's hips lifted, meeting each one of Stephan's firm strokes, his muscles fluttering from the spasms racking his body.

"And if you'd let me, I'd have you on my arm at the gala so everyone in my family knew just how lucky I was to be with you."

Stephan worried that he'd gone too far with that last wish. Was he baring too much of his soul by letting Carter this far in? Especially when he knew he couldn't stay in this little haven Carter had created for himself.

He didn't have the chance to ponder it further, because Carter's body arched in the water, his cock pulsing in Stephan's hand as his release erupted into the air and slapped against the water on its descent.

And when Carter's body went limp against him again, Stephan took a few moments to take his own pleasure, holding Carter against him because he needed him near. He always needed him near.

And as they sat for a moment, catching their breath, and trying to find the strength to pull themselves from the tub, Carter turned in his arms and nuzzled his neck and whispered, "If that was your way of asking me to attend the gala with you, the answer is yes."

Fifteen

Stephan sat in the limousine currently parked in front of Carter's brownstone. He hadn't needed to arrive so early. After all, his date lived a few houses down from him. But knowing how this evening would unfold once he and Carter stepped out of this car and into Borough Hall, he was antsy.

He was a coward for waiting this long to tell Carter everything. He knew that. At first, he'd lied to himself, citing the fact that his stay in the States was temporary. He would leave, and it didn't really make sense to cause Carter all that unnecessary grief. But then he'd talked with Ace about Carter and then talked to his mother to start opening the lines of communication and then it became clear to him that, even if he did leave, he owed Carter the truth.

Why? First, because Carter deserved to know the truth. But also, Stephan needed to work his way free of all these secrets and lies so he could find peace again. Knowing that didn't make things easier for Stephan, especially since it was likely he would lose everyone he loved by the end of this evening, including Carter.

That was a hard pill to swallow, and Stephan had to admit he was terrified to face that reality. That fear had led him to putting this off until now, the very last possible moment.

"Grow a set, Devereaux-Smith. Tell this man the truth before you hurt too many people to count."

The privacy window dropped and Darren, his driver, spoke. "Did you say something, Mr. Devereaux-Smith?"

Stephan shook his head at the sound of his driver's voice, realizing he'd spoken those words aloud.

"No, Darren. I was just making a list of the things I need to do tonight."

"Yes, sir."

Darren turned around and raised the privacy glass again. Stephan took a breath, cherishing the silence until he saw Carter step out onto the top step, looking good enough to eat.

His fit form was covered in the clean lines of a dark gray A. Sauvage tuxedo whose subtle but clean lines accented every inch of Carter's delicious physique.

It should've been impossible for that man to be finer than he already was, and yet, him wearing that tuxedo made Stephan take deep slow breaths in an effort to control his response to him.

Stephan stepped out of the car and walked up to the steps to meet Carter.

"Everything about the way you look in the tux is making me want to skip this shindig and take you back to my place."

"Oh no, buddy." Carter shook his head. "I put in absolutely too much work to look this good. You are taking me out as promised."

"I'll make it worth your while." Stephan stepped closer and Carter put up a hand on his chest to stop his forward momentum.

"I'm sure you would. But this is the first time I've been to something like this in a while. I'd forgotten how much fun they can be. I'm actually looking forward to it, so, rain check on the fun and sexy times, okay?"

Stephan swallowed and stepped aside as he watched Carter retreat down the steps. How was it possible that he felt like even more of an asshole now than when all of this deception began. Carter was looking forward to this. Ripping this chance away from him would be so wrong.

As the driver held the door open for the two of them and Stephan slid in behind Carter, his conscience checked him.

It might be wrong to rob Carter of his excitement tonight. But it would be outright cruel to let him walk into this clusterfuck unknowingly.

"Hey, is everything all right?"

No, it wasn't. Not by a long shot.

"Carter," Stephan took his hand, bringing it to his lips and placing a soft kiss there. "We can't go to this gala together. At least, not until I tell you the truth about who I am and what being with me will mean for you."

"My name is Stephan Devereaux-Smith. I am the nephew of the renowned Ace Devereaux. And if you step out of this limousine and into Borough Hall tonight, this sheltered life you've built yourself in Brooklyn will be over before they serve eggnog cocktails and start playing the Temptations' 'Silent Night.'"

Cold, frigid cold spread through Carter as he listened to Stephan Smith,—correction, Stephan Devereaux-Smith of the Brooklyn Devereauxs come clean about all the lies of omission he'd let Carter soak up over the last three weeks.

Three damn weeks.

Carter was numb, and the only thing that broke through the pinpricks sticking every inch of skin he possessed was the heat of Stephan's thumb gliding over his hand.

"You lied to me " Carter spat as he snatched his hand from Stephan's. "Why?"

Stephan flinched when Carter took his hand back, as if someone had thrown some scalding hot liquid at him.

"For many of the same reasons you keep your identity on the low. I come from a very powerful and wealthy family. There are people who would use the opportunity to get close to me to access what I have and what I can offer them."

"I've never wanted a damn thing from you, Stephan."

"I know that. But by the time I was sure of that, you'd told me about what happened to your wife and Hollywood, and I knew you wouldn't have anything to do with me if you knew who I was. We'd planned to keep it light and fun. It was never supposed to be…"

"What wasn't it supposed to be? Tender, caring, powerful? Because that's what it was to me Stephan. I let you in and you lied to me."

Carter spoke through clenched teeth. He wanted to yell, to break the glass of the limousine with his bare hands. But years of training in Hollywood had taught him to always keep his cool when he was in public.

"Fine, you didn't think this was going to be anything but fun at first. I'll give you that, because I felt the same. But why let it continue. Because the last time we were together, that wasn't just random fucking, Stephan. You made love to me like I was the most precious thing in the world to you. Why would you lie to me, keep me bound to you when you knew I would never risk being with you if I was aware of the truth?"

"Because I realized I was falling for you. Because I didn't want to lose you."

A single tear slid down Stephan's cheek, breaking the smooth calm of his expression. It was enough to thaw Carter's insides the tiniest bit so that he wanted to reach out and comfort Stephan.

But he couldn't. This man had lied to him. And worse yet, he'd been willing to put Carter and his daughter at risk just to have what he wanted.

Carter sat with his back stiff against the seat cushions, giving a slow nod to encourage Stephan to continue.

"I ran into Lennox the day I went to Borough Hall to secure the venue. He mentioned you, and I realized the connection you had to him and my cousin Amara then. I knew then I couldn't keep lying to you."

"If that were true, why would you ask me to this gala? Why would you try to set me up like that?"

Stephan wiped his open palm down the length of his face and huffed. "I didn't mean to invite you. In the heat of passion I told you everything I would do if you were mine. I never dreamed you would see it as an invite and accept it."

"So you let me buy into this fantasy, Stephan?"

"I wanted it to be real. I wanted us to be real."

Stephan leaned in closer, and his nearness made Carter dizzy with want. He was mad enough to crush rocks in his fists, but he still couldn't fight the fire that Stephan always lit in him.

"I want to show you to the world, Carter. I wanted to have this night with you to prove to you we could survive this, and that I would never let anything happen to you. I wanted you to see that if we could do this here, then maybe I'd be able to convince you to come back to Paris with me."

Carter's brain short-circuited as he tried to follow Stephan's logic. "I have a child. I can't just uproot her entire life for good dick, Stephan. Parenting doesn't work that way."

Stephan swallowed, returning to an upright position. "That's the thing, Carter. I was hoping for once, I'd found someone who saw me for more than my name and more than my dick. I wanted you to want me…for me. I'm so sorry I lied. And I know I don't deserve your forgiveness, but I'm gonna ask for it anyway. Because to me, you are more than your name, and you're certainly worth more than your dick, even though I'd categorize it more as superb than just good."

"Are you really trying to be fucking funny right now?"

Carter wished they were standing outside of the car because then he'd be able to pace as he tried to wrap his mind around what was happening. But Carter didn't make public scenes. He didn't do anything to draw attention to himself, and Stephan knew that. That's why he'd told him this news inside the car. So Carter would have to remain calm and listen to him.

Too bad for him Carter was a master at relaying his anger while keeping his face, features and body language neutral from prying eyes. Thank you, Juilliard.

"Did you actually just sit here and have the nerve to tell me what you want?"

"Carter—"

"Shut it," Carter spat and held up his finger. "Don't say one more word. All this time, I've been handling you with kid gloves and bending over backward to respect your privacy, never once pushing you to share beyond what you were ready, because I cared about you, and because I understood what it felt like to be violated in such a way. All this time I just wanted to give you whatever it was you needed, even if I ached so much to know more about you that it tied my head in knots. All of this effort I'm putting out there to take care of this beautiful sad man my kid's dog nearly assaulted, and this whole time you're a damn Devereaux?"

Carter banged his hand against the panel of the door, too angry to notice the throbbing sting that remained afterward.

"You must've been laughing your ass off at me. I mean, it's obvious you had me dick whipped, I bet that was a laugh and a half for you too."

Carter's words felt like acid, bitter and corrosive, as he hurled them at Stephan.

"I never laughed at you. I loved you. Everything about you made me want to be better and tell you who I was. But I knew if I did…"

"You knew I'd leave. You knew I would never put my family's safety at risk to be with you. So you said to hell with my wishes, you'd just do what you wanted anyway."

"Carter…" Stephan leaned over, planting his forearms on his thighs. "I never would've allowed anything to happen to you or Nevaeh. I wasn't disregarding your safety, Carter. I was trying my best to navigate your fear. Fear has kept me away from my family for two years and it almost cost me this beautiful thing that we share. But I can't run anymore, Carter. And I'm begging you to stop running too. Please, just give us a chance."

"I would've given you anything!"

Carter's voice rose, banging off the interior of the limo,

shaking the tenuous control until the mask fell and tears burned as they slid down his face.

"I'd have given you anything you asked for if you'd just trusted me and respected my boundaries. Because that's what love does, Stephan. It doesn't manipulate, it respects, it honors. But if you could lie about this, if you could touch me like—"

Carter couldn't finish that sentence. If he did, the memories of just how often and deeply Stephan had touched him both physically and emotionally would overwhelm him.

"I can't trust you, Stephan. After everything I've lost, everything I've been through, I need to be able to trust that you will always have my and by extension my daughter's best interest at heart." He waved his finger between the two of them. "The way you've handled this tells me I can't trust you with my heart, and I for damn sure wouldn't trust you with her safety. So, whatever you thought we had, however you saw this ending, I'm done. I will not be taken for a fool. I will not be willingly gullible for you ever again."

And then Carter did the second hardest thing he'd ever had to do. He pulled away from Stephan when he reached out to grab him, and he stepped out of the car, taking the stairs two at a time and rushing inside his front door. When the door was closed, and he was certain he was safe from the magnetism that always pulled him toward Stephan, he let his head rest against the cold wood and wondered how the hell he'd ended up here.

Sixteen

Breaking up with someone that was never his boyfriend was a real bitch.

"If you wake that baby up after I had to nearly tie her to the bed after she was so excited from watching you get runway ready, I promise you're not gonna like me very much."

Carter hadn't even realized he'd been making that much noise as he reached for a decanter full of liquor with one hand and tumbler with the other.

"Gracie…" His voice was sharp and raw, and he could see her flinch from the way his harsh tone wrapped around her name.

He cleared his throat, trying to keep his anger at bay. "I don't want to be disrespectful, but I need to be alone right now."

Gracie had loved him like a son and moved her life all the way from California to New York for him because her daughter had loved him. Repaying all that kindness with a short temper and a slick mouth because Stephan had pissed him off wouldn't do.

"What are you even doing here? Shouldn't you be at the Christmas party you were helping to plan?"

Carter carelessly poured liquor into his glass, not even caring what variety it was. As long as it burned going down, that's all he required of it at this moment. He took a large gulp, hissing at the sting traveled down his throat and to his gut.

He went to pour another, but before he could tip the bottle, Gracie grabbed it and held it out of his reach.

"Can't a man drink in peace in his own damn house?"

Gracie looked over her shoulder at the empty space behind her, then turned calmly back to him.

"I don't know who the hell you think you're talking to, but it ain't me. And since I know your mama would take a slipper to your head if she heard you talking to me that way, I have no doubt you know better."

She was right. His mama's *chancleta* never missed, and if she heard him carrying on like some ogre stomping all over his house and taking this disrespectful tone with Gracie, he had no doubt he'd have caught a flip-flop to the head by now.

"I'm sorry, Gracie. Stephan and I had a fight in the limo and I refused to go to the gala tonight."

He walked over to his recliner near the fireplace, needing to be surrounded in something familiar, something he knew would never betray him. Up until a few minutes ago, he was beginning to feel like Stephan had become like his recliner, a sure thing he never had to worry over.

God, how quickly did things change?

"What happened? You seemed so excited about the night."

"I was." He leaned over, bracing his elbow on his thigh and letting his hand slide down his face. "But then…"

"Then what?"

"I found out Stephan has been lying to me about who he is."

She sat quietly, waiting for him to get it all out in one angry rush, and he was grateful for that, because he wouldn't have been able to relay the whole tale otherwise.

"He knew how Michelle died. He knew what celebrity, fame, and notoriety cost me. He knew what my selfish need to be part of that world stole from all of us. Why would he do that?"

"Carter?"

Gracie's voice was soft and soothing. Such a gentle sound that was meant to soothe him, but it nearly broke him instead.

"Carter," she said again. "Come here, baby."

His gaze met hers, and he saw the warmth of a mother, and his rage and anger morphed into guilt that hung over him like a thick cloud, nearly suffocating him.

He tried to resist her request. He'd taken enough from her. He didn't deserve her sympathy too. But when she nodded her head, he couldn't resist. He took the few steps to close the distance between them and sat on the floor, his head resting at her knee.

The first stroke of her hand in his hair cracked the last bastion of his resistance. With it, the unshed tears he'd been fighting to hold back fell too.

"I remember the day my daughter met you. You were brought down to the CT to get a scan to help diagnose your appendicitis. She was the tech that night and she had a little boy in the waiting area who was terrified and wouldn't let her come near him. But he saw you and realized you were his favorite action hero, and you used your celebrity to make that child feel brave, safe, and calm so he could get his scan done."

"I can't believe Michelle told you that. I was just trying to help."

"No." Gracie continued as she smoothed her hand through his hair. "You were being kind. You didn't want to see that boy suffer, and even though you were in pain yourself, you wanted him to be all right. Michelle knew then that you were the type of man she could love."

He remembered that night well. He'd been in so much pain, but calming that little man had seemed way more important than his own situation. And when Michelle had finally been ready to tend to Carter, she'd been so tender with him, he'd known then he never wanted to be without that feeling in his life.

"She was such a beautiful soul, Gracie, and I took her away."

"No." Gracie scratched lightly at his scalp. "You loved her for as long as God allowed you to. What happened to my daughter was a tragic accident. It wasn't your fault, Carter. The paparazzi who chased her into the street were at fault. Not you, and not your celebrity.

"Now that we've gotten that out of the way, let's move on to your young man. A Devereaux, huh?"

Carter nodded, taking in a slow breath to try to stop the tremble in his voice.

"Yeah. One of the wealthiest and most famous families on the planet. How did I not know this?"

"Because maybe Stephan didn't want you to see his fame and his money? Maybe the only thing he wanted you to see was his heart? Is that really any different than why you moved back to Brooklyn? So you and your daughter wouldn't have a spotlight and a microphone shoved in your face at all times?"

"You don't even know the man well. How can you take up for him?" Carter knew he sounded like a petulant child, but he wanted to wallow in his self-righteousness just a bit longer, and Gracie calling him on his shit wasn't really helping him do that.

"I know the man that my daughter loved. I know she would've done anything to love you for the rest of her life. And if my angel loved you that much, then a man like Stephan Devereaux-Smith, someone who's been raised to recognize quality and luxury, there's no way he couldn't do everything in his power to keep you near. That includes omitting who he is because he's afraid to be marked as guilty by association in your eyes."

Carter groaned. "I really hate it when you do that."

"Do what?" He could hear the smile in her voice even though he couldn't see her face from this position.

"Make sense, he muttered, groaning again when she chuckled."

"Carter, you can't hide from the world forever. You were blessed enough to have my daughter, and the universe is offering you another chance to have something beautiful again with another special person."

"How do you know Stephan is special? You've barely met the man?"

She rubbed his head again and he nestled deeper into her knee, still unable to move. In the first few days after Michelle's death when he was overwrought with grief, he'd sit at her knee and it would make all the noise stop for just a few seconds. Being this close to someone who loved his wife as much as he did, it helped him endure an unbearable load.

"Because you loved a woman who had the biggest, brightest heart in the world. There's no way you could settle for someone whose spirit wasn't equally as loving, brilliant, and kind."

God, this woman. All these years later, she was doing it again. Making him feel like a son instead of a broken man. Putting him back together when the outside world tore him apart. Carter didn't know how he'd gotten so lucky to have both the best mother and mother-in-law in the world, but he knew he wouldn't let either of them go for anything in the world.

"So, I'm gonna need you to go wash your face, brush your hair, and get the Visine out of the fridge, because love is waiting, and it wouldn't do to find you looking like who did it and ran."

He barked in laughter until Gracie shushed him. When he recovered, he stood up and kissed her on her cheek and gave her a big hug. Now, all he had to do was go to this party and get his man. Fame had stolen so much from him. He'd be damned if his fear of it caused him to lose another thing.

Stephan waited outside as long as he could, looking for Carter. He'd known Carter was angry. He couldn't blame him after keeping the man in the dark like that. But still… somewhere deep down he'd hoped…

Too riddled with guilt to even continue that line of thought, he looked down at his watch and realized he had to get inside if he was going to do what he planned to do before the extended branches of the Devereaux family arrived. This was a Brooklyn Devereaux issue and it needed to be dealt with internally before anyone else added their two cents.

He was about to turn around when he heard a familiar voice. "Were you waiting for me?"

"Hello, Mother." Stephan's heart lurched in disappointment. It wasn't his mother's appearance that disappointed him. He was actually happy about that, considering what he had planned. His mother needed to be here, and given the amount of acrimony she held for her brother, Stephan hadn't known for certain that she would show up.

She needed this.

They all needed this, and after losing the man he loved because of his role as the secret bearer, Stephan needed this too. Not because he was looking for absolution. He wasn't. But he loved Carter, and he had every intention of fighting for him. He couldn't do that until he'd buried all of his past.

Holding on to it had made him come to Carter with only half-truths. But after tonight, he would be free to be honest with Carter because he could finally be honest with his family, and most of all himself.

"Mother, I'm pleased you're here."

He leaned in, kissed her cheek, and offered her his arm to hold as they entered the building.

"I almost believe you mean that, son."

"I do. I know that you've been hurting for a really long time and I wasn't here to help you deal with that. I just hope after tonight you can understand why I haven't been here, why I needed to be away, and how sorry I am for leaving you all alone."

Her eyes widened, softening her features. Her mouth was slightly ajar, and if he weren't seeing this for himself, he wouldn't believe the sincere surprise written all over her face.

"Thank you for that, Stephan. But you weren't the cause of my pain. Ace was."

He patted her hand. "A discussion for another time. Right

now, we need to meet up with the rest of the family before this party officially begins. And Mother?"

She arched a brow, waiting for him to continue.

"No matter what happens tonight, know that I love you."

She stared at him for a long moment. He couldn't blame her for her silence. Martha was a lot of things, but gushy and emotional wasn't one of them. He'd spent his life modeling the same behavior because he thought it would make her more comfortable around him. But he hadn't counted on how much it would eat at his soul not being truthful about what he felt.

"I… I love you too, son." She whispered those words to him, patting his arm softly to reinforce them, making them more real.

When they stepped inside of the main hall, Stephan stopped, looking around the room, top to bottom, side to side, taking in all the individual touches that he'd worked on with Carter.

The white silk curtains that covered each wall and the sparkling gold shimmer woven into the canvas made the room look like it was bathed in snow. The matching linen tablecloths and gold flatware, goblets, and napkins were the perfect accents. Decorative white lights hung on artificial white branches through the room, creating a soft, warm glow throughout.

It was more than he ever could've done on his own in the short amount of time they'd known each other. Three weeks shouldn't have been enough time to pull this off, but with Carter's help, he had. Three weeks shouldn't have been enough time to fall in love, lose his heart, and lose the man he loved at once either, but apparently Stephan was an overachiever, so he'd managed that too.

Once his eyes reached the dais, they settled upon all of the members of the Brooklyn Devereauxs.

Ace sat in the middle of the dais with his brother David sitting to his right. There was an empty chair to Ace's left, and when he heard the small gasp escape his mother's mouth, he knew she understood that chair had been held for her.

Ace's son Deuce, his daughter-in-law Destiny, and his granddaughter Trey and her husband, and Ace's ward, Jeremiah, were standing in front of the center of the dais. Amara's mother, Ja'Net and her father Angel were standing with Amara and Lennox directly in front of David, and Lyric stood to the left with her beau, Josiah, directly in front of the empty chair where Martha was intended to sit.

All three children of Si and Alice Devereaux were still present in the world, and all their living offspring were here too.

It was the most heartbreakingly beautiful sight he'd ever witnessed. He stood there, quietly taking it in, committing every smile, every feature to memory just in case he never had the opportunity to see them again.

"Mother, please—"

"Stephan, I don't understand. What's happening here? Are you all right?"

He shook his head. "No, I'm not. And I haven't been for a long time. But hopefully, after I say my piece, I will be."

He swept his hand in the direction of her seat, asking once more if she would acquiesce. With cautious steps, she moved toward the dais and gracefully took her seat next to Ace.

The room was crackling with anticipation. They all knew the history, the battles that had been forged between these siblings and their offspring, but only Stephan knew why the war began in the first place.

"Thank you for coming here early tonight. The rest of our large clan will be here soon, so I should probably get on with this."

He shoved his hands in his pockets, fiddling with his billfold to help him find the words he needed. Words that he'd buried for so long.

"We have not functioned like a family for a very long time. We've functioned as a business. We've even functioned as competitors. But we have not been a family in recent times. And we need to fix that now."

He looked at Ace, who sat with a weary smile on his face and unshed tears in his eyes, closing his eyes and signaling his permission for Stephan to proceed.

"Time is not on our side, and we may never be in one place again once we leave this room."

The proof of their understanding shone in their shimmering eyes and their tense faces.

"As I'm sure you're all aware, two years ago Uncle Ace received a call from Jamaica Defense Force's Coast Guard, informing him that my brother Randall had died and someone would need to come collect his body.

"What you don't know however is the reason they called Ace, is because the details of Randall's death weren't as you've been led to believe."

He felt rather than saw Lyric's eyes on him, and his hands wanted to immediately reach for her, comfort her from the blow he was about to throw at her. But he couldn't; she as well as everyone in this room needed to hear this.

"Wait," Lyric began. "You said they'd called Ace because Randall had been operating a Devereaux Inc. vessel that was titled to Ace. If that wasn't the case, I was his wife and next of kin, Stephan. If something was amiss why didn't they call me?"

"Because they thought you'd died with him?"

"What the hell?" Her jaw tightened and her nostrils flared, and Stephan couldn't tell if it was disbelief or anger contorting her calm and tender features into something unrecognizable to him.

Questions were still dancing in Lyric's eyes, but the dark steel of Josiah's held acknowledgment as Stephan watched him step closer to Lyric, wrapping a protective arm around her.

"They thought you died with him because he was listed at the resort as Mr. and Mrs. Randall Devereaux-Smith. Believing you were both dead, the authorities contacted Ace because the vessel was his."

Stephan tore his gaze away from Lyric and found his mother's "The woman was an employee of Devereaux Inc. When we contacted her sister, she said Randall had taken her sister on the trip because they wanted to spend her birthday weekend together without prying eyes."

Stephan stepped closer to his mother and Lyric, the two women he'd tried his best to protect, silently asking for their forgiveness as he continued.

"I asked Ace to use his power and influence to cover things up so the two of you would never know what happened. You were both devastated already. Randall was everything to the both of you, and I didn't want the circumstances of his death to steal the joy his memory brought you."

"And that's why you left?"

Lyric slowly took his hand, tightening her grip on it before she spoke. But instead of anger, it was as if she was trying to give him something, someone to hold on to.

"My lie, it pit my mother against her brother because Randall told her Ace sent him on an unexpected business errand. It blackened me with guilt. I knew if I stayed, Lyric, my guilt would've forced me to tell the truth. You weren't ready for that. Neither of you were.

"My mother held Randall on a pedestal—he could do no wrong, and you loved him to distraction. I just... I couldn't take that away from either of you. So I asked Ace to lie instead.

"But because of my lie, my mother hated her brother..."

"And you got to be exiled away from the people you love?"

His sister-in-love was always so perceptive.

"Stephan, he was your brother." Lyric's voice held so much love and compassion for him, he wanted to wrap himself up in it. But he wasn't the victim here, or at least, he wasn't the only one.

Lyric held on tighter. "You were grieving too. All this time you were trying to protect us, who was there to protect you?"

"Ace," his mother said as she turned her head toward her brother. "You covered my dead son and gave the one who remained the resources and support to protect me and his brother's wife."

It wasn't a question. Martha spoke, even without any sort of confirmation, as if she knew this to be truth. From her erect posture to the stern, clear sound of her voice, she knew that Stephan wasn't lying.

"All these years you let me hate you because my son asked you to help him protect me."

"You are my little, sister, Martha. I would've borne any pain I had to soften the loss of your son."

And that's when it happened, a tear slid down her face, and Stephan could see the wall his mother had built between herself and her older brother crumbling with each tear that followed.

"I'm so sorry, Ace. All this time I've wasted hating you."

"It was better for you to hate me—" his voice was shaking with a mix of relief and love "—than to break your heart all over again after losing your boy."

Ace's words triggered something in the room: parents found children, hugging them just a bit tighter. And when Martha and Lyric each held one of Ace's hands, Stephan knew he'd accomplished what he'd come here to do. Set the record straight, unload all the guilt and trauma of the last two years, and find a way to sanctify his soul.

Unfortunately, the irony was that the moment he set himself loose from one lie, he was shackled by the heartache of revealing the truth to the man he loved. Feeling overwhelmed, unburdened, but not yet free, he stepped out into the hall.

This was the first step. He'd told the truth to his family, hopefully opening up a path of healing across generations. Now he just needed to figure out how to fix things with Carter. Because more than ever, his soul ached to be both unburdened and whole, and only Carter held the missing piece.

Seventeen

"Carter, is that you?"

Carter turned around to see his best friend Lennox exit the main hall. Carter had arrived a few moments earlier, but when he'd heard Stephan's heavy and somber voice confessing to his family, Carter had stepped away, not wanting to intrude.

"Yeah, man, it's me."

Lennox looked him up and down, paying close attention to Carter's outfit. "What are you—"

Carter lifted his hand. "Man, it's a really long story, one I don't have to time to tell right now."

"You need something?"

"Yeah, to fight for my heart." At that moment, Stephan stepped into the hall. He pointed at Stephan. "And right now, my heart is standing in the middle of the floor, looking like he's about to collapse."

Lennox looked at Stephan and then back at Carter with bewilderment in his eyes.

" Do you remember what I told you about love when you and Amara were going through it."

Lennox answered in the affirmative. "That no matter the risk of pain, love is always worth it."

"Yeah, well," Carter continued. "let's just say I had a huge reminder of that tonight. So, as much as I would love to stand here and break things down for you. I need you to step aside and let me talk to Stephan Devereaux-Smith because he's the man I love."

Lennox's gaping mouth was proof that after all these decades of friendship, Carter still had the power to shock his friend. A fact he would lord over Lennox's head if he wasn't so eager to make things right with Stephan.

Carter stepped in Stephan's direction, and Lennox grabbed his arm to stop his momentum. "Once this is settled," Lennox mock whispered, "I better get all the damn details or it's gonna be me and you and Amara, and trust me, you don't want that smoke."

Carter laughed because the little he knew of Amara, he was certain of that fact. She was persistent, bold, confident, beautiful, and the best damn corporate lawyer he'd ever met. And considering the way she'd owned Lennox and twisted his emotions into a pretzel, he figured the safest bet was to never get on her bad side.

"I'm so damn mad with you."

Stephan watched as Carter walked closer to him and the rest of the world melted away.

"Just when I was beginning to open back up to another person, feel safe with another person, you lied to me and made me question whether I could trust you. Made me think that you loved me and I could love you."

"I did lie to you about who I was, Carter, and I was wrong for that. But never...never did I lie about loving you, about wanting to make a home with you. My feelings were always real."

Carter stepped closer, and with every inch he gained, Stephan's heart thudded against his chest in anticipation.

It was just like their first meeting all over again—his brain was fuzzy, and his heart was pounding, and it was hard to think and breathe. But standing in Carter's presence was worth all of the discomfort, because to bask in his glow transcended any pain.

"I know your feelings are real." Carter laced his fingers into Stephan's, anchoring him where they stood. "That's the only reason I'm here now. I know what it's like to lose love, Stephan. I know what it is to have to live with the finality of goodbye. I'm mad as hell that you lied to me, even by omission. But knowing how much I love you and that you're still alive, there's no way I could waste this gift between us."

Carter looked up at him, leaning in slowly, letting his forehead touch Stephan's briefly before Carter lifted his chin with a finger, and placed a sweet, delicate press of his lips to Stephan's, nearly rendering him incapable of a verbal response.

"You're gonna be in the doghouse for a long ass time." Carter eagerly shared that detail. Stephan was so afraid this was all a dream and interrupting Carter would mean he disappeared like a puff of smoke, he simply nodded.

"But no matter how long it takes for us to get right again, I need you to know that as much as I fuss at you, I'm gonna love you just as hard. And that will be a good thing. Because it means we'll have to take our time and really get to know each other and each other's families. Because if the tail end of that conversation I heard you having with your people was any indication, your family is just as messy as mine.

"That's for damn sure." Stephan nodded. "Does this mean you're going to forgive me?"

"It means I'm willing to do the work so that I can forgive you and we can get past this. You're my person, Stephan. I can't let you get away just because I'm angry with you.

"I promise, I will do everything to keep you and Nevaeh safe."

"You'd better." Carter stole another kiss. "Because, between Gracie and my mother, those two women could make a body disappear and no one would be the wiser."

"I'll be on my best behavior." Stephan pulled him into his arms, needing to feel the weight of Carter's body against his. The heft, it meant this was real, that Carter was really here, that he hadn't lost the most important thing in his life due to his own stupidity and fear.

"Good," Carter replied. "Now that that's settled, I think it's time you made some introductions. Because if I don't give Lennox the deets, he's already threatened to sick his lawyer wife on me."

Stephan clucked his tongue. "Take it from someone who grew up with that woman. She will ruin you, and then go back to eating her favorite snack while scrolling on the internet like nothing ever happened. Trust me, you don't want no parts of that."

"But I do want every part of you."

Such simple words, but their meaning held their weight in gold inside Stephan's heart. Carter Jiménez had given Stephan a reason to walk out of the dark and find the light in his lover's arms.

"Damn, baby." He tightened his hold on Carter, so grateful to have him here like this in the open where the world could see. "You really do know how to make a brotha feel loved."

Epilogue

Nine months later...

They'd dated for six months, getting to know each other's families, and Stephan had taken that time to fall deeper in love with Carter, and to have his heart stolen again, this time by Nevaeh. She'd taken to Stephan so easily, and it just reinforced for him that he'd found the perfect love for him.

After six months of dating, they'd gotten engaged. Stephan throwing himself a birthday dinner and using it as on opportunity to ask Carter to marry him. Since the Devereauxs didn't have a history of long engagements, they'd married two months after their engagement at a small ceremony in the family room of Devereaux Manor.

Ace demanded he would sit by Stephan's side as one of his best men, just like he did Jeremiah's on his wedding day. There was no way Stephan would refuse his decree. And so, on the happiest day of his life, Stephan was surrounded by all the people he loved, including his mother and his beloved Ace, who had found their way to reconciliation since Stephan had finally told the truth about Randall's death.

Since things happened so quickly, he and Carter had decided it was too soon to broach the subject of adopting Nevaeh, but Stephan knew deep in his heart, that's what he wanted, if Carter and his beautiful stepdaughter would allow it. Until then, he'd just use this time to love on them both, show them both he was ready to make the necessary sacrifices to love and be loved by this family. The one he was born into, including the newest member of his family, Amara and Lennox's baby girl, Omari Devereaux-Carlisle. And the one he'd married into with two more mothers, a precocious little princess, and his husband.

Now, here they were, together again with all the people they loved, one month after saying their vows and nine months after declaring their love for one another at Ace's Christmas Gala. Here they sat, hand in hand, watching as thousands gathered to pay their respects to Jordan Dylan "Ace" Devereaux, I, as he lay in state at Brooklyn Borough Hall. It was an honor rarely reserved for civilians. But his contributions were so great, his beloved city wanted to send him off with the pomp and circumstance of a king.

Stephan looked at his family seated in somber reverence before the ebony casket with its gold bearings. In the first row, his uncle David and Stephan's mother, Martha, Deuce and Destiny, Jeremiah and Trey, sat together. Lyric and Josiah, Amara, Lennox, and their baby, Omari, Stephan, Carter, and Nevaeh were seated in the second row. Right behind them was his older cousin Ja'Net and her husband Angel.

As he glanced around, he could see all of them holding tight to one another, bearing the great weight of such a significant loss. They were hurting, but the love that shone between each of them was going to keep them safe and bound together through ache of grief.

He knew this, not just because he knew these people, because that's what he had, what he felt so strongly as Carter and their little girl surrounded him, making the hurt just that much more bearable.

He ran his hand over the intricate braiding pattern he'd done in Nevaeh's hair last night. His little angel had climbed up next to him on the couch, bringing him the hair tools, asking him if he'd braid her hair so she could be pretty for Uncle Ace.

The sweetness of that gesture had nearly broken him. But as he parted and greased each section before cornrowing each braid, the love Ace had begged him to seek, surrounded him, holding him together when his heart threatened to break apart for Ace. And while he'd braided her hair to perfection, Carter had sat next to him, touching him, kissing him, letting him know he was loved.

"Hey, you doing okay, baby?"

Carter squeezed his hand, lending Stephan his strength. It was then that he realized how right Ace was when he told him he needed to find someone who would replenish his joy when it was waning.

That's who Carter was. From the very first he'd taken care of Stephan when he'd needed it. And every chance Stephan had, he'd repaid Carter's kindness. Because, yes, he needed someone to pour into him. But he also needed to care for the person that cared for him too. It's the only way it would work. It's the only way Stephan would allow it to work.

He cupped Carter's cheek, tracing a gentle thumb across

the skin there, and he smiled, leaning over to softly press his lips against his husband's.

"I love you Carter Devereaux-Smith. Thank you for loving me."

Carter touched his forehead to Stephan's and said, "Thank you for letting me."

* * * * *

AN OFF-LIMITS MERGER

NAIMA SIMONE

To Gary. 143.

To Connie Marie Butts.
I'll miss you forever
and love you longer than that.

Prologue

Tatum Haas laughed, reaching for the bottle of Riesling and refilling her near-empty glass. The happiness inside her resembled the golden wine. Light. Sweet. Perfect. She'd been waiting for this night since her first meeting with Mark Walker at one of the endless fundraiser galas that demanded Tatum's attendance because her mother sat on the committee. That event where they'd met, though, had been different. She'd found the man who would change her life forever.

Yes, that night—and all the wonderful, sweet and romantic evenings and days following—had led her here. To the evening before she would finally be Mrs. Mark Walker.

She couldn't contain her smile as she lifted her glass for another sip.

Everything was…perfect.

"I know what that smile means," said her best friend, Nore Daniels. "You're either thinking about Mark or this right here…" Nore teased, picking up her fork and diving into the decadent plate of seafood pasta in front of her.

Tatum grinned.

Still chuckling, Nore jabbed her fork in the direction of the hotel suite door. "You're the only one with a key to the suite, right? Dara will sense you having fun, or—" she gasped dramatically "—eating a carb, and your soon-to-be mother-in-law will bust up in here and shut this down. That woman can sniff out joy like a great white smelling spring breakers on a beach. And the result is the same. Carnage."

Tatum shouldn't laugh; it only encouraged Nore. And Dara Walker would be her mother-in-law as of tomorrow. But hell, Nore wasn't wrong. Dara had been over-the-top with the preparations for the wedding. And this girls' night with her best friend and maid of honor had been her only respite—or escape.

"No worries. There's only one key to this room. And I might've told everyone we're staying at the Four Seasons instead of The Liberty." Tatum picked up her fork and twirled the pasta around the tines before slipping the food into her mouth. And closed her eyes on a hum. "This is obscenely good." She dug back into her plate. "That it's damn near the first thing I've eaten in a month without Mom watching me probably has something to do with it."

How sad that at twenty-eight and almost a married woman, Tatum felt *pasta* was her form of rebellion. She shrugged, as if she could dislodge that irritating, disloyal thought.

"Sneaky. I like it." Nore squinted at her. "And your mother is a lovely woman, but she doesn't know shit if she's trying to make you starve yourself. You're gorgeous just the way you are."

Tatum smiled. "Mark believes that, too."

"I adore Mark," Nore said, "but the most important thing is *you* know that."

Tatum stretched an arm across the table and squeezed her friend's hand. "I do. I promise."

And this summed up why they'd been best friends since

college. Through ten years, living in different states and all the other messes life had thrown them, nothing could diminish the friendship and love they shared.

"Oh before I forget." Nore jumped up from the couch. "Be right back." She raced from the living room, disappeared into the bedroom they were sharing for the night and reappeared a couple of minutes later carrying a small white box wrapped with a silver bow. "For you. I hope you didn't think I forgot."

Tatum softly laughed, accepting the present. She didn't need to lift the lid to know what lay inside. Delight bubbled inside her. "I didn't think you would," she murmured, removing the bow and then the top. "I'm not going to lie. Wearing this is one of the things I've been most looking forward to about tomorrow."

During a girls' trip that summer, Nore had dragged Tatum to a pawn shop with the intent of selling the engagement ring from Nore's jerk of an ex-fiancé. Instead, Nore had spotted this gorgeous and unique brooch. Gold and silver were molded into tiny delicate flowers of turquoise, pink and ruby red, and diamonds and seed pearls dotted the petals and vines. They created a border around a stunning portrait of a woman. While a wide-brimmed hat hid most of her features, her back and regal profile were visible, as was the smooth light brown skin of her cheek, mouth, chin and elegant neck. It was definitely a statement piece, and her best friend had taken one look at the Victorian brooch and bought it as a wedding gift for Tatum. Her something old *and* new.

"What're you doing?" Nore laughed as Tatum pinned the jewelry to her sweater. "Isn't it some kind of bad luck to wear that before your wedding day?"

"Please." She waved off Nore's question, brushing a finger over the enamel portrait. "Something this beautiful and with such a romantic legend attached to it couldn't be bad luck."

Tilting her head, Tatum grinned. "So tell me again how it's just a fairy tale?"

Nore rolled her eyes but nothing could hide the happiness that emanated from her as if a beacon shone from under her skin. "All right, so maybe the legend isn't sentimental bullshit. I mean, could someone make an argument that finding the brooch and me meeting and falling in love with Joaquin was purely coincidental? Sure. But you know what, Tate?" A soft smile curved Nore's mouth. "How we came together? How we pushed through? It's been nothing less than magical to me. So, yes, I'm a believer in whatever enchantment or love that brooch holds. And I also believe it's found its rightful place with you."

Tatum traced the jeweled flowers, thinking of the beautiful tale attached to the piece. According to the saleswoman, the daughter of a Barbadian Parliament member had traveled with her father to London. Once there, she'd fallen in love at first sight with an English baron. The two lived and loved for many happy years and he'd had the jewelry piece commissioned as a symbol of his love for her. Because of that devotion, the story claimed whoever possessed the brooch would experience the same kind of love. They would find their soulmate, and though the path would be troubled, they'd ultimately find a lasting, true love.

"Thank you, Nore. This means the world to me. And so do you."

"Nope." Her friend shook her head, wagging her finger. "No, ma'am. You're not going to have me up here crying and looking haggard tomorrow. Feelings. Ew." Nore scrunched her nose. "Hell no, I—"

The peal of Tatum's cell interrupted Nore, and still grinning, Tatum picked it up, glancing down at the screen. She barely contained her grimace when Dara's name filled the caller ID. Her mother-in-law-to-be must've figured out Tatum and Nore's disappearing act.

Preparing herself for the upcoming nice-nasty tirade that only a society maven could deliver, Tatum pressed the answer button and lifted the phone to her ear. "Hi, Dara," Tatum greeted, smothering a laugh as Nore rolled her eyes. "I'm so sorry about the hotel mix-up—"

"Tatum."

Everything in her went still. As if a primal part of her recognized that something important had happened. But also that the "something" would be earthshaking. Life altering. And her brain was granting her one last moment of normalcy before her world shattered around her.

"Tatum," Dara repeated, her voice huskier, still trembling.

"Yes. I'm here."

Nore's gaze sharpened, a frown drawing her dark eyebrows together.

"Honey, I need you to come to Mass General as fast as you can, okay?"

Tatum's pulse spiked, and acidic fear flooded her mouth. If the mention of the hospital hadn't sent her heart racing, then the *honey* from Dara Walker would've—the reserved older woman never used endearments.

"Dara," Tatum whispered. Then swallowed, tried speaking again, but her voice didn't emerge any stronger. "What's wrong? Is it…?" She couldn't voice it. Because that would make this burgeoning nightmare real.

"It's Mark, Tatum," Dara said, confirming Tatum's biggest fear.

Her nightmare.

"No." Tatum shook her head as if Mark's mother could see the gesture. As if the motion, the objection would somehow unravel Dara's words. Make them untrue.

"Please, Tatum. Get here as fast as you can. He's in surgery, but I don't—" Her voice cracked.

"I'm on... I'm..." Tatum's suddenly dry throat wouldn't allow her to finish the sentence.

Nore reached out, plucked the phone from Tatum's stiff fingers.

"Hi, Dara. This is Nore. What's going on?" She paused, her worried golden-brown gaze fixed on Tatum. Alarm flared in her friend's eyes as she listened to Mark's mother. "Don't worry—I'll get Tate to the hospital. We'll be there in ten minutes. See you soon."

Sheer panic propelled Tatum to her feet. She shot out of the chair, gripping the edge of the table to steady herself, and Nore grasped her elbow.

"I got you. You go to the door and the elevators. I'll be right behind you with your shoes, coat and purse. Right behind you, Tate." With a gentle but firm shove, Nore pushed her toward the suite door.

Tatum didn't remember leaving the suite or arriving at the hospital. The next couple of hours passed in a blur of low voices, dread, anxiety and confusion. She and Nore sat in a small private waiting room along with Mark's and Tatum's parents, as well as her sister, Mia. Maybe Dara called them, or even Nore had on their way to the hospital. Tatum had ceased to be aware of anything but the fear that wrapped around her lungs in a brutal, suffocating grip.

Please, God, let Mark be okay. Please let him live. I can't lose him. Not when we're just about to start our life together. I didn't get to say I love you to him...

Surging to her feet, she scrubbed her hands up and down her arms. Just as she paced to the window, a low voice spoke from the other side of the room.

"Mr. and Mrs. Walker?" A petite Black woman in scrubs

and a surgical cap approached Dara and Leo, her lovely features calm, composed.

Mark's parents rushed over to the doctor, and Nore appeared at Tatum's side while her parents formed a steady wall on the other. *Go over there*, a voice screamed inside her head. *Go be with them*. But she couldn't move.

"Yes." Leo Walker curved an arm around his wife's waist.

"I'm Dr. Jennifer Danner. I operated on your son." She met the Walkers' gazes, and the compassion in the doctor's eyes ripped a hole in Tatum's chest even before she continued speaking. "I'm sorry. He didn't make it. Your son suffered massive brain injury from a ruptured brain aneurysm. We tried everything we could to save him but he's gone. I'm very sorry."

A horrific wail rebounded off the walls of the waiting room, and Dara collapsed in Leo's arms. That terrible, agonized sound echoed in Tatum's head, her chest, her belly. Her own knees liquefied beneath her.

Time ceased to matter, ceased to exist. There were only those two words.

He's gone.

He's gone.

The pain ripped through her.

He's gone.

He's gone.

"Oh fuck."

Nore's stunned yet furious whisper sliced through the smothering blanket of grief. Blinking, Tatum stared at her friend's dark frown as she peered at the cell in her hand. Her tongue couldn't move to ask her what was wrong, but just as she thought the question, Tatum noticed her sister peering at Nore's phone, shock suffusing her expression as well. And when Mia glanced at Tatum, uncharacteristic pity in her dark gaze, grief temporarily shifted to dread.

Her cell vibrated in the pocket of her cardigan, and for a moment, Tatum considered not looking at it. Nothing good waited for her on that phone. Yet, her numb fingers closed around the steadily humming cell.

A social media notification with Mark's name underneath it. God, that hadn't taken long. But they couldn't know he was de— They couldn't know *that* yet since they'd just received the news, right? No, all they could report was he'd been rushed to the hospital…

She pressed her thumb to the screen.

"Tate, no. Don't—" Nore grabbed her hand.

But it was too late.

Funny.

Just seconds earlier she'd believed the pain pulsing through her like a raw, open wound was the worst pain she'd ever experienced. She'd been wrong.

TheSpilledTea, a popular social media–based tabloid company, had been thorough.

Pictures of Mark on a gurney.

Images of his parents, of Tatum and Nore arriving at the hospital.

But it was the story underneath that sent her spiraling into agony.

Mark Walker, heir to one of the largest communications corporations in the country. Fiancé to Boston socialite Tatum Haas.

Anonymous 911 call by mysterious woman.

Found naked and unresponsive in hotel room.

Eve of wedding.

Obvious signs of sexual tryst.

No. She hadn't believed a more brutal pain than loss existed. But when a woman discovered the man she loved, the man she'd been prepared to devote the rest of her life to had spent his final moments inside someone else… Well, she understood two things in that moment.

One, she'd been fooling herself. She'd never experienced true agony until now.

And two. When your heart had been betrayed and broken, that so-called thin line between love and hate evaporated.

Oh no. Fuck that thin line.

Hate and love were so inextricably melded, she couldn't separate one from the other.

But hate…

Hate had an edge.

One

Ten months later

A. Armani suit. Wool.

   B. Barbara Harrington. CEO of Mouton Publishing.

   C. Cartier watch. Panthère de Cartier, to be exact. A twenty-thousand-dollar price tag.

Tatum scanned the throng of guests crowded into the gilded ballroom of the historic hotel as she unhurriedly wound a path through them. Huge crystal-and-gold chandeliers were suspended from the cathedral ceilings, reflecting light off the many jewels adorning hair, ears, necks, even dresses. Narrowing her eyes, she swept her gaze over the ringed balconies high above the floor. Satisfaction whispered through her.

   D. Denise Jacobs wearing a Dior gold-and-pearl collar necklace. Two points on that one.

Tatum had become somewhat of a pro at this alphabet game she played at social events. What had started as a method of surviving the torturous appearances her parents insisted on had turned into a fun challenge. Once or twice, she'd even reached *Z*. It seemed pathetic that this had become her idea of a good time. But after the last ten months of blocking out the whispers, the gossip, the humiliation and pain, she didn't care how sad her coping mechanisms were. Whatever worked to get her through these evenings and back to the sanctuary of her home. So, she'd cling to her game.

E. Emerald green cocktail dress. Okay, that was weak…

"Did they ever figure out who he was screwing in that hotel room when he died?" a not-so-hushed voice asked behind Tatum.

Ice slid through her, and it required every bit of her battle-scarred but iron-strong control not to flinch. Or turn around and find out the identity of the avaricious gossiper.

"No. And it's been almost a year since he died. You'd think they would've discovered *something* already. It's damned hard to keep a secret for long in this city," another woman said with a chuckle.

"Well, I *did* hear that was *far* from his first affair. Apparently, he'd been a bit—" a small laugh partially covered by a delicate cough "—popular."

The second woman scoffed. "Especially with other men's wives, if what people are saying is true. Maybe that's why the 911 caller was never found. If I was cheating on my husband, I wouldn't come forward either. Can you imagine *that* conversation with the police?"

A delicate hand grasped Tatum's elbow and gently but firmly pushed her forward.

"Since I was raised with you, I know you were taught it's rude to eavesdrop," Mia drawled, steering Tatum away from the conversation. "Especially when you're ear-hustling on two little bitches who don't have the manners or common sense to even look around and see who's listening."

"How else am I supposed to know what people are saying?

We were also taught that knowledge is power," Tatum said, her conversational tone belying the bitterness, hurt and... helplessness swirling inside her with no outlet. Well, grabbing champagne glasses from the passing server and smashing them to the floor would be an outlet, but not a constructive one. And that would be breaking her parents' cardinal rule.

Do not make a spectacle.

Or rather, even more of one.

Because apparently, being the would-be bride of a man who had died bare-ass naked during sex in a hotel suite the night before his wedding was the very definition of a spectacle.

And yet, they kept making her attend these social gatherings, trotting her out in public as if the demise of her engagement—no pun intended—was a spectator event.

Tatum was the local fair rolling into town; every time she walked into a room, a giddy and greedy excitement traveled through the crowds. Her pain, her shame, the remnants of her pride seemed to be the most popular ride.

"Now you're being deliberately obtuse. I swear, sometimes I think you're punishing yourself by listening to that bullshit," Mia snapped.

Tatum waved off her younger sister's theory, scoffing, covering the brief ache tightening her chest. How could she explain that witnessing the gossip was her own form of rebellion? Her small way of recapturing just a small piece of the power she'd lost ten months ago in that hospital waiting room? Confronting those women or walking away would've smacked too much of running. But standing there, letting the gossip strike her skin, absorbing the tiny blows...

Yes, it sounded silly—confident, sexy, gave-zero-fucks Mia wouldn't understand. And because they'd never been as close as sisters only two years apart should be, Tatum didn't attempt to explain it.

It was times like this when she really missed Nore. Her best friend would've simply got it...got her.

"I'm not a masochist, Mia," Tatum assured her. "Blame our parents. This is why they have me here. Less punishment, though, and more inoculation. The more I'm exposed to the stares and comments, the less sensitive I am. Builds up my immune system."

Mia glanced at her, the corner of her lip curled in a faint sneer. "You take such satisfaction in playing the victim."

Tatum's footsteps stuttered, and she slowed to a halt, her gaze centered on her sister, studying the same dark eyes their mother had bequeathed to them.

No, she and Mia didn't share a tight relationship, but since Mark's death, Mia had been less abrasive and more compassionate, even her defender in some situations, such as the one she'd just tugged Tatum away from. But then, there were other occasions when Tatum could almost believe... She shook her head.

"You know, I can't decide if you're mad at me or mad on my behalf. Because I haven't done anything to deserve that remark," Tatum murmured.

Mia huffed out a breath and glanced away, a tiny muscle flicking along her jaw. After a moment, she looked back at Tatum. "Look, I'm—"

"Girls, we've been looking for you," Regina Haas announced, approaching them with a smile and a warning glint in her eyes.

And as soon as Tatum noticed who accompanied her mother and father, the meaning behind that cautionary gleam became clear.

Leo and Dara Walker.

Dammit.

"It's a crush in here. Which is great for the Hearts and Hope Foundation," Tatum smoothly said, referring to the children's cancer organization that would receive the funds from the evening's donations and silent auction. Shifting her attention to Mark's parents, she forced her lips into a smile. "Hello, Leo and Dara. It's wonderful to see you."

Dara moved forward to clasp Tatum's arms and brush a kiss on each of her cheeks. "You, too, Tatum. We've missed you."

To the casual listener, the older woman's voice carried a warm tone, but Tatum caught the subtle note of censure. A band around Tatum's chest tightened as if someone were turning a screw, and the muscles in her face trembled from the effort of maintaining her smile.

"I'll take the blame for that." Her father settled a hand on her back. "Having Tatum in the office has been a godsend and I've been monopolizing her time."

Why should she apologize for carrying on? For not dedicating her life as a shrine to Mark's memory?

Immediately on the heels of that thought, guilt crept through her. It wasn't that she didn't still care about Dara and Leo. How couldn't she? They'd been in her life as long as Mark had. But after... They'd expected her to grieve like them. But she couldn't. It was impossible. While they had lost a beloved son, Tatum had lost the man she'd loved, learned of his cruel betrayal, been abandoned to suffer the consequences of his actions. Yes, she grieved, but her feelings were much more...complicated.

She reached for the brooch she'd pinned at the bottom of the deep vee of her neckline, grazing her fingertips over the cameo. It was the first time she'd worn it since...that evening. Why had she decided to wear it tonight of all nights? She couldn't explain. To persuade herself she was over her pain, her grief? That she wasn't defined by her past?

It was an epic fail.

"That's understandable. Dara has accused me of throwing myself back into work as a way of coping with…" Leo cleared his throat.

And only the flash of sadness in his eyes prevented Tatum from commenting that she actually enjoyed her position at BayStar Media, that it wasn't just busywork to avoid thinking about Mark.

Constantly biting her tongue and pretending to be broken over a man who hadn't given a single, solitary damn about breaking *her*—it chafed.

And she was developing rug burn.

"I was going to call you this week, Tatum," Dara said. "Leo and I have decided to create a foundation in Mark's honor. We're offering scholarships and paid internships at MassComm to incoming college students in the Boston area."

"That's wonderful," Tatum murmured.

And it was. For the students benefiting, the opportunities would be invaluable.

Dara smiled. "I'm glad you think so. We're hosting a ceremony and dinner in a couple of months to announce the foundation. We debated holding it on the anniversary of Mark's… passing, but Leo and I think this will be a chance to commemorate such a solemn and painful time with something positive and hopeful. I believe Mark would've approved." Dara's smile trembled a little. "We would love if you would attend as our guest speaker. No one knew Mark better than you, and it would mean so much as the woman he loved and as the person who loved him if you'd speak on his behalf."

Tatum stared at Dara, stunned.

Did she…? She couldn't really expect…? There was no way she…?

As she shifted her gaze from Dara's expectant expression to Leo's steady look, Tatum's belly constricted around a terrible, painful ache. Yes, Dara did expect Tatum to get up in front of hundreds of people and pretend that Mark hadn't

ripped out her heart, that she hadn't suffered the embarrassment over the last ten months... Pretend that Mark had been
a loving, devoted partner when everyone in that room would
know the truth...

They expected her to lie to cover Mark's reputation even
if it cost her what precious little remained of her own.

Heat rolled through her, streaming up her chest, neck and
face. She forced her hands to remain straight at her sides
when her fingers almost curled into fists. With her light
brown skin, she couldn't hide the slashes of red that stained
her cheekbones. It'd been one of her mother's greatest de-
spairs that Tatum had never learned to control her face as
every good socialite should. And right now, her face probably shouted *hell no*.

"Of course she will. It's so kind of you to ask." Her mother
rushed into the silence to assure the Walkers. "Just let us
know when the dates have been firmed up and we'll all be
there."

"If you'll excuse me, please." Tatum didn't offer a reason
for leaving; she lacked the mental or emotional bandwidth to
conjure one up, and she doubted *this is some bullshit* would
do. Besides, she couldn't even utter that. Not when she could
barely *breathe*. Turning on her stiletto, she walked away from
the small group and wound her way through the crowded
ballroom, no destination in mind.

Anger propelled her forward. Anger at her parents, at the
Walkers—at fucking *everyone*, including herself.

Stop being this pawn on their chessboard. Do something.
Say *something. Find your backbone.*

Backbone. She locked down the caustic chuckle that
abraded her throat. What a joke. At some point in the past
months, she'd lost that as well as the strength she'd always believed to be one of her prized qualities. Maybe she'd buried her

spine in the ground with Mark. Along with her pride. Along with her trust in people…in her judgment. In her herself.

Dammit.

She should've stayed home tonight.

She should've…

Shaking her head, she increased her pace, her footsteps keeping time with the desperate beat of the pulse pounding in her head.

There was no point in thinking about should haves. Just as there was no point in wishing she could turn back the hands of time and open the eyes she'd willfully kept shut.

No matter how desperately she wanted to, she couldn't outrun this mess.

Mark had given her no choice but to outlive it.

Two

What the fuck did I do to deserve ending up here?

Bran Holleran held his thin cigar between his finger and thumb, clamping it between his lips. Squinting his eyes, he puffed on it, the chocolate and Jack Daniel's notes swirling over his tongue. He savored them before blowing the smoke out into the cool late-September night.

Was it rude to be out here on this deserted balcony when the social event he'd been invited to attend by the investor he was in Boston to woo—yes, woo, dammit—was inside? Yes. Rude as hell. But was he ready to reenter that ballroom thick with people who reeked of money, blue blood and condescension?

No.

This shit wasn't him.

Galas. Tuxedos. Diamonds that cost more than his whole house. Ten-thousand-dollar plates.

Yeah, he was cofounder of Greer Motorcycles Co., the high-end motorcycle manufacturer, and a multimillionaire in his own right. But none of that changed who he remained at heart—a man whose passion was building custom motorcycles and riding them on long stretches of road. A man who'd rather have a thick rare T-bone steak and a cold beer than a lump of fish eggs on a cracker and a glass of wine.

Yet here he was. In Boston at some high-society party instead of back in Seattle, Washington, either in his office or at Greer's factory working on a new custom build. Logically, he understood why he'd been chosen to come here instead of Joaquin Iverson, his friend and cofounder. Joaquin had recently become engaged, and his fiancée's event-planning company was also based in Seattle. It'd made more sense for Bran, who didn't have any personal attachments and could work long-distance, to temporarily relocate cross-country.

Still didn't mean he wasn't asking God whom he'd offended to end up in his version of hell.

Lifting the cigar to his mouth again, he closed his eyes. He didn't smoke often, but the indulgence helped him relax, and right now, surrounded by all these people with their fake high-pitched laughter, mind-numbing small talk and cardboard food with too many sauces, he needed to *relax*.

Fuck. He had a whole month of this.

He puffed harder.

The striking of heels against stone alerted him to the end of his solitude before he heard the sensual, husky notes of a woman's voice. Irritation flashed through him, but so did something else. Something edgier, darker that became even more restless and insistent as that throaty voice drew closer. He couldn't even catch the words, but he didn't need to. That voice...

Pure sex. The kind that got so hot and sweaty you had to throw the covers off so they didn't get twisted up around you. The kind that permeated the room with its own perfume.

Plucking the cigar from between his lips, he stared hard at the shadow that drifted toward him. His gut clenched, hard.

Anticipation.

This eagerness usually only wound its way through him when he sat down and prepared to work on a bike. Until this moment, as he stared into darkness, he'd believed nothing could compare to that.

Damn, he'd been wrong.

"Is it so inconceivable to think, for just one moment, that I don't want to live my life in the past? That I want to move on and not be your son's fool, pathetic fiancée for the rest of my days?" A growl rumbled out of her, and it echoed in his chest, in his gut. Lower still over his awakening cock. Disgust flickered inside him. He was forty years old, for God's sake. Not a wet-behind-the-ears kid whose dick bricked up with the slightest turn of the wind. Yet, he didn't move as she continued with her tirade, oblivious to her fascinated audience. "The audacity of me to hope my life would be my own? Dammit, you know this is your fault. Maybe if you'd put your foot down, and oh I don't know, placed your needs ahead of someone else's for once, like they do, you'd be free, if not happy. God, what would that feel like?"

A sigh whispered on the air, and the woman moved out of the shadows to the edge of the balcony, into the direct beam of the moonlight.

Goddamn.

Emerald green slid over a tall, slender frame with curves his palms itched to track. The dress should've been demure—it covered her from shoulder to wrist and draped to the floor with a small train in the back. His younger sister, Dani, who owned a bridal shop and had drilled a few dress details into his head, called the design a mermaid style. But when the woman turned toward him, all thoughts of *demure* jumped over the edge of the balcony—along with his ability to form coherent thoughts.

A deep vee plunged between her small, perfect breasts, displaying golden brown skin from the elegant column of her neck to well below her breastbone. Unlike most of the women back in the ballroom, she only wore a glittering pair of earrings. Not that she needed more jewelry. All that gorgeous skin would've rendered even the Hope Diamond gratuitous.

A silver belt accentuated a small waist and the flare of her hips. Impossibly long legs pressed against the dark green material, and both his cock and his imagination would have to be on permanent vacation not to stir at the thought of those limbs wrapped around his waist—or his head.

She shifted, and he dragged his gaze up the beauty of her body to her— His breath lodged in his throat. *Damn.*

If her body was stunning, her face… He slowly lowered his cigar so nothing could obstruct his view. Her face was a work of art.

A glimmer of recognition flashed inside him, but it winked out like an extinguished flame under a ruthless wave of lust. Lust and awe.

Delicately arched eyebrows over thickly lashed almond-shaped eyes. Cheekbones high and sharp. A proud, patrician nose with a very faint smattering of freckles across the bridge that prevented it from crossing over into arrogance. A graceful jawline he suspected could turn stubborn. And a wide, lush mouth that shouldn't have him ordering his cock to stand down like he was a horny-ass teenager. He was too damn old for that shit. Too damn old for *her*, given that she couldn't have been older than twenty-five or so.

His gaze lingered on the full, sensual bottom curve of her lip.

Apparently his dick ascribed to the "age is just a number" school of thought.

"This is ridiculous," she murmured, almost too low for him to catch. "I must be just as ridiculous."

"I don't know. I've been called worse." The words escaped him before he realized he'd intended to speak.

"Oh my God." Her body jerked, and she snapped her head in his direction. Her hand flew to the base of her throat. "What the hell?"

He brought his cigar back to his lips and puffed on it, blowing smoke out several seconds later, then continued as if she hadn't spoken. Or wasn't staring at him in wide-eyed shock. "I've been called worse," he repeated. "Done worse. You out here talking to yourself might seem, well…questionable to you, but other people may consider it normal behavior and a healthy way of working through your issues."

He didn't know who was more surprised—her or him. He and Joaquin were such great friends and business partners because they communicated through motorcycles, monosyllabic words and grunts. It was their love language. Neither one of them indulged in—or needed—lengthy conversations with one another. They weren't built like that.

Bran definitely wasn't. He didn't talk much, or tease. Didn't flirt. Even before Roma, he hadn't been that guy, but *after* his ex-wife, whatever inclination he'd had to try and behave differently had gone scorched earth by his divorce.

Yet here he stood in a shadow-enshrouded balcony talking to a stranger and toying with flirting.

And his only excuse was *her.*

Like a living flame, burning bright against the dark night, she seemed to *seethe* with emotion. And he was a kid warned away from a hot stove, longing to touch that fire. And only once his skin had been licked by its heat would he know to back away…or crave its bite again.

"It's also rude to cut in on other people's private conversations," she bit out. "Even if it's with themselves."

A bark of laughter barreled up his chest, but with effort he shoved it back down. Because that made no damn sense. It was funny as hell, though. Which served to spike an unwanted curiosity about the stunning woman before him. Right alongside that inconvenient lust.

A combination that any man who thought with his brain rather than his dick would run away from.

"Rude?" He shrugged. "Maybe." He cocked his head. "But then, I was here first. So technically, that means you're violating my space. If you want privacy, there are other balconies where you can have a one-on-one argument. Given what I saw of this place, you have about ten more to pick from."

She frowned. Even as she glared at him, his body tightened in anticipation that had him feeling like his skin had shrunk on his extra-large frame.

"You're looking like you want to jump, baby girl." He brought his cigar back to his lips as he delivered the warning on a low silken murmur. "And the way I'm feeling right now, I might be in the mood to catch you. Be sure that's what you signed up for, though. Don't let the suit fool you."

Her soft catch of breath caressed his ears, stroked over his chest—and lower. Though he couldn't quite detect the color of her eyes, the slight widening of them and the parting of her lips denoted her shock. At his words? Probably. Just looking at her—her beauty, flawless body, clothes—and the company she kept behind them in that ballroom, he seriously doubted anyone had ever dared to speak to her as he'd just done.

Hell, had anyone ever dared dig their hands in that long, thick hair that fell over her shoulder in a perfect dark sheet? Pull on it, tug her head back and mess up that immaculately applied lipstick until it stained both of their mouths and skin?

No. He'd bet his 1973 Norton Commando 850 that none of the men back there sipping their champagne and ogling the waitstaff had ever given that to her.

"Excuse me?" she whispered. "Don't let the suit fool me?" From one instant to the next, her frown cleared and a smile curved her plush mouth. And no one could've missed the edge sharp enough to draw blood. "Well, would a trash can do? It seems like that would be a better fit for your manners. Especially since you obviously believe it's okay to disrespect me."

He'd been right. Touching that flame didn't have him wanting to back away.

He stepped closer.

Again, she wasn't quick enough in concealing her reaction, and she retreated a step before drawing up short. That delicate but stubborn chin hiked up, and apparently not satisfied, she recovered the ground she'd given up. And he glimpsed her eyes for the first time.

It could've been the moonlight that made the brown appear almost black, but somehow he doubted it. And as he stared down into those damn-near-bottomless depths, he found himself battling the urge to retreat, to stumble back a step before he dove into her with a recklessness that was completely alien to him.

Her gaze lowered from his, skimmed over his face, beard, not betraying a blink at his long hair pulled back into a bun before taking in the black-on-black Tom Ford suit. When she returned her regard to him, her dark eyes didn't reveal her thoughts, and for the first time in more years than he could remember, he cared about a stranger's opinion. Because if it wasn't about a bike he designed or manufactured, he usually didn't give a fuck.

But now, staring down into a pair of inscrutable brown-black eyes, he did.

And that unnerved him more than he cared to admit.

"Disrespect you?" He exhaled, turning his head so he didn't blow the chocolate-flavored smoke in her face. Arching an eyebrow, he said, "That was an invitation and a disclaimer. You're the one in a mood, baby girl. I was just letting you know I might want to indulge it. If upfront and honest talk offends or scares you, then that would be a 'you' problem. Because again—" he jerked his chin to the side, indicating the space around them "—my balcony first."

Yeah, he was being deliberately...provoking.

And if he were honest, it surprised him. True, he did possess a blunt a manner, but this? Something about her... He wanted to poke, prod. See if she would hide behind that icy, polite demeanor with the nice-nasty edges or slip and allow him to see more of that fire.

He didn't come here—to this event, to Boston—for this. To tease some mysterious, unknown woman on a dark balcony. A woman he wouldn't see again after tonight. He didn't come here to wonder what those perfectly manicured nails would feel like biting into his bare shoulders or back. To discover if those eyes would grow even darker with lust.

To wonder if that flash of fire he'd glimpsed would burn just as bright, as hot if he sank hard and deep inside her...

Yes, no doubt about it, he was being deliberately provoking. But to what end? Her emotion?

Or her lust?

Because fuck him, if he didn't want both.

Not that he had anything against a one-night stand with a gorgeous woman. Hell, that pretty much summed up his relationship history in the last seven years since his divorce. But as much as he hungered to find out how that throaty voice would sound wrapped around his name as she screamed in orgasm, an equal amount of disquiet crept through him.

There might be a man who could fuck her and walk away without being greedy for another taste.

He had the sneaking suspicion that man wouldn't be him.

She closed her eyes and drew in a breath, and again, a niggling sense of familiarity flickered in the back of his skull. Did he know her? Had they met? Couldn't have. No way in hell he would've forgotten her.

She pinched the bridge of her nose, shaking her head.

"No. Just…no." She lowered her hand and opened her eyes, wrinkling her nose. "An invitation? To what? Maim you? Because that line can't possibly work. What self-respecting person has fallen for it?"

"Not a line." He shrugged a shoulder and set his cigar on the ashtray resting near the stone ledge. "Just offering you an outlet. And the chance to place your needs first, as you claim you have a problem doing." Sliding his hands in the front pockets of his suit pants, he murmured, "Just from the observation of a random eavesdropper, there isn't anything foolish or pathetic about you. I can't speak on the 'fiancée' part, though."

Pain glinted in her eyes so brightly, he couldn't have mistaken it for anything but what it was. And the sight of it pierced him like the heel of her stiletto to his chest, cutting off his banter and his breath.

"Hey, baby girl—" he said, voice low, shifting closer to her.

"Don't call me that."

She probably meant to snap at him. But the words emerged as a low rasp.

"Okay," he said, deliberately softening his voice. Instead of backing away like he should, he leaned against the stone railing, studying her, seeking to defuse the situation and extinguish the hurt in her gaze. "What should I call you, then? What's your name?"

Her lips parted—whether to give an answer or to tell him to go to hell, he didn't know—but he didn't get the chance to find out. At least not from her.

"Tatum, I've been looking all over for you."

This woman he recognized as soon as she stepped through the wide French doors, and as soon as Mia Haas said, "Tatum," that nagging sense of familiarity finally clicked into place.

Tatum Haas.

The best friend of Joaquin's fiancée, Nore.

The daughter of the man Bran was in Boston to see as an investor in Greer Motorcycle's newest model.

Well, damn.

A wide pit yawned in the bottom of his stomach, then stretched higher toward his chest. In the emptiness echoed disappointment and the shadow of loss. He shook his head and straightened, stepping away from the woman who'd gone from pure temptation to off-limits in the blink of an eye.

Yeah, who was he kidding? She was still pure temptation.

"Ms. Haas, it's good to see you again," he said, turning to Silas Haas's other daughter, the one he'd met in Seattle. The beautiful young woman had attended the launch party for their first electric model, the KING One, months ago. And later, when Bran and Joaquin had taken the first meetings with BayStar about a possible investment for their new line of cost-friendly motorcycles, Mia had sat in on them. He nodded at her now. "How're you doing?"

"Well, Mr. Holleran. But please, it's Mia." She smiled, and he noticed the resemblance between the two women. Both shared the same eyes and bone structure, although Tatum stood a couple of inches taller and Mia boasted a slightly curvier frame. And Mia's mouth didn't put him in the mind frame of sin, sweat and begging. "Since you're in Boston for the foreseeable future," Mia continued, "and we'll be working together, I hope I can call you Bran."

"Of course."

"I take it you two know each other," Tatum said to her sister, not looking at him at all.

For some reason, he wanted to grasp her chin and turn her head toward him, force that almost-black gaze to him.

But that was foolishness, too, for several reasons.

Didn't stop his fingertips from tingling, though.

"We do," Mia said. "Mr. Holleran, or Bran," she corrected herself with a soft chuckle, "is one of our newest clients. Bay-Star is investing in his company, Greer Motorcycles. I'm surprised Dad didn't mention it to you."

If he hadn't been watching Tatum so closely, he might've missed the slight clenching of her jaw. But he didn't miss it. And though it fell under the category of "not my business," he couldn't help but wonder what that was about.

"Well, Mr. Holleran." Tatum turned to him, her mouth stretched into what she probably would mistakenly label a smile. He, on the other hand, knew bullshit when he saw it. Especially when it sounded like she'd swallowed glass. "It would seem like we aren't really strangers."

"Not at all," he said. "Some might even consider us in-laws." He tilted his head, his regard falling to the brooch pinned to the bottom of the plunging vee between her breasts. "I should've recognized that, if nothing else. It's a distinctive piece. Nore Daniels wore it the first time we met at my best friend Joaquin Iverson's birthday party."

Tatum blinked, confusion clouding her eyes. But a moment later, realization dawned.

"You're—" She shook her head, frowning. "No, that's not possible. We would've met long before now."

"Not really. The first time you visited Seattle after Nore and Joaquin met is when they were…"

Tatum snorted. "I believe what you're trying not to say is when Joaquin fucked up."

"Yes, that." No point in defending his friend. Joaquin had screwed up but thankfully he'd pulled his head out of his ass before it'd been too late. "And since then Nore has flown out here to see you. Sorry, I didn't recognize you."

"Yes, well, Tatum's had quite a lot going on lately, which is why the rest of us have circled the wagons, so to speak. Not that we mind. That's what family is for, after all." Mia moved forward and slid her arm through his. "Which reminds me, Tatum," she continued, glancing over her shoulder at her sister. "Mom and Dad sent me to find you since you abruptly ran off. Dinner and the silent auction are about to start."

"You two go ahead. I'll be right behind you." Tatum waved her hand, her voice even, as devoid of emotion as her face.

And he hated it.

This wasn't the woman he'd been sparring with for the last twenty minutes. He wanted her back, not this solemn version with her fire banked.

But it wasn't just that.

It didn't sit right with him to walk away with Mia and leave Tatum alone. There was something—a tension, a rigidity—that had entered their space, entered Tatum since her sister had joined them on the balcony. And though he only possessed a barely there connection to Tatum through mutual friends, and their initial meeting had contained more vinegar than honey, he couldn't leave her behind.

"We'll wait." He removed his arm from Mia's. "When you're ready."

Mia stiffened, but he ignored it, his attention focused on Tatum. She, in turn, stared at him. An emotion flickered across her face, but it appeared and disappeared before he could crack its meaning. Not that he spoke fluent Tatum Haas.

Not that he cared to.

Shit. Lying had to be bad for the digestion.

"I wasn't aware I required an escort," she snarked, then jerked her head toward his cigar, which still smoldered on the ashtray. "You don't want to forget to put that out and take it with you."

"It's a cigar, baby girl, not a cigarette. You don't 'put it out.' You allow it to die out gracefully."

"That doesn't sound pretentious at all. And I told you don't call me that."

The bite returned to her voice, and satisfaction hummed under his skin.

"And you never gave me a name to call you in its place," he reminded her, and her full mouth firmed in annoyance. What did it say about him that he enjoyed it? "Are you ready to go in together, or are we hanging out here longer?"

An emotion gleamed in those dark eyes and once more he had to check the overwhelming urge to pinch her chin, tilt her head back and study that gaze, mine it for all its secrets.

But experience had taught him the brutal lesson of giving in to impulse. Once a person had his life dragged from one end of hell and back, he heeded every warning.

And Tatum Haas was a walking, breathing caution sign wrapped up in a neon red alert. The blinking kind.

Fucking danger ahead.

That chin he'd imagined cupping lifted, and that reserved mask slid back into place. "Pity is not on the dinner menu for this evening. I don't need or want yours," she coolly informed him, then strode past him and her sister.

The aloof socialite veneer was impeccable. And he might've believed it and felt put in his place if he hadn't glimpsed those eyes.

Yeah, they betrayed her hurt and ruined the whole charade.

"You'll have to excuse my sister," Mia said as he watched Tatum disappear back inside the ballroom teeming with people. "I promise you we all really do have better manners." She laughed softly. "She's had a tough year—"

"Yes, I get that." Glancing down at her, he nodded. "You said dinner's about to start? We should probably get in there so you can get to your table and I can find mine."

"Oh. Uh—" she gave her head a slight shake "—yes, you're right." A frown flirted with her brows before her expression cleared, and she recovered with another smile. "We should head in."

Mia probably wasn't used to being interrupted or, given her beauty, men not hanging on every word she uttered. But Bran didn't want to hear what she had to say about her sister. Yes, he was very aware of just how "tough" Tatum's year had been. Her best friend was engaged to his. Of course, Joaquin had shared some of the details with him.

But getting the story from Mia—or anyone here—smacked too much of gossip. Didn't matter that she was Tatum's sister. And not only had he outgrown that shit when he graduated high school, but there seemed to be something else he couldn't quite put a finger on...

He lifted a shoulder and moved forward, mentally shaking off that nagging sense of...whatever. He was here in Boston to lock in his investor and oversee a couple more opportunities for their new model.

That was it.

Not to meet or engage in dangerously flirtatious banter with prickly younger women who talked to themselves.

Not to imagine how said prickly younger woman looked midorgasm. Especially when she was the daughter of the investor he needed.

And definitely not to entangle himself in a ménage with him, her and the ghost of her dead fiancé.

No. The sooner he got his business handled and got out of Boston, the better.

Three

Monday mornings were a torture all their own, especially precoffee, but being summoned to her father's office—still with no coffee—tipped this one over into a special level.

Grinding her teeth, she studied the steadily rising numbers of the elevator as it carried her to the executive floor. Not that she minded seeing her father; she loved Silas Haas and had been a self-admitted daddy's girl from the time she'd been born. But ever since Mark's death, there'd been an indefinable change in their relationship. As if when he looked at her, he didn't quite know what to make of her. Like Mark's infidelities and death had tainted her, irreversibly changed her from the daughter he'd once known and left him with…her. And Silas seemed to be out of his element in how to handle her. So he'd opted for wavering between kid gloves and tough love and her mother went with ignoring the entire episode.

Was it any wonder Tatum's stomach had decided to make a jailbreak for her throat?

She had no idea which version of her father she'd encounter this morning.

Both of them saddened and irritated her.

She didn't need to be "handled." She needed... She needed them to see her as a person and not a scandalous tragedy.

The elevator slid to a stop and the doors opened. Sighing, she stepped onto the floor that housed all the offices for the senior-level executives of BayStar Media. *One day*, she promised herself, surveying the closed heavy oak doors with their embossed gold doorplates and individual assistant desks guarding their sanctuaries. A conference room with floor-to-ceiling windows, a large table with mounted tablets and surrounded by leather chairs, and a huge screen occupied one side of the area. And at the end of the corridor sat the corner office of BayStar's CEO and the grandson of the founder, Silas Haas.

As she approached her father's closed door, his executive assistant, Brenda, glanced up from the computer screen on her desk.

"Good morning, Tatum." She smiled, the blunt ends of her sleek blond bob brushing her jaw as she nodded. "You can go on in. He's expecting you."

"Thanks, Brenda." Before Tatum headed in, though, she reached into her purse and removed a small paper bag, then set it on the top of the desk. "Here you go. For Ryan and his new collection."

The other woman's lips rounded in an O as she accepted the gift. While other ten-year-old boys might be consumed with video games, cartoons or sports, Brenda's little boy loved to collect. Everything from book series to trading cards—if they caught his attention, he collected it. Right now, he was focused on gathering a key chain from every state in the US.

"What's this...?" Brenda removed the Washington State–shaped key chain with landmarks engraved on it, including the Space Needle and Mount Rainier. She grinned, her green eyes bright. "Tatum, you didn't have to do this."

"Of course I did. When Dad told me about Ryan's newest collection, I had my best friend go right out to the store, buy me a key chain and mail it to me. Tell him I need a picture when it's complete."

"I definitely will. Thank you again. He's going to love it!"

"You're welcome." With another smile, she continued toward her father's office, trying to hold on to that bit of joy. She had a suspicion she'd need it.

After a couple of raps on the closed door, she waited several seconds before twisting the knob and entering. Her father sat behind his massive, ruthlessly neat glass-and-chrome desk, glancing up when she stepped into the room.

He welcomed her with a smile before standing and rounding the desk, arms outstretched, and the band constricting her chest loosened a fraction. If he'd called her here to drop some kind of bomb, he probably wouldn't have greeted her with such warmth. Silas had always been an affectionate parent but also a firm one when required. Still, this side of him reassured her that she wouldn't face bullshit this morning.

Thank God.

Maybe she could get that coffee now.

"Good morning, Tatum. You look well. How're you doing?" He met her halfway across his cavernous office, gripping her upper arms and pulling her into a quick embrace, then brushing a kiss over her cheek.

"Good, Dad. I can't complain. How're you?"

He stroked a hand down his blue-and-gray-striped tie and his thick, muscular stomach. Big and wide-shouldered, he more resembled the linebacker he'd once been for Notre Dame than a CEO. Silas remained in shape, and Tatum had inherited their height from him.

"Fine, fine. Have a seat." He waved toward the couch, table, armchairs and service station loaded down with a coffee urn, cups and saucers and smaller sugar and cream pots. "We're just waiting on your sister."

Tatum arched an eyebrow as she strode toward the sitting area and the nectar of the gods, otherwise known as coffee. No one could ever call her a morning person, and she owned it. A couple of minutes later, she stirred liberal amounts of cream and sugar into the fragrant brew and lifted her gaze to her father, who sat behind his desk once again.

"Any hint on what this impromptu meeting is about?" she asked, raising her cup to her mouth for a careful sip.

"Patience, Tatum. Y'know, your mother and I—"

"Almost named me that, I know." She laughed at the family joke that her parents had teased her with so many times because she lacked that particular virtue. Carrying her cup and saucer, she sank down onto the couch. "While we're waiting on Mia, I've been meaning to ask you—"

"Sorry, I'm late," Mia announced, breezing into the office. "Traffic is terrible this morning." Smiling at her father, she strode toward Tatum and dumped her purse and bag on one of the armchairs before approaching the service station. "Can you catch me up on what I missed?"

"I waited on you to arrive to start," their father said, a note of disapproval in his tone.

Frowning, Tatum slid a look at Mia, who appeared unbothered, her attention focused on pouring coffee. If Tatum's impatience was a Haas joke, then Mia's inability to arrive anywhere on time was another one. So why did her father seem annoyed? Hell, by now they all cushioned time into anything involving Mia.

"If you two are ready, I'll begin." He joined them, claiming an armchair across from Tatum as Mia lowered to one adjacent to the couch.

"BayStar has an investment opportunity with a high-end motorcycle manufacturer based out of Seattle. Mia, you're already familiar with Greer Motorcycles, and Tatum, from what I understand, Nore is engaged to one of its owners. From a business aspect with BayStar, we've been in talks with Joaquin Iverson and Bran Holleran for months about investing in a new line they're about to launch—their second launch of a new model within a year."

He passed Tatum and Mia a tablet each, and on the screen was a report on Greer Motorcycles, the company's history, solvency and a summary of the investment proposal.

She lifted her cup of coffee for another sip, hiding anything her face happened to betray at the sound of Bran's name. Stunned didn't begin to cover the blast of ice that had hit her when Mia mentioned Bran being a client of BayStar's. Tatum would've remembered it if her sister had talked about him before. Just as she remembered every single detail having to do with Bran Holleran.

Unbidden, her mind drifted to him, the cofounder of Greer—she knew this as she'd read a short bio on him. The perfunctory facts neatly summed him up: forty years old, custom bike builder, twenty years' experience in his field, owner of one of the best custom-build companies in the southern US before he collaborated with Joaquin Iverson to establish Greer.

The black-and-white details in no way captured the charismatic, sexual gut punch that was Bran Holleran.

Even now, a shiver danced down her spine as a vision of him from Saturday night wavered in front of her. A wave of heat poured through her like fresh lava. She gritted her teeth against the rush of warmth, but it was pointless. Just as trying to not think about the man was pointless.

Bran Holleran hadn't just gotten under her skin. He'd crept into her mind and taken up residence.

Like a damn squatter.

When he'd stepped out of the shadowed corner and into the moonlight, she'd been struck senseless. That hadn't even happened when she'd met Mark, and up until the moment she'd laid eyes on Bran's striking features, Mark had been the handsomest man she'd seen.

Handsome.

Could she get more bland?

Handsome didn't begin to describe the wide, strong brow, or the stark, almost harsh cheekbones and jawline. Or the bright blue of his gaze that incongruously reminded her of fire under heavy, dark eyebrows. Didn't start to cover the bold slash of nose some could've called hawkish but she labeled domineering. Definitely didn't properly describe the carnal delight that was his mouth. God...

She downed more coffee but it didn't stop another wave of heat swamping her. Just the thought of those firm, wide lips bordered by that thick salt-and-pepper beard had her fighting not to squirm.

What would that facial hair feel like brushing over her skin? Over her breasts? Her inner thighs? Would it be abrasive and leave a burn behind, reminding her he'd been there? Or would it be soft, a silken caress like gentle fingertips?

Clearing her throat, she refocused on the present...and not on the ache pulsing between her thighs.

"That's not a red flag?" she asked her father. "Two launches in a year could be a sign of them expanding too fast."

"If this was another company, maybe. But not them. And they're two entirely different products. One was their first electric motorcycle and this one will cater to a different demographic. And you have their numbers in front of you. Greer doesn't *need* our investment to roll this out, but they want it in more of a partnership. We can offer them money as well as the resources that come with BayStar Media. And Greer is a sound investment for us."

"And if I may add," Mia interjected. "Between the two founders, they bring a combined thirty years' experience in the motorcycle industry—twenty years with Bran and ten years with Joaquin Iverson, and that's not counting the number of years Joaquin spent racing bikes. They know their industry and client base. And in the decade Greer Motorcycles has been in operation, they've grown to a multimillion-dollar business. They've been all custom builds until now. And they're seeking to move into mass production with this new line. Just from the research I've done, I believe they can do it successfully, and BayStar would profit as an investor."

"All true, and I agree with you." Silas nodded at Mia, then looked at Tatum. "Mia mentioned you met Bran at the fundraiser Saturday night."

Annoyance glimmered inside her, and she resisted glancing at her sister. Logically, her sister relaying that Tatum bumped into Bran shouldn't have bothered Tatum. It shouldn't have struck her as Mia tattling or trying to get in their father's ear. Shouldn't have…

But it did.

And she hated that.

"Yes, we did. And we spoke briefly," Tatum admitted. "Definitely not long enough to cover a new partnership with BayStar."

Her father nodded. "That's fine. You'll be rectifying that in the future." He paused. "Because I'm placing you over this investment project. And you will be the liaison for BayStar while Bran Holleran is in Boston."

A beat of silence pounded in the office, and Tatum didn't know who was more shocked: her or Mia. Blinking, she stared at her father, then looked at Mia, who gaped at Silas as well.

"Dad, I don't understand." Mia shook her head. "What do you mean?"

"I'm sorry, Dad, I'm not sure I understand," Tatum said

at the same time, objecting with her sister but for different reasons.

Mia because she obviously felt blindsided, and Tatum because she didn't want this responsibility. More specifically, she didn't want to have anything to do with Bran Holleran.

"Just what I said. Tatum, you will take point on the Greer Motorcycles account." He leaned back in his chair and set his tablet on the side table next to him. "Everything you need to know to catch you up to speed is in what I just sent you. Including the marketing projects we have set up for Greer so far. It's going to be your responsibility to use our resources to secure more for this investment. You'll report your progress directly to me."

Overwhelmed. As she stared down at the tablet, the date on it blurred. For a moment, she considered dropping the device to the floor and power walking from her father's office.

Since Mark's death, Silas had treated her like his glorified intern, keeping her close, doling out tasks but not allowing her to stray too far from under his wing. There was a marked difference in how he treated Mia, her younger sister, like a competent, capable employee, and Tatum, like a broken bird he didn't trust to leave the nest.

And now, he'd thrust her out.

It was what she'd wanted; she'd hated his coddling. But... yes. Overwhelmed.

"Hold on, Dad, please. Just hold on." Mia scooted to the edge of her chair, holding out a hand, palm up. She loosed a short, sharp chuckle. "You can't be serious. Greer Motorcycles is my account."

"If Mia already started working on this—"

Her sister threw Tatum a narrow-eyed glare. "I don't need you to defend me," she snapped.

Well, hell. She'd been trying to side with her. They wanted

the same thing, after all—Tatum off this account and Mia back on it.

But, as always, Mia tended to see Tatum as the competition, sometimes even the enemy, rather than an ally. Her sister took sibling rivalry to another level. Always had, even though Tatum had wanted nothing more than to be close to her.

"I've made my decision," Silas said, voice flat, final.

Yet Mia refused to let it go.

Slashing her hand through the air, she insisted, "Dad, I did all the legwork and research on this project. I flew out to Seattle to attend the launch of the KING One and to meet with Bran and Joaquin. I already know this deal, so it doesn't make sense that you would just remove me from it."

His eyes hardened. In one moment to the next, he changed from Silas, their affectionate and protective father, to Silas, decisive and sometimes ruthless CEO of BayStar Media.

"As an employee of BayStar, you did what was requested and required of you. But not once did I say you would take lead on this deal. I asked you for research and to accumulate information, that is all. You took it upon yourself to fly out to Seattle and hold an initial meeting with Greer and informed me after the fact. Just as you attended their launch just weeks after—" Silas shot a swift look at Tatum before returning his attention to Mia "—after everything that occurred. That was inappropriate and I certainly didn't ask you to go. But again, you did so on your own."

"Only because I noticed Greer Motorcycles on your agenda for discussion with the board and I decided to take the initiative. As you've taught us."

"If you'd believed I would've agreed with your actions, you would've been up front with me beforehand, Mia, not after. That includes the meeting you took with Joaquin and Bran, placing me in the awkward position of having to pretend I'd known about it all along. I don't operate that way.

And if you weren't my daughter, you would've been fired. Too many times you've acted like a lone wolf, and I won't reward bad behavior."

He turned once more to Tatum, and pinned her with a steady, hard stare.

"You're heading this deal. The fact is, Tatum, everyone—our employees, the board, shareholders, the public—needs to see you are more than this…incident with Mark. That you can not only handle this responsibility as an officer in this company but that you can successfully close the deal. This is the opportunity for that."

Hurt shimmered inside her. Hurt and a humiliation so deep it seemed grafted to her cells. A humiliation that didn't belong to her but had become hers all the same.

"This is bullshit," Mia hissed.

"Tread carefully, Mia," Silas snapped.

"No." She bolted to her feet, her body nearly trembling with outrage. "I've worked on this deal, but now I'm being kicked off because *she*—" Mia flung a hand in Tatum's direction "—has a PR problem? Like I said. This. Is. Bullshit."

After snatching up her bag and purse, Mia stalked out of the office and slammed the door behind her. Tatum didn't move, the reverberation of the noise and her sister's anger vibrating through her. Her heart pounded against her sternum and the beat filled her ears.

"Dad," Tatum murmured. "Why're you doing this?"

"I explained my reasons." He rose from his chair and crossed the room to his desk. "Your sister will get over this. In the meantime, you should have all the information you need to get rolling."

"Mia is not just going to get over this, Dad. And I can't say I blame her. This isn't fair. Not to her. Not even to Bran Holleran or Joaquin, who are probably comfortable with her as the representative of BayStar—"

"You need this. Do you understand me, Tatum?" he asked, stopping in front of his desk and turning around to meet her gaze, his own as uncompromising as his tone. "You. Need. This. Professionally and personally. You went through a serious upheaval this past year, but you know as well as I do that people are sympathetic for five minutes. Then they start looking at you. What did you do? What's wrong with you? And because you've never addressed it, speculation has only increased, not diminished."

Anger and pain speared through her, and she sucked in a breath. "None of what happened with Mark is my fault," she said, hating that her voice shook. "And I can't control how people look at or think about me."

"No, it wasn't and no, you can't. And none of it is fair, Tatum," he murmured.

She bit the inside of her cheek to stem the flow of words. Words that would've been vitriolic and undeserved had she yelled at him not to "handle" her. Not to treat her like she was this fragile thing that would shatter at the slightest harsh comment.

Unbidden, her mind flew to Bran Holleran. He hadn't treated her like that. He'd spoken to her with a rawness in that rough-road voice that had made her feel substantial, grounded... whole. There'd been nothing careful or curated about his speech. He just hadn't given a fuck, and it'd been...liberating.

Exhilarating.

And it was that exhilaration that had her nervous to be in his company. Some women might be thrilled to have the sweet song of excitement buzz through their veins, hum under their skin.

But most women hadn't been so burned by a man that the thought of trusting one with anything again—her body, her feelings or, God forbid, her heart—ranked up there alongside cuddling with a homicidal shape-shifting clown.

"But," her father continued, dragging her attention back to the here and now, "at the risk of being cliché, life isn't fair. Even less when you're a woman and a very convenient and visible target for a man's failures. So as wrong and burdensome as it is, the challenge to change the narrative falls on you. And I have to own part of the blame in this. I've treated you more as a daughter than an employee, and that's how people have come to view you. But if you're honest, Tatum, you haven't fought too hard to come from under my wing. You've become comfortable. Too comfortable, even though both of us know you're capable of taking over my job if you wanted it."

"That's not tr—" she automatically objected, but when her father arched an eyebrow, the protest died on her tongue. She frowned. Had she been complacent? *Yes.* The answer shimmered in her head, whisper soft but definite. "I can see why you'd say that. I did sit back and lick my wounds, and maybe I let it go on too long. But I've never been satisfied with leaning on you or letting you coddle me, Dad. I've never been content to sit on my behind and collect a check without earning it."

"I know that, Tatum. No one knows that more than me." He paused and his gaze switched to a picture on his desk. She couldn't see it from her position on the couch, but she didn't need to. Her father'd had the framed photo of his family—her mother, her and Mia—sitting on the desktop for as long as she could remember. "Now's your chance to show everyone else. To prove it to everyone else."

He slid a hand into his pants pocket and rubbed the other over his head. "I had also planned on telling this to you and your sister together, but since she left..." He frowned, shooting a glance at the closed office door as if Mia still stood there. "I guess I'll have to find her later and share this with her. But Greg Mendahl is retiring at the end of the year. I will be promoting someone from within to the position of chief operating officer, and I would like that to be one of my daughters. Both of you have worked for this company full-time for years and interned since you were teens. You've been here longer than Mia, but as unfair as your sister believes I am, I also can't just give you the position based on that. Especially when she's been kicking ass here at BayStar these last few months. Do you even want the position, Tatum?"

"Yes, of course."

She didn't need to think about her answer. Some little girls imagined being models or actresses or doctors. She'd only wanted to work with her father at her family's company and continue the legacy of her great-grandfather. Tatum *enjoyed* her job.

She refused to allow Mark's death—no, Mark's *betrayal*—to steal another dream from her.

"Of course I want the position," she repeated, her voice stronger, more certain this time.

"Good." He nodded, a gleam in his dark brown eyes. "I've already contacted Bran Holleran and told him to expect your call."

She returned his nod, not allowing her expression to reveal the trepidation twisting inside her. Just the thought of seeing the tall older man with the piercing blue eyes and big body had an avalanche of emotions crashing through her.

Nerves. Irritation. Fear.

Excitement.

The last two she resented like hell.

Because once again, her future depended on a man. A wild card.

And she didn't like it.

She didn't like it at all.

Four

Damn. And he'd thought Seattle traffic was bad.

Bran shook his head as he hit the lock button on his key fob and strode up one of Beacon Hill's famous cobblestone streets. Not only had he hit afternoon lunch traffic but he'd also circled the block six times looking for a place to park in this historic Boston neighborhood.

At any other time, he would've slowed his pace to take in the stately brownstones with their flower boxes, iron gas lamps and grand architecture from the turn of the century. Whenever he visited a new city, he loved to tour the corners and areas that made each place distinct. And this one, where history seemed to emanate from the brick of the streets and buildings, was one of those areas. But he couldn't today. Not when he was already five minutes late for his appointment. And something told him the person waiting on him not only valued punctuality but would be looking for anything to strike a mark in his con column.

He shook his head as he passed an array of antique shops, cafés and boutiques on Charles Street and approached the

Italian restaurant Tatum had suggested for their lunch. To say he and Tatum Haas had started out on the wrong foot would be akin to saying the Bermuda Triangle was a lost and found section.

As he stepped inside, scents of oregano, basil and thyme greeted him, and he couldn't help inhaling the delicious aromas deep into his lungs. His stomach growled in approval. He scanned the restaurant, surprised at its emptiness. Given the location, the elegance of the place and the promise of the scents emanating from the kitchen, he would've expected the restaurant to be bursting at the seams with people. Had he mixed up the time or the location?

"Good afternoon, sir. Are you Mr. Holleran?" an older man in a black suit and white shirt asked, walking up to him.

"Yes." Bran scanned the vacant area once more. "I'm supposed to meet Tatum Haas here."

The other man nodded and swept a hand to his right. "Yes, sir. She's already arrived. If you'll follow me."

Several moments later, they entered a private dining room that could've been borrowed directly from the movie set of a Tuscan villa. Stone walls, antique lamps, terra-cotta tile, and pots of red and purple flowers had him longing for another trip back to the country of his grandfather's birth. But as beautiful as the setting might be, nothing could divert his attention from the woman rising from the circular table that could easily sit ten or twelve people.

He'd only seen her in evening wear but she looked just as stunning in a simpler royal blue wrap dress. With her long dark hair pulled back in a high ponytail, nothing hindered her refined features from view and he studied the beautiful face that had been haunting him the last couple of days…and nights. He'd halfway convinced himself the depth of those dark eyes, the sharpness of her perfect cheekbones and the prurient lushness of her mouth were his imagination or a trick of the shadows.

The joke was on him.

"Mr. Holleran," she said in that smoky voice that seemed damn near inappropriate for daytime hours. She glanced away from him and smiled at the older man next to him. "Thank you. We're ready to begin now."

"As you wish." The maître d' dipped his head in acknowledgment. "I'll send your server in now."

Tatum lowered into her seat and Bran settled into a chair across from her.

"Thank you for meeting with me on such short notice," she said.

"Of course." He nodded. "But is what we're about to discuss so top secret you had to rent out the entire restaurant?"

She arched an eyebrow, and he found himself waiting, *anticipating* the retort she would deliver. Trading barbs with this woman was better than some of the best sex he'd ever had.

"While I can assure you BayStar Media considers you an important client, closing a restaurant to speak with you isn't really necessary." She picked up the glass of water on the table and sipped from it before continuing. "But since the owners here are longtime friends of the family, they allow us to use their restaurant for lunch meetings before they open for the evening. They have excellent food and it's one of the most popular places to eat in Boston. I thought you might appreciate experiencing one of our attractions even while we're working."

The words were pleasant enough, but that proper tone with its sprinkling of icicles… It told him if he didn't like her choice, he could choke on it.

Why that had lust thickening in his veins, he couldn't explain. Before now, he'd never cottoned to that opposites at-

tract bullshit. But now? Comparing her smooth, buffed edges
to his rougher ones… Her upper-crust, champagne and cav-
iar background to his blue-collar, beer and steak fries one…
Her aloof reserve to his don't-give-a-fuck approach… Yeah,
they were as different as night and day. Yet, no woman had
stimulated his mind and his body like Tatum Haas. Not even
his ex-wife.

And since he would be working closely with Tatum on
a project that meant expansion in another direction for his
company, that "stimulation" was not a good thing.

On the contrary. It meant, he'd either keep his dick in his
pants or he was fucked. And not in the way that part of his
anatomy was used to.

"I'm appreciative," he said, picking up the wine list. As if
that signaled their server, he appeared at the table, and they
placed their drink requests. A Riesling for her, and a Sam
Adams for him. "I don't know any other way to be, so can
I speak freely?"

Because nothing about her escaped his notice, he caught
the slight tensing of her body. And the very deliberate loosening of it.

"Yes. If we're going to be working together for the length
of time you're in Boston, I think we should be honest with
each other."

"Is this—" he waved a hand back and forth between them
"—going to be a problem?"

"I'm not sure what you're referring to by—" she mimicked
his gesture "—this."

Cocking his head, he studied her. "What happened to honesty?"

"I can assure you I'm perfectly capable of handling Greer
Motorcycles' account."

"I didn't imply you aren't. The question on the table is do
you *want to*."

Her full lips firmed for a moment before she nodded. "Yes. I wouldn't be sitting across from you if I didn't want to be here. Believe me, Mr. Holleran, this investment with Greer is as important to me as it is to you."

Well, that was telling. Not as important to BayStar Media, but to *her.*

"Okay, then," he conceded, although he was far from satisfied with her answer. "How about we start with you calling me Bran."

After a brief hesitation, she nodded. "Fine. And please call me Tatum."

She paused, leaning back as their waiter returned with their drinks. They took a couple of minutes to place their lunch orders, and then she returned her attention to him. The impact of that dark gaze struck him like a kick to the chest. He lifted his beer to his mouth, but the cold alcohol did little to alleviate the lick of heat curling and twisting low in his gut.

She's a good ten years younger than you, at least, he reminded himself. And she was no doubt still grieving her dead fiancé. From what Nore had mentioned, the two had been very much in love. Hell, even if Tatum wasn't his business liaison with BayStar, she still remained too young and in love with a ghost.

He didn't need those fucking complications.

"I've read Greer's biography and a little about Joaquin Iverson and yourself. Can you tell me more about the company and the new line of motorcycles you'd like us to invest in?" she asked, lifting her wineglass to her mouth.

Even Moses appearing before him and wielding a stone tablet of commandments couldn't have stopped Bran from watching those lips part around the glass rim. Never in his life had he wanted to trade places with a wine flute, but damn. Here he was.

Tightening his grip on the bottle in his hand, he sipped more of the alcohol and immediately wished for another beer. It might take a few to get through this meeting.

"As you probably know, we've been in business for ten years, almost eleven now. Joaquin, who was one of the top professional racers, had already been a customer of mine when he approached me about starting a high-end motor-cycle manufacturing company. I owned a smaller custom-build business at the time and stepping into this larger arena was definitely higher risk—especially since the majority of new companies don't see profits for years—but that's life," he said with a shrug. "And neither Joaquin nor I have ever played it safe, so I decided to join him. We have an excellent team around us and we managed to turn Greer into a multi-million-dollar business. We recently launched our first elec-tric model, and the sales have been outstanding so far. We've been beyond pleased with it and the customer response."

Her fingers drummed against the bowl of her glass, and it momentarily distracted him. It wasn't possible, but he swore he could feel the pulse of that touch on his chest, his abdo-men…and lower. He shifted in his seat, fighting the urge to reach across the table and cover her hand with his to stop the movement.

Or to tangle those slim, elegant fingers with his longer, thicker ones and savor the differences between them before lifting each fingertip to his mouth and acquainting it with his lips, his tongue.

Shit.

He'd asked her if it was going to be a problem working together.

He should've been posing that question to himself.

"Can I ask why Greer is rolling out two new motorcycle models back-to-back? I'm a layperson who freely admits she doesn't know anything about bikes, but is it fiscally sound to do this? Are you afraid of oversaturating your client base?"

"That's a good question." He folded his arms on the table and leaned forward. "And the answer is no, we're not, simply because the customer who will or has bought a custom build from us or purchased the KING One isn't the same client who will purchase this newer model." Her eyes brightened with interest, and the delight of discussing his passion warmed him. "Until now, every motorcycle we've manufactured has been a custom build, meaning the client contacts us, discusses what they specifically want in their bike and, after it's completed, we deliver it. Because we work so closely with our customers, we manufacture anywhere from two to three hundred bikes a year. But this newest model will be different. Not only will it be our first cost-friendly line, but it will also be mass-produced. This is a new direction for us but Joaquin and I both agree that between the quality of our product and the name recognition behind Greer Motorcycles, it will be a success."

"Hold that thought." Tatum turned to the chair next to her and picked up a tablet, then started tapping on the screen several times. "Have you considered an ad campaign surrounding the…" She frowned slightly. "What is the name of the new model?"

He held up a hand and shook it back and forth. "We've been going back and forth on a permanent one. The KING One was easy—we named it after Joaquin's father. But we've tossed around a couple. For now, we're leaning toward the Greer Rocket."

"No."

He blinked. Shock rippled through him. He stared at the top of her head as she tapped something else into her tablet. Hell, she hadn't even bothered to look up when she dismissed the name for *their* bike.

"Excuse me?" he asked.

"I said, no." She finally raised her head and met his gaze, and even though annoyance whipped through him, a part of him still found the wrinkling of her nose adorable.

Damn. He was in a professional meeting. He had to leave adjectives like *sexy*, *beautiful* and *adorable* at the fucking door.

"What do you mean 'no'?"

"No offense, and I'm sure all of you at Greer know your business, but that's a terrible name."

He stared at her. "When someone says 'but,' what they really mean is forget everything I said before 'but.' Now I'm about to tell you what I really think."

"I watch *Dr. Phil*, too," she drawled then tilted her head. "Of course, you're old enough to remember when he was on *Oprah*."

He snorted. "So you're not only insulting the professionals' choice of name for their product but you're taking potshots at my age. Nice." He tipped his chin toward her tablet. "Just tell me what problem you have with the name while I order you a glass of milk to go with lunch."

The corner of her mouth kicked up, and so did his temperature.

"I'm sure you have your reasons for the Rocket, but since we agreed on honesty between us, I hear that and think of a vibrator."

Holy shit.

Somehow, he managed not to choke on his tongue or fall out of his seat. But no way in hell could he prevent the barrage of erotic images from bombarding his head. Her, gorgeous brown skin dewy with sweat, long hair a dark tangle haloed around her head, eyes closed, body straining...

Kill. Me. Now.

He couldn't unsee that image. Especially with the word *vi-*

brator seeming to echo in the room as if it had been shouted in a wind tunnel.

"Excuse me?" he croaked.

She shrugged a slim shoulder, seemingly oblivious to the arousal she'd detonated like a bomb. "Sorry. Not sorry." She held up a hand as if stopping him from speaking. *As if I could speak.* "And I know what you're getting ready to say. A motorcycle is called a crotch rocket. But other than being really obvious and unimaginative, the name will draw more smirks than praises."

He tipped his beer bottle up, taking a long, *long* sip.

"Well then, what do you propose?" he finally asked.

"So glad you asked." Smiling, she flipped the tablet around and showed him an image of the prototype he'd sent over to her father and sister. "Tell me what you see when you look at this."

"A standard bike powered by a 399 cc, air-cooled, two-valved single-cylinder engine with a fuel injection that provides amazing response practicality. It's light and compact and is well suited to both beginner and experienced riders. It's also the perfect bike for a custom build. So a client can add customizations if they'd like."

She nodded. "Okay, my turn. Do you know what I see?" Flipping the tablet, she peered down at the screen. "A really kick-ass-looking bike. Ooh. And it's shiny and black. Looks fast. Vroom." He barely managed to swallow his bark of laughter as she glanced back at him, that eyebrow arched once more. "What name can we come up with that crosses the divide between all the cool details you just provided and my 'vroom'?"

"I'm guessing you have one?" He waved a hand, gesturing that the floor was hers.

"As a matter of fact, I do." She smiled, setting the tablet down on the table. "Greer Motorcycles presents The Gauntlet.

A gauntlet protects, shields and is essential to armor. That's the message you want to send your customer. It's a steady, reliable bike that will protect you on the road, an essential addition to your collection. But also, it's a challenge to all of the established motorcycle manufacturers that your new line is coming for their spot and their clientele."

Goddamn.

She was good.

"Well?" She dropped her hands to her lap, her shoulders straightening. No, bracing. Did she expect him to reject her suggestion? Did she doubt herself? "What do you think?"

"I think I should call Joaquin and let him know our model has a new name."

Her lips slowly curved upward into a wide smile, and the delight there gleamed in her dark eyes. Once more, all the air escaped his lungs, driven from them by shock. And desire.

God, that smile.

As if a hand pressed against his chest, he leaned back in his chair, pinned by the beauty and power of it. Was this really the first time he'd seen her smile?

Yes. The answer came, swift and certain. Because if he'd been on the receiving end of *that* before, he would've not only remembered, but would've been doing everything in his power to elicit its reappearance.

Clearing his throat, he reached for his beer again and then offered up a little prayer of thanks as the server entered the room with their food. Maybe if he stuffed his mouth with veal parmigiana, there'd be fewer chances of him uttering something stupid—and too revealing.

Like how her smile should either be outlawed or canonized because no one should wield a superpower like that.

Or how the joy lighting those brown-black eyes had him greedy to see what lust would do to them. Darken them until her gaze appeared almost obsidian? Or brighten them even more until they burned him with their heat?

Then… Then he remembered why she probably didn't smile as much. Why he'd glimpsed more hurt and barrenness in her gaze than joy.

When a person lost their partner to death—even under the worst of circumstances—it left wounds, scars. An emptiness that was impossible to fill. He should know; he'd had a front-row seat to that kind of mourning after his stepfather died. It'd been four years, and his mother still hadn't wholly recovered.

He needed to keep that at the forefront of his mind. Remember that he hadn't arrived in Boston to get involved in any kind of entanglement. Especially when it seemed like both of them carried so much baggage they rivaled a damn airport.

"I'm glad you like it." She picked up her fork and cut into her lasagna. "So my father mentioned other opportunities you're looking into while here. Do you need our assistance with any of them?"

For the next forty minutes, they ate and conversed about the deal to have their motorcycle featured in a movie filming in Boston the following week. It would be great promotion and a chance for millions of people to view their newest model before it even rolled out.

As they finished up their meals, their waiter returned to remove the empty plates and replace them with two big slices of cheesecake covered in strawberry sauce and fruit. Like with her meal, Tatum dug into the dessert with relish and appreciation. And her low hum of pleasure vibrated over his skin, beneath it. Damn, did anything this woman do not strike him as fucking hot?

"What happened to your sister?"

Her fork hovered above her food, her gaze lifting to his.

As if a door shut, those eyes that had been so bright with interest only seconds ago became shuttered, closing him out of her thoughts.

"I'm not sure what you mean," she said, that cool note returning to her voice.

"Until the call from your father, I was under the impression Mia would be handling the deal with BayStar. Is there a reason behind the abrupt change from her to you?"

She set the eating utensil beside her plate and straightened until it seemed her spine fused with the chair back.

"No reason other than Silas preferred I take over. If you have any questions, I'm sure he'll be willing to answer them for you. But I doubt he would've placed someone inept over this account when closing it would be extremely beneficial to both you and BayStar."

Her tone remained even, neutral. And not a curl of her lip, a flare of her nostril or a flicker of emotion in her eyes betrayed her. Yet something...

The subtle stiffness of her shoulders.

The slight hike of her chin.

Her hands, which had been on the table, were now under it, out of view.

Funny how he noticed those tiny details when before now, he'd only paid that close attention to motorcycles. They were more interesting and less bothersome than people.

But Tatum Haas was proving to be different from most "people."

"Are you this prickly with everyone or am I special?" he asked.

For a moment, she didn't reply. But then her eyes briefly closed and she turned her head to the side. When she finally returned her gaze to him, the inscrutable expression had disappeared and the faintest hint of a smile curved her mouth.

"I'm a little scared to admit that it might be with everyone." Shaking her head, she said, "I apologize. I do want to see this investment happen. I think there's something special here for both Greer and BayStar."

Bran nodded and debated whether or not to bring up the elephant in the room that they both seemed determined to waltz around.

What the hell. He mentally shrugged. He'd never been much of a dancer anyway.

"If any of this is due to Saturday night, we should have a conversation to clear the air."

"Yes, we got off on the wrong foot." Tatum picked up her fork again but didn't resume eating the dessert. "But that's in the past. It doesn't affect the here and now."

The hell it didn't. His encounter with the fiery, combative woman on the balcony had flipped a switch in his body, and he'd been inconveniently fascinated since then. And this aspect of her—the sharp, creative businesswoman—only deepened that absorption. Deepened the need winding its way through his veins straight to his cock.

No, he might not act on that grinding lust, but he couldn't deny its existence either.

He had control of his dick, though, not the other way around. And he would be damned if he allowed an attraction—he had to snort at that anemic description—to derail his purpose in being here and working with her.

"Good." Then because a disconnect obviously existed between his brain and mouth, he murmured, "Do you want to talk about why you're prickly?"

"No." Her answer, flat and definite, came immediately and carried a whole lot of *shut this shit down* behind it.

Yeah, he heard the message as clearly as a shout and would heed it. He caught something else, too. Her pain. Her anger.

He'd been through a rough and ugly divorce. And while the end of a marriage could be compared to a death—of a relationship, a certain lifestyle, a dream—it wasn't the same as an actual death. This woman bore the scars of losing not just her future and the man she'd loved but the man she'd believed him to be.

If working together on a deal that was crucial to his company's expansion wasn't enough reason not to become involved with Tatum Haas, then playing second fiddle to a memory—that was a battle where there could be no winners.

No, he'd stay here for the month needed to settle business for Greer. Then he'd leave for home, where he belonged.

Now if he could just get his cock to cooperate.

Which would be easier if he stopped staring at that beautiful temptation of a mouth. Or those soulful almost-black eyes. Or the sleek fall of her hair. Or the slim yet tight curves of her body.

Shit. He just needed to stop looking, period.

Tatum flattened her hands on either side of her dessert plate and studied them as if they held answers. Finally, she lifted her head and met his gaze, and a small fissure zigzagged through the resolutions he'd just cemented in his head. His grip tightened around his fork, but that measure of control didn't erase the desire to feel her soft skin beneath his fingers. To sweep his thumb over those cheekbones and somehow erase the shadows from her eyes.

Fuck.

Thoughts like that belonged to a younger man tasting his first sting of love. Not to him, an older divorced cynic with more miles and experience than a 1984 Harley Davidson Shovelhead.

"Mia mentioned you would be in Boston for the next few weeks, and we'll no doubt communicate often. But it would be best if we kept our interactions strictly professional. It's… simpler that way."

Though he'd already arrived at the same conclusion, irritation crept through him.

"That won't be a problem," he said. Forking up cheesecake and fruit, he steered the conversation back to the newly christened Gauntlet. Right where it belonged. "I'm supposed to be on the set of the movie next week…"

No. Not a problem at all.

Five

"There you are," Nore greeted Tatum from the laptop screen. Her best friend sat on her couch, legs curled under her, popcorn in her lap and glass of wine on the coffee table in front of her. In other words, ready for their monthly Movie Night. "I thought I was going to have to start calling your phone off the hook to hunt you down."

Tatum laughed, sinking to her own sofa. After breaking open a microwave bag of cheese popcorn, she dumped the snack into a bowl she'd brought into the living room. Picking up her own glass of wine, she toasted her friend. Though they were literally on opposite sides of the country, they had a standing "date" every second Thursday night of the month—Movie Night.

After Mark died, Nore had let Tatum miss a couple of their get-togethers. But she hadn't let Tatum get away with that for long. On the third month, Nore had flown to Boston, invaded Tatum's house and didn't leave for a week. Much like Tatum had done for Nore when her friend had been going through a rough time with Joaquin.

That's the kind of friendship they shared.

And it'd helped to ground Tatum, keep her sane during one of the darkest periods in her life.

"Now, you know I was going to be here. Can't have you jumping on another flight to see me. Hell, I might not get you out of my house next time." Tatum grinned and dumped a bag of M&M's into her popcorn.

"Please. You love when I come visit." Nore waved her hand and then leaned forward, squinting at her through the screen. "Daaamn, woman! A whole bag of M&M's? All right, this is obviously an emergency. Movie Night can wait a few minutes. What's wrong?"

"Why does something have to be wrong just because I'm indulging in a few snacks?"

Nore tilted her head, and her skepticism reached through the laptop. "In college, I came back to our dorm room to find you eating a bag of sour cream 'n' onion chips with mini Snickers thrown in. That's when you found out Lawrence Collins had been seen taking another girl to his room at a frat party not hours after declaring his undying devotion to you. Several years ago, you tore up a pint of strawberry ice cream with chocolate chip cookies and Twix mixed in. A coincidence that you'd discovered your ex Richard had kissed Mia at your family's annual July Fourth party? I think not. And then, what about—"

"Fine." Tatum scowled at her friend, holding up a hand to stop Exhibit C. "You might have a small point."

"Small?" Nore snorted. "I'll let you have that one. But just go ahead and spill. Who's the man—and why the hell didn't I know there even *was* a man?—and what did he do?" She jabbed a finger at Tatum. "And later we're really going to dive into how we, as women, need to stop being emotionally out of control over another person and letting it manifest in binge eating. That shit is old. If you want to eat your weight in snacks because that's just what you feel like doing or because it's fucking Monday, great! Awesome! Do you and I'll probably join in. But allowing someone else that control? Nope. We're done with that, sis." She inhaled and blew it out. "Okay, that's me getting down off my soapbox. Now. Dish. And no judgment because that's not what we do either."

The need to object rose inside her. But she couldn't lash out at her friend or even tell her to mind her own business. Because Nore was right; Tatum couldn't deny it. And it took a true friend to tell her the truth and hold up a mirror so she could be the best possible her.

Didn't mean she wasn't going to eat this bowl of popcorn, though.

"The reason I didn't mention a man is because there isn't a man—at least not how you're meaning." At Nore's squint, Tatum huffed out a breath. "Bran Holleran is here in Boston," she said by way of explanation.

"Yes." Nore drew the word out. "I thought I mentioned he would be out there for a few weeks? Joaquin told me they approached your company for an investment opportunity and Bran is out there to finalize that, among other things, for their new motorcycle." She shook her head. "But what does that have to do with—*oh*. You and Bran?" she asked, leaning forward. "How? What? When? Was it *good*?"

A bark of laughter escaped Tatum and she leaned back from the barrage of questions, holding her palms up. "Wait a minute, wait a minute." She chuckled again. "First, there isn't a me and Bran. We met last weekend at a fundraiser and let's just say that was…memorable."

"How memorable? 'Fond memory that gives you fuzzies' memorable? Or 'Hey, future kids, your mom had a hot dirty past and she regrets nothing' memorable?"

"Nore. Seriously."

"What?" She shrugged, lifting a hand of popcorn to her

mouth. "I love Joaquin with all my heart but that doesn't mean I'm blind. The man is sexy as hell with that salt-and-pepper hair and beard, striking blue eyes and big body. He's *Roadhouse* Sam Elliott meets *Sons of Anarchy* Charlie Hunnam. Tell me I'm wrong."

Nope, she wasn't wrong. And as an image of Bran at the restaurant table—that tall frame sprawled in his chair like a king on a throne—flitted across her mind, her body co-signed the sentiment. Bran Holleran wasn't just sexy—he exuded sex. With each syllable drenched in that deep rough-and-tumble voice with its hint of the South. With each shift of those wide shoulders and each stride of his long, powerful legs. With every movement of his wide, carnal mouth.

With every too-incisive, too-knowing stare of those beautiful, bright blue eyes.

"Yes, he's a good-looking man," Tatum conceded with a straight face. "But mostly he just gives me the urge to take off my shoe and break a heel going upside his head with it. And you know how much I love my Manolo Blahnik stilettoes. The truth is our meeting was more along the lines of *Ten Things I Hate About You*."

"You do realize those two end up together in the end, right?"

"Nore." Tatum groaned then laughed. "We are not Heath Ledger and Julia Stiles. More like Tom and Jerry," she muttered. "But anyway, we totally rubbed each other the wrong way. Only after, do I discover he's here in Boston because of BayStar. That's not the end of it, though. Dad removed Mia from the account and assigned me to it. So now I'm working directly with Bran and it's…" She frowned, her mouth twisting.

"Uncomfortable?" Nore supplied.

"Yes." She huffed out the answer. "And that might be a bit of an understatement."

"Why? Because you two exchanged some sharp words?"

"Yes. No." Tatum frowned. "I don't know."

Nore didn't immediately reply, but Tatum could practically feel her regard through the laptop screen.

"What?" Tatum pressed her friend. "You're usually not one to be at a loss for words or hold back. Just say what's on your mind."

Nore blew out a breath. "Okay, here's the thing. I'm usually not a proponent of you being uncomfortable, but right now? I'm thankful for it. Other than work, you haven't shown much interest in anything—or anyone. And if Bran is making you feel, *period*, then I'm all for it. I don't care if it's anger, irritation or homicidal tendencies. Wait." She scrunched up her nose. "Maybe I do care about the last one. I couldn't come visit you in jail. It's such a depressing place."

"Nice to know your concern has its limits," Tatum drawled. "And I love you, but I'm not remotely interested in getting involved with Bran or any other man. I don't think I need to explain why."

"It's been almost a year, Tate," Nore murmured. "And I'm not saying there's a time limit to grief. But I also hate to see you a prisoner to the pain and anger of Mark's death. He's still controlling you from the grave."

Silence echoed between them, and Nore's words ricocheted off the walls of Tatum's skull. Like an accusation. Or a revelation.

Again, she yearned to deny her friend's words. But she couldn't. There were some days she felt *consumed* with powerlessness and resentment. Overwhelmed by it. Especially when others wouldn't let her forget that she would always be Mark Walker's Jilted Fiancée. Or Mark Walker's Almost But Not Quite Widow.

Closing her eyes, she pinched the bridge of her nose. "I think…" she whispered then trailed off.

"You think what? You know you can talk to me about anything and it stays here, Tate," Nore reminded her.

Opening her eyes, Tatum sighed but instead of meeting her friend's gaze, she stared at her untouched glass of wine. "I think," she softly began again, "if I just knew everything. If there weren't any more secrets. He lied and left me in the dark the entire time we were together. And now that he's gone, I still don't have the truth. I continue to play the fool because, in a way, he's still lying to me. If I knew..." she repeated, then shook her head.

"What will it change, Tate?"

"For once, I'll feel like I have control over my life. I won't sit here every day with my stomach in knots waiting for the other shoe to drop and blow my life to pieces again. If I know everything—Why did he treat me like this? How long was it going on? Who was the other woman?—then I won't continue to feel like a blind idiot who chose a man who didn't choose her back."

"Babe." Nore sighed and set her bowl of popcorn next to her. "You need to acknowledge that you might never discover the answers to those questions. And then you're going to have to find a way to be okay with that. Mark being unfaithful wasn't a reflection on you. It speaks more about his lack of character than yours. Yes, I hate to speak ill of the dead, but I won't lie either. You are and never have been a fool. And anyone who says differently? Fuck 'em."

Laughter bubbled up inside Tatum, momentarily lightening the weight on her chest. "I hear what you're saying, Nore. I honestly do, and I'll try. But contrary to popular opinion, getting under a new man isn't always the answer to getting over the old one."

"So don't get under him—yet." Nore grinned. "All I'm saying is if you're so busy focusing on the past and holding on to it, you'll never be free for whatever or whoever comes into your life." Nore tilted her head. "You still have the brooch, right?"

Tatum tried not to roll her eyes…and failed.

"Oh God, Nore, please don't start that." She shook her head, picking up her glass of wine. "Yes, I have the brooch, and I'm holding on to it because my best friend bought it for me as a gift. But my well for believing in fairy tales has run completely dry."

Nore squinted at her. "Oh so when I had it, you believed in the legend. But now you don't?"

"The night you gave it to me, my fiancé died and I discovered he'd been a manwhore our entire relationship. So no, I don't believe in it."

"Have you ever stopped to consider that maybe—just maybe—Mark wasn't the true love you were meant to have? That your real soulmate is still out there?"

No, she hadn't considered that. And though the story attached to the brooch was romantic, she'd meant what she told Nore. Legends, fairy tales… They belonged to other women, not her. More importantly, she wanted no part of them. It'd been the stars in her eyes that hadn't allowed her to see the lies right in front of her.

No. She'd never put herself in the position to fall for another man's lies again.

Mark had taught her a valuable lesson.

Never give everything to someone else and risk having nothing left but shattered pieces of herself. She couldn't afford to repeat her mistakes. Next time she might not have anything left to pick up. And she refused to be that weak woman again.

"How about I make a deal with you?" Tatum held up her glass toward the screen. "If my soulmate comes along, you'll be the first to know."

Nore held up her own glass. "I'm going to hold you to that.

Then I can intervene before you provide him with a dissertation on why soulmates don't exist."

Laughing, Tatum lifted her wine to her mouth for a deep sip. "I wouldn't give him a dissertation. Now, maybe a three-page, single-spaced essay…"

Snorting, Nore set down her glass and grabbed her bowl of popcorn, moving it back to her lap. "Let's get this movie going. But be warned." Nore jabbed a finger at her. "I'm not done with you."

"You wouldn't be my best friend if you were."

Six

Bran stood outside the metal fence with black netting. He scanned the crowds that had gathered in the area, but didn't spy a specific lovely face. Glancing down at the watch on his wrist, he noted the time. Still about ten minutes before the time he'd given Tatum. And she could've hit traffic on her way out to Weymouth from Boston. No doubt it was even thicker as she approached The Hangout, the huge former fighter jet hangar behind him that had been transformed into a soundstage for the blockbuster movie that had just started filming.

An electric charge seemed to fill the air, emanating from the people hoping to catch a glimpse of one of the stars or some of the action behind the fence. Hell, he couldn't blame them. He didn't get starstruck easily, and yet excitement hummed through him at being a part of this Hollywood magic, even if peripherally.

Just as he started to glance at his watch again, he caught movement out of the corner of his eye. And the buzz in his veins jacked higher. Shit. That didn't bode well. But he didn't glance away from the slender woman striding up the street with a confidence that had his gut knotting with arousal. His heart drummed out a sonorous rhythm, one that echoed in his cock. Heat surged over his skin, and the soft breeze of late September did nothing to cool him. Because this particular warmth wasn't due to the outside temperature.

Damn.

It'd been a little over a week since he'd last seen Tatum and his body reacted as if it'd been years. No. Didn't bode well at all.

Stuffing his hands in the pockets of the black hoodie he wore under a dark blue blazer, he walked forward, meeting her halfway. It was either that or continue ogling her like a creep.

She's eleven years younger than you. When she was a junior in high school, you were getting married.

He silently repeated the reminder like a mantra. A warning. His ex-wife had been five years younger than him, and the longer they'd been married, the more that age gap had widened.

"Tatum," he greeted, sweeping a glance down and taking in her dark red wide-legged jumpsuit that accentuated the sleek lines and sensuous curves of her lithe frame. "Good to see you again."

"You, too."

She stretched out her hand toward him and his stomach tightened. Damn. He'd been trying to avoid touching her for a sense of self-preservation. Reluctantly, he clasped her hand in his, and the press of her smaller, softer palm to his larger, rougher one... Yeah, it shouldn't have been sexual. But it was. He couldn't help looking down at their hands and imagining how it would be with their bodies aligned together, his larger frame wrapped around her more slender one. The need to cover her, surround her...protect her clawed at him.

As soon as possible, he dropped her hand and returned his to his hoodie.

"I'm sorry about running late. Finding parking around here was terrible. I didn't count on that," she said. "I noticed all the crew parking signs and didn't want to risk getting towed."

"No problem. You're good." He turned and fell into step beside her as they headed back toward the entry point. "I appreciate you taking the time out of your day."

She shrugged. "It's only a half-hour drive. And besides—" she tilted her head toward him, smiled "—it's not every day I get invited to an actual movie set."

"True." He arched an eyebrow. "And of course, you get to see your investment for the first time," he added, tone dry.

"Oh of course. There's that." The corner of her mouth quirked. "Speaking of our investment... Have you spoken with Joaquin about changing the name of the motorcycle?"

"Yes, I did as soon as we finished up our lunch." He couldn't contain his smile as he thought back on the video call with his partner and friend. "His exact words were, 'Well, damn. Can we hire her?'" As Tatum laughed, he forced his gaze not to linger on her pretty mouth. "I guess you can say he was for it. Our new model is officially called The Gauntlet. The changes in marketing and design are being implemented right now."

She didn't reply but her soft smile might as well as have shouted her delight and pride. Inside the pocket of his hoodie, he balled his fist, his nails pricking his palm. Nice try, but the tiny bite of pain didn't erase his need to trace that full bottom lip.

Damn, he wanted to feast on that smile.

Minutes later, they entered the gate with their passes, and Bran led her across the lot toward the former hangar. Trucks and steel construction containers occupied the perimeter of the property. Crew and staff strode to and from the building, and the set appeared to be its own small town.

Breaking his own rule about touching her, Bran set a hand to the small of her back, and he ground his teeth at the blast of heat that punched him in the chest and slid its way through his body.

"We have permission to visit the set today but I wanted to take you over to the trailer first and let you see The Gauntlet up close," he explained, guiding her toward one of the trucks.

"I would love to," she said. "I don't think the notes I read included how your new model ended up being included in an upcoming film. Other than the obvious promotional reasons, it must be exciting for you to see your product on the big screen."

"Yeah, it is. And after twenty years in this business, I didn't think I'd be able to experience another first."

"You're lucky," she murmured. "I experience new firsts all the time."

He glanced down at her, but she didn't look up at him or elaborate on that enigmatic statement. A part of him wanted to stop right in the middle of the lot, turn her toward him and demand an explanation. Tell him about the subdued note in her voice.

Give him names, times and locations so he could handle every person who dared cause the thread of pain in those words.

But he'd stopped going around beating up people on behalf of others in grade school. No, wait. High school. In his defense, though, when Michael Wheeler decided to put his hand on Bran's sister's ass, the football player had pretty much asked to have his own ass delivered to him.

Mentally shaking his head, Bran refocused on their conversation.

"This way." He jerked his chin toward a trailer on the right side of the lot. "You asked how we managed to get our motorcycle in the movie. It's a case of who I know. Which for me happens to be someone with the casting company. They were looking for certain cars to rent and they also needed a motorcycle for a chase scene. She'd been a longtime client of mine, and I'd built several motorcycles for her. So when she called and asked about one for the film, it was the perfect opportunity."

"Longtime client?" she asked. "Is she from the South, too?"

He slid her a glance. "If you're going fishing, at least let me give you a rod."

"Fine." She held up her hands. "Busted. But can I point out that a gentleman would've just answered the question instead of calling me nosy?"

"Well, there's your answer. I never claimed to be a gentleman." He smirked at her low snort. "And no, as far as I know, Tracy is LA born and bred. And I'm from Georgia. Although I haven't lived there for at least a decade. My mother's still there, though."

"Really? Your mother?" she echoed, surprise ringing in her voice.

"Yes, I do have one of those," he drawled. "Contrary to the bio on Greer's website, I didn't spring from a god's skull. That's just a press release."

"A good one, too, although I thought the picture of you in full armor was a bit much."

"Shit. I told marketing that might be a little over-the-top." Their gazes met. And they grinned.

But in the next instant, the air between them grew charged, electric, and their wide smiles ebbed then disappeared.

"You should do that more often," he murmured.

"You do realize how condescending it sounds for you to tell me I should smile more, right?" she asked just as softly.

They'd come to a halt in the middle of the lot, and for him, they could've been the only two there. That's how focused, no, *consumed* he was by this woman.

"I heard it as soon as I said it, and I apologize. It does sound incredibly patronizing." He paused. "Still, I'll say I hate why you've probably lost that smile."

She didn't reply, but her mouth firmed. Surprise and another more enigmatic emotion flickered in her eyes before she glanced way from him. *Dammit.* Why had he mentioned the death of her fiancé, even peripherally? To insert distance between them? To remind himself *why* he needed to insert that distance? Both?

As he dragged a hand over his head, his fingers bumped the bun on top of his head. There could've been a less clumsy way of him doing that without causing her pain. *Asshole*, he hissed at himself.

"There's the trailer," he said, dipping his head toward the truck containing Greer's new model. "I let them know we're on our way."

Fifteen minutes later, he wheeled the motorcycle down the ramp then popped the kickstand, halting it in front of Tatum.

"This is it," he announced proudly. Maybe even a little reverently. "The Gauntlet."

"It's beautiful. Can I?" Tatum's hand hovered over the handlebar.

"Of course."

With a nod, she stroked a palm over the chrome panel and the seat. He felt that touch over his skin, his chest, his ribs, his hip. Struggling not to shift and fidget under the oddly sensual action, he switched his attention back to the motorcycle, taking his time to catalog and scrutinize every detail, ensuring nothing was amiss.

"It's bigger than I imagined," she said with a low huff of laughter. "More... I don't know, sexy, if that's a thing."

Yeah, it was.

"I can't speak for all riders, but for me it can be sexual having all that power between your legs and being in control of it. There's the absolute freedom of it, too. Nothing but you and the elements. The wind pressing against your skin and roaring in your ears like a lover. Yeah, it can be sexy as hell."

Her lips parted, and her tongue peeked out to slide over her the bottom curve. What would she do if he reached across this bike, cupped the back of her neck and captured that mouth with his own? Traded her moan for his? Part of him was willing to say *fuck it* to every reason why he shouldn't.

"So." She cleared her throat, grazing her fingers over the seat again. "In the file, the model is black. But this is red. I remember you telling me they would all be mass-produced the same."

"They will be. But one great feature is they're the perfect basis for custom builds. Like this one. Take a look." He pointed out elements on the bike. "The Gauntlet has good bones, and specifically for the movie, we added lower super-bike-style bend handlebars as well as a tuck-and-roll seat and trunk. We then streamlined the rear fender a bit and have the red paint on the panels. It has amazing torque and power. I test-drove it myself, and it's an incredibly smooth ride." He swept a hand over the immaculate chrome.

"You really love what you do, don't you?" Tatum asked, and he didn't need to look at her to catch her smile; he heard it in her voice. Although, hell, he really liked looking at her.

And the sight of her lips curved in pleasure was just so damn pretty.

Still… He fought not to fidget under the warmth in her eyes.

"I know you're now the president of your own company but looking at you with the motorcycle, hearing you talk about each and every detail…" She shook her head. "No one could miss your joy, your passion for it. You really love the art that goes into building and designing a bike."

"I do. Each one is its own challenge and accomplishment."

She studied him, and this time he surrendered to the need to avoid her inspection. God, a woman over a decade his junior had him ducking his head like a boy half his age. Who was he again?

"I read that you used to own your own custom-build business. You probably don't have as much time to be hands-on with Greer as you did then," she said.

"Most of my time is spent in the office rather than the garage or warehouse. But I still approve every design because you're right. It's a matter of pride."

"But you miss it."

"I miss it," he softly admitted. "Owning a small business is different than running a larger company. Less…intimate, although I can name almost all of our employees and consider several of them close friends. But yeah, I do miss getting my hands dirty. If I didn't have my own collection of bikes, I'd probably go a little crazy." He jerked his chin toward her. "And you?"

She tried to control her flinch. The movement was almost imperceptible, but Bran noted it.

"And me what?"

"You brought up passion and joy. What's yours? Working for your family's company? I've heard you're good at it."

A sardonic caricature of a smile twisted her lips, and he instantly detested it. That didn't fit, didn't belong on her.

"Really? Who told you that? Nore?"

"No." He crossed his arms over his chest. "Your father, actually, as well as several of your coworkers and employees. They admire and respect you. Why would you think they don't?"

"Did I say that?" she asked, voice tight.

"Yes, Tatum, you did."

A tense quiet descended between them, taut and so fucking loud with her denial, her pain, her...*screams*. They rang in his ears.

"Just say it," she whispered. "Ask me."

"Tell me," he whispered back. "I don't want to hear it unless you willingly tell me."

"Maybe..." Her lips flattened and her jaw clenched. After a moment, she continued, her voice a shade lower. "I'm already this figure either to be pitied or condemned. A cautionary tale or a salacious piece of gossip. Maybe I don't want to be either with you. Maybe I just want to be who I was before my life imploded."

She's not yours to comfort.

His mind understood that, but his body ached to do differently. His hands tingled with the need to cup the back of her neck and slide into her hair. His chest itched to have her pressed against it. His thighs tensed, ready to brace her negligible weight against him, embrace her strength and absorb it into his own.

He gave his head one short, hard shake then lowered his arms to his sides.

"And who were you before?" he asked.

She blinked, as if surprised by the question. For a long moment, she met his gaze then dropped it to the motorcycle, tracing a finger along the curved handlebar. What did it say about him that the stroke shivered down his rib cage?

It said he was in deeper shit than he cared to acknowledge.

"I was a successful businesswoman who didn't doubt her purpose. A professional who inspired confidence because I was confident. A woman who knew she was loved and desired and cherished the security of it. A woman who had the world at her fingertips."

She inhaled a breath, lifting her head. And it was a good

thing he didn't know where her ex-fiancé was buried because he might go dig him up, kill him, then drive him six feet deep again. For causing that pain in her almost-black eyes, the bastard deserved it.

Loosing a short, jagged laugh, she pushed her long hair over her shoulder, then straightened those same shoulders. As if she were shrugging on emotional armor, her reserve seemed to settle piece by piece. The hike of her chin, the subtle shifting of her body away from the motorcycle and him, the smoothing of her expression.

And he resented every slight alteration that enclosed her behind that impenetrable wall of ice.

"Betrayal by someone who is supposed to love you doesn't strip away the core of you," he quietly said. "Does it beat you down until you're fucking screaming for mercy? Does it make you question every decision you've ever made and have you wondering if you can trust yourself, much less anyone else? Hell yes. But change who you are at the very core of your being? No. We don't come out the same—but shit, when people are in accidents, they don't either. They're scarred, in pain and need to go through rehab to relearn everything they once did so easily. It's the same thing when someone violates your faith in them and puts your whole worldview on its ass. But underneath all the bullshit, you're still you. Scars and all."

"You said 'we,'" she murmured.

He frowned. "What?"

"You said, 'We don't come out the same.' Like you personally know what it is to be changed by betrayal."

Her mask slipped—just enough for him to catch. And if he hadn't, he might not have answered her question. But if tearing back the curtain on his own past would punch a bigger chink in that steely armor... Yeah, he'd do it.

"I've been married. And divorced." He dipped his chin.

"You don't go through that and not come out on the other side without some bruises."

She stared at him, and he glimpsed the curiosity in her eyes.

"Just say it," he said, returning her words from moments earlier. "Ask me."

Her lips parted, and though he didn't enjoy delving into the bloody wreckage that had been his marriage, his gut tightened as he prepared to do just that. For her.

"I—" She frowned and, bowing her head, removed her phone from the pocket of her jumpsuit. "Sorry, I need to take this." She tapped the screen and then held the cell to her ear. "Hey, Dad." Tilting her head, she slightly turned away from Bran. "Yes. I'm in Weymouth with Bran Holleran. We're visiting the movie set." She pinched the bridge of her nose as she listened to whatever Silas Haas said on the other end of the line. "This can't wait?" she asked, and it sounded like the question came through gritted teeth. "Dad, I'm not—" A pause. "Fine. I'll be there in an hour or two." Pause. "No, it cannot be sooner since I have to drive back to Boston... See you soon."

Bran cocked his head. "Change of plans?"

Annoyance and something else—something murkier and complicated—flashed across her face.

"Yes." She shook her head. "I'm sorry, Bran. An...emergency has come up and I need to return to Boston." Glancing down, she once more touched the seat of the motorcycle then dropped her arm. "Thank you for introducing me to The Gauntlet. I think Greer has a great product and I'm even more excited about this project."

"I'm glad." He studied her, taking in the taut line of her jaw. "Everything okay?"

She smiled, and he had to swallow his growl at the phoniness of it. Again, he strong-armed down the urge to take that pretty mouth. This time to erase the blasphemy curving it.

"Yes, just something I have to see to. But—" she waved a hand over the motorcycle "—do you think it would be too much trouble to take stills of this model? I'd love to include them in my presentation to the board of a customized version of The Gauntlet. Show its versatility."

"I can arrange that."

"Great." Nodding, she said, "I really do apologize for leaving so suddenly. It's rude at best and unprofessional at worst. If…"

She trailed off, and his chest burned with anger at whatever in that phone conversation caused the strain that damn near vibrated from her.

"You don't owe me an explanation, Tatum."

Her lips twisted, and how sad that this hard, self-deprecating curl seemed more honest than the smile she'd just given him.

"Yes, I do, but thank you for not requiring one." With a soft sigh, she circled the motorcycle and strode off in the direction of the gate.

For several long moments, Bran stared after her, watching her elegant figure walk farther and farther away. He hadn't been privy to that phone conversation, didn't know exactly what had been said to cause the sudden switch in demeanor from wary but open to closed off and defensive. Didn't matter to him.

What did matter was he had to grab a hold of the handlebar, grasp a physical reminder of why he'd traveled to Boston. Business. An investment. Company growth.

Not to protect a beautiful but lonely woman from whatever harm she was heading toward.

No. He wrapped his hands around both handlebars and released the kickstand.

His business might be *with* Tatum Haas, but she *wasn't* his business. He'd leave the superhero shit to the directors of the film.

Besides, in the end, who would save *him* from *her*?

Seven

Hell had been depicted as a lake of fire.

Or a land of flames and brimstone.

Even a bottomless obsidian pit.

For Tatum, hell was a dinner party.

A dinner party with polite, well-mannered guests, laughter as tinkling and bright as the cutlery, and free-flowing wine that led to freer-flowing tongues.

Regina Haas didn't need a reason to host a get-together. *Oh Meghan Markle and Prince Harry are being fabulous again over on IG? Dinner party to celebrate!*

Tatum smothered a sigh, peering down into her half-empty glass of wine. Apparently, a side effect of Merlot was bitchiness. Huh. That probably wasn't included on the label.

She loved her mother; God knew she loved her mother. But they'd never been as close as mother and daughter should be. Regina was all beautification committees, fundraiser boards and country clubs. And Tatum was a Netflix-and-chill workaholic. She swore the proudest she'd made her mother was when she'd become engaged to Mark. And now that Tatum was a not-quite-jilted-but-definitely-disgraced almost bride, they'd returned to that limbo of being related but having no idea what to say to each other.

Which explained Tatum's presence at yet another torturous dinner party where, by not-so-happy coincidence, she would end up sitting next to an eligible bachelor. That she stayed and didn't complain was the bone she threw to Regina for being the stain on their family reputation and the punishment she inflicted on herself for... Hell, she could take her pick.

"I don't know what that wine's said to offend you, but I think I'll pass."

An electric current charged through her, and she stiffened under the shock of lust. Dammit. Without her permission, her lashes lowered, and she inhaled the intoxicating scent of chocolate, oak and sex. Pure, raw, wild sex.

Only one man possessed that scent.

And even though it'd been three days since she'd last savored that particular aroma—three days since she'd left him to be dragged back into her past—it had the power to set her ablaze.

Damn, she should be running in the opposite direction. But like any prey trapped in the sight of a powerful, sleek beast, it was much too late for that. Besides, if she were honest, she wasn't entirely sure she wanted to flee.

But she was entirely certain she desired to be caught.

More wine.

Lifting the glass, she slowly turned around and met Bran's bright blue eyes. And pretended her breath didn't snag in her throat.

"Hello, Bran."

"Tatum." His gaze dropped to her glass. "I usually count on the alcohol to get me through shit like this, but it doesn't seem to be helping you. So maybe I'll pass up the wine and request the hard liquor."

"Smart move. Especially since Mom invited Colleen Howell. Sweet lady but she's at the bottom of her second martini. By the time dessert is served, she'll have offended every marginalized community and explained exactly how this world is going to hell in a handbasket. Spoiler alert. If it were up to her, we'd all be extras in *The Handmaid's Tale*."

He blinked then cocked his head. "Where I'm from, we don't usually combine 'sweet lady' and 'racist' in the same sentence. And we for damn sure don't invite them to sit down and break bread."

She snorted. "Well, welcome to my world, where the only thing more rude than being a racist is confronting one and making them feel uncomfortable about their bigotry."

A frown creased his brow and once more he glanced down at her glass. "Exactly how many of those have you had?"

She heaved a sigh and took another sip. "Not enough." When his frown deepened, she admitted, "Two. And counting."

A corner of his mouth kicked up and the heat swarming through her veins added to the effects of the alcohol. She almost braced herself against his wide chest, but at the last moment, she caught herself and tightened her grip on the glass stem.

Maybe drinking around this man wasn't the wisest decision. His singular potency reduced her to a lightweight.

"Well, it looks like I need to catch up. Especially if you're going to be dropping truths all evening, I'm going to need it." He lowered his head, so she had an up close and personal view of the black striations in his blue eyes. His minty breath ghosted over her cheek, and holy... Please, God, let that moan have echoed in her head instead of aloud. "For the first time I'm looking forward to this evening."

He straightened and gestured toward the circling waiter,

and even the flick of his fingers had her gulping down the remaining wine in her glass.

What was it about him that had her so…fascinated?

The thick, long dark hair he'd bound in a tie at the back of his head? The coarse yet neat beard sprinkled with strands of gray? The sensual dichotomy of bold, craggy facial features and a plush mouth? The big, wiry body that radiated strength and power? She was no stranger to good-looking men. Men with flawless beauty that seemed almost otherworldly. But that didn't pertain to Bran Holleran.

Even in a perfectly tailored navy blue suit that fit his frame as if he'd been stitched into it, he exuded a carnal, corporeal *roughness* that spoke of virility, sexuality, dominance.

In other words, Bran Holleran was so damn *touchable*.

"I've been thinking about you the last few days," he said after requesting a whiskey from the server. "Is everything okay? You mentioned an emergency when you left."

She swallowed, battling back the wave of nausea that crashed into her. She set her empty glass down on an end table, the fruity Merlot suddenly too much.

Emergency. Anger roiled inside her chest, spreading like destructive flames. A scream tickled the back of her throat, but as she did with all her emotions when it came to Mark, his lies, his death, his parents, she swallowed it down. The "family emergency" had turned out to be Mark's mother finally cleaning out his apartment and calling her parents to send Tatum over as emotional support. She had slowed down communicating with Dara and Leo months ago. It might have been selfish. It might have made her cold and unfeeling in their eyes. But for Tatum's own sanity she had distanced herself. And after the other day, she should've stuck to her resolution. But she'd caved to the pressure.

And now she paid for it.

"Fine." She tipped her head back to meet his gaze. "Everything's fine."

"Liar."

Shock tripped through her at his blunt accusation. Shock and an electric charge of pure lust.

What the hell?

"Excuse me?" she rasped.

No man—not even Mark—had ever been so direct and bold with her. Whether out of manners, the weight of her last name or the money that backed that name, the men of her acquaintance had always been unfailingly polite...at least to her face.

Maybe they just didn't care enough to be so flatly honest.

Mark hadn't.

God knows she would've rather had his honesty than his perfect manners any day.

As the reverberation of that truth shook her, Bran cocked his head. "Are you lying as a way of telling me to mind my business? Or has 'fine' become a habit?" Eyes narrowed, he shook his head. "I can't tell which one."

"Stop it." She hated that it emerged as a plea.

Almost hated *him* for it.

But if she'd learned anything about Bran in the last couple of weeks, it was that his hard exterior reflected a laser focus that could be intimidating or exciting when pinned on her. At this moment, those bright blue eyes elicited a desperation inside her.

Desperation for him to cease this emotional full court press.

Desperation for him to continue pressuring her, to make her answer. To make her lance a wound that threatened to poison her.

A wound that everyone else in her life pretended not to see.

"Okay, Tatum. I'll back off." Just as relief and disappointment flooded through her in equal measure, he murmured, "For now."

"Bran, I'm so glad you could make it." Mia approached them, and with a smile that could only be described as sultry, she set a hand on Bran's muscular upper arm. A bristling tension invaded Tatum, and damn, that wasn't good. Not good at all. "It's wonderful to see you again."

"Hello, Mia," he greeted, turning and at the same time dislodging her hand from him.

Whether the move had been intentional or not, a fierce satisfaction whistled through her. That and another razor-sharp slice of relief. She could try to deceive herself but the sour slide of jealousy through her belly wouldn't allow it.

She detested seeing her sister intimately touch Bran.

The stark, terrifying realization had Tatum edging away from him mentally and physically. From them both.

Or she tried to.

The big hand at the middle of her spine prevented her from moving.

Mia's gaze dropped to where he was touching her, and her mouth tightened at the corners. Her sister cut a glance at Tatum, speculation gleaming. A denial rose to Tatum's tongue, but she swallowed it down. What was the saying about a guilty man running when no one pursued him? Besides, it would be a lie.

There was nothing professional about the arousal pulsing inside her like a beacon.

"We haven't seen that much of each other since you've been in Boston," Mia said, returning her attention to Bran. "How're you liking our city so far?"

"It's beautiful. I'm still working remotely from my hotel room, but outside of that, I've done a little exploring. I even took one of the guided tours. There's a lot of history here."

"Guided tours?" Mia chuckled, and Tatum stiffened, recognizing the edge to it.

Her sister, with her beauty and charismatic personality, dominated attention and a room. But the flip side of that meant she could sometimes be a mean girl when she felt challenged. Tatum had been sliced by that acerbic wit more than a few times. And as Mia slid an amused look in Tatum's direction, she prepared herself to be on the receiving end of her sister's sharp tongue once again.

"Tatum, really?" Mia shook her head, giving Bran a rueful smile. "You have to forgive my sister. It's been a while for her, so she's probably forgotten things like hospitality and client care. But no worries. I'll have a packet of sights, events and entertainment sent to your hotel. We can also arrange for an employee from BayStar to accompany you, if you wish." She shrugged a bare shoulder. "And of course, you still have my number. If you'd prefer to have someone familiar tag along rather than a stranger, don't hesitate to call. I'd love to introduce our city to you."

Tatum stared at her sister, disbelief and more than a little hurt seizing her in an ironclad grip. She could barely move—hell, *breathe*.

You have to forgive my sister. It's been a while for her...

Mia's words reverberated in Tatum's head, growing louder with each ricochet off her skull, drowning out the hum of chatter in the room. With Tatum being older by just two years, there'd always existed some sibling rivalry between them. Not on Tatum's part, but from the time they were young Mia had believed they were in some kind of competition.

If Tatum made the honor roll, Mia had to hit the dean's list.

If Tatum joined the cheerleading team, Mia had to be captain.

If Tatum earned the position of senior vice president at

BayStar, Mia had to aim for the same but in a shorter amount of time.

Still, Mia had never undermined Tatum in front of others. Had never deliberately hurt her.

Had definitely never thrown her under the bus. What the hell? Why would she…?

Oh you know why.

She only had to take one look at her sister's face, at her body language. At the soft smile that carried a hint of invitation, the gleam of admiration in her brown eyes. At how she canted her petite, slim frame toward Bran.

Mia wanted Bran. At the very least, she was attracted to him.

Oh God.

Tatum's stomach bottomed out. Dread and another darker, far more complicated emotion rushed in to fill the void. She deliberately flattened her hand against her outer thigh, determined not to press her palm against that strange, awful ache in her belly.

Part of her grappled with the need to shift away from Bran. He was her client, dammit. *Her client.* Didn't matter that just one look at his bold, almost harsh features and soft, wide mouth detonated an explosion of heat across her nerves.

Didn't matter that when he gazed at her with those electric blue eyes, she glimpsed something Mark and the circumstances of his death had stolen from her.

Desire. Hope.

Or maybe she was just projecting.

The fact that she wanted to hold on to that desire, clutch that hope as if it were an endangered species, blared a visceral warning to avoid him—that gaze, his touch, his fucking scent—at all costs.

Yet… She didn't move. Didn't shift away when the smart, wise thing would have been to put the length of the room between them. Because something more desperate than her fear resided deep inside her, restless, insistent. Ravenous.

"Thank you for the offer," Bran said with a nod. "But I actually enjoy exploring a city on my own."

Disappointment flickered in Mia's eyes, but she still maintained her smile, though Tatum noted the slight strain around it.

"Well, know the offer stands." Mia switched her attention to Tatum. "The Walkers have arrived. Mom wanted to make sure you spoke to them."

It was Tatum's turn to force a smile. "Great. I'll go find them in a few minutes." Or not.

Annoyance vibrated through her. Her mother hadn't thought of giving her a heads-up that Dara and Leo would be attending tonight? Of course she hadn't. Just like her mother had pressured her father into calling Tatum about helping Dara and Leo clean out Mark's place, her mother had exhibited quite clearly whose side she fell on when it came to this whole shit show called Tatum's Life. No, Tatum wouldn't be marrying their son, but Regina Haas didn't want to lose the social or business connections. Didn't occur to her mother that constant contact with Mark's parents inflicted a pain on Tatum that left her scarred.

"Just a warning," Mia continued. "Dara was telling Mom about that foundation they're creating…and how you haven't returned any of her phone calls or made time to discuss the ceremony." She arched an eyebrow. "You might want to start thinking up an excuse—or escape route—now."

With a small smirk, Mia walked off, and though Tatum wanted to snatch her sister up and demand to know her problem, she instead scanned the room, doing exactly what Mia suggested. Searching for an escape route.

God, she was such a coward.

"This foundation must be secretly funding crimes against humanity."

"What?" Tatum startled. She'd almost forgotten Bran still stood behind her.

No, that was a lie.

"I said this foundation must be up to no good if your re-action to your sister's announcement is anything to go by. Here." He gently encircled her wrist, lifting her arm and pressing his glass of whiskey into her hand. Wrapping her fingers around the glass, he said, "Drink. You look like you need it more than me right now."

She should've balked at the command. She damn sure shouldn't raise the whiskey to her mouth.

But she didn't balk...and she did drink. And she imag-ined that even as the bold, smoky flavor hit her tongue, she could taste his specific flavor underneath the nut and cara-mel notes. A shiver danced through her as she thought about her mouth covering the same place his had touched. And as the whiskey burned a path to her stomach, she briefly closed her eyes, savoring the heat.

When she lifted her lashes, her gaze crashed into his. The blue seemed to crackle with an inner fire, and its flames licked at her breasts, belly...her clenching sex.

God.

The damp flesh between her legs spasmed even as her nipples beaded.

Was he aware of how he stared at her? Like he could con-sume her in huge greedy bites and return for a second serv-ing.

Screw it. She took another sip of whiskey.

"What's wrong, Tate?"

His use of the nickname only Nore used jarred her. And unlike the familial affection Nore elicited, the sound of the shortened version of her name on his lips had a whirlpool of need eddying low in her belly. Because she could imagine him whispering the nickname in her ear as he surrounded her, covered her...pushed inside her.

She considered lying, brushing off his question and then finding an empty corner where she could avoid him and the Walkers. That had become her MO when she couldn't brazen out a situation, after all. Hide, as Mia had mockingly accused.

So yes, she should've followed that tried-and-true method.

Instead, when her lips parted, the lie didn't emerge. The truth did.

"The Walkers," she began, haltingly at first, but after a deep breath, the words tumbled out, damn near tripping over one another. "The Walkers are Mark's parents."

His face remained impassive but she caught the slight softening around his mouth and in his eyes. "Okay." His gaze roamed over her face before meeting her eyes again. "You don't get along with them?"

She huffed out a breath that abraded her throat.

"If only it were that simple. No." She shook her head. "I think I might prefer it if they hated me," she murmured then loosed a low chuckle. "That sounds terrible, doesn't it? But that's how I feel sometimes—terrible, heartless. Because only a terrible, heartless person would rather their almost in-laws despise them than be this...lodestone for their son, for their grief, for the expectations. No one has guidelines for how I should feel toward the people who would have been my mother-and father-in-law if not for their son being caught with his dick hanging out in a hotel room. Literally."

Her chest rose and fell. But God, if it didn't give her a small measure of relief saying it aloud.

Bran shifted, placing his big, hard body between her and the rest of the room, shielding her from curious stares.

"Drink again, baby. Finish it." He nudged the side of the

tumbler with a bent finger. "Then go get your coat, leave and wait for me outside. I'll make your excuses to your parents."

"What?" she rasped, blinking up at him.

She'd heard his words but didn't fully grasp their meaning.

"Go on and finish that, Tate." He nodded toward the drink and then waited until she did as told. As the alcohol spread its warmth through her, he removed the glass from her hand and set it on the table beside her empty wine flute. "Now go." He jerked his chin in the direction of the living room entrance. "I'll be right behind you."

"I don't understand—"

"It's obvious you want to be here as much as I do. Except I hate this pretentious bullshit and you appear to be here under coercion or out of duty—which are two sides of the same coin to me. So I'm about to go find Silas and let him know that you weren't feeling well and I'm dropping you off at your house. Head out now so it'll only be me lying." When she didn't move, still too stunned that he was honest to God attempting to *rescue* her, he cupped her hip and squeezed. *"Go, Tatum."*

The contradictory kindness and firm command shattered her numbness, and her body moved as if guided by his instruction, even before her mind settled on obeying. She didn't stop to speak to anyone or to grab her coat, all of her attention focused on the front door and the quiet and freedom beyond it.

She craved it, could nearly taste it, and her eyes stung from the relief that coursed through her as she opened the door and stepped out into the night air. She didn't flinch or shiver against the cool breeze, too relieved to feel it. Eventually, she'd have to answer to her mother for skipping out on this dinner party, and it wouldn't be pretty. But right now? Right now she couldn't find it within herself to care. Not when for at least one more night she could shrug off the weight of grief, of shame, of imagined responsibilities.

Tonight she could be free, unburdened.

Behind her, the front door opened and then a large hand pressed to the small of her back. She didn't need to glance over her shoulder or inhale his scent to identify him. The ripple of lust undulating down her spine announced who stood behind her, who touched her.

"Where's your coat?" Bran asked, and moments later his sports jacket covered her, enveloping her in warmth and his sweet, earthy scent.

"I didn't want to stop and get it," she murmured, lifting her hand to grasp the lapels of the jacket and tug them closer.

Not because she was cold. No, because she wanted to sink farther into this sensory embrace.

"Ready to go?" He replaced his hand on her back.

"Yes," she said, descending the stairs. But because she had already thrown caution to the wind tonight and wildness sang in her veins, she tipped her head back and met his bright gaze as she stepped off the final stair. "But I don't want to go home."

He studied her for a long moment, then slowly nodded as if he'd come to some sort of decision.

"Okay, I'm game. Where would you like to go? This is your city, not mine." He tilted his head, and she tried and failed to prevent the shiver that worked its way through her at his hooded gaze. "Take me to your favorite place in Boston."

Back out now. Don't do this. Abort mission.

"I can do that," she whispered.

Damn.

Eight

"This is your favorite place in Boston?"

Bran surveyed Rowes Wharf, taking in the lights reflecting off Boston Harbor's dark water. Their perch on the low wall provided a great view of the huge arch over the waterfront as well as the marina, restaurants and a floating stage. At a little after eight, people were gathered in the restaurants, but only a few brave souls sat at the tables and chairs outside. It was cooler out here so close to the water but Tatum, still wearing his sports jacket, didn't seem to feel it. From the small smile that curved her pretty mouth, she didn't appear to feel anything but relaxed.

Good.

His chest constricted, and he curled his hands tighter around the edge of the wall.

He didn't need to close his eyes to conjure up an image of Tatum's beautiful features pulled tight with pain. Her sister's words had struck a nerve, but it'd been that verbal hemorrhaging of words—of truth—that compelled him to take her out of her parents' home.

He'd spent enough time with Tatum to realize that any one of those guests catching a glimpse of her vulnerability would probably be her nightmare. Hell, surprise had rippled through him when she unloaded all of that in front of him. Surprise, followed closely by a fierce surge of protectiveness. The same protective urge that had insisted he wrap her in his own clothes when she stood on the front stoop in nothing but the beautiful body-conforming off-the-shoulder dress. Even if just for a few brief moments she'd allowed him to see the Tatum Haas behind the curtain. To see her stripped-down, bare, exposed. And he didn't take that lightly. Not with this woman.

Silas had seemed to accept the story of Tatum being ill and needing to leave. But Bran could admit to himself that even if the older man had argued, nothing would've stopped him from taking Tatum out of that home.

He didn't care to analyze why.

"It's one of them," Tatum answered his question. "I also love Boston Common but it isn't too smart to go there after dark." She lifted her take-out coffee cup that he'd bought on their way out here. After a careful sip, she tilted her head back, eyes closed. That same faint smile played with her lips, and Bran slid his hands inside the front pocket of the hoodie he'd pulled on in lieu of his jacket. He fisted his fingers but they still tingled with the need to trace the line of her full bottom lip. "But I've loved coming here since I was a little girl when Dad chartered a yacht for my mom's birthday. This sounds silly now, but the wharf reminded me of Atlantis. Like a separate country floating on water. I had a pretty big imagination back then."

He scanned the waterfront again, this time viewing it through the eyes of a child.

"I can see that," he murmured, wanting her to continue talking.

She chuckled and for the first time that night, it sounded genuine. Satisfaction winged through him.

"Then the arch seemed like the gateway to another world, and I suppose a little of that wonder still exists. That, the water, the ships... It's like here, all things are possible. You can sail off, visit different places, be someone different, and never return if that's your choice. Or you can leave for a little while and always return home. It's a place of choices and possibilities." She loosed another of those soft rolls of laugher, accompanying it with a shake of her head. "I'm going on and on and probably sounding too fanciful for a grown woman."

"What does being an adult have to do with it? It's a shame that more of us don't maintain that whimsy or imagination."

She arched an eyebrow, a glint of amusement in her dark gaze. "You're a little too old to believe in mythical cities. Do you believe in Santa Claus, too?"

He shrugged. "I haven't seen any concrete evidence proving Atlantis doesn't exist. And back off Santa. He's a global treasure."

Her smile widened, and she shifted her attention back to the water and the marina. After several moments of silence, her soft sigh drifted on the night air.

"Are you going to ask me?"

Bran didn't pretend to misunderstand her. "No," he said, voice blunt. She switched her regard from the waterfront to him. "This—" he waved an arm toward the water "—isn't about quid pro quo. If you want to talk to me, fine. I'll listen. But if you want to debate the existence of Nessie next—which by the way, is real—or just sit here in silence, that's fine, too."

She stared at him, her lips slightly parted.

"I'll give you Nessie," she said, voice a little hoarser. Clearing her throat, she nodded then fell silent again. "Please ask me," she softly requested.

He studied her, the desperation threading through her voice there in her nearly black eyes.

Please ask me.

The three murmured words echoed in his head, a loaded appeal. There was too much he wanted to know about Tatum. And in this case, knowledge wasn't power. It would be his weakness, his downfall. The more he discovered, the harder it would be to preserve the distance he so needed with her. Curiosity mated with the hunger and lust twisting in his gut...

Yeah, a smart man knew mixing business with pleasure when he would be leaving in a matter of weeks was a destructive move. He shouldn't ask her anything. Shit, shouldn't be out with her in the first place.

But here he was.

And even as every self-preserving instinct within him roared in disgust, he asked, "What happened with your fiancé?"

A visible shiver racked her, and he almost—almost—rescinded the question. But she'd requested this of him, which told him she *needed* this. Needed to lance this festering wound. So he waited.

"He died from a ruptured brain aneurysm on the night before our wedding day. I'll never forget sitting in that hospital waiting room, receiving the news that the man I loved was no more. He was gone. I would never hear his deep voice, his laughter. Never inhale his scent. Never be touched by him again."

She fell silent once more, clasping the edges of his jacket, pulling it tighter around her as if trying to sink into the dark blue material.

"I'll also never forget that just minutes after finding out I'd lost my fiancé, I discovered the paramedics had found him unresponsive and naked in a hotel suite. From the condoms in the room, both used and unused, it was obvious he hadn't been there alone. The night before he was supposed to stand up in front of our family and friends and pledge his fidelity to me, he'd been fucking another woman."

Her eyes briefly closed, and pain flickered across her face, momentarily tightening it. But then she lifted her lashes, and the stark, naked hurt in her eyes had him fisting his hands harder. Touching her wasn't only inappropriate but it might also stop her from talking. And he sensed talking was what she needed more than comfort.

"It would've been one thing to hear the news in private, that the man I'd been loyal to had betrayed me. But I didn't. I discovered it through media outlets and on social media. Apparently, a call had been placed to 911 by an anonymous woman, and we assume she was the person he was with that night. My grief, my pain, my anger—it was all on display for public consumption. I couldn't even mourn him properly because I couldn't—can't—figure out a way to separate the man I'd loved from the man who betrayed me in the most cruel, hurtful way possible. Then there were the reporters, cameramen and keyboard warriors scrutinizing my every move, every expression, every word. If I didn't say anything or didn't cry, I was a coldhearted bitch and deserved him cheating on me. If I did show emotion, I was weak, crying over a man who obviously didn't love me enough to stay faithful. And then there was Mark's parents."

The confession poured from her in an unimpeded stream. Hurt, anger and, yes, grief throbbed in her voice, and it confirmed what he'd suspected all along. She still hadn't gotten over Mark Walker. There was too much emotion there, too much confusion left unresolved. While he sincerely doubted Tatum would intentionally hurt another person, anyone she became involved with would bear the weight of the baggage she carried.

Fuck, he hurt for her.

"Tell me they don't blame you for his actions," he said, voice sharper than he intended.

She crossed her arms over her chest. "No, they don't. As inconceivable as it sounds, it might be easier if they did. Don't get me wrong, I fully understand that they lost a son—their only son. And God yes, they should grieve, should be in pain. But they're his parents. I'm the woman he betrayed, lied to, humiliated. Their emotions are more clear-cut than mine. But they expect me to mourn as they do, to be his loving, devoted fiancée in life and death. And it's impossible. But they can't see that or don't want to face it. They've ignored how he hurt me, and want me to ignore it, too."

"Is that where this foundation that Mia mentioned comes in?"

Nodding, she loosened her arms and gripped the edge of the low wall, subtly rocking back and forth.

"Yes. At the fundraiser gala a couple of weeks ago, they announced to me and my family that they were starting a foundation in Mark's name, where they would offer scholarships and internships at their company to graduating college students. They asked me to be the guest speaker." She huffed out a sound caught somewhere between a rough exhale and a jagged laugh. "Be Mark's voice as his loving fiancée."

Damn. Even though he'd never met Mark's parents, that didn't prevent annoyance from pricking him. Of course, he sympathized with them—how could he not?—but they were either oblivious or willingly blind to the burden and pain they inflicted on Tatum.

"Are you going to do it?" he asked.

"No. I don't know." She swept a hand over her hair. "My mother already accepted on my behalf before I had a chance to say yes or no. I probably will."

He frowned, twisting to face her more fully. "Why? I can

tell you don't want anything to do with it. You're not obligated to his parents."

A half smile quirked the corner of her mouth, and instead of humor, it possessed a shitload of self-deprecation.

"You're frustrated with me. I can hear it in your voice," she murmured. "Not that I can blame you. I'm frustrated with myself. But the Walkers own MassComm, and they're one of BayStar's business partners. That's why my parents were so thrilled about our relationship. It would've been like the merger of two media empires. And even though Mark's gone, they want to retain that connection. My father for business reasons and my mother for social. And no, I didn't ask for any of this, but they are on the receiving end of the embarrassment and unwanted negative attention because of me. So in a way, I am obligated to mitigate the damage. That's my responsibility."

"You mean your penance."

She sucked in a breath, and her chin snapped up as if he'd delivered a verbal blow. Blinking, she stared at him for several seconds.

Then breathed, "Yes."

"So you're paying the price for someone else's crime, and you're okay with that?" He didn't wait for her answer but pressed on. "Who in your life led you to believe that your feelings, your thoughts, your *heart* are expendable? Your voice, *you* are just as important as the man everyone lost. Just because you're alive and available, *tangible*, doesn't depreciate your life. And if they—your family and Mark's— can't see it, then that's their issue not yours. And no way in hell should you take on that burden. You're only responsible for you. Your man fucked up. Fucked up bad. He just so happened to die and escape the consequences of his cowardly behavior. Last I checked, reparations for screwing around have never been in anyone's will. So why the hell should you be expected to inherit his debt?"

He ground his teeth, trying to extinguish the anger flickering in his chest like flames.

"You're really upset. For me," she whispered, and the note of awe in her voice only stoked those flames.

Reaching out, he broke his own rule about touching her and cupped the back of her neck. He drew her forward as he leaned in, meeting her halfway. His nose nearly bumped hers, and he could taste the hint of coffee and hazelnut on her breath. Without his permission, his fingers flexed against the side of her throat. It wouldn't take much pressure to guide her forward the negligible amount to take her mouth and see if her kiss delivered on the promise of that taste.

"No," he ground out. "I'm not upset. I'm pissed. You. Did. Nothing. Wrong. And fuck whoever would try to make you believe you have to clean up the mess your ex made and left behind."

"I don't think we're supposed to speak ill of the dead."

"Fuck that, too," he said bluntly. Her eyes slightly widened, but he continued, "Dead or alive, I'm calling you out on your bullshit. And for him to screw around on you—betraying your trust is bullshit. So he can get it, too."

"He can get it, too?" A smile slowly curved her lips then spread into a full-out grin. "You know you're cute when you're defending my honor."

"I'm forty fucking years old. I'm not cute."

"I don't think the two are mutually exclusive."

They stared at one another, and he couldn't stop himself from stroking his thumb up and down her neck. This close, he didn't miss her shiver at his touch. And damn if that tremor didn't ripple down his own spine…and over his cock.

He leaned back. Away from her. Away from temptation.

"Thank you," she murmured.

"You don't need to thank me for telling you the truth."

"I'm not," she said. "I'm thanking you for tonight. For…" She glanced at the water. "This. Thank you for this. It's…"

"You're welcome," he said.

She tilted her head, and those nearly black eyes roamed over his face.

"What? Just ask me what you're thinking." He could read the question in her gaze.

"Why did you—I hate to say *rescue me*, because I've never been some damsel in distress. Although lately…" She shoved a hand over her hair again, and he wanted to replace her fingers with his, feel the slide of the thick dark strands.

"Lately what?"

"Not important." She waved a hand, and when she gave him that forced, fake smile after he'd already witnessed the beauty of a genuine one, he almost growled a warning to her. "So why did you take me out of there tonight? Not that I don't appreciate it," she assured him, "but you were willing to lie to my father—your potential investor and business partner—to do it. Why?" she pressed.

"Because the people who should've noticed you were hurting didn't. So I did what they couldn't or refused to do."

She probably tried to control her flinch but didn't succeed. Neither did she conceal the spasm of emotion that crossed her features. He didn't mention either; her pride wouldn't thank him for saying anything.

Shaking her head, she murmured, "Why do you—"

"Care?" he finished for her. "That you even have to ask that pisses me off even more." His mouth twisted into a snarl that echoed in his head. "I have no doubt you can rescue yourself, Tate—something tells me you've been doing it a long while. And most people enduring what you have this past year would've broken. But that doesn't mean you can't loose the reins of control and let someone claim them. Doesn't mean you can't lean on them and allow them to bear the weight. That doesn't make you weak. It just makes you human."

"Is that what you did tonight? Give me someone to lean on?"

He studied the gleam in her eyes, the sinking of her teeth into her bottom lip, the unconscious lean of her body toward him.

Fuck.

Hot desire pounded through him, knotting his stomach, throbbing in his dick. His thighs tightened against the primal ache, and he inhaled a low, deep breath. But fuck if her sultry scent, which reminded him of sun-warmed sands and perfumed skin, didn't permeate his nostrils, his throat, his lungs.

"You're asking the wrong question, Tate," he said, and there wasn't a damn thing he could do about the gravel roughness to his voice. "You leaning on me, loosening some of that control... It isn't about me giving that to you. It's about you accepting what I'm offering. That's why you could never be weak. You had—and have—all the power."

"We're still talking about this evening at the dinner party, right?" she whispered.

Did she know her gaze dropped to his mouth? Lingered there?

Did she have any idea how close she was to having him showing her what he could do with his mouth?

No, to both.

She couldn't. Otherwise she wouldn't continue to sit there with him, with all that vulnerable soft heat in her eyes.

He would be the worst kind of asshole if he crossed the space separating them and took those slightly damp lips, introduced her to his tongue, to the greed barreling through him like a storm-whipped wind. No, he couldn't claim to have been the best man in all his forty years.

But tonight... Tonight he'd aim to be.

Goddammit.

He slowly stood, stretching his hand out to her. And the anticipation howling inside his head couldn't have been a clearer warning that touching her—even an innocuous palm pressed to palm—was a mistake.

But one he was willing to make.

Tatum stared at his hand for a long moment before she slid hers over his.

Yeah. Mistake.

He locked down the moan crawling up his chest and into his throat. Damn, if he didn't feel that soft caress down his chest, his abs and wrapped around his flesh. Touching this woman, whether it was her hand, the small of her back or her vulnerable nape, foretold a danger he should heed.

But apparently, experience didn't equal wisdom. Because as he gently pulled Tatum to her feet, none of the warnings and admonishments he'd given himself mattered. Not when her scent called to something wild in him. Not when her slender, wickedly curved body brushed his. Not when those dark brown eyes issued an invitation her mouth would deny.

"I should get you home," he said instead of answering her loaded question. Especially since he couldn't definitively state that his response would've been *yes*.

"Right. It's getting late." She nodded, slipping her hand free of his grasp, turning away.

But not before he caught a glimpse of the rueful twist of her lips. Yeah, she hadn't missed his avoidance. And as he followed behind her along the wharf, he shook his head.

Sometimes retreat didn't mean cowardice.

Sometimes it presented the wisest course of action.

He'd keep telling himself that, and hopefully soon he'd believe it.

Nine

Tatum stared at the contents of her walk-in closet as if the array of dresses, pants and blouses were the Riemann hypothesis instead of her options for Sunday brunch at her parents' place. Honestly, she'd rather sit down and attempt to solve the Millennium Prize Problem than attend the weekly meal with her family.

She winced.

Guilt crept through her, but she couldn't deny the truth. Ever since she'd disappeared from the dinner party on Friday night, her mother had been blowing up her phone, vacillating between passive-aggressive comments about ungrateful children to outraged criticism for embarrassing her—and leaving her dinner party unbalanced. Her father hadn't called at all, which portended a more ominous conversation.

Oh yes, she couldn't *wait* for brunch.

Sighing, she grabbed a pair of eggplant-colored highwaisted pants and a lavender lace shirt before she could change her mind. About the outfit and brunch. While her parents' chef would be serving roast beef as the entrée, Tatum knew she would be the main course.

Because the people who should've noticed you were hurting didn't. So I did what they couldn't or refused to do.

Bran's words from Friday night haunted her, and as she closed her eyes, his voice gained volume and speed in her head. Part of her wanted to dig that...that indictment out of her brain. To erase it as if it never existed. Because it charged her parents, Mia, the Walkers with not just leaving her out there exposed and unprotected, but maybe with being complicit in inflicting the hurt.

Then there was the other side of her that embraced it. Inside—so deep inside—something unfurled, reaching for those words, for him. Because he'd *seen*. He'd called a thing *a thing* even when she'd been afraid to say it. Felt guilty for thinking it.

But his bald, frank manner hit her as both intimidating and liberating.

And wholly addictive.

Like the man.

Exhaling a breath, she slid a hand over the back of her neck, recreating his hold on her, attempting to recapture the hot brand of it against her skin. Molten heat flowed through her at the memory. Now, like then, her breasts swelled, nipples tightening. She lowered a hand to her belly, pressing against the ache there, the same ache that had been there Friday night. Her thighs tightened against the heavy beat of arousal between her legs...assuaging it, stirring it? She curled her fingers, refusing to alleviate that needy pain.

Because stroking herself, making herself come to the memory of her client remained a step she wasn't willing to take.

Or was afraid to take.

Maybe. Because every encounter, every minute with him seemed to weaken her resolve.

Dropping her arm, lest she surrender to temptation, she exited her closet and tossed her clothes on her bed.

As she shrugged out of her robe, her cell phone rang on her bedside table. She side-eyed it for a moment. Had to be her mother ensuring she didn't plan on skipping brunch. Resentment flared in her chest but instead of smothering it like she usually did, she allowed it to kindle, her hurt blowing air on it.

Just for a moment. Then she squelched the rebellious, disloyal emotion and strode over to pick up the phone. Surprise struck her, and she blinked, peering down at the screen as if the name there would change.

No matter how long she stared, though, it remained the same.

Finally, she answered the call, lifting the cell to her ear.

"Hello," she said, her heart's rhythm filling her ears.

And yet Bran's "Hello, Tatum," clearly cut through the white noise. The sound of his deep rumble of a voice moved through her in a sinuous glide, leaving electricity in its wake.

Sinking to the edge of the bed behind her, she tightened her grasp on the phone. "Bran, this is a surprise. Is everything okay?"

"Yes, everything's good," he said. "You've just been on my mind."

She closed her eyes, ordering her body to stand down. Demanding her heart not jump in that juvenile way. Fear slunk into her chest, winding around her ribs. The last time the traitorous organ in her chest did this exhilarant trilling, she ended up with not just a broken heart, but a broken *world*. She couldn't trust her instincts. And yet...

And yet she didn't reprimand him for talking to her in such a personal way.

Didn't end the call.

If she were honest with herself, that ship had sailed the moment she'd walked out of her parents' house Friday night.

"I don't know if that's a good or bad thing," she murmured.

"Good," he assured her, and the low, dark rumble of *good* had her teeth sinking into her bottom lip to hold back a moan. "I want to show you something. Are you busy?"

"Right now?" She glanced around her bedroom as if the *something* had materialized there. That twisting spiral of excitement was a bad sign. "Today?"

"Yes, to both," he said, humor in his tone. "Are you free?"

No, I'm expected at brunch with my family in an hour.

The reply sat right there on her tongue. All she had to do was speak it. And she would because spending any more time with Bran outside of BayStar's office or in a professional setting was plain foolish. Not to mention, she couldn't just flake on her parents, no matter how much the thought of facing their disappointment had her belly in knots…

Who in your life led you to believe that your feelings, your thoughts, your heart *are expendable?*

Again, more of Bran's words returned to haunt her and a burst of frustration and…and helplessness mired with anger and pain echoed in her chest.

Did she consider her feelings, her basic needs of protection, acceptance and understanding expendable?

God, yes.

The answer blared loud and clear in her head. In her soul. When did she prioritize her own desires, her comfort? Her… joy?

Now. That's when she started. Now.

Even if it was just for this one time.

"Yes, I'm free," she said, throwing caution—and common sense—to the wind. "What do you have in mind?"

"Don't worry, you'll see. Just wear something comfortable and warm. I'll be there in half an hour."

"Half an hour!" she objected. But she was objecting to herself because he'd ended the call. And staring at the screen only wasted precious minutes of the time she had to get ready. "Dammit," she muttered, tossing the cell to the mattress and leaping to her closet.

Twenty-eight minutes later, she descended the stairs of her brownstone to the first floor and the foyer. Just as she moved off the last step, the doorbell rang, and for the briefest moment, she stiffened, her stomach fluttering like a whole net of trapped butterflies.

She couldn't see through the solid wood door but only one person could be standing on the other side.

Inhaling a deep breath that did nothing to calm the storm brewing inside her, she approached the door and opened it before reason could convince her otherwise. Though she knew Bran would be waiting on her stoop, the impact of him still propelled the air from her lungs.

She'd seen him in a flawlessly tailored suit, in business casual pants, shirt and jacket. And he'd been beautiful in all of it. But in this—in a black leather jacket, a black T-shirt, faded blue jeans and scuffed motorcycle boots—he was stunning. A visual and elemental blow to the senses.

Her fingertips itched to trace the craggy lines of his face thrown in sharp relief by the thick dark and gray strands secured at the back of his head. Instead, she shifted back from the door and waved him inside.

"Hello, Bran. Come in. I just need to grab my jacket."

"Thanks." His blue gaze swept over her thick cream sweater, black jeans and knee-high riding boots as he stepped into the house. "You look perfect."

"Thank you." She rubbed her hands down the front of her thighs. "You didn't give me much direction other than comfortable and warm. So…" Her hands fluttered, and dammit, she was babbling *and* fidgeting. *Stop talking and move*, she silently ordered herself. "I'll be right back."

Leaving him in the foyer, she headed down the hall to the closet. A minute later, she returned, shrugging into a hip-length camel-colored leather jacket.

"Ready," she announced, and Bran's gaze shifted from scrutinizing her foyer to her. Once more, she fought not to fidget under that steady, unwavering stare and barely won the battle.

"You have a lovely home," he said.

"Thank you." She turned, surveying the space and attempting to view it through his eyes.

"It's…you."

She jerked her regard back to him, surprise whispering through her. "Thank you. Again," she murmured. "I'm a little afraid to ask what that means," she half joked.

Only half. Because part of her really wanted to know what he saw when he looked at her home. And the other part… Well, she feared he saw too much. And that he would be right.

"It's elegant, beautiful and thoughtful. It's clear every piece has been chosen carefully. But it's also comfortable. That living room is just that—a *living* room. I wouldn't be afraid to sit on the furniture. It looks like you not only actually use it but enjoy it."

She'd been right to be afraid. Vulnerability crept over her, and she almost patted her chest to make sure her flesh still covered her bones and heart. She hated this sense of exposure.

And yet she couldn't deny the bloom of pleasure that radiated from behind her rib cage, spreading wide.

Unlike some people did, when she'd bought the brownstone, she hadn't rented out the ground floor or upper level. Nor had she hired an interior designer. Mark hadn't understood it, and often told her she was wasting time and her efforts when she could easily hire someone to do the job faster. But this was her personal haven, her sanctuary. She'd selected each piece that graced the walls and occupied the floors and corners. From the dove-gray chaise longue under the George Inness landscape in the foyer to the custom bookshelves and reading nook in the living room, they all had been handpicked by her. And yes, enjoyed by her.

"It seems like your talents are wasted on custom design for motorcycles and should be focused on being a mentalist." She tossed out the nonchalant, teasing comment as she moved toward her front door, not willing to analyze his theory or how it affected her. "Ready to go? I can't deny I'm curious about where you're taking me."

He studied her for a long moment then dipped his head and followed her out of the house. Once she locked the door, he cupped her elbow and guided her down the front steps.

But she drew up short on the bottom one, her lips parting in shock.

"What...? Are you...? You can't..."

A low chuckle rumbled from the man next to her.

"I'm sorry. I didn't catch any of that." He continued striding over the sidewalk to the curb—and the motorcycle parked there. "But if I have to guess, I'm going with, this is The Gauntlet in the so-called flesh. Yes, I intend to take you on a ride on your potential investment and oh yeah, I'm very serious. Did I get it right?" He arched an eyebrow, a smirk tugging the corner of his mouth.

"Yes, you covered it all." She flicked her fingers toward the motorcycle she'd seen on the movie lot. "You don't really expect me to get on that, do you?"

He slowly nodded. "I do. How else to fully judge the product you're considering financing? If you're going to stand up in front of your board and talk about The Gauntlet, then you have to experience it."

"Using reason isn't going to get me on that bike," she muttered, crossing her arms and glaring at him and the motorcycle.

"Tatum." His soft tone carried a note of steel. "Come here."

That voice shouldn't work. That dominant order should have her rebelling, not moving her feet in his direction. Yet moments after he commanded it, she stood in front of him, tipping her head back to meet his bright blue gaze.

"I would ask you if that usually works, but here I am, right in front of you, showing that it works," she grumbled.

He bent his head, lowering it until his lips grazed the rim of her ear. "Which one are you really scared of, Tate? Riding the bike or that you might actually enjoy riding the bike?"

A shiver rocked down her spine as she emotionally shrank away from his question. He was almost correct. She was afraid she might enjoy riding the bike with *him*. And because she couldn't allow him to guess that, she hiked her chin up and stepped closer to the bike.

"Sorry to disappoint you, but neither."

"I could never be disappointed in you, Tatum," he said, and while she reeled from that murmured admission, he removed a matte black helmet from the bike's trunk and moved in front of her.

Still speechless, she stood, unmoving, as he fit the gear over her head and then instructed her on how to mount the motorcycle. After she perched on the seat, he threw his leg over, his big body sitting in front of her. He freed a helmet identical to hers from the handlebars, covered his head with it then glanced over his shoulder.

"Ready?"

"Yes," she lied.

"Hold on to me," he ordered.

And the moment she'd craved and dreaded arrived.

Craved because she got to wrap her arms around him,

press her chest and abs to his wide back…her sex to his firm, gorgeous ass.

Dreaded because she got to wrap her arms around him, press her chest and abs to his wide back…her sex to his firm, gorgeous ass.

Once she did this, there was no turning back. There was no forgetting how hard, solid and warm he felt. There was no unimagining how that hard, solid and warm body would press hers into a soft mattress.

After slowly sliding her arms around his trim waist, she locked her fingers and pressed them against the ladder of his abdomen. *Damn.* She'd never been more painfully aware of another person in her life.

The motorcycle roared to life and, *holy…* Behind the helmet, she closed her eyes and her lips parted on a gasp. She'd never sat on a washing machine stuck on the spin cycle, but *oh God* this delicious hum between her legs *had* to be why that activity remained so popular.

Bran eased out from the curb, the speed sedate over the cobbled road and onto Charles Street.

This isn't so bad. Not bad at all.

Then about ten minutes later, he exited onto the interstate and…

"Oh my God!" Her scream echoed inside the helmet, joining the thunderous pounding of her heart.

"You good?" Bran shouted, the wind carrying his question back to her.

"Oh my God!" she yelled again, and he laughed, long and loud.

Her laughter joined his.

The world flashed by them in a Technicolor blur, the wind a muted howl through the helmet and an almost sensual pressure against her body. And the power… On this great, rumbling machine, holding on to this equally strong beast of a man, she harnessed power, wielded it and walked the fine edge of becoming its casualty.

Teetering on that threshold was emboldening, terrifying…

Exhilarating.

Roaring down the highway, no cage of iron, chrome and glass between her and the elements, she could understand why some people chose the road and their motorcycles as a way of life.

The farther Boston grew behind them, the lighter her chest and shoulders became. And as the landscape changed from urban to farmland and forests, the weight of worries, responsibilities and duty sloughed off like a rough, too-tight, ill-fitting skin. Bran slowed and exited the interstate toward Taunton. Tatum took in the Taunton Green, the city square, as well as a couple of parks and historic buildings.

After a short break to stretch their legs—okay, *her* legs—they left Taunton, winding their way back through more countryside until their surroundings shifted once more as they neared South Boston.

"Castle Island?" she yelled minutes later, grinning as Fort Independence appeared in the distance.

Bran nodded, and she shook her head, still smiling. It'd been years since she'd been to the attraction on the shore of Boston Harbor. It was a little too cold for swimming at the beach, but the site also contained a playground, a gift shop, a food court and a wonderful ice cream parlor. Visitors could also tour Fort Independence, one of the oldest fortified sites of English origin in the US.

Delight raced through her as Bran parked in the designated area and cut the motorcycle's ignition. He dismounted, his thick thigh muscles bunching under the faded denim, and she swallowed a sigh at the sensual display. Sliding her hand into his outstretched one, she climbed off the bike, her own thighs trembling after riding for so long.

"You okay?" he asked, not releasing his clasp on her hand.

"Yes, I'm fine."

Only then did he reach out and remove her helmet. And though she could've done it herself, she allowed the gesture. He'd taken care of her, from unknowingly aiding her escape from an uncomfortable brunch to this joyous experience, to ensuring she was comfortable with several minibreaks during the ride... Bran had protected and pampered her. He'd given her a peace and respite she hadn't realized she so desperately needed.

And thank God it wasn't over yet. Because she didn't want to return home and have this day end. Not yet.

"Is this one of your tourist adventures?" she teased as he secured the helmets to the motorcycle.

He shrugged but humor gleamed in his blue eyes. "Sue me. I'm a cliché." He jerked his chin toward the entrance. "C'mon. One of the last tours is about to start."

For the next forty minutes, they walked around the huge fort and the grounds. Tatum didn't listen to their guide, knowledgeable as she was, as much as watch Bran listen to her. He was so attentive, seemed so captivated by the stories and facts the older woman relayed. That intense, focused expression shouldn't have been so hot, but damn, it was. She couldn't help envisioning how he employed that same focus and intensity when he slid inside a woman, when he dragged a scream of pleasure out of her.

Okay, maybe staring at him wasn't such a good idea. Old gray stone. Yes, a much better visual. Definitely safer.

"You enjoyed that," she said as the guided tour ended and their group scattered, some to explore on their own, and others no doubt headed to Sullivan's for lobster rolls and ice cream.

"I did. I'm a bit of a history buff. Always have been. The love of it was one of the things my family and I shared. Growing up, we didn't have a ton of money, but every summer we decided on a city or town and we'd load up in the car, my dad would hitch the trailer with his bike—and later mine— to the back and we'd take off. The only requirement for our destination was it had to be historic. We'd visit all the different sites, do a couple of ghost tours. A Holleran vacation wasn't complete without a ghost tour." A smile softened his firm, wide mouth. "Those are some of my best memories."

"That sounds amazing," she murmured, strolling toward the fort's exit. "So you and your family—you're close, then?"

Yes, she was fishing, and to herself at least, she could confess to a hunger for any information not included in his bio or his BayStar dossier.

"We are. My father died four years ago—"

"Oh, Bran, I'm so sorry," she murmured, setting a hand on his forearm.

A muscle flexed under her palm, and he covered her hand with his, squeezing slightly. "Thank you. It's been rough, especially for my mother. They were married for thirty-eight years when he passed. She's still adjusting to a life without him."

He was quiet for a moment, a slight frown creasing his brow, but then he gave an abrupt shake of his head, and his expression cleared.

"Even though I've been in Seattle for a decade now, Mom and my sister Dani come out to visit me pretty often. It's not as regularly as I'd like, but Dani owns a bridal shop, so she can't just up and leave. But I go home to see them, too. And then we call each other several times a week. We all make an effort to keep in touch."

"That's how Nore and I are with each other. We call all the time but we also have monthly video chats set up."

He snorted. "I know about your movie nights with Nore. Joaquin ends up hanging out with me so he doesn't accidentally overhear something he shouldn't. Hearing you two debate the career longevity of Manuel Ferrara and his contribution to film might've scarred him for life."

"What?" She held up her hands, shrugging. "You mean to tell me Joaquin has a problem with his wife watching porn?"

"Hell no," he said, a half grin quirking the corner of his mouth. "He had a problem listening to his precious Nore and her proper friend describe said porn star's best moves and rate them one through ten. One being vanilla and ten being 'holy shit I think I just got pregnant with octuplets.' Your words, a direct quote, I believe. My poor friend. I think he lost some of his innocence that night."

Tatum barked out a crack of laughter and couldn't stop. She halted in the middle of the walkway, clutching her stomach. Wiping a tear from her eyes, she steadied herself against the fence as her hilarity eased.

"In my man's defense, though, he fully supports his fiancée watching porn. He's just firm on not hearing you two discuss it."

"That's fair." She snickered. "Wait until I tell Nore—"

"Oh no you don't." Bran jabbed a finger at her. "That was told to you in the utmost confidence. She doesn't know about that and it's going to stay that way."

Grinning, Tatum heaved an exaggerated sigh and tipped her head back. "All right, *fine*. But she's my best friend. One of our rules is we don't keep secrets from one another."

"Yeah, well, I broke a code telling you that, so you'll keep this one," he warned.

He narrowed his eyes at her, and she held her hands up to her chest, palms raised.

"I said fine. I just want it known I'm doing this under duress." Too bad her wide smile belied that accusation. She pushed off the fence and started walking again, and Bran fell into step beside her. She slid a look at his strong profile highlighted by his thick salt-and-pepper beard. "Nore has mentioned you before, and while I knew you and Joaquin were business partners and pretty close, I didn't think you were best friends. Not like me and Nore."

"Joaquin is a good man, and I'm lucky to call him friend. He got me through one of the toughest periods of my life. Stuck beside me when not many people would've," he murmured.

"Your father's death?" she asked.

Bran glanced down at her, and pain flickered in his bright eyes. Her fingers tingled to touch him, to offer him comfort like he'd given her on the wharf. She hesitated, the small tic along his jaw a warning that she heeded.

Never would she have attributed the word *brittle* to Bran. And she still couldn't. But staring into his face with the shadows clouding his gaze, smooth skin pulled taut over his sharp bone structure, his wide mouth flattened into a grim line and that tiny muscle continuing to jump at his jaw…

He appeared to be a man on the edge of a break.

Inexplicably, she feared touching him would trigger that event. So she kept her hands to herself. Though a primal instinct deep inside cried out for her to do just the opposite.

"Yes, he supported me when my father died, but that's not what I mean. He stood by me through my divorce. And by rights, he didn't have to—hell, shouldn't have. Not after the damage my personal life wreaked on Greer, especially in our infancy. You don't fully understand the depth and scope of someone's love and loyalty until you've fucked up so bad others have walked away. And that person sticks. Not because of a contract. Not because of a business. Because they believe in you, trust you when they have every reason not to."

A thick trepidation gathered in her chest. For him, not herself. Nothing about his words suggested this story was a happy one.

"If you want to talk to me, fine. I'm here and I'll listen. But if you want to debate why I scored Manuel Ferrara's doggy style a solid eight or just sit here in silence, that's fine, too."

He blinked, and some of the shadows evaporated from his eyes as she threw his offer from Friday night—albeit the porn version—back at him. His mouth softened, losing some of the tightness at the corners.

"I can honestly say that might be the best offer I've received in a long time. At least in the last five years."

"Tell me, then," she whispered.

He turned, curled his fingers around the top of the fence as if he needed something solid to hold in this tumble back into his past. Then he lifted a hand and gestured toward her, beckoning her closer.

"Come here, Tate," he said, his voice low, rough, like it traveled over churned-up road. "Please."

She could no more resist his request or that tone than she could resist his earlier invitation to join him for the day. Something inside her was weak, vulnerable when it came to this man, and later, she would find a way to shore up her defenses against him. But not now.

She took his hand, and a moment later, he maneuvered her so she stood in front of him, her back to his wide, hard chest, his long arms caging her on either side. His chin brushed the side of her head, his mouth moving against her hair. The need to spin around, wrap her arms around his waist and bury her face in his jacket, inhale his scent yawned wide inside her. She longed to transfer her strength to him, as silly and impossible as it sounded. But this wasn't about her; it was about him. So she remained facing away from him, understanding without being told that he didn't want her to see him as he relayed this tale.

"We met when I was twenty-seven and she was twenty-two. Not only did I marry a younger woman but I was a total cliché and married an employee. Roma worked in my shop, and not long after she was hired, we started dating. We'd only been together two months before we eloped. To Vegas." His humorless chuckle, heavy with self-deprecation, brushed the top of her ear. She closed her eyes, hating the sound of it. "At first, we were happy. She quit working after we married, which I didn't mind. My mother didn't work outside the home. She was a homemaker. And my parents were full partners in their marriage. If that's what Roma wanted, then I was fine with it. But I soon discovered she didn't want to work outside the house—or in it. I offered to pay her tuition if she wanted to go back to college and complete her degree but that didn't interest her either. Only one thing did. Shopping."

Damn. She didn't need a crystal ball to foresee where this was headed. Glancing down, she stared at his hands and the knuckles blanched from his tight hold on the railing. She covered his hands with hers, intertwining their fingers. Her belly dipped when his lips grazed the rim of her ear, her hair. Keeping her emotional distance from this man was proving to be a hopeless endeavor.

"I owned my own business. I was successful. And when Joaquin and I decided to start Greer, we planned on the company being even more successful. And it was. But those first few years were building ones, and even with the capital we raised and our own fund we invested, they were tight. But that didn't stop Roma from spending. Every day, I'd return home from work and there would be bags littering our room and another bedroom that she used for her closet. Of course I'd heard about that kind of thing before, but seeing it, experiencing it? That was some shit. And no matter how many times I'd sit her down and talk to her about budgeting, it didn't stop her. Soon, we were in debt. Deep in debt."

He loosed another of those grating chuckles, shaking his head. The sound scraped over her senses, her skin and, screw it. She tried to turn around, look at him, but he stiffened his arms, caging her between his body and the fence.

"No, let me get this out. And I can't do that if you... If you're—"

"Okay, Bran," she whispered. "Whatever you need."

He pressed his forehead against the crown of her head for several moments, and they stood there, silent, the ripples of the lapping water in the harbor, the hum and laughter of people in the distance the only sounds.

"I grew up poor," he continued quietly. "Yeah, we had road trips in the summer, but there were times when grilled cheese and tomato soup was on the menu three times out of the week because it was lean at Dad's garage. I knew what it meant to go without because Mom had to make a choice between bills for that month. So money isn't that big a deal to me. But the other things..." He shook his head, and she braced herself for those *other things*.

"I don't know if it was a maturity issue, but she became resentful of the hours I spent working, which, admittedly, had increased after founding Greer. But I'd been attempting to build a life for us, and when she felt ignored or neglected, she wouldn't just spend money, she'd also come to the office and cause chaos by accusing me of cheating with our employees, verbally abusing the female staff by taking out her anger with me on them. She acted out in a bid for my attention, but the people around me were the casualties. Some of the employees she targeted quit. We lost a couple of early business contracts because her antics got back to them. Joaquin should've ended our partnership then. Hell, I would've. But he didn't. He not only kept me on as his partner but he also remained my friend, my brother as I made the hardest—and yet not the hardest—decision in my life. I ended my marriage."

"Bran, I'm so sorry," she said.

It struck her that she'd said the same thing about the loss of his father. But in a way, wasn't it another kind of death? She should know. She *did* know.

"Don't be. I gladly paid half my worth to divorce her. Money well spent."

Jerking her grip free of his, she spun around and tipped her head up to look into his face. Somewhere in the back of her mind, she conceded she was only able to look at him because he allowed it. That knowledge should not have sent a curl of heat twisting low inside her, but it did.

A grim smile curved his mouth and Tatum shook her head, lightly thumping a fist against his chest, right over his heart.

"Don't do that," she said. "Don't dismiss that relationship like it didn't impact you. Like it didn't have good, even happy moments. It's those moments that made the demise of the marriage hurt. Just because it ended ugly doesn't detract from the joy. I think the joy, the hope—they are why we're so angry when it falls apart. Because the love should've been enough to make it work. But we don't live in snow globes or pretty glass castles. Love and beautiful moments don't make a relationship. They aren't enough to sustain a marriage."

"Is this your version of a pep talk? Because if it is, you suck at it." He arched an eyebrow and rubbed the pad of his thumb over her cheekbone. The innocuous caress echoed in her sex, directly over her clit, and she trembled. Damn, even when he insulted her, this man did it for her. "You're too young to be this cynical."

"Not cynical. I'm only telling you what you already know. And it has nothing to do with age. Deliberately sabotaging the career, livelihood and dreams of the person you're supposed to love and support is a character flaw. I'm sure she had legitimate complaints—you working too many hours, probably not paying enough attention to her when you were home, being a man—but she chose an illegitimate way of reacting to those issues. Instead of sitting you down and telling you about yourself, she destroyed your finances, your stability and your future. Yes, she was immature. But she was also a fool."

Anger burned through Tatum, and right on the heels of it streamed embarrassment at her vehement defense of him. Damn, she should mind her business. Seriously, who was she to judge, when her own relationship had been such an epic failure? If anything—

The soft brush of lips over hers snatched her from her thoughts, and she gasped. Heat blasted through her from that barely there kiss but, oh God, it damn near rocked her back on her heels. Unable to help herself, she touched the tip of her tongue to her bottom lip and tasted him. Tasted his addictive earthy flavor. She smothered a moan. From the way his gaze dropped to her mouth and narrowed, she almost believed he heard that aborted sound.

"Why?" she whispered, and his scrutiny lifted to meet her eyes.

"Why what?" he asked and the growl in his voice rasped over her skin like calloused fingertips.

"Why did you…?" Instead of completing the question, she pressed her fingers to her mouth.

"I can give you the answer that wouldn't send you running scared or I can give you the truth that will damn us both. The choice is yours."

He stepped back from her, as if granting her physical space to make her decision. And she appreciated it. His scent, his intense gaze, his big frame surrounding her—they clouded her brain, permeated her senses until her head swam, full of *him*.

Her heart battered her rib cage, and the wet flesh between her legs pulsed with a heavy, aching beat, casting its vote. Her sex was all on board Team Truth, but her head… It threw warning after warning, reminding her of what happened the last time she'd let her guard down and trusted a man.

Reminding her she couldn't trust *herself*.

"The first answer," she murmured, shifting backward until the fence poked into her lower back. "Give me the first answer."

He studied her, and it bordered on intrusive. Or maybe that's just how it felt because she wanted to remain hidden from him, feared he would perceive just how much she secretly craved his truth. The self-destructive part of her longed to be damned. By him. With him.

God. What did that say about her?

"Thank you," he finally said, pinching her chin and tilting her head back even farther. Every part of her—her breath, her blood, her damn soul—stilled, waiting. For his next words, his next touch...the next brush of his mouth. "I kissed you as a thank-you for listening, for making me feel safe. For not judging me even though I acted like—" a quick smile lifted the corner of his mouth "—a man. Thank you, Tatum."

"You're welcome."

He cocked his head, and stepped forward, claiming the space both of them had inserted between them. From one second to the next she went from inhaling fresh air with a hint of rain to chocolate, oak and sex.

"When or if you want to know the other answer, call me. Come to me. But be ready for the truth, Tatum."

His stare kept her pinned in place for several long, taut moments. A sense of foreboding slid along her veins, flooding them. And underneath, electrifying, was excitement. Cruel, foolish excitement.

Moving back, Bran jerked his chin.

"You mentioned something about ice cream?"

Ice cream? He seriously expected her to just go eat ice cream after he turned her inside out with that ominous warning? But she said, "Yes."

"Have you ever had Sullivan's?"

"No, but I'm very much looking forward to it."

Their gazes caught again. Were they still talking about the restaurant? She didn't know...and was too much of a coward to ask.

"Well, let's go get ice cream then," she murmured.

She pushed off the fence and started down the walkway, and Bran fell into step beside her. Relief should've been her companion as they headed toward the building housing the food court. But it wasn't. Instead, frustration and disappointment weighed on her like an indictment.

She'd made the right decision, the responsible decision, for herself and for her family. So why did she feel like she'd let herself down in her desperation to run toward the sensible and safe thing?

Ten

Bran aimed the remote at the mounted television, turning it on. Two news anchors conversed but he paid the program little mind. All he needed was noise to dispel the quiet in his hotel suite. Funny how he'd never really minded the quiet before. Especially after Roma left, he'd learned to value it. After all the arguing and screaming, he'd equated quiet with peace.

But after spending the day with Tatum, talking with her, hearing her laughter, her shouts against the wind while on the back of his motorcycle—yeah, it was too quiet. Instead of comforting, it suddenly seemed suffocating.

Tapping the volume button, he filled the room with the chatter of the weatherman forecasting rain tonight and a cold front predicted for tomorrow. Good thing he'd taken Tatum on that ride today because Monday would've been too cold.

And you would've missed having that beautiful body curved around you and her hands branding your skin.

He couldn't even tell his subconscious to shut the hell up because it was right. Even now, he could feel the phantom heat of her breasts against his spine, her fingers and palms pressed to his chest and abdomen, searing him through his jacket and shirt.

It'd been the ride from hell and one of pure, undiluted pleasure.

Having Tatum on the back of his bike had been only one of his fantasies. The other...

Setting the remote on the glass coffee table, he scrubbed a hand over his face, but it did nothing to dispel the images flashing across his mind like the dirtiest movie reel. Twisted sheets around tangled limbs. A slender, sleek body arching tight over him as he gripped curved hips. Long, toned arms and legs wrapped tight around his neck and waist. Perfectly manicured fingernails denting his shoulders...

Giving his head one hard shake, he grabbed a cigar and matches off the table and strode across the sunken living room. He climbed the one step into the dining area with its long table and eight tall-backed chairs. The opulence of the suite rolled right off him as he crossed to the French doors that led to the balcony. After twisting the knob, he stepped outside and within moments had the lit cigar to his lips. Puffing on it, he swirled the chocolate-and-whiskey flavor in his mouth before blowing out the cloud of smoke. He squinted at the view of downtown Boston, but the usual calm when he relaxed with his cigar didn't fill him.

Not when thoughts of the day tracked through his mind.

Fuck that. Thoughts of Tatum.

He stared down at the lit end of the cigar, not seeing the red embers. Instead, he saw the joy on Tatum's face as she removed his helmet. Heard her delighted scream as he revved the bike's engine and took off down the interstate. Inhaled the woodsy, citrus scent from the back of her ear as he rubbed his chin against her thick, long strands. Felt the comfort and heat of her body as he caged her between his chest and the fence.

Damn, he should've never thrown down that dare. He'd screwed himself with that move. Now all he could do was torture himself with images of what could've happened between them if she'd said yes. Because that's what her asking him for the truth surmounted to—her saying yes to them returning either back here or to her home. No, she'd done them both a favor.

Just as he brought the cigar back to his lips, a knock sounded on the suite door. He narrowed his eyes on the balcony doorway as if he could determine from there who would be bothering him at this time of night. Hell, who would be bothering him, period. He only knew a few people in Boston, and none of them would be here.

Sighing, he set the cigar on an ashtray and strode back inside. Curling his hand around the knob, he pulled the door open.

"Yeah—Tatum?" He transferred his grip from the knob to the frame, his fingers aching in protest at the tight hold. "What're you doing here?" he unintentionally growled.

"I…" She blinked, her fingers twisting in front of the same jacket she'd worn earlier. As if becoming aware of the tell, she glanced down then dropped her arms to her sides. "I'm sorry to drop in on you unannounced. If it's a bad time…"

She started to turn, but before his mind had even issued permission, he grasped her lower arm.

"No." He jerked his hand back and tunneled his fingers through his hair, briefly fisting the strands before lowering his arm to wave her inside. "No," he repeated. "It's fine. Please, come in." She hesitated, and he couldn't blame her. Not with how he'd just spoken to her. But he stepped back and dipped his chin. "Tatum. Come in," he repeated, voice lower, and damn, he tried for softer. But couldn't be certain he achieved it.

Still, she slowly nodded then entered and he clenched his jaw as her scent assailed him. If he had half a brain, he'd order her to leave. Nothing good could come from the thickening of his cock just from one good hit of her. But he, who'd learned the hard way not to be impulsive, didn't tell her to exit. Instead, he closed the door and followed her farther inside the suite, studying the proud line of her shoulders and back, the subtle yet sensual sway of her hips.

He was fucked and he hadn't laid one finger on her.

Tatum paused beside the dining room table, surveying the elegantly appointed rooms. In the last few years, this kind of luxury had become his norm. But no matter how many zeroes in his net worth labeled him a millionaire, the young kid from small-town Georgia would always reside inside him, and that part would never get used to opulence. Though he currently stayed in one of Boston's most expensive five-star hotels, a small voice couldn't help reminding him how much money he'd save in one of those chain motels across town. All he needed was a clean bed, a shower and a working TV.

He shifted his scrutiny from the suite to Tatum. Now, she belonged here, in these surroundings. Nothing about Tatum Haas said chain hotel. Her skin deserved to grace only the highest thread count Egyptian cotton sheets. Only the best food prepared by top chefs should cross her lips. Only the best view of the city should greet her every morning.

Another reason he should escort her out of here. He could give her pleasure if she allowed him—give it to them both— but the man she needed, the man who'd enjoy galas and dinner parties, the man born of her world... That could never be him. And more importantly, he didn't want to be that man.

"Beautiful place," she said, finally turning to look at him.

"It is." He crossed his arms over his chest. "What're you doing here, Tatum?"

She slid her hands in the pockets of her jacket then swept one hand over her dark hair. The jerky movements relayed her nerves, as had the hand twisting at the door.

"Do you want something to drink?" he offered, because shit, he could use one. And it looked like she could, too. "Water, wine, scotch?"

"Scotch, please," she said, and he didn't miss the relief in her voice.

He nodded. "Why don't you take your jacket off? Unless you plan on having that drink and then running?"

A smile flirted with her mouth. With a silent, fierce curse, he pivoted, stalking toward the built-in bar in the living room. If it felt like he was running away from her and his obsession with that mouth, well… That's because he was running away.

Once he'd set two short glasses on top of the bar, he poured two fingers of scotch each from the crystal decanter and, inhaling a deep breath, turned. Tatum had removed her jacket and stood next to the couch. He approached her, offering her the drink. Their fingertips brushed as she accepted it, and he put a stranglehold on the groan that clawed up his throat.

Yeah. He should've definitely shown her the door.

Sipping the scotch, he welcomed the burn and studied her over the rim.

"You good?" he asked.

"Yes, thank you."

"Do you want to pretend we're talking about the scotch?"

Another of those smiles played with her lips and she shook her head. "I don't think I'll ever get used to how you speak to me," she murmured.

He frowned, lowering his glass. "Have I offended you?"

"No." She shook her head again and took a healthy sip, not even wincing at the potency of the alcohol. "On the con-

trary. Whatever is on your mind, you speak it. Is some of it
blunt and a little shocking in its frankness? Yes, but that's
also why it's so…refreshing. I'm used to barbs wrapped in
compliments. Insults gifted in pleasantries. The truth so en-
tangled with lies that it's impossible to tell one from the other.
Whether you're delivering praise, criticism or an opinion, it
is what it is. And that's rare."

"That's sad." And no, he didn't speak all of what was on
his mind. Especially with her. He would be in a shitload of
trouble if he did.

"It is, isn't it?"

"Is that why you're here?" he pressed, because dammit,
she *still* hadn't answered his question. And though he suspected the reason, he needed to hear it from her. Hear it in
that sex-and-moonlight voice. "You're here for the truth?"

Lust ignited inside him, having already been at a sim-
mer since he'd opened the door to her on the other side. He
locked all his muscles against the onslaught of it, willing her
to laugh off his question.

Willing her to give them both what they needed but, goddamn, had no business taking.

"Yes, that's why I'm here."

Fuck.

Her answer stroked down his chest, his clenching abdomen, his throbbing cock like a seeking hand.

"Give me the truth you didn't earlier today. The one I was
too scared to ask for. I want it now."

"What's different between now and then? What changed?"

"You're stalling," she softly accused, taking another sip
of scotch. "And I might've been scared before, but it's you
now. *You're* scared to answer *me*."

He didn't—couldn't—deny either allegation.

"What changed, Tate?"

She chuckled, and the smoky sound was molten heat in his

blood. Gone was the nervous, fidgety woman who'd shown up at his hotel room door. She'd been replaced by an assured temptress, confident in not just herself but the obvious hold she had on him. Was he glimpsing the Tatum she'd been before her fiancé's death and infidelities had dented her heart and confidence?

The person he'd come to know—the smart businesswoman, vulnerable woman—was irresistible to him. And this version?

This version left him speechless and breathless.

"I shouldn't savor this, but I can't lie. I am." She stared down into her glass for a brief moment. "All this time, I thought it was only me feeling a little terrified, off-kilter and uncertain. But it isn't only me. You're right there with me. Tell me I'm lying," she demanded.

"You're lying," he said, partly just to see what this Tatum would do.

And partly because conceding that she was right—that she terrified him, left him standing on uneven ground—threatened to put him right back in the place he'd been seven years ago when he'd been powerless to stop the shitstorm shaking up his world.

Yeah, she scared him that much.

"I do believe this is the first time you've lied to me," she murmured. And smiled. "Good."

He didn't need to ask what she meant by that; he'd given himself away. So he remained silent. And just watched, fascinated and more than a little wary as she set her tumbler on the end of the coffee table and approached him, not stopping until only a breath of space separated his chest from hers.

"I came over here because I was sitting in my big, empty, too-quiet house trying to convince myself that being there was what I wanted. That it was the right thing to do and the right place to be. That it was safe. But the longer I sat there with the silence and the loneliness, what was right, safe became less and less important. I've always done what was expected of me, followed the rules my entire life. And where has it gotten me? Alone, afraid and quiet. For once, I wanted—*want*—to be selfish. I want to be loud."

If her admission hadn't snatched the air from his lungs, those nearly black eyes with their steady, unwavering stare would've. She stood emotionally naked before him. Shame crept inside him. Because he'd been too afraid to do the same.

He stepped back.

And stripped off his T-shirt.

Her soft gasp brushed against his bare chest as he moved forward, reclaiming the space he'd placed between them. He cupped her cheek with one hand and the whimper that escaped her damn near triggered one from him. Her lashes fluttered, and he bent his head, brushing his lips over the lids before trailing a caress over her cheekbone.

"You want the truth? I don't know if you do because I don't want it." He pressed a kiss to the skin just below her ear, absorbed the delicate shiver that trembled through her. Swallowed a hiss of pleasure as she gripped his waist, her palms against his naked skin. "From the moment you stepped out on that balcony, I've fantasized about you. Wondered if all that fire, all that attitude you threw would burn me alive if I ever got you under me...over me. Fantasized about being on the receiving end of that mouth, those teeth. Fantasized about you marking me with both."

He shifted his hand from her cheek to her head and burrowed his fingers in the thick strands, savoring her hair sliding over his sensitive skin. This time, he didn't hold back his groan. He gave that to her in return for her whimper. "I have no business saying this to you, and you have no business listening. You should tell me to go to hell and walk right out of this room. Because I'm going to be a complete asshole and put the weight of it on you. Because left up to me, I'm picking you up, wrapping those long mind-fuck legs around me and taking you into that bedroom. And not to discuss. Not to talk. We're going to fuck until both of our bodies give."

Her quick, heavy breath broke against his collarbone, and he knew her answer before she uttered a word.

"I don't want to talk either." She lifted her lashes, met his gaze. And the lust in those dark eyes—*damn*. "Fuck me," she whispered.

As if those two words snapped the threadbare restraints on his control, he did just as he promised. Bending down, he cupped the backs of her thighs then stood, hiking her into his arms. Without prompting, Tatum embraced him with her legs, her arms locking around his neck. He spun around and stalked toward the bedroom, desperation and lust lending him a focus that he'd only experienced with motorcycles.

"Wait."

Though every nerve ending screamed in denial and his cock throbbed in protest, he stopped. Searching her face for any sign of doubt, of discomfort, he waited as she requested.

"You're not the only one to dream," she whispered, threading her fingers through his beard, scratching her nails along his jaw. He gave her another moan because goddamn, it felt good. *She* felt good. "One kiss," she said, her gaze dropping to his mouth. "Can I have just one kiss before we—"

He crushed his mouth to hers.

She'd never have to beg him for this. Not when he craved it so bad his fucking toes ached with the need.

And that first taste… God, his knees almost buckled and took both of them to the floor. Sweet. Heady. And immediately addictive. Just one hit. That's all he needed to know he would always hunger for this particular flavor. *Her* flavor.

Her lips parted for the thrust of his tongue, and he took full advantage. Diving deep, he sucked and licked. Dueled and danced. The more he had of her, the more he tasted, the more moans she gave him, the more he needed, demanded.

It might've been a mistake giving in to her. The odds of them making it to the bedroom had severely decreased. And he didn't care. With the lust roaring in his ears, pumping in his veins, he'd take her on this floor and thank God for each rug burn.

She jerked her mouth away from his, and he wasn't too proud to admit he chased her. But she buried her face in his neck and muttered, "The bedroom. Please."

He didn't need any further encouragement. Within moments, he entered the dimly lit space and laid her on the mattress and followed her down. Then taking her mouth again. And again. And again. By the time he lifted his head, her lips were swollen and wet from his and they strained and rocked against each other. Hell, if she weren't still fully clothed and he didn't have his sweatpants on, he would be buried inside her, finally discovering for himself if the clasp of her sex was as tight as his imagination assured him it was.

Cradling the back of her neck, he helped her sit up. Fisting the bottom of her sweater, he tore it over her head and dropped it to the floor behind him. A black lace bra cupped her perfect small breasts, and he bent his head to sip from her flesh. One of those whimpers he was already addicted to echoed in his ears as she tangled her fingers in his hair, holding him to her. Urging him to taste more, take more. Or maybe he was just projecting. Either way, he accepted the offer.

Opening his mouth over the firm flesh, he reached behind her and unhooked the bra then peeled it down her arms. Satisfaction and need coursed through him as he molded her breasts to his hands, squeezing and plumping. He licked a path to her nipple and sucked her deep and hard, drawing on her, circling the beaded peak with his tongue. She arched into him, pressing her flesh into his mouth. Her hands scraped his scalp, his shoulders, his back, restless, urging. On a hum, he switched to the other breast, his fingers tugging and tweaking the damp tip as he again lost himself in her.

Her hips jerked, writhed. Tatum spread her legs wide, cradling him between them, grinding her sex against his abdomen. Damn, he wanted that hot, wet flesh against his skin. On his fingers. In his mouth.

Need and urgency bombarded him, and he sprang off the bed. Bending down to scatter kisses down her torso, he gripped the button on her jeans. He paused, glancing up at her, waiting a moment. If this wasn't what she really wanted...

"Please," she whispered.

A groan rushed through him as he knelt on the floor, removed each boot and then stripped her jeans down her legs. With a finger hooked on each side of her black lace underwear, he drew them off as well, slower, revealing her like a gift. And she was just that. A beautiful gift he'd never expected and damn sure didn't deserve.

"Bran," she breathed, her thighs tensing under his palms. She slid her own hands down her legs to tangle her fingers with his.

He shook his head. "Tell me to stop or move those hands, baby." He grazed the back of one hand with his lips. "The choice is yours."

After a moment, she dropped her arms to the mattress. Her body shook as she slowly widened her legs, and he could feel the effort it took for her to deliberately relax. He rewarded that trust with a hot open-mouthed kiss on her inner thigh.

As he inhaled deeply, her intoxicating musk filled him, and his stomach cramped with hunger. God, he just needed to satiate it. Or he could try. Fuck, he wanted to try.

Palming her thighs, he spread her wider and buried his

mouth against her sex. Her sharp cry bounced off the walls, resounded in his ears, echoed in his chest, his gut. The sounds were almost as delicious to him as the succulent flesh under his tongue, his lips.

With a growl, he devoured her, attempting to get his fill, but even as he lapped at her clit, stroked a path between her swollen folds, he knew it was in vain. He could never get enough of her taste, of that small bud of nerves flinching and swelling under his hungry licks, of her liquid desire in that tight, hot channel. No. He was destined to become a fiend over her.

Pursing his lips over that engorged nub, he sucked even as he slipped two fingers inside her, groaning at that smooth, slick clasp. She quivered around him, and fuck, his dick pulsed, already feeling those tiny spasms over his own flesh. He reached down and fisted himself, trying to alleviate some of the pressure so this didn't end before it began. But he miscalculated. With her in his mouth and his fingers buried inside her, his hard grip only propelled him toward orgasm.

"Get there, baby," he growled, licking her, circling her clit with the tip of his tongue. He thrust inside her, harder, faster. Curling his fingers, he rubbed her, grinding his knuckles against her feminine lips. "Give it to me."

With a long, low moan, she came, her sex gripping him in a chokehold. And he almost followed her. Taking several precious moments, he continued to stroke and rub, giving her the full measure of her release. But as soon as she slumped back against the sheets, he slid free and stood. And removed his sweatpants. After quickly grabbing a condom from his wallet on the bedside table, he ripped the foil package open and rolled the protection down his cock. Later, he might be embarrassed over the slight tremble in his body as he climbed over her. Later, he might deny the twist of anxiety in his gut as he kneed her legs farther apart and hooked her knee over his hip.

Later, he might ignore the small prayer he raised up as he notched the head of his cock between her soaked folds.

Later, later, later...

Right now, though, he admitted she shook him. He admitted being inside her scared and thrilled him.

He admitted this was important to him.

Threading his fingers through her hair, he smoothed it away from her face, fisting the strands. Unable to *not* kiss her, he took her mouth, and she didn't avoid him. Didn't shy away from tasting herself on his tongue and lips. And God, that was sexy as hell.

"On you," he said, trailing a kiss over her cheekbone to her ear. "When you're ready."

"Inside me, Bran," she whispered, her hands tangled in the hair at his nape. "Now."

He didn't need any further encouragement. Thrusting, he buried his cock deep inside her, and despite his best effort, a groan ripped free of his chest. God*damn*. It was like diving into the sultriest sauna and the most refreshing pool of water. How had he gone...?

He cut that thought off, clenching his jaw.

Sex, he reminded himself, pressing his forehead to hers, eyes squeezed closed. It's sex. Amazing, fucking soul-tearing, mind-altering sex. But still...

"Tate? Baby," he growled. "On you," he reminded her. If the too-tight clasp of her core hadn't alerted him that she struggled to accommodate him, the quivering of her slick muscles and the fine tremble in her legs would've. "Tell me when I can move."

"One minute," she rasped, her arms tightening around him. "One minute."

"No hurry, baby."

Oh fuck, he was going to die. But he'd go happy.

He sucked the delicate line of her jaw and nipped before tracing a path down her neck and sipping from the shallow bowl in the middle of her collar bone. With a hum of pleasure, he kissed her again, lowering his hand and cupping one of her beautiful breasts. Shaping it. Squeezing it. Rolling her nipple.

Her hips rolled, pulsing, and lifting his head, he asked—begged, "Ready, Tate?"

"Please, yes," she moaned.

"Thank God."

She chuckled, but it ended on a gasp as he withdrew and drove forward again.

"Again," she breathed. "Oh my God, again."

He obliged, pulling free of her silken grip then powering back in. She sucked him inside, squeezing him, working him. How had he gone forty years without knowing this kind of pleasure? Rearing back, he hiked her thighs over his legs, cupping her ass, holding her steady for his hard, quick thrusts. Her cries poured out of her in a nonstop stream, and he accepted each one as a challenge to fuck her more, harder, bury his cock higher, deeper.

"Bran. I'm—" She gasped, and before she could finish the warning, her sex clamped down on him, rippling over him, milking him.

She came, hips writhing, body shaking, and on a gritted curse, he fell over her, one hand flattened next to her ear and the other still cradling her thigh. He pistoned into her again and again and once more before erupting and following her into a desperate, powerful orgasm. Electricity crackled up his back, nailed him in the back of the neck then traveled back down to sizzle at the base of his spine and even in the soles of his feet.

As he tumbled forward, gathering Tatum close and pressing his nose to the crook of her neck, he had one thought.

He'd fucked up.

Because once wouldn't be enough.

Eleven

Déjà vu.

Sighing, Tatum glanced down at her phone, glancing at the text message she'd received climbing into her car. Her father "requested" her presence as soon as she arrived at the office. Something told her that Monday was about get a lot Monday-er.

This impromptu meeting was about business or her ditching brunch yesterday. At the moment, she didn't feel equipped to discuss either.

The elevator slid to a halt, and the doors opened. Striding out, she barely managed not to wince at the unfamiliar twinges in her thighs…and the flesh between them. Heat poured through her with each reminder of the night before. Of the man responsible for the soreness. And those were the invisible souvenirs. This morning, as she showered, her fingers had glided over the smudged bruises on the insides of her thighs, on her breasts. Without her permission, her fingers lifted and glided over the one on the curve of her breast and hidden under her dress. She flushed.

"Woman, get it together," she muttered under her breath.

She'd snuck out of Bran's hotel before the sun rose, leaving him in the sheets they'd tangled together. That had been more difficult than she would've believed; a part of her—a large part—had wanted to stay in the king-size bed with him, his big body curled around hers. Because that craving had yawned so wide and deep inside her, she'd hurried out of there like Lucifer himself had been snapping at her ass. And not sexy Tom Ellis Lucifer. But the big horned fire-and-brimstone baddie.

Coward move, yes. At the moment, had she felt like she was running, if not for her life, then for her self-preservation and sanity? Yes.

So she could be excused.

But the joke was on her. Because she escaped the hotel room but couldn't outrun her body. Or her mind, where memories from the night before replayed like a movie reel.

Shoving those thoughts to the back of her mind as she approached her father's office—because it was bad form to have a meeting with her dad while thinking about the hottest sex ever—she smiled at Brenda.

"Good morning, Brenda," she greeted the executive assistant.

"Good morning to you, Tatum." She smiled and nodded her head toward the office door. "Your father and sister are already in there."

"Thanks." Still smiling, Tatum kept it until she turned around and then frowned.

Her father hadn't mentioned a meeting with her and Mia. If this was about yesterday, why would her sister need to be in attendance? After giving his door a quick rap, she waited until he called out then entered.

"Morning, Dad." She closed the office door as Silas and

Mia both looked in her direction—he from behind his desk and Mia from the armchair in front of it.

Why did she get the feeling she'd just interrupted something?

Stop being paranoid, she immediately berated herself. It was her father and sister, not coworkers gossiping around the watercooler—if they had a watercooler.

"Hey, Mia," she said, her voice not betraying the disquiet gelling inside her belly. "Dad, I hope you have coffee ready. It's already a Monday," she teased, crossing the floor to the vacant armchair next to her sister.

"Coffee's over there." He dipped his chin in the direction of the sitting area, but Tatum didn't turn and glance over there, much less rise from her seat. Call it a survival instinct, but she didn't feel like she could remove her attention from either her father or sister. And God, that sounded plain awful. But she still didn't look away from them.

"Thank you." She paused and crossed her legs, flattening her hands on the arms of the chair. "What's going on?" Her twisting stomach wouldn't allow her to beat around the bush.

"What happened with brunch yesterday?" her father asked in return.

Seriously? This was the office. He was calling her on the carpet about missing a meal. They couldn't have done this by phone call? Though she'd suspected this might be the reason behind the early-morning meeting, it didn't annoy her any less. At some point during this past year, she hadn't just been viewed as broken but her parents had also started treating her as if she were nine instead of twenty-nine.

And yes, she was partly to blame because she'd been so mired in her own anger, pain and grief that she'd permitted it. But this had to stop. *Had* to stop. The coddling, the admonishments, the ambushing, the pushing... When did *she* get to push back?

"Dad." She inhaled a breath and slowly, deliberately released it. "I love you and Mom, but I explained to you both yesterday why I didn't come over."

"You said something came up," he said, templing his fingers under his chin, his dark gaze narrowed on her.

"Yes, and it did."

"On a Sunday?"

"On a Sunday," she repeated, and a tense quiet descended on the office when she didn't offer a more detailed explanation.

Finally, Silas sighed. "Tatum, I'm not sure what's going on but I'm concerned."

She tilted her head, frowning. "Forgive me, Dad, but I'm truly confused. You're concerned because I missed one family meal? At the most, it's rude to cancel at the last minute, but a meeting that smacks of an intervention? That's a little extreme."

"First, disappearing during your mother's dinner party Friday night and having a client take you home. No word from you on Saturday. Then you cancel yesterday, and when your sister went by your house to check on you, you weren't home. Not Friday evening or Sunday," he said, and even though his voice remained calm, she couldn't miss the accusation and disappointment there.

"Okay, let's talk about it, Dad," she said, leaning forward, propping an elbow on her knee. She met his gaze with her own, her heart thumping like a wild thing behind her breastbone. "Truth? I didn't become ill Friday night. I was anxious, frustrated and uncomfortable in the home where I should've felt safe and welcome. Instead, once again, you prioritized business and appearances over my well-being, my concern, my simple *feelings*, and invited Leo and Dara Walker."

"Are you serious, Tatum?" He scowled, flipping his hands up, and though her father would never speak it, the gesture clearly read, *What the fuck?* "Do you really expect me to end a business arrangement because of… Mark's death? That's ridiculous, immature and unprofessional."

"No, I don't expect you to end your business relationship with them. But I do expect and deserve loyalty. Keep it business—deal with them here in the office or in professional settings. But always inviting them into spaces I consider safe is a violation of our relationship. It would be one thing if their purpose was MassComm. But every time, without fail, they pressure me to remain in the role of Mark's fiancée, unwilling to see how it tears me down. But if they either can't or are unwilling to see it, you and Mom do. You know what it does to me, and yet you continue to place me in that position because of *business*."

The silence in the room roared in her ears, echoing the frantic pounding of her pulse and heart. Her chest rose and fell on her rapid, agitated breaths, and she struggled, but finally won, to bring it under control. She refused to give her father the ammo of accusing her of being "emotional."

Even though, goddammit, she was emotional. If parents not protecting their child but opting to throw her to the wolves didn't call for *emotion*, than she didn't know what did.

"It's been almost a year, Tatum," he murmured, and she hated the compassion in his eyes.

Resented it.

She'd needed his compassion the first time the Walkers asked her to speak at Mark's funeral when the betrayal and pain had been fresh. She'd needed his concern when he'd called her, pressuring her to go over to Mark's old apartment to help clean it out and be dragged down a memory lane that had been all lies. She'd needed his protection when they'd impressed upon her again to speak at their foundation in his honor.

She'd needed her father, her parent. And he hadn't been there.

But Bran had. He'd shielded her from her parents' demands, their expectations, their thoughtlessness.

He'd done what none of her family had in almost a year, as her father had pointed out.

"We can't be responsible for wrapping you in cotton, Tate," Mia said, backing their father. So this was the side her sister had chosen today. It'd wavered over the months, flip-flopping. "You can't avoid them or anyone else, for that matter. Life is going on while you're stuck in the past."

"Stuck in the past?" Tatum loosed an abrupt, dry chuckle. "That's the problem, isn't it? I'm trying to move forward but I'm not allowed. And Dad—" she shifted her gaze back to her father "—if you can't even say what happened, how difficult do you think it is for me? 'Mark's death.' He didn't die in a car accident or have a heart attack. He had a brain aneurysm and died naked in a hotel room while screwing a woman that wasn't me, the fiancée he was supposed to marry the next morning. The fiancée he'd been cheating on for months, possibly our entire relationship. Those are the facts. No one—" she slid a hard look at her sister before returning her regard back to Silas "—gets to determine how I deal with it."

"Does part of you 'dealing with it' include becoming involved with a BayStar client?" he asked, his voice softer but no less demanding.

Shock shoved her back against the chair. Ice splintered inside her chest, and she couldn't move. She stared at her father, vocal cords encased in a deep freeze.

What...? How...?

"Answer me, Tatum. Are you—" he paused, his lips firming into a grim line "—intimately involved with Bran Holleran?"

"Why would you ask me that?" How did he know? Or

was he only fishing for information? Either way, she couldn't admit the truth. Not…right now. Guilt flared inside her, yet she didn't avoid his gaze, but met it. "Tell me what this is really about. I miss a Sunday brunch and suddenly I'm called on the carpet for what, exactly?" She tilted her head. "Sabotaging an account or attempting to acquire it by getting on my back? That's a big leap isn't it?"

"The fact is I've heard of…concerns about his demeanor toward you. And with you being in a vulnerable position—"

"Oh this is great." She leaned her head back and barked out a harsh laugh. "Dad, either you believe me capable enough of working in this company and possibly one day helming it or you don't. The only thing riding a fence gets you is splinters in the ass."

"Now just a minute," he snapped, flattening his palms on his desk and leaning forward. "I'm your father—"

"Here, you're my employer," she snapped back. "And tell me one thing I've done to jeopardize this account. One act of impropriety. Name it."

He glanced at Mia, and it was fleeting, but Tatum caught it. And understanding dawned. So bright and clear, she narrowed her eyes on her father then Mia.

"Oh I get it now. The source of the *concerns*." She arched an eyebrow and smiled and didn't try to soften the sharp edges of it. No, those edges reflected the jagged points of hurt in her heart. "How about you confide in me, Mia, instead of carrying tales to Dad? What is it about Bran Holleran that worries you?"

Mia sighed, rolling her eyes as if exasperated by Tatum and the discussion. "I just mentioned to Dad how he was a little handsy Friday night—"

"Handsy?" Tatum snapped, scrolling through her memories to the night of the dinner party. "In what way?"

"Tatum, stop being so obtuse. He touched your back—"

"And you touched his chest," Tatum shot back. "So if he was inappropriate, what were you?" Mia's lips parted, but Tatum shot up a hand, halting her next words. "Next, Mia— because that's bullshit and you know it—what is the rest of your evidence that is so dire it facilitated this *meeting*?"

She fought to grab a hold of her temper, but she suspected this was less about concern over any potential predatory advances and more over their rivalry. Both professional and personal. Mia was undoubtedly still angry about Dad removing her from the account. And… And Tatum hadn't forgotten the way her sister had looked at and touched Bran. With familiarity and more than a little interest.

There was an agenda here. And it was all Mia's.

"I came by your house Friday night after dinner to check on you and drove over on Sunday. You weren't home either night. And when I tried calling you and Bran, neither of you answered. I doubt that's just a coincidence," she sneered.

"Oh so we've taken to doing drive-bys on each other? While your concern is certainly—" Tatum's lip curled in a mocking smile "—touching, I can't help but wonder why you dropped by my house when you haven't before. Did it occur to you that I didn't want company? Or that if I was out, that it was my business and I didn't have to log my whereabouts with you?"

"Sarcasm gets you—"

"Gets my point across," she interrupted. "And another question. Why are you calling Bran Holleran? The account was assigned to me, so I can't think of any reason you'd have for contacting him."

Mia's chin lifted, and her smile, though small, was smug. "We have a friendly personal relationship."

Tatum didn't allow her sister or father to witness how that self-satisfied, arrogant answer affected her. How it punched her in the chest, leaving a hollow ache behind. Leaving jealousy behind. This had ceased to be about business.

This was about her not feeling emotionally safe with either of them.

"Are you removing me from the Greer Motorcycles account, Dad?" she asked, switching her attention back to her father. The calm, flat tone didn't match the cacophony of anger, disappointment and hurt clashing inside her like an out of tune orchestra.

Everything in her stilled as she waited for his answer.

After a long moment, he exhaled. "No, Tatum, you are still on the account. But—"

"No." She rose from her chair and forced her hands to remain at her sides instead of clenching into fists. Or worse, crossing over her chest, telegraphing her vulnerability. "No buts. Yes, I've had a difficult last few months. But my track record at BayStar can hold up against any employee here. If it couldn't, you wouldn't have risked having me handle Greer Motorcycles in the first place, no matter my relation to you. So either you trust that I wouldn't do anything to deliberately harm this investment or you don't."

Not waiting for his reply, and not glancing at her sister, she strode across the office and, after pulling open the door, exited.

But she couldn't leave the guilt and powerlessness so easily.

She couldn't outrun herself.

Twelve

"So are we taking turns popping up on each other?" Tatum stopped at the end of her front walk, meeting the ice-blue gaze of the man sitting on the top step of her home.

"If that's what you want to call it," Bran said, rising, and she tried—damn, she tried—not to soak him in. But she failed. Miserably. She couldn't stop from taking in his tall, wide-shouldered frame clothed in a black pea coat, dark blue sweater and jeans.

A ball of heat coalesced just under her navel and she glanced away from him, focusing on a spot somewhere over his shoulder. Just for a few seconds while she got the need under control. She should've expected that seeing him for the first time after having him inside her would carry more impact.

But God, she'd seriously underestimated just *how* powerful.

She couldn't look at him without seeing that beautiful, rugged face tightened in lust as he came and went rigid above her. Couldn't see him without feeling the phantom brand of his chest to her back and his hand on her thigh, holding it high as he thrust into her from behind. Couldn't see him without feeling his hard, big body surrounding her as they fell asleep.

A shaky breath shuddered out of her and she forced herself to meet his gaze again.

"What would you call it?" she asked, climbing the steps until they stood next to each other.

She didn't wait for his answer but unlocked her front door and entered then held it open for him to follow. Call her paranoid, but after the morning she'd had, privacy on her front stairs had become more of a theory than reality.

Once she'd dumped her bag and purse on the chaise longue, she shrugged out of her coat and hung it on the newel post of the staircase.

"Are you done?" he asked, his smoke-and-midnight voice dancing down her spine.

She halted on her way to the living room and spun around to look at him. The hurt, the anger, the fear from earlier swelled inside her, threatening to take her under. All day, she'd wanted to call him, to hear his voice, to…to have those long, muscled arms around her, cradling her as they'd done the night before. But she couldn't. Couldn't give in to that need, couldn't lean on him.

Last night was last night. In the past, and it had to stay there. Because she could so easily become dependent on him, and even if he weren't her client, Bran was leaving Boston in a matter of weeks. And who was she kidding? A man scarred by his divorce and a woman left damaged by death and lies didn't make for a healthy relationship.

They should end this now and walk away…

"No," she whispered. "I'm not done."

She stalked over to him, thrust her fingers underneath the bun low at his nape, dragged his head down as she rose on her toes and took his mouth. Not bothering to contain the whimper that clawed free of her, she parted her lips and thrust her tongue into his mouth, taking control of the kiss.

Taking. Taking. Taking.

And he gave. God, did he give.

His hands lightly cupped her hips and he let her have her way with his mouth—nipping, sucking, licking, rubbing. She couldn't get enough of those firm lips with a touch of softness. Drawing back, she grazed his full bottom lip with her teeth, easing any sting with a long, luxurious swipe of her tongue.

Desperation and hunger stole through her, and if she could've crawled up his rangy body, or better, inside him, she would've. But she settled for tugging free his long, dark hair, burrowing her fingers in the strands. Pulling him down again, she reclaimed his mouth, enjoying every scratch of that salt-and-pepper beard over her skin. Not caring that tomorrow might tell the tale if she weren't careful.

She was far past careful.

Ripping a page out of his book, she stepped back from him and slid her feet free of her heels. Keeping her gaze fixed on his gleaming blue eyes, she reached for the tie at her waist, loosened her dress and unwrapped herself. The front fell open, revealing her purple demi bra and matching thong. Without a word, she shrugged, and the material slipped soundlessly to the floor. Still maintaining their visual throwdown, she slowly bent at the waist, reaching for the silk top of her thigh-high stocking.

"Don't." She paused at the hoarse command, her fingers hooked into each side. A shiver rolled over her at the lust burning in his eyes, tightening the skin over his brutal bone structure so he appeared carved from the hardest, most beautiful stone. "That's mine."

That's mine.

He referred to the action of removing the lingerie—he

proved it by striding forward and sinking to his knees in front of her, his hands brushing hers aside.

Yet…

Yet, the command—no, the claim—reverberated inside her chest, and much lower in her sex. Branded her. She'd never believed she would want to belong to someone again, not after the last time had ended up a cruel lie. Mark hadn't been hers; he'd been several somebodies'. And she hadn't been his. How could she be if she was interchangeable?

So she'd given up on that dream, convinced herself she didn't need it.

Until this moment. Until Bran uttered *mine*.

A yearning so wild, so fierce swelled inside her, she had to swallow back a cry. A cry that would've been misplaced in this foyer, where only lust and hunger reigned.

Tunneling her fingers through his thick hair, she scraped her fingernails over his scalp, hoarding the low rumble of pleasure he gave her in return. His hot mouth was high on her thigh just above the lacy top of the stocking. Kissing the skin, he rolled the lingerie down and repeated the caress and the gesture on the other leg.

His palms cradled her hips, and he leaned back on his heels, staring up at her, and maybe she was projecting but it almost looked like reverence in those ice-blue depths. The emotions she'd been fighting all day coasted up her body, swirling, merging, and she blinked against their force. That look called her strong and indomitable and she felt anything but.

"Baby?" he murmured, his calloused palms stroking down her thighs to the back of her knees. With a slight pressure, he bent them and brought her down to the floor, straddling his powerful thighs. Those same hands cupped her face, tilting it down so she had no choice but to meet his gaze. "What's wrong? Talk to me, Tate."

She shook her head. Not now.

Right now she just wanted to burn with him. Drowning in the pleasure only he seemed capable of eliciting from her body.

Circling his wrists, she drew his hands down to her breasts, urging those big palms and long, elegant skillful fingers to cover her. Squeeze her. Make her come. And forget.

Maybe he heard her plea, or maybe the need to touch her surged as hot in him as it did in her. She didn't care. Not here.

As he shoved the bra cups under her breasts and played with her flesh like she was an instrument he was set on fine-tuning, she kissed him again. Thrust her tongue to engage in another erotic game of hide-and-seek. And below, she rocked against the hard, thick—*God*—long length of his cock. Back and forth. Up and down. She was so wet and was probably making an utter mess of her insubstantial thong and the front of his jeans. It didn't matter. Nothing mattered but him and the pleasure that streamed through her like liquid fire.

"Don't think I don't know you're using me to get off, baby," he murmured against her flesh, flicking a glance at her even as he swept the flat of his tongue over her nipple. Rubbing his thumb around the other tip, he lowered one hand to his jeans and undid them. He slowly reclined on the foyer floor, pulling her with him. Threading his fingers through her hair, he cradled her head and this time, his kiss left her breathless and weak, limbs trembling. "Don't hold back, Tate."

He lowered one hand back to his jeans, jerked the zipper down and pulled his cock free. Hiking his hips up, he shoved the denim down until it gathered just under his ass. Palming his aroused flesh, he stroked a hand up its length, the wide bulbous tip disappearing in his fist before appearing seconds later, glistening with precum. His body arched and strained into the rough caress, and her mouth watered at the thick cock now gleaming with the evidence of desire *she'd* stirred. Desire for *her.* "Fuck it, baby," he urged. "Use it. Use me. That's what I'm here for. For you."

She covered his mouth with her hand. That mouth, that tongue, was temptation, and if he didn't stop talking, his dick wouldn't be the only thing she would beg him for. His raw honeyed urging would propel her right over the edge into release if she wasn't careful.

Lifting, she hovered over his cock…then slid down. And oh God, down. A moan slipped free from her, and the hand not covering his mouth tangled in her own hair. Oh damn. He was… He could… She couldn't…

Oh but dammit, she couldn't stop. The pleasure/burn spurred her on, didn't cause her to halt. She wanted all of it, all of *him*.

"Fuck. Tate." Bran jerked his head to the side, out from under her hand, and he gripped her hips, stopping their steady pulsing. "No condom," he ground out.

She hung her head, her fingers digging into his broad shoulders.

"Pill," she breathed, meeting his bright gaze. "I'm on the pill. And I'm clean. I checked after—*oh God.*"

He thrust hard inside her, stealing the rest of the air from her lungs. Her back arched, her nails denting his skin. Fingers fisted her hair, tugging her head down, and dazed, she stared at him.

"It's just you and me here. No one else." He held her to him, rocking his hips in a tight circle as if trying to screw inside her. Or something. Damn, she couldn't tell anymore. She barely knew who *she* was any longer. "And I'm clean, too. Thank God. Because to go my whole fucking life without feeling this…" He withdrew and plunged inside her again, and she tipped her head back, whimpering. "Yeah, this was worth waiting forty fucking years for."

She'd waited twenty-nine to feel this…free. And she reveled in it. Threw herself into it with abandon. She rose off his cock, stopped when only the tip stretched her entrance, then dropped back down. And damn, she almost came from that alone.

Almost.

She lost herself in each plunge, each roll, each grind. Beneath her, Bran strained and arched into each stroke, each filthy slide of skin against skin, flesh over flesh. They raced together toward that inevitable, cataclysmic end, even though she ran away from it. Chased it. Dodged it. Chased it. Dodged it.

But when he reached between them and rubbed his thumb over her clit, that's all it took for her to detonate and release into the oblivion of ecstasy. She shook with it, cried out with it.

Gloried in it.

Beneath her, Bran pounded into her, his strokes uneven, fevered, and when he exploded, coming and pouring into her, she sank down onto his sweater-covered chest.

She didn't want to move.

And she didn't have to.

There was a freedom in that, too.

"Okay, you win." Bran leaned against the kitchen wall, arms crossed over his bare chest, while she cooked them omelets. Simple but filling food after two bouts of hot sex. "You won the fucked-up Monday contest."

"Thank you." She performed a half curtsy, almost flashing him from under the hem of his sweater. "I'd like to thank the little people..."

He snorted, his wiry body straightening as he crossed to her glass-fronted cabinets and opened the one with plates. After liberating two, he walked over and held them out for her, and she slid the eggs onto them. While he carried them to the table in the breakfast nook, she grabbed knives and forks. They sat and dug into the food, and several moments passed with nothing but the scrape of utensils against plates filling the silence.

"This is delicious," he praised. Lifting his wine—because they were classy like that—he pushed the empty plate away from him.

"Thank you." And no, she wasn't blushing.

"I'm not saying I'm surprised..." He arched an eyebrow, the corner of his mouth quirking. "But where did you learn to cook like that?"

"Why wouldn't I know how to cook? Just because we had a chef in our house?"

"Yeah."

"You're right." She grinned. "Nore taught me in college. She refused to watch me waste money on takeout and restaurants after we moved off campus into our own apartment sophomore year. She made me learn simple meals so I could feed myself. Like normal people. Her words, not mine." She laughed, shaking her head.

God, she missed Nore.

"She misses you," he said, and she glanced sharply at him. Did he grant amazing orgasms and read minds? A regular Renaissance man. "Before I met you, I knew one main thing about you, Tatum Haas. You're loved."

She bent her head, slicing into her omelet. Not because she was suddenly so famished—no, to hide the sting of tears. *You're loved.* Sometimes she forgot that. And sometimes she needed the reminder because she felt so unlovable.

"That's why we're best friends. I love her, too," she murmured.

"I could see that without ever seeing the two of you together. I think that's the only reason she put up with your sister when she came out to Seattle."

Tatum jerked her head, blinking. "What?"

He nodded. "Maybe Nore hasn't said anything, but when

Mia flew in for our launch party, they were just cordial. I got the feeling Nore doesn't really care for her."

"No," she murmured, frowning. "She's never said anything."

Although, now that she thought back on it, Nore would beg off from spending time with Mia back in college, claiming Tatum should spend time with her sister. Her frown deepened, and she resisted the urge to grab her cell and call her best friend. Had Mia said something to Nore? Made her feel uncomfortable?

"Knowing Nore, she wouldn't. Of course—" he shrugged "—I could be off. I've only seen them together twice, and both times were in Seattle. For the launch and when she visited Greer for the initial meeting about an investment with BayStar." He set his glass down on the table, propped his crossed arms in front of him and leaned forward, his gaze steady on hers. "Those were the only occasions I've talked to your sister outside of the times here in Boston. With you. There's no relationship between us other than a professional one. Definitely not one that I instigated or encouraged."

A knot that she hadn't even been aware of unfurled deep inside her. Mia had planted seeds of worry and distrust when she'd intimated earlier that she and Bran were closer than business associates. Given what Tatum had endured with Mark… It had instilled an insecurity inside her that she hated because it wasn't her.

She didn't want it to be her.

"You didn't have to lie to your father about us, though," he added.

Setting her fork down next to her plate, she huffed out a self-deprecating laugh. "One, who I sleep with is none of his or Mia's business. And two, yes, I did."

He cocked his head. "Why?"

"Because I'm a PR problem." This time her laugh abraded

her throat. Standing, she grabbed their plates up and then carried them to the sink. "We've talked about why I replaced Mia on your deal. But I wasn't completely honest." She flattened her palms on the counter, staring down at them before lifting her head and meeting his unwavering gaze. "My father replaced Mia with me because, as my sister puts it, I'm a PR problem. The board, our employees, the public—they need to build confidence in me and stop seeing me as 'the tragedy.' So you were my chance to rehabilitate myself and prove I'm able to handle the upcoming open position of COO."

She leaned against the counter. After inhaling a breath, she exhaled it then smiled. It felt brittle on her lips.

"So no, I couldn't tell him that you and I had slept together. Because he wouldn't have seen two consenting adults. He only would've seen me continuing to be a broken, needy PR problem. One so desperate for male validation because of my dead fiancé that I fucked a client. And he would've viewed you as the man taking advantage of his vulnerable daughter. And what we've both worked so hard for wouldn't mean a damn thing. Not to mention, Dad isn't above smearing your name in the business community."

Bran pushed back his chair and rose to his feet. In moments, he stood in front of her, his arms bracketing hers, his chest a breath away from hers, his face lowered until their breaths nearly mingled. To glimpse the anger and frustration there. The simmering lust.

The…

She dipped her gaze to his chin. Here she went, projecting again.

Not being strong on her own but needing a man to want… and love her again. Weak. She'd promised herself she'd never be that weak again. She *owed* that to herself.

"Let's get one thing straight, Tate. I respect your father as a businessman. Neither me or Joaquin would've approached him about investing in Greer if we didn't. But he can't make or break my career. And anyone who would believe you're some vulnerable, fragile creature who can't hold her own in and out of the boardroom is a fucking idiot and not worthy of trying to impress. I don't give a good goddamn about their opinion of me nor do I need their business. I've never hidden behind anyone before—man or woman—and I won't now. So don't use me as the reason for not being honest with your family. And one more thing."

He pinched her chin, tilting her head back. "Not all men lie. Not all men cheat. Not all men will fail and abandon you."

"I know that," she whispered.

"Do you?" He dropped his hand and stepped back. "I have to wonder about that."

Clearing her throat, she ducked her head and rounded him. Because while she did believe that not all men would betray or disappoint her, a tiny, whisper-soft voice insisted that was a lie. At least for her. Insisted she couldn't trust another man because she couldn't trust herself.

She was the problem.

"I'll be right back. I'm going to grab some clothes and return your sweater since it's getting chilly in here."

It was as good an excuse as any. She really needed a moment that wasn't chocolate, oak and sex infused. Not granting him time to object, she dipped out, climbed the stairs to her bedroom and exchanged a black lounge outfit for his sweater. After several minutes, she descended the stairs and reentered the kitchen, a smile back in place.

"Here's your— What're you doing?" she rasped, shock freezing her in the kitchen entranceway.

His sweater fell from her numb fingers as she stared at Bran as he rose from a crouch, holding a small cardboard box, and inside were a black cell phone and a brown leather wallet, among other items. Dimly, she noted the top of the box on the floor along with a watch and thin gold chain. Still, the nausea churning in her belly, the acid racing for the back of her throat claimed most of her attention. Bran glanced at her over his shoulder, but the emotional riot inside her must've been reflected on her face because he dropped the box with the phone and wallet to the table and strode the short distance to her.

"What the hell, Tate? What's wrong?" He cupped her jaw. "I'm sorry about the box. It was on the chair and I didn't notice it until it dropped on the floor. I got most—"

"That's Mark's phone," she breathed, staring at it as if it might lunge out of the container and hiss at her. "Not his regular one. The day I had to leave the movie set? It was because his parents called my mother and father to have them convince me to help clean out his place. I hated it. Every second, I hated being in the space where we'd eaten together, relaxed together, made love." She choked on a bitter laugh. "Or I was making love. But I stayed and his mother insisted on giving me the box of his effects from the hospital. Including that phone. I immediately recognized it's a burner phone. It was so obvious, and there's only one reason for a man in a committed relationship to have a burner."

He lowered his hand from her face and nodded, his eyes narrowed, thoughtful. Glancing down at the phone, he studied it for several moments before returning his regard to her.

"It's not my business, but when I picked it up, the screen illuminated. After ten months, this phone should be dead. You charged it?"

Embarrassment spread through her like a stain, and she bent on the pretense of picking up his sweater when she couldn't meet his gaze.

"Tatum?"

"Yes," she snapped. Then softer, rubbing her forehead, said, "I'm sorry. Yes, I did." Jerking her arm down, she hiked her chin up, and knew she looked defiant, defensive. But she couldn't help it. That had been her MO for the past months. "I don't know. I've never known," she said.

Circling him, she headed for the wine she'd abandoned on the table. She picked it up and sipped. But she wasn't thirsty; she was stalling.

"You've never known what, Tatum?"

"Who he was with," she blurted. "The police didn't find the woman who called 911—the woman he was having an affair with. And I know it's crazy and self-destructive, but part of me just believes if I knew…if that last part of the mystery was solved, then I could let this anger, this resentment go. I could truly move on. But it's the not knowing…"

She set the glass back on the table and wrapped her arms around herself.

"You can tell yourself that but we both know that's bullshit. Look at me," he ordered, and she obeyed. "You're torturing yourself. Punishing yourself," he said, and though his words were harsh, his soft tone belied them. "What happens if you meet this woman? What will it prove? What will you tell yourself? Everything mean, ugly and hurtful you can think of? You will be mean to yourself, heaping that toxicity on the only innocent person in this whole shitstorm of lies. And one of those lies, Tatum? That you'll let it go. That you'll heal once you know who was lying in that bed with Mark."

He rounded the end and cupped her elbows, giving her a small, gentle shake. Then he pulled her close, ignoring her crossed arms, and brushed a kiss over her forehead.

"You'll heal once you realize the fault lies with people who aren't here to be accountable for it. And you'll start to let go when you accept one unfair, fucked-up thing." He cradled her face, his thumb rubbing over her bottom lip. "Baby, Mark cheating on you with another woman had nothing to do with you. To him, it probably wasn't even personal. What's more, if he were here, he'd most likely swear up and down he loves you. And it might even be true. That sounds crazy to you because *you* were hurt, *you* were betrayed, *you* were about to be his wife. But it's true. That's because he had something missing inside him. Integrity. Honor. Loyalty. Selflessness. The ability to put someone else above himself. So you see, it had nothing to do with you and every fucking thing to do with him."

She blinked. Blinked again, battling the sting in her eyes. Sinking her teeth into the inside of her bottom lip, she tried to contain the tears. His words reached right into her chest, fisted her heart and squeezed until she couldn't breathe.

"No, baby. Don't hold back. Not with me. You're safe here. Right here." His arms enclosed her, his hand sliding into her hair and cradling her head, pressing her face to him. "Let it go without any fear of judgment. Let it go."

As if she only needed those words, the sob ripped free from her. Like a lanced wound, the rage, pain, helplessness, insecurity and fear poured out of her, and she clutched him to her, her haven in this chaotic, scary storm.

She let go.

And he held her.

Just as he promised.

Thirteen

Bran stepped off the elevator on the floor that held BayStar's executive offices. As soon as the doors opened, a young Black woman smiled at him.

"Mr. Holleran." She extended her hand. "I'm Tara, Ms. Haas's assistant. If you'll follow me, she's waiting for you in the conference room."

Shaking her hand, he nodded. "Thank you, Tara. It's nice to meet you." He followed her down the hall and dipped his chin again when she stopped in front of a closed door on the left. "Thank you again."

"You're welcome." With a smile, she left him to enter the conference room, and Mia Haas glanced up from papers on the long table, giving him another smile, this one much warmer than her assistant's.

"Bran." She strode toward him, her arms outstretched. When he halted her progress and aborted what would've undoubtedly been an awkward hug—awkward in that he wanted no part of it—he clasped both of her hands between his. He shook them once and released her.

Her smile dimmed but held firm. He'd admire her for her composure if anger didn't burn a hole in his gut.

"I was surprised to receive your request to see me, Bran. Pleasantly surprised." She swept a hand toward the chairs lining the table like soldiers. "Please, have a seat."

"No, thank you. This won't take long."

She frowned, tilting her head. "I hope everything is okay. Is there a problem with the Greer account?"

"No, everything's perfect there." He studied her, searching for the signs among her loveliness that might reveal the heart—or lack of it—that existed beneath. But nothing. Not one. Damn. Clue. He removed his cell from the pocket of his blazer, located his contacts and scrolled until he found hers. He recited the number. "That's your number, isn't it, Mia?"

Her frown deepened and she leaned a hip against the edge of the table, crossing her arms over her chest. "Yes, that's mine." Flicking a hand toward the cell, she asked, "I'm sorry, but I don't understand. What does my phone number have to do with why you needed to see me?"

Slowly, he shook his head. "I hoped—"

The door to the conference room suddenly opened and Silas stepped inside, his gaze shifting from Bran to Mia, and his dark eyes held a wealth of suspicion. Even though, when he greeted Bran, none of that leaked into his voice.

"Good morning, Mia, Bran." Silas closed the door. "I passed Tara on the way from my office. She said you two had a meeting. Bran—" he slid his hands in his pants pockets "—are you having issues with the deal? Maybe we should get Tatum here—"

"You'll probably want to hold up on that until we air this out." He returned his attention to Mia, holding up his phone again. "Your telephone number. Apparently from the phone you used to call me when I was in Seattle."

"Yes, I already said that was my number. I still don't understand what that—"

"Why was your number in Mark Walker's burner phone? As a matter of fact, you were the last person he called on the night he died."

"What?" Silas barked, striding forward. Bran felt him draw nearer rather than saw him. Because he didn't tear his stare away from Mia. "What number?" Bran didn't have to look back at the phone again to recite it, since the night before, when he'd first glimpsed it on the burner phone's log, the thing was branded into his memory. "That's not Mia's cell number," Silas objected.

"It is." Bran dipped his chin toward the quiet woman whose brown eyes seemed to darken with anger...and maybe some trepidation. "She just confirmed it. Another burner phone, right?"

She didn't reply, but she didn't need to. He had his answer. Had everything he needed to know.

"You were the woman who called 911 that night. You were the one with Mark in that hotel room, and then after making sure the ambulance came for him, you showed up at the hospital as if you hadn't been the woman screwing your sister's man behind her back."

"The hell?" Silas snapped. "That's not true! Mia, say something, dammit. Tell him this isn't true. You would never do that to your sister. I don't know how family treats one another where you're from, Bran, but here we love each other. We're loyal—"

"Dad," Mia quietly said. "Stop."

"Yes. Please stop."

Bran pivoted sharply on the heel of his motorcycle boot. *Shit.* They'd all been so focused on their conversation, none of them had heard the door open or see Tatum enter.

Damn, he wanted to go to her, wrap his arms around her.

Shelter her from what was about to come. But he couldn't. He'd tried but he couldn't protect her from the storm that was about to wreck her life. Again.

Tatum moved farther into the room and closed the door behind her. She halted in front of her sister, and Bran tensed, ready to intervene if Mia took one step toward Tatum.

"Go ahead, Mia. Dad's listening, and so am I. Is Bran right? Were you the woman with Mark? Were you with my fiancé behind my back?" she asked, voice even. Too even.

Bran's body rebelled at *my fiancé*. Stupid as hell, but a primal part of him rejected her claiming anyone else. Anyone but him.

Shit.

Clenching his jaw, he shoved the inconvenient and disquieting thought aside for the moment. Although there was no ignoring it for long.

"Mia," Silas rasped. "Sweetie, no."

Mia's gaze flicked to her father then back to Tatum. Her expression didn't reflect any emotion. Not fear or remorse... Yet, her eyes contradicted the aloofness. They gleamed with a sheen of moisture that Mia blinked against.

"Yes, it was me," Mia admitted, tone cool. "I was with Mark that night. And yes, I had been seeing him behind your back for the last year."

Except for her shoulders and back stiffening, Tatum didn't react. But Silas's rumble of shock and outrage filled the room. He moved toward his daughter, slamming his palms down on the conference table across from her.

"No," he snapped. "No, I won't believe it. I won't accept that you would betray your sister like that. And that you'd lie about it, not just to her and to us and the police, too. No daughter of mine would do that."

"Oh so you remember I'm your daughter when it's convenient for you?" Mia murmured, her lips twisting into a wry smile. "Sorry to disappoint you, Dad, but a daughter of yours did lie and cheat. I don't know how, but you're going to have to find a way to deal with that."

"Is that why you did it?" Tatum asked, speaking for the first time since her sister's heartbreaking announcement. "To get back at Dad for some perceived slight? Or did you do it to hurt me?"

"Both." Her voice lost some of that ice. "You have no idea what it's like growing up in the shadow of the perfect Tatum Haas. That shadow is so long and wide, a person is invisible in it, can never step outside of it. Anything I did you'd already done or had done better. I have never been enough. At home or here." She jabbed a finger on the table. "So yes, I slept with Mark, to take who you believed was yours. To finally be on equal footing with you, even if it was in secret. But that backfired. I fell in love with him. But he wouldn't call off the wedding. In the end, he still wouldn't choose me. And even after his death, you're the poor-is-me fiancée. You're the tragic figure when you weren't the only person to love him. Or the only one he loved."

"You've witnessed firsthand the hell the last few months have been. And you can still stand there and complain because people didn't know you were the side chick? That you're not getting the 'attention' I'm receiving?" Tatum laughed, and Bran nearly winced at the serrated edge of it. "Forget Mark. *You* betrayed *me*. Your sister. Every day for the last ten months, you've made a conscious decision to look me in my face, remain silent through my pain and continue to lie. And somehow you're still making yourself the victim."

"Tatum." Mia's mouth trembled and she sank her teeth into the bottom lip. Glancing away from her sister, she shook her head. "I'm sorry. I've wanted to tell you the truth. It's been hard for me, too—"

"Boo-fucking-hoo." Tatum slashed a hand through the

air. "Save it, Mia. Because you haven't changed. God," she chuckled, "there's sibling rivalry, but deep down you must really hate me to do something so dirty, so callous and cold to me. I can never trust you again."

"Tatum…" Silas turned to her, his dark eyes sad. The man seemed to have aged at least ten years in just seconds. Lines creased his cheeks, and he appeared…tired. Ashamed. "Please, take a moment. Don't say anything you might regret later. What Mia has done is terrible, and I still can't believe—" He bit off the rest of the sentence, his head briefly dropping. "But she's still your sister and we're family. We always will be."

Anger roared through Bran and he turned to Silas with a snarl. Once again, he was abandoning Tatum instead of having his daughter's back. The other man might not see it that way, and yes, he was in a difficult situation, but standing up for one daughter didn't mean he loved the other less. It meant he was fucking *parenting*.

"Don't bother, Dad." She held up a hand, palm out. "You're embarrassed over her actions. You're horrified. But this isn't your wrong to forgive, and you won't make me absolve her of it so you and Mom can continue to have the perception of a happy family at dinner. Don't even ask it of me. One day I might forgive you," she said, returning her attention to Mia, "but today is not that day. Especially when I doubt if you're more remorseful over the pain you've caused or just getting caught."

"Tatum, please," Mia whispered. "I am sorry I've hurt you."

"I don't believe you. But worse? I don't believe you wouldn't do it again." Stepping back, she inhaled an audible breath and looked at her father. "Dad, I think you will understand if I take a personal day."

Without waiting for her father's agreement, she spun

around and strode from the room, her shoulders straight, head high. Like a fucking queen. Bran didn't bother addressing Mia or Silas but followed Tatum down the hall to her office. She didn't turn around and look at him when he closed the door.

"Did you intend on telling me what you discovered about Mia and Mark?" she murmured.

"Of course I did," he said, approaching her from behind. "I would've never kept something like that from you."

He wanted to reach out to her, draw her back against his chest. But her stiff posture—and the fact that she wouldn't look at him—didn't invite his touch.

"Last night, you must've looked at the burner phone while I was upstairs. You recognized Mia's number then. Why didn't you tell me last night?" She finally turned around to face him, and shit, the pain in her eyes. He briefly closed his own, but this wasn't about him. And she deserved answers. "Did you think I was too weak to handle the news that my sister had been fucking my fiancé behind my back?" she continued. "Did you think I'd break?"

"Tate, no, nothing could be further from the truth. I just didn't want to inflict anymore hurt on you before I was sure. This morning, I called her, asking to meet to make sure I didn't have it wrong before telling you."

"So everyone in my life has been treating me like a helpless baby who can't fend for herself. Or a china doll that will break at the slightest tap. And you did both."

His jaw clenched, and he inhaled a deep breath. Let it out. *Fuck*.

"You're right," he said. "I shouldn't have tried to shield this from you. It's your life, your decisions and, though this has to hurt almost as bad as Mark's death, you're strong enough to handle it. I messed up, Tatum, and I'm sorry."

"Yes, that's been said a lot this morning." She pinched her

forehead then rubbed it. "If you don't mind, I'd rather never hear those words again."

"Tatum." He moved toward her, his hand outstretched, but she backed away from him. "Let me hold you, please."

"No." She shook her head, hands up in front of her. "Don't... Stop. I don't want to be held. I want to be left alone."

A band constricted around his chest and he fought past the tightness to breathe, to not say *fuck that* and storm her. Drag her into his arms and hold her until her body lost that unnatural stiffness.

Until the fear creeping inside him dissipated.

"Okay, I'll give that to you," he slowly said. "I'll just call later—"

"No, don't," she interrupted. "I need space. To think, to..." She briefly closed her eyes, her fists clenching beside her thighs. "I'll contact you when I'm ready."

"Will you, though?" he murmured, the fear swirling, gelling into a hard knot behind his rib cage. "You told me once that you value my honesty. I don't believe in playing games or saying one thing when I mean another. So your turn, Tatum. Be honest."

Her nostrils flared, eyes narrowing on him. Shaking her head, she warned, "You don't want that. Not right now, Bran."

"I'll be the judge of that."

But she might be right; given the pounding of his pulse and the bracing of his body, he might not be ready for the blow.

"As fucked up as that was—what I just walked away from—it revealed something to me that I've been in denial about. I wear fucking blinders when it comes to people. I am like that defenseless baby because I can't trust myself. Not only did I choose a man who lied to me and cheated on me for at least a year, but I couldn't even see that my sister was the same. I made excuses for them both. I'm dangerous to myself, and I'm so damn tired of being the casualty of my own willful blindness. I can't do it anymore."

"And your solution is to, what? Go scorched earth with every relationship in your life? Baby, life is about risks. It's about taking a leap and hoping the person you love is either with you in the fall or will at least teach you how to land softer next time."

"You're talking to me about risk? Don't be a hypocrite, Bran. When was your last long-term relationship since your divorce?" she jabbed.

"Last night. The night before that. Three weeks before that when I met a woman on a balcony. A woman who challenged me professionally then personally. A beautiful woman who has me believing in second chances."

He stated the truth baldly, laying his heart out there for her. And goddamn, his timing sucked, but she had to know she wasn't defective. She'd *changed* him. Was she perfect? No. But she was his. And he wanted to be claimed by her. He needed to be hers.

"I don't believe you," she whispered, shaking her head. Turning from him, she thrust her fingers through her hair, disheveling the strands. "I don't believe you," she repeated.

To him? To herself? To them both?

"No, you don't *want* to believe me. There's a difference."

"It was a mistake." She whirled back around, and only the desperation in her voice and eyes kept him from snapping at her. Instead, pain and disappointment mushroomed in his chest. Shoving until they filled his lungs, his head. "We shouldn't have become involved in the first place. You know that. I do. And you're leaving for Seattle, anyway. We were never meant to happen or be permanent. Neither one of us wants permanent."

"Anything else you want to throw out, Tatum?" he murmured. "You're too young for me. It's unprofessional. I could lose the investment deal." When she didn't say anything but remained stubbornly quiet, he huffed out a soft, harsh chuckle. "Spoiler alert, Tatum. This deal could go to hell and I wouldn't care. If it came down to the choice of not knowing you, not loving you or funds for a motorcycle? You'd win every time. Business deals come and go, but there's only one you. You're younger than me. Yeah, maybe we shouldn't have become involved. We can't change any of that. And more importantly? I wouldn't. Every. Time," he bit out. "You."

He finally crossed the room and strode straight up to her, not stopping even though she shuffled backward. Her ass bumped the edge of the desk and still, he kept going, lifting his hands and cupping her face.

"I love you. You don't want that from me. But my love isn't conditional on your acceptance. I can't make you love me, though. I can't erase the fear, the hurt. But I won't stay here imprisoned by it either. Not even for you. When you're ready to truly be free, to not be ruled by the past or allow it to dictate who you are, come find me." He pressed his lips to her forehead then leaned back, smoothing his thumbs over her cheekbones. "Remember, Tatum. Either they write your story or you do."

With that, he released her and walked out of the office.

Because in spite of his big talk, he couldn't bear hearing her say she didn't love him.

Fourteen

The peal of the doorbell echoed throughout Tatum's home. Staring at her security system's image of who stood on the other side of her front door, Tatum longed to ignore the sound.

I can't deal with this.

Not when it hurt her to move, hell, to *breathe*.

Only one day had passed since the confrontation in the conference room with Mia and then in her office with Bran. She didn't possess the emotional bandwidth for more. Yet, she unlocked the door and opened it, meeting Dara Walker's gaze on the other side.

"Dara," she said to Mark's mother. "This is a surprise."

"I called you at the office, but your assistant said you weren't in. Then I tried calling your cell but it went straight to voice mail. I apologize for dropping by unannounced but I needed to speak with you, Tatum. It's important."

God, she wanted to close the door. Instead, she stepped back and allowed her almost mother-in-law to enter. Though she seriously doubted Dara's definition of *important* measured up to hers.

"Tatum." Dara entered the living room and sank down on one of the chairs next to the couch. "Your father contacted Leo and me. He told us about Mark and… Mia." Dara closed her eyes, shaking her head. "I still can't believe it."

Believe that your son had sex with his fiancée's sister or that your son was a liar and cheater?

The question sat on her tongue like a hot lump of coal, but she swallowed it. Lowering to the sofa, she didn't say anything.

Dara sighed. "I can't imagine how you're feeling right now. And I won't presume to. But—" she paused, reaching out and cupping Tatum's knee "—your father also said under the circumstances, you shouldn't be expected to speak at the event we're planning for our foundation. And that he nor your mother would be attending."

What was she saying? Her father had actually stood up for her? He'd placed her feelings above his business and social association with the Walkers? Shock rippled through her, followed by a hesitant, buoyant joy. And relief. She would've never expected that of him or her mother. But…they had. They'd put her first.

"Now, I can understand how receiving the news you have can leave you reeling," Dara said, squeezing Tatum's knee and reclaiming her attention. "But I'm asking you not to act too hastily. I know you're angry with your sister, as you should be, but this party will benefit students who're going to college. That should be the focus. And you and your family not attending would distract from the purpose. We *need* you to speak and for Silas and Regina to attend."

"No, you mean you need us to show up so people don't speculate about why we're not in attendance. Because if I don't attend, people may believe I'm angry with Mark for not being faithful. They might remember he's not perfect."

Dara frowned, straightening, her hand falling away from Tatum's knee.

"Wait a minute. I understand—"

"Stop saying that," Tatum interrupted, trying her hardest to strap down her temper. "You don't understand. If you did, then you would stop asking me to pretend your son didn't hurt me to my core. Didn't hurt me with someone I loved. Out of all the people in this city, this state, he slept with my sister. If you truly understood, you wouldn't ask me to sacrifice my pride and feelings on the altar of your son's reputation. You wouldn't expect me to grieve like you but grant me the room to mourn in my way, even if you don't agree with it."

Dara blinked, her lips parting, but no words emerged. Her fingers fluttered to the base of her throat, and guilt twinged in Tatum's chest. But she smothered it. No, this needed to be said. It was past time. And more, Dara needed to hear it.

"I loved your son, Dara. I loved him and was getting ready to pledge my heart, fidelity and future to him. And he would've stood up there and mimicked those words knowing he'd been with my sister the night before and probably had every intention of being with her in the future. I get to be mad about that. I get to not want to praise him and ignore his failings. I get to do all of that even if it makes you uncomfortable. Because yes, he was your son and you love him unconditionally and can look past what he did. I can't. I not only have to mourn the man I lost but the man who I believed him to be. And I refuse to live quietly anymore or pretend to be the long-suffering fiancée. You celebrate your son's life. I'm going to move on from your son in death just as I would've done if I'd discovered his betrayal if he were alive."

Dara rose, and Tatum followed suit, preparing herself for a vitriolic diatribe. But it didn't come. Instead, the other woman grasped Tatum's hand in hers.

"I'm sorry my son hurt you. He was wrong, and you did

nothing to deserve that kind of pain or disloyalty. And I'm sorry that we haven't been considerate of your feelings. All we saw—" Her voice cracked but she cleared her throat and squeezed Tatum's hand. "Please forgive us, and in your time, please find it in your heart to forgive Mark. Not for me or even his memory, but for yourself. You deserve to be free."

With one last squeeze, Mark's mother turned and left the house, leaving Tatum standing there stunned and, *God*, lighter than she had been in, well…nearly a year.

It hadn't been discovering whom Mark had been with that had removed the burden from her heart, her soul. No, it'd been finally speaking her truth. It'd been having her own back and finding her own strength.

It was finally…forgiving herself.

Forgiving herself for not seeing Mark's lies.

Forgiving herself for being angry.

Forgiving herself for being silent.

Forgiving herself for loving someone who hadn't loved her the same.

And that was okay. There was nothing wrong with loving. The defect didn't lie with her.

I love you. You don't want that from me. But my love isn't conditional on your acceptance.

She closed her eyes, Bran's words both a balm and an indictment. By grasping so tightly to the past, the bitterness and hurt, she'd almost let a new, fiery, protective love slip through her fingers. She'd hurt Bran—and she couldn't deny it as his eyes didn't lie. The *man* didn't lie—because she'd lashed out, afraid to trust that maybe, out of the worst possible situation, something and someone truly beautiful had come into her life. And she was worth them.

Oh God, she loved Bran Holleran.

And no, the fear didn't magically disappear when she admitted that to herself, but surrounding that kernel of doubt and uncertainty was hope. Hope and love.

Bran had said she was responsible for writing her own story.

Well, she was, staring right now.

Hopefully, he would be there at the happily-ever-after.

Fifteen

"So can you fly back home for a couple of days?"

Bran squinted against the late-morning October sun as he stepped into the revolving entrance of his hotel. These things were death traps waiting to happen. He didn't care what anyone said.

"Yeah," he replied to Joaquin's question as he moved into the hotel lobby. "That's not a problem. I can catch an early plane out tomorrow. Can you send me all the details on the client and what he's looking for?"

"Done," Joaquin said. A pause. "You good?"

Bran drew up short, his jaw clenching for a moment. He'd called his friend the day he'd left BayStar's offices, and Joaquin had listened as Bran relayed everything that had happened since he'd arrived in Boston. Joaquin hadn't torn him a new one about Bran becoming involved with Tatum, hadn't dug into him over not keeping things professional. He'd just stayed on the phone as Bran drank then asked him if he needed to come home. Joaquin offered to take Bran's place in Boston. Because that was the kind of man and friend he was.

But Bran had turned him down. There was no outrunning himself. No matter whether he returned home or stayed here, Tatum would be there with him. There was no escaping her either.

"Yeah, I'm fine," Bran answered.

"All right, then. Once I have your flight information, I'll have it sent over to you."

"Sounds good. I'll see you tomorrow."

He ended the call and tucked the cell in his coat pocket. Maybe going home for a couple of days would be good for him, though. He hadn't even been able to sleep in his own hotel room because the bed, the living room, the dining room—every area reminded him of Tatum. And though the suite had been cleaned several times over, he swore he could still catch her scent. Hear her voice...

"You're leaving?"

He stiffened. Well, damn. His imagination wasn't that fucking vivid. Turning, he locked down the swift surge of joy and lust as he stared down at Tatum. He glanced away from her for a moment because, God, she was beautiful. And it'd been nearly a week since he'd seen her, touched her. But her presence here at the hotel didn't mean shit. He loved her, but yeah, after that last morning in her office, he was wary as hell.

"Yes." He watched, a little confused and a lot interested when she frowned and her fingers twisted together. Her tell. "What're you doing here, Tatum?"

"Looking for you," she said, then tilted her head, frown deepening. "You told me to come find you when I was finally free. And now you're just—" she waved a hand in the direction of the hotel entrance "—leaving?"

"And are you?" he pressed, ignoring her last question. Because damn that. The first part of her statement was the most important. "Are you free?"

Her expression smoothed. Inhaling an audible, low breath, she nodded. "Yes, I am."

"Since when?" He crossed his arms over his chest, challenging her.

He loved her, had prayed to hear those words from her and he wasn't even a praying man. But still… He didn't believe in miracles. And this turnaround—it smacked too much of a miracle. And the thing about them? They tended to be disproven and unbelievable.

"Since I realized all the things you listed that Mark lacked—integrity, honor, loyalty, selflessness, the willingness to be self-sacrificing—you possessed. Every one of them. That man was you. And I was so afraid of being disappointed, hurt and abandoned again that I couldn't see or accept the chance to love again. To *be* loved again. I don't want to exist in the past anymore. I don't want to be handcuffed to the memory of a dead man. Instead, I want to live for the man who I not only deserve but who deserves me."

His heart pounded in his chest, the frantic beat roaring in his ears. She said everything he'd hoped to hear. But a part of him—that part still hurt from her rejection—was afraid to speak. Afraid that she would rescind those words. Afraid he would believe in them only to have her take them away.

"You should know that I requested my father hand over the Greer Motorcycles account to someone else," she said.

"What?" He stepped forward, scowling. "Hell no, Tatum. I'm not working with someone else. You deserve the credit and the promotion your father promised. I won't let you do that."

"You won't let me?" she repeated, a small smile flirting with the corner of her mouth. "It's done. They will be presenting the deal to BayStar's board next week and I expect it will be pushed through fairly quickly. It's an amazing product. But—" she inhaled a deep breath and then exhaled "—I can't accept that promotion for COO. Because I already have a new job, starting in a few weeks. As of yesterday, I'm now a partner in the Main Event."

The Main Event? Nore's event-planning business? But that would mean...

"You're moving to Seattle?" he rasped, disbelief and hope, so much goddamn hope, mingling and swirling inside him.

"Yes. I'm not running away, though. I've spoken with my family and have made this decision from a place of strength, not vulnerability. I'm making the decision to start over because it's never too late. Because you're in Seattle, my best friend is there. My happiness and peace are there. My future is there."

She reached in her pocket and pulled something free. When she stretched her palm out, the distinctive brooch he remembered from the night they met perched there.

"Nore bought this for me last year. As a wedding gift. See, there's a legend attached to it. The owner will be led to their soulmate. Their path won't be easy, but they'll be destined to find a lasting true love. I'd believed Mark's death destroyed my belief in magic, in love. But you restored it, Bran," she whispered, and he couldn't deny the love that shone in her dark eyes. "You brought the magic of love, trust and belief back into my life. And I want to give all of that back to you. If you'll let me."

He didn't bother answering.

Damn near leaping at her, he swept her into his arms and crushed his mouth to hers. And when her arms closed around his neck and her lips parted for his kiss, joy burst inside him like the brightest sunshine.

"I love you, Tatum," he growled against her lips. "Give me your heart because you have all of mine."

"You already have it." She scattered kisses along his jaw,

his chin and finally his mouth. "It's been yours all along," she said then sealed that vow with another kiss.

Did he believe in the legend of that brooch? He didn't know, probably not.

But he believed in her.

He believed in them.

And that was more than enough magic for him.

* * * * *

COMING SOON!

We really hope you enjoyed reading this book. If you're looking for more romance be sure to head to the shops when new books are available on

Thursday 9th November

To see which titles are coming soon, please visit

millsandboon.co.uk/nextmonth

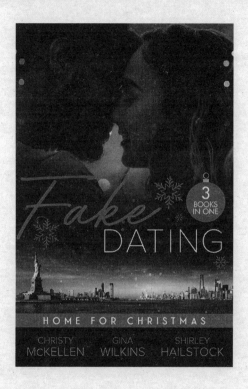

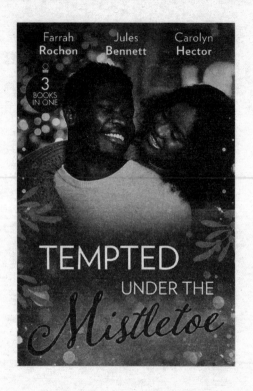

LET'S TALK
Romance

For exclusive extracts, competitions and special offers, find us online:

f MillsandBoon

𝕏 @MillsandBoon

◉ @MillsandBoonUK

♪ @MillsandBoonUK

Get in touch on 01413 063 232

MILLS & BOON

THE HEART OF ROMANCE

A ROMANCE FOR EVERY READER

MODERN
Prepare to be swept off your feet by sophisticated, sexy and seductive heroes, in some of the world's most glamourous and romantic locations, where power and passion collide.

HISTORICAL
Escape with historical heroes from time gone by. Whether your passion is for wicked Regency Rakes, muscled Vikings or rugged Highlanders, awaken the romance of the past.

MEDICAL
Set your pulse racing with dedicated, delectable doctors in the high-pressure world of medicine, where emotions run high and passion, comfort and love are the best medicine.

True Love
Celebrate true love with tender stories of heartfelt romance, from the rush of falling in love to the joy a new baby can bring, and a focus on the emotional heart of a relationship.

Desire
Indulge in secrets and scandal, intense drama and sizzling hot action with heroes who have it all: wealth, status, good looks…everything but the right woman.

HEROES
The excitement of a gripping thriller, with intense romance at its heart. Resourceful, true-to-life women and strong, fearless men face danger and desire - a killer combination!

To see which titles are coming soon, please visit

millsandboon.co.uk/nextmonth

GET YOUR ROMANCE FIX!

Get the latest romance news, exclusive author interviews, story extracts and much more!